LONELY CRUSADE

Lonely Crusade

CHESTER HIMES

THE CHATHAM BOOKSELLER
CHATHAM, NEW JERSEY

Copyright 1947 by Chester Himes

Reissued 1973, by The Chatham Bookseller
by arrangement with Chester Himes

Library of Congress No. 73-84810
ISBN 0-911860-35-5

For my brother-in-law

HUGO JOHNSON, C.M.M., USN

LONELY CRUSADE

Chapter 1

L̲EE GORDON was the happiest man in the world that afternoon. His happiness was contagious, infectious, affecting every person in the office. Smitty the union council secretary beamed with the good feeling of a man who has just done a noble deed. The other union officials present grinned with good fellowship; and the two white women secretaries looked up with friendly smiles.

Lee Gordon had just been hired by the union council as an organizer. His first assignment, to which he would report in the morning, was at the Comstock Aircraft Corporation, where an organizational campaign was then under way.

To a white man that spring of 1943, with war wages hitting their peak, this job, paying only forty-two, fifty a week and offering no more than a future in a union, might have meant very little.

But to Lee Gordon it meant a new lease on life. Not only did it mean the end of a long and bitter search for dignified employment, but also vindication of his conviction that a man did not have to accept employment beneath his qualifications because his skin was black. And in a very personal way it meant that he could hope again to be a husband to his wife.

To other Negroes also it had a special meaning. It was the sort of job to which they refer so proudly as a "Negro First"—in this instance the first appointment of a Negro to the position of a full-time organizer in a Los Angeles union. Reporters and photographers from the three Los Angeles Negro weekly newspapers had covered his appointment. By the time the next editions had been read, Lee would become an important figure in the Negro community. Various civic and church groups would invite him to address their meetings; social clubs would invite him to join.

There were white people also—politicians, Communists, and members of various race-relations committees—who would realize the importance of this job to Negroes, from whom Lee would receive overtures of sorts.

All of this Lee Gordon knew. He felt a sense of satisfaction. With inner exultation he also felt vindicated in his stand against the Communists, whose insidious urging that he accept a laborer's job to help defeat fascism had become obnoxious in the end.

But when he had left behind the supporting tolerance and the democratic camaraderie of the union officials, his high spirits dampened. Awareness of his race began leaking into his consciousness. And when he boarded the streetcar crowded with white Southern warworkers that war spring of 1943, being a Negro imposed a sense of handicap that Lee Gordon could not overcome. He lost his brief happiness in the sea of white faces.

For now the very thing that had, at first, inspired it brought a sudden fear. The elation at having secured this job was now replaced by the frightening realization that he, a Negro, was holding it—that he had once again crossed into the competitive white world where he would be subjected to every abuse concocted in the minds of white people to harass and intimidate Negroes. He was afraid, as much of the fact that he would go and subject himself to this, as of what would happen to him once he had become subjected. Now suddenly he hated this urge in him that always sent him sowing in the fields where the harvest was nothing but hurt. Yet he would go, he knew. And be afraid, and hate his fear, and hate himself for feeling it.

He was a fool, he called himself. To keep going back where he was not wanted. Where the penalties for just going were so great. But he would go, he knew.

He wished he didn't have to go. It certainly would not be for the money; he could earn twice as much doing the labor he had refused. Nor would it be for the prestige in the Negro community, which a few short minutes ago had been a cause for pride. For now he was not moved by the desire to be a big shot on the South Side.

Although he believed in unionism, and admired the union's democratic stand—never so much as that day—yet he would not subject himself to the exquisite mental anguish of the Negro out in the main white stream purely for the love of unionism, he knew.

Nor would it be the sense of satisfaction he had first experienced that would make him go, he now realized. In a way, it would be more satisfying if he did not go at all. He had always found it more satisfying to reject the conditions of existence prescribed for him by white people than to accept them.

No, it was something more. He did not know exactly what it was. But it would make him go. But it would charge him to. He knew that he would pay for it in this fear that rooted in the bog of all his protestations and strangled every noble purpose he ever had. Because fear was the price he paid for living.

And fear was the price he was paying now, ten hours later, as he lay tense and unsleeping beside his sleeping wife. The fear in him was something that a dog could smell. He could do the work, he told himself. That, in itself, would be no problem. And he could get along with the white workers if they would give him a chance. But his mind kept conjuring up visions of rebuffs, humiliations, sneers, scorn, rejection, exclusion—all of the occupational hazards of a black face. He could see the hostile faces of the white workers, their hot, hating stares; he could feel their antagonisms hard as a physical blow; hear their vile asides and abusive epithets with a reality that cut like a knife.

He closed his eyes in an effort to shut out the thoughts. Beside him his wife snored slightly in her sleep, drawing his attention. She lay half on her side facing away from him, her head resting on her outflung arm. Although her dark hair and brown skin were barely discernible, he could imagine the tight rows of curlers and the greasy face. He felt resentment that she should go through this each night, making herself distasteful to him so that she would be presentable on her job.

Where, before, her snoring had been but a distraction, now it became nerve-racking. She could sleep, he thought. What did she care about his new job? Since she had become a women's counselor for the Jay Company with her little cute office and white secretary, she was not interested in anything else. Only in being more beautiful than her secretary, so that the white bosses who might drop into her office would notice that she, also, was feminine. In being refreshed to cope commendably with the messy problems of the black proletariat. In being cool and poised in order to appear the "great" Negro woman she was—in her little pool. So let her sleep, he thought. Who was he to burden her with his problem? She was concerned only with the problems of her company employees. Would he never realize it?

He had told her of his job upon her return from work that evening. How he had been given the tip by Andy Carter, an old schoolmate then practicing law, that the union council was looking for a Negro organizer. The frantic manner in which he had gone about digging up references, exerting what little pull he had left.

In answer to her question, what had he related as experience, he replied truthfully that the chief reason they had hired him was to represent his race. Although he had suspected her of needling since he had posed a similar implication when she had gotten her job.

He had named the union officials whom he had met to see if she remembered any from her brief period of union activity. And then had told her of their reaction—that they had seemed to like him.

But he had not told her about his fear. He had never told her how much he was afraid of going into the white world in quest of what he felt was rightfully his. Not always afraid of anything that he could name, define, put his finger on—seldom that. Afraid, for the most part, of his own fear, of this emotion that came unbidden to him and that he had no power to dispel. He had not told her this because that had been something else he had been afraid to do. But now suddenly he wished that he had.

"Ruth!" It was an involuntary exclamation, startling to himself.

For an imperceptible moment her snoring stopped, then it began again in slightly increased tempo. But now she was awake.

From outside came the soft, dismal sound of rain, underlining his fear with a loneliness that sapped at the core of his will. A sudden weakness enveloped him. He felt at bay, repressed, incapable, and infinitely alone.

"Ruth!" He called her name coaxingly.

Receiving no answer, he ran his hand over her breasts and

stomach, sought caressingly the familiar tufted mound. But there was no passion in his actions—only an effort to find passion.

During times such as this, when faced unavoidably with the consciousness of his fear, he felt a sense of depression that reduced him to sterility as if castrated by it. Paradoxically, it was these times, more than ever, he desired to have sex.

But she refused to move or give any sign that she had awakened. For she knew what was happening to him; she felt his lack of desire, his fear, and impotency that was even now trampling down his every endowment of manhood. She knew that he found relief only in brutality, and she hated him for it.

She had been absorbing Lee's brutality for six long years. At first, she had been convinced of his essential need for it. Hers had been a confidence in his ability to eventually come through and in some way find the verification of manhood he seemed eternally to be seeking. For a time—so many long and wasted years it now seemed —she had kept faith in this confidence, and in her own therapeutic quality to relieve. She had not minded absorbing his brutality, allowing him to assert his manhood in this queer, perverted way, because all of the rest of the world denied it. But at so great a price, for it had given to her that beaten, whorish look of so many other Negro women who no doubt did the same. Even now, under the rigid discipline she applied to herself, she had not entirely lost it.

But now her faith in him was gone. Now she did not believe that anything would ever help Lee Gordon. And she herself was through with trying.

"Ruth!" It was a demand for a reply.

"What is it, Lee?" she answered wearily.

"I was just thinking."

"About what?"

"Oh, about my job."

"What about it, Lee?"

"I think I'm going to like it."

She did not reply, and in the silence his loneliness returned. Eight years before, when they had married, he had thought that she would be the answer to his loneliness. She had been the promise of a new, happy life.

For a brief, hurting moment he recalled the funny, crazy times they used to have in bed on rainy nights like this, that first year of their marriage. They had lived in a tiny back bedroom, so cramped for space that only one could dress at a time; and when they had been in a hurry to go some place, the other had to dress in the bathroom.

For the most part he had been out of work, and many times the nights had been filled with hunger. But never with emptiness like this.

And often when they had had the money to buy food, they had chosen wine instead. For with the wine they could lie together in the warm, dark nights and imagine things. This was the best, the highest they could reach in that dark-toned pattern of existence. It had seemed like something burnished—almost silver, almost gold. Really, it had been tin foil. But when both had caught it at the same time, it had been beautiful in a way. All the pageantry and excitement of life in white America had been there—the Rainbow Room and the Metropolitan Opera on an opening night; Miami and Monte Carlo, de luxe liners and flights by night. And doing noble, heroic, beautiful things for her, and at her pleased smile, saying: "Only because I love you."

At other times they had lain abed and read to each other. It had been a pleasure just to listen to her voice. She had taught him to enjoy literature, as she had taught him so many other deep pleasures of existence, and had introduced him to such men as Tolstoy, Dostoyevsky, and Balzac.

Together they had felt the tragic thanatopsis of their little dog's death. They had exulted together on warm spring days in the incomparable glory of just living. And they had seen burlesque shows on Main Street together.

Together they had laughed. It had seemed then as if nothing on earth could have pried them apart.

Gone now, in the pages of America. . . .

Well—yes, Lee Gordon thought. When you were a Negro, so many things could happen to keep you from fulfilling the promise of yourself. No doubt he had been some sort of promise to her that he too had never fulfilled.

Yet now he was of a mind to blame her for all of it. He had acquired the habit of blaming her for most of the things that happened to him, knowing as he did that she was not to blame.

"Don't you want to celebrate?" he forced himself to ask.

"I'm tired, Lee. I had a hard day at the office."

"You're always tired—especially when I want something. I'll be glad when you quit."

Again she withdrew in silence. He fought for dominance, struggling to force submission into her living flesh. But he could feel no desire, and she could show no response. He conjured up lust-provoking visions of other women he had seen and desired, women of the street, women of his imagination. It had no effect. He hated her because he could feel no desire. She hated him.

Yet he had her anyway, because she was his wife. And as his wife, the vessel of his impotency, into whom he must release his slow, numbing sense of panic.

Even in this, he failed. For it was as self-abuse, repulsive and never ending; and even ending was all the same as when it had begun, passionless, unrelieving, and as unemotional as spitting on the street. Nor did the fear abate.

Now it was through. He had awakened her and made her listen. And then had raped her without desire. Maybe some day he could tell her why he had done it, and she might forgive him, he thought. But now, bone tired with the first thin rottenness of remorse beginning to leak into his mind, the only thing he wished to do was go to sleep. She must be unutterably weary, also, he thought.

But he came back to it inescapably, dreading it as he did so, as a man will come back to a place where he has committed a brutality to view in horror his own degradation.

"Smitty said I'd get a raise if we're successful at Comstock," he said. "Then you can quit your job and stay home. You won't have to be tired all the time."

"Oh, Lee, let's don't start quarreling." The thin thread of exasperation in her voice was near the breaking point.

"I'm not quarreling. I'm just commenting on my job."

"You used to hate the union when I was active in it," she reminded him.

"I just didn't want you running around with all those lousy Communists."

"Is that what you intend to do?"

"Look, why is it you always try to belittle everything I do?"

"I am just reminding you of your attitude when I was interested in unionism."

"At least I'm not going to get so involved that I bring it home to bed."

"Then what are you doing now?"

"I simply remarked that you should be able to stay home and be a wife after I get my raise."

He could not tell her how much it hurt him for her to have a better job than he had ever had. Nor what it had done to him inside for her to have supported him since he'd been out of work. Now if she could not understand herself, to hell with her, he thought.

"Oh, Lee, please let's go to sleep!" she cried.

"Go to sleep then!" he shouted. "I'm not stopping you!"

She turned her back and drew the covers. Soon she was asleep.

He lay and listened to the rain. He was not only a coward, but a beast, he berated himself—lower than a dog. The bravest thing he had ever done was to rape his wife. What tortured him now was the cold, sober realization of the extents his fear could drive him—as if always he lived on the border line of his own restraint.

Maybe it came from knowing too much, he tried to rationalize. From having read too many newspapers, magazines, and books, and having studied his American history too well. Had he never known the long history of brutalities toward Negroes, he might not now be so afraid, he told himself. But as it was, every time he read of a white mob lynching a Negro in Mississippi, he felt as if they had lynched Lee Gordon too.

But all this fear now just because of one, small, insignificant job was senseless, he told himself. Just a case of stage fright, first-night jitters that anyone, white or black, might experience on the eve of a new, strange job.

He would think of something to refute this fear, then relax, and go to sleep, he decided. Tomorrow he would have forgotten it. But he could think of nothing that would make him unafraid.

Chapter 2

L EE GORDON came suddenly awake, blasted from his sleep. The darkness had not lifted, and for a moment he wondered what it was that had awakened him. It seemed as if he had just dozed off. As he turned sleepily to settle back again, a sense of urgency arrested him. He cocked his head to listen but heard only the faint traffic sounds that filtered from the night.

Lord, he had a headache, he thought, rubbing the flat of his hand hard across his forehead. The ticking of the clock called his attention. Turning, he switched on the night light to check the time. The face of the clock showed twenty-five minutes until seven.

He jumped from the bed in a crowding sense of panic and began dressing in frantic haste. How he had forgotten to set that alarm, he did not know. Smitty had said he'd call for him at six-thirty; he would be there any minute. It would never do to be late on the first day.

He was pulling on his undershirt, debating whether he would have time for a quick shave, when the horn sounded again. Now he realized that it had been the sound of the horn that had awakened him. Emotions rippled across his face and settled it in slanting lines; and the abrupt halt of haste glazed his eyes.

Well . . . he had done it, he thought. He had kept the record straight. A "nigger" was never on time. He hated this. It was as if he had begun with failure.

Drawing on a bathrobe, he crossed the living-room to the front door. A sense of inner disparagement weighted down the edges of his self-confidence. Now the day was harder to face.

Opening the door, he called: "Okay, Smitty, just a moment!" The rain beat out a dismal melancholia, muffling his voice. Gray darkness veiled the coupé at the curb. He wondered if Smitty had heard him. As he waited for the answer, the wet coldness penetrated his thin bathrobe. He shuddered as if a foot had stepped on his grave. Then he closed the door and returned to the bedroom to finish dressing.

Ruth sat propped up in bed. "Was that Smitty?" she asked.

He glanced quickly at her, then glanced away. "Yes."

Remorse assailed him, and for a fleeting instant he was inclined to apologize for his brutality of the night.

But her next words, "Didn't you know that he was going to call for you?" brought annoyance, and the inclination passed.

"Yes, I thought I told you," he replied in a monotone.

"Have you eaten breakfast?"

"No."

"You should have set the alarm."

"Which is now apparent," he muttered, realizing now that he would have to go without a shave.

She started to arise. "I'll make some coffee."

"It's too late now." His voice was accusing.

"It won't take but a minute," she persisted.

He compressed his lips and jerked on his coat.

"You shouldn't go without your breakfast," she said disapprovingly.

"I wouldn't have to if I had a wife."

She sat back, withdrawing from him. Now as she looked at him with quick anger, she suddenly saw him and realized with deep shock how much older he looked than when she had last noticed him. It was as if he had aged ten years during the past nine months. The cut of his features, which had first attracted her, were angled thin now, and there was a bitterness in the droop of his mouth that marred his whole appearance. In the light of the low bed lamp his tall, thin frame looked gaunt. The realization that she had not actually seen him for all that time, although living with him in the same house and sleeping with him in the same bed, brought a sharp pang of guilt.

"Do you have everything you need, Lee?"

Her voice drew his stabbing stare. "What the hell do you care?" he thought.

But aloud, without inflection, he said: "Yes."

"Now don't get angry and impatient with everyone," she cautioned. "Give yourself a chance."

He turned the full impact of his contempt on her. "Lord, you've gotten important since you've become a counselor. I'd hate to be around you if they made you manager of the joint. Well, listen, suppose you tend to your job and let me tend to mine?"

She lay back and looked away from him, feeling the full, hard brunt of his rejection. She had been foolish to say anything at all, she upbraided herself. She should have realized that he would take advantage of it to hurt her again. Mentally she washed her hands of the whole proceedings—let him do as she wished.

He slipped into his trench coat, jammed on his hat, and turned toward the door.

But now it was she who could not let it go. "Aren't you going to kiss me?" she called.

The question startled him. Then it brought a blind, cornered rage against her subtle pressure. This dirty, despicable, underhanded trick, he thought. Only a petty woman would stoop to such a thing. For she knew that he did not want to kiss her. She never kissed him when she left for work. But she knew also it would cost him more in peace of mind to refuse. It was her sly way of forcing him to accept the token of her Godspeed after he had rejected the accompanying counsel.

So he turned and came woodenly and with blank face across the room and bent toward her. In the moment intervening she had put passion into her manner. Now prone with one of her large, ripe breasts overflowing in brown warmth the blue night gown, her lips flowering prettily against the darker brown of her heart-shaped face, she looked more desirable and voluptuous than in many a long, lonely night. But he did not see her. He put his flat, cold lips to the pressure of her kiss, and when her arms came up to encircle him, he broke quickly away.

Outside, the horn sounded three times. Coming as it did against Lee's cornered fury, it planted the first seed of discord in his attitude toward Smitty. His impulse was to just stop still and let him wait. But he shook it from his mind and continued outside. At the steps he stiffened, then took a deep breath, braced himself, and went down the walk in the rain. It was like stepping into another world.

Smitty opened the door of the coupé and greeted him in a deep-toned, inflectionless voice: "It's not that I'm rushing you, Lee, boy, but we want to get out to the plant before the day-shift boys go inside."

Lee felt a sudden defensiveness under the flat, unsmiling scrutiny of Smitty's light blue eyes, which protruded from the pink and white roundness of his face like painted marbles.

"Oh, I was waiting," he said, adjusting himself in the seat and closing the door. "But a couple of last-minute things came up I had to do. You know these wives." Now, addressing a white person, there was a difference in his speech, something of a falter, a brief, open-mouthed hesitancy before sound, the painful groping, not quite a stammer, for the exact word.

Turning the car into the northbound traffic on Western Avenue, Smitty replied: "We've got a job ahead of us."

It was not intended as a reproof, but Lee took it as such. "Oh, I know. But my wife doesn't seem to understand the importance of unionism."

"Many people don't. It's our job to convince 'em."

Although Lee did not look at Smitty, he could visualize him sitting there, his big, paunchy body uncomfortable in a suit that had been wrinkled from the first day he had put it on, gripping the wheel in his two big, white, flabby fists more as if wrestling the car than driving it. Yesterday, he had felt an unconscious liking for Smitty, but now it was gone. He felt restrained by his slow-motioned seriousness, compelled against his will to make it some concession.

"It seems that Negroes should be convinced already—all the union's done for us."

As quickly as he said it, he wished that he had not. It had come, he knew, from a strange, involuntary urge to please, to dissemble, to impress Smitty with his acumen. He hated this in himself yet many times lately he had caught himself doing it.

But Smitty had not heard; driving had claimed his attention.

The rain fell in a steady, windless downpour. It came drearily out of the dark-gray sky and filled the streets to overflowing. It drummed on the car top, splattered on the hood, poured down the windshield in rivulets, making driving perilous.

Lee lowered the window on his side to stop the windshield fogging, and the spray wet his face and hands, beaded on his raincoat. The coolness felt refreshing to the hot haze of his mind, but the tight defensiveness continued to nag him.

At Washington Boulevard they turned west, taking their position in the long line of warworkers' cars. Headlights glowed yellow in the gray gloom, and from the flanking murk a drab panorama of one-storied, stuccoed buildings unfolded in monotonous repetition. At every intersection a streetcar ahead forced them to a stop.

"Let's see if we can't get by," Smitty said, gunning the coupé through the curb-high flood.

Cutting back to the center of the street after they had passed, they narrowly missed the streetcar; and the motorman clanged furiously, frantically on his bell. Lee's heart caught in his throat. But the physical tension abruptly loosened the tightness of his mind, causing him to give a spurt of laughter.

"Sunny California," Smitty muttered.

"That's what the post cards say."

"How long have you lived here, Lee?"

"I was born here. Didn't I tell you?"

"I believe you did at that. Then you know about the history of unionism here."

"Well—not too much. Only that the road has been rocky."

"Didn't you tell me that you hold a union card?"

"Not now. I joined the Cannery Workers when I worked in the cannery. But that was only through the spinach season—about a couple of months—then I let my membership lapse."

"That's been part of the trouble here; the work has been too seasonal."

"The cannery and agricultural workers haven't been so difficult to organize, have they?"

"Not the workers, no; but the golden sons and daughters have fought us at every turn in the road."

"I thought you were getting those workers pretty well organized."

"We're bringing 'em into the fold. But they're not the only workers in California. They're just the only ones who want to admit that they're workers—aside from the dock hands, of course."

Lee gave a perfunctory laugh. "Well, now that industries are coming here, we've got a whole new group of workers," he said.

"Have you ever stopped to think, Lee," Smitty began ponderously, "that ninety per cent of the people are workers?"

"Is that so?"

"I don't mean that all are workers in the sense of industrial workers, agricultural workers, office workers, and such. I mean in the professions, in the sciences—doctors, lawyers, technicians. Why, half of the staffs of managements are workers. Any person who does not own the business from which he derives his income is a worker."

"That sounds like Marx," Lee commented.

"I don't give a damn who it sounds like. I said it, and it's true. And sooner or later we're all going to realize it, and they're going to realize it, too."

"Well—yes. But the industrial workers are the ones who must be organized first."

"Yes, that's the ticket, now," Smitty nodded. "That's why this job is so important." He slapped the steering wheel in emphasis. "This is the beginning. We're going to organize every worker in a war industry. But it's always important at the beginning."

"Yes, that's the hard part," Lee agreed.

"This job is big, boy. There is a possibility that the future of the union may hang on it."

"I can see that." From the sound of his voice Lee appeared alert and attentive, but he was scarcely listening. He wanted to arrive and get over the first shock of strangeness, to see what sort of fellows the local officials were, and to learn of their attitude toward himself.

But Smitty continued as if carried away: "This country is virgin—industrially virgin. Five, ten years maybe, it might be the center of gravity of American industry."

"It could easily be."

"Good country for industry. Big, warm—low taxes, cheap living —the Pacific opening up the whole Asia market. In ten years the whole auto industry might be located here—if the native fascists haven't scared off the labor by then."

"Well—"

"That's our problem, to keep the workers here. And the only way we can do it is to organize 'em."

"That's right."

"Lee, you might say the fate of the working class of the world depends on us here. As Comstock goes, the West Coast goes. As the West Coast goes, the nation goes. As the nation goes, the world goes."

Lee felt a desire to laugh, but he realized that Smitty was serious. "It's a big job, all right," he hastened to agree.

"Your people have a big stake in it too."

"Yes, I know that."

Smitty nodded approvingly. "I think you're going to be a great help to us, Lee."

"Well—I'm going to try."

"Unionism is the only answer," Smitty declared dogmatically. "All the rest is so much crap."

But Lee had finished with echoing.

In silence they passed a drive-in restaurant, possessed of no glamour in the rain; then came into the glass-fronted, neon-lighted extension of a business district. A housing development, seemingly deserted, grew out of the gloom. Beyond was a rolling expanse of gray-green, dimensionless meadowland fusing with the gray horizon. But as they neared, the meadow assumed angles and shape and dimensions, and revealed itself as the huge, flat, sprawling assembly of camouflaged buildings that was Comstock Aircraft Corporation. A knot caught in Lee's chest. He felt small, insignificant, incapable.

Turning into a muddy driveway beside a one-room, unpainted shack, Smitty parked behind another car. Lee opened the door, stepped out, and stood breathless in the rain waiting for Smitty to come around and lead the way inside.

A white glare coned from a green-shaded droplight over a motley scene. Men and women of varying ages and several nationalities crowded about an oil burner, talking above the voices of each other. All wore the uniform of California, jacket and slacks, with Comstock badges pinned to their lapels. The air was hazy with cigarette smoke, stale with the smell of dampness, rank from the fumes of the oil burner. But the general atmosphere contained a note of militance, the positive character of people assembled for a purpose.

A rough pine table, stacked with union literature, stood along the wall. Two chairs flanked it. One man sat apart on the corner of the table, a foot propped on a chair, stolidly smoking a cigarette. Unlike the others, he wore a shiny blue serge suit complete to vest, a soiled gray shirt, and a green tie. No badge was in evidence on his clothing. About him was the air of settled implacability.

Voices greeted Smitty as he came into the room—quips, curses, questions. But when Lee followed, a silence came. The silence passed as suddenly as it had come. But now the voices had a different sound. There was a quality in the difference that Lee could always hear.

But the first person Lee saw was the man who sat apart. Their glances crossed, and from where he stood Lee could feel the force of this man's stare—neither hostile nor friendly, but stripping away the layers of all subterfuge.

Then Smitty drew his attention to make an introduction: "Lee Gordon, Marvin Todd. Marv's our acting chairman of the local."

Lee extended his hand to a tall, blond man with glassy blue eyes. "Hello, Marvin."

"Hah!" Todd gave the single explosive epithet and turned away.

Slowly Lee withdrew his hand as silence again descended upon the room. Now it was not fear he felt, but a stricture of the soul, the torture of the damned, a shriveling up inside, an actual diminution of his organs and the stoppage of their functions.

Disapproval fashioned the expressions of the others. But blood reddened Smitty's face with apoplectic rage. For an instant it seemed as if he would call Todd back. All the workings of his slow, ponderous mind were visible in his face—the furious incredulity at Todd's outburst of prejudice, the tortured sympathy for Lee's predicament, the indecision as to what steps he should take, the deep aversion for the entire racial scene, bafflement, hesitancy. . . . Until then, Lee had been watching him. Now he looked away. He did not want to see the compromise he thought might come next, for after that he would not have anything at all for Smitty.

For a moment longer the silence hung, pregnant with expectancy. The man in the blue serge suit slid from the table and crossed the room.

"I'm Joe," he said, extending his hand to Lee. There was the slight indication of an accent in his voice, which made his words seem battened down.

Lee never shook a hand with more gratitude.

Relief flooded Smitty in red and white waves. "Joe's the man." The words poured out of him. "Joe's the big boss, Lee. I'm only his helper. Joe Ptak, Lee Gordon."

For an instant Lee was conscious of the attention of the others in the room. Then he forgot them in the hard, calloused pressure of Joe's grip, in the cold, level scrutiny of Joe's slate-gray eyes.

"Hello, Joe."

Joe Ptak nodded without replying. There was an impenetrable aloofness in his manner, an uncompromising rejection of human instability. His body was stocky, barrel-chested, rooted in the earth; his face was blunt with features that seemed hammered and his head was square.

Still scrutinizing Lee, he raised a cigarette with his left hand from which the first two fingers were gone, parked it in the corner of his mouth. Then he ran his two remaining fingers through his bristling shock of iron-gray hair, and turned away.

Voices came back into the room, and Smitty resumed the introductions.

Lee met Benny Stone next, a short, curly-haired Jew with sharp, dark eyes, who was acting financial secretary of the local. Benny's effusive greeting brought a recurrence of the old troubling question: On what side did the Jew actually play? Was Benny's effusion a slap at Todd or a pretense for Joe?

But it went from his mind as he turned to meet the others—the three Mexicans and two white women and other white men—all of whom were volunteer organizers, waiting for the day shift to begin. They were cordial but not effusive, and beyond the simple salutation there was nothing any of them had to say.

With the business of the introductions over, Smitty said a few words to Joe and left. Lee was alone; no one spoke to him and no conversation included him. He took off his raincoat and, holding it over his arm, went to stand by the stove. A searing sense of inadequacy assailed him as he struggled desperately against consciousness of his race.

He was too tight, he told himself. Making too much of a mountain from a molehill. There was no need to be so tight, no sense in it. No one was going to shoot him. No one was even thinking about him. That silliness of Todd's was nothing—a vulgar exhibition by an ignorant white. It had not hurt him, and all it had done for Todd was to bring down disapproval.

But the old suspicion that there is always a conspiracy against a Negro crowded back into him. His thin black skin kept feeling white eyes—measuring him, calculating, conspiring. And his futile, sterile pride was bleeding.

The sound of the whistle came as a reprieve. Quickly the room emptied of all but he and Joe. Hanging up his coat, he turned to Joe.

"Well, what do we do?"

"Take it easy," Joe replied.

But shortly the room was filled with volunteers form the graveyard shift. Joe did not introduce him, but Lee had the emotional advantage of having been there first, and his manner was more relaxed.

At Joe's direction, he sat at the table and copied the names, badge numbers, department numbers, and home addresses of workers who had joined, or had promised to join, the union, dictated to him by the various volunteers. As before, several were Mexicans, but he identified the majority of whites as Southerners by their speech.

At the last, some one said in a softly modulated voice: "I, too, would like to join the union."

Lee glanced up to see a dark-brown, scholarly appearing man of middle-age, dressed in khaki coveralls and wearing a miner's cap. His features had the taut-skinned, high-cheekboned structure of an Indian's, but his eyes were a soft, limpid brown. So many contradictions were apparent in the man that Lee looked startled.

"You are accepting Negro members, are you not?" the man asked in a precise, persistent tone.

"Oh, indeed!" Lee shouted in embarrassment. "Sure, that's

why I'm here. We're certainly glad to have you. Now what is your name—and let me have your address, too."

"Lester McKinley," the man replied, giving him an address on the West Side.

When Lee had finished writing, he extended his hand. "My name's Lee Gordon. I'm an organizer here."

"I'm glad to meet you, Mr. Gordon," McKinley said soberly shaking his hand. "If you require any assistance at any time, please don't be hesitant in calling on me."

"Why, thank you," Lee replied gratefully.

"*Labor omnia vincit*," McKinley quoted. "Labor conquers all things." A smile flickered across his somber features, then he turned, and without looking at any of the others, leisurely left the room.

"Well . . . scholar or mountebank?" Lee Gordon asked himself.

And then a white voice cut across his consciousness: ". . . naw, not there, I was in niggertown." There was no malice in the voice, only the forgetfulness of a Negro's presence. But it put Lee right back where he had been with Todd.

For a long moment he sat rigid in recurring torture, afraid that if he looked up he'd see a white man's grinning face. Then he decided to appear as if he had not heard. From the literature on the table he selected a tiny booklet: *Your Union at Work*. He turned the page and read: "We, the Workers, realize that the struggle to better our working and living conditions is in vain unless we are united to protect ourselves collectively against the organized forces of the employers. . . . We, the Workers, form an organization which unites all workers in our industry on an industrial basis and rank-and-file control, regardless of craft, age, sex, nationality, race—"

At the word *race*, his mind left the printed page so that now only his eyes were perceiving the words. His mind was lost in the black, senseless, depthless morass of race—gone!

"You ever work in a steel mill?"

The question jerked Lee out of it. Joe waited for his reply.

"No, I never did," Lee said.

The day-shift volunteers had gone; they were the only two left.

Joe held up his left hand. "I lost these in a steel mill in Youngstown, Ohio."

Lee looked at the two-fingered hand, then at Joe's granite-hard face. As it had been with Smitty, again he felt the compulsion to adjust his personality, somewhat in the manner of a foil, to Joe's; to say the thing that was expected of him. He didn't know what to say.

"I didn't get a cent," Joe grated. "I got fired. The shop wasn't organized."

"That was tough," Lee sympathized inanely.

Joe gave him a look, and a fire lit up in his slate-gray eyes. "A lot of these punks drawing union pay don't even know what a union is."

Lee winced. But Joe was not referring to him; for the moment he had forgotten Lee's presence.

"They could-a had 'em all organized, if they'd organized the unemployed," he went on. It seemed to rankle deep inside of him . "They could-a organized 'em then. They could-a organized 'em on WPA. Now they got to do it the hard way. So who do they send but me?"

"Oh, you're from out of town?" Lee again spoke foolishly just to fill the silence with sound.

This time Joe saw him. "Let's get some beer," he said abruptly.

"I'll settle for coffee," Lee said with a smile.

The rain had stopped. But the gray murkiness of a Los Angeles March morning remained, cold and depressing. They slopped through the puddles silently and turned into a bar and grill. As always, Lee suffered his moment of suspense over whether he would be refused service. But the bartender waved to Joe, and he became relaxed. They sat in a booth and ordered. The coffee went through Lee like a drug, sharpening his brain and refashioning the day with a more rounded perspective.

Tilting the bottle to his mouth, Joe set it down empty and called to the bartender: "Send me two more; that was a boy."

Lee laughed dutifully. "Say, Joe," he asked suddenly, "just who am I supposed to take orders from?"

"From me," Joe replied. "I'm the organizer."

But this was not what Lee wanted. He knew the general setup. The organizer was assigned by the national union to organize a shop. He was given full charge. But in the locality where he was to work, he could elicit the aid of the local union council, use its resources in the field and its assembly halls for union meetings. In this case, it had been Joe who had asked for help with the Negro workers. The union council had decided to hire a permanent Negro organizer to be used in turn by all locals within its membership.

"What about the local officials? Todd? And Stone?" Lee wanted to know.

"They're to take orders from you. But who gives the orders and who takes 'em ain't what's important."

"Well then, am I supposed to work with them? Or do I work alone?"

"You work with everybody. It's the rank and file that builds membership—the volunteers. No volunteers, no union. You get the volunteers. They'll get the members."

"Oh, I can do that all right. I just wanted to know about Todd."

"To hell with him!" Joe said.

Now Lee felt better. "I just wanted to know."

Joe gave him a penetrating look. "Forget it." He dismissed it from the conversation and launched into the vital business: "Now let me define the issues for you. This is how it is. We got mostly new workers here—new to industry, that is. Most of 'em are from the South, against the union on general principles. They been taught the union is a part of Russia; they believe what they read in the papers. On top of that, they're making more money than they ever made. And they're working under better conditions. The company keeps 'em hopped up on patriotism. Some of 'em are so ignorant they believe it's treason to join the union. They got recreation rooms in the joint, bands to play while they eat; and they even have dances. Better'n an Irish picnic. They don't even have to buy newspapers any more; the company gives 'em one free—*The Comstock Condor*—you'll see it. You read it and you'll learn what a son of a bitch I am."

Lee laughed. Joe said: "This is dry talk," and called to the bartender, "Make it two more."

Waiting until he was served, he tilted a bottle, emptying it, then went on: "There is a man named Foster." At the mention of the name, a new quality came into his voice—respect underlined with bitter hatred. "If you want a job making twice as much as you do now, go over and tell 'im you're working for me."

"Looks like they got it in for you," Lee commented.

"But Foster don't work like that. He gets the others to do the dirty work—the personnel officer, a little rat named Porter. To hear Foster tell it, he's the best friend the union's got."

"Oh, I thought he was the personnel director."

"He's the executive vice-president in charge of production. That means he runs the joint. He's a retired millionaire from back East. I used to work in his steel mill. He took over the job out here when the war broke out; I guess he owns a lot of stock. There was a piece of crap in the *Condor* saying: '. . . he talks softly and carries a big stick.' I suppose he thinks he's another Teddy Roosevelt. But the workers swear by him.

"Now we can't agitate. That would be unpatriotic. But how the hell can you organize without agitating? The hell of it is, we don't have nothing to agitate about. They got the union system of seniority and upgrading in the plant. There ain't no problem there. Right now labor is at a premium; the company needs 'em. Employment ain't no problem. They give 'em insurance, accident benefits, everything we can offer but future security. Right now they ain't thinking about the future. And that's all we got to sell. Foster knows it. So he ain't worrying. He lets us do the worrying.

"But we got to organize 'em. We got to build up a strong local and do it fast. In a couple of months we'll have a labor board election. And we got to win it. It's important from the long view. This employment ain't gonna last forever. If we don't have a strong union when the war's over, there's gonna be hell to pay.

"Listen, man—Lee—whatever in the hell your name is—listen, I'll tell you, it's so important we can't afford to lose. It's more than just my two nubs—I can do more in a steel mill with my two fingers than most men can with six. It's the future of the world. All those boys dying and these rotten fascist bastards—" Emotion choked him. He swallowed it, and said, "To hell with it! Our work is to get it done, not to talk about it."

When Joe paused to light a cigarette, Lee noticed that Joe's hand was trembling. Joe dragged deeply, flicking out the match. Then he was calm again.

"Now this is how it is," he began again. "They got thirty thousand workers on three shifts. Twenty-nine thousand ain't never belonged to any kind of union. They ain't got no company union; that would at least be something we could fight. And ain't no other union putting in a bid. All we got to fight is high wages and prosperity." He went off again: "If they'd listened to me five years ago." Then he came out of it.

"There's about three thousand colored workers. That's Foster again. His even ten per cent. Most of 'em are new workers, hired after the others. Most of 'em are doing labor—that's because they're new, see. Just enough been upgraded to prove there ain't any discrimination. From what I know about the colored workers, discrimination is most of what you got to work on. So I know your job ain't gonna be easy.

"On a job like this, the union can't show any special interest in your people or we antagonize the Southern whites. Don't look for none.

"The Communists will be after you. Just be prepared. In case you don't know, this is how they'll work. They'll get somebody to make friends with you—either another colored man or a white girl. Then they'll try to recruit you. Anyway, they'll try to control you. But as long as they don't catch you agitating on discrimination, they'll help. They got that unity crap going and they won't want you around agitating. Now take their help. It can be good. They got better inside contacts than you'll ever get. But don't let 'em run your show. Play the discrimination, and play the Communists, too. It's all in not letting 'em see you. If it's another colored man they send out for you, he'll be a dumb son of a bitch, anyway. Just remember, you're organizing for the union, not for Joe Stalin. Watch out they don't undermine you or double-cross you. And don't you fight 'em, for God's sake. Let me do that. It's up to you how you do it. But it's gotta be done. We'll need that colored vote to win an election. That's your job. You got to get 'em. The next meeting will be in two weeks. The leaflets announce it. When the shift changes today, go down to No. 2 gate and pass some out. Try to get some colored workers at the meeting. After the first come, others'll follow. Do the best you can. When you need help, come to me. If you believe in the union, you can convince others. If you don't, you can't That's the score, brother," Joe concluded. "Now how 'bout some chow?"

The spell of Lee's complete attention was broken. His thoughts diffused rapidly. His emotions lost sharp definition and spread into confusion. Contemplation of the job Joe had outlined nurtured his sense of inadequacy. He could not bear the thought of food. But when it came, he ate.

At ten minutes of four, Lee carried an arm full of leaflets down to the No. 2 gate. The sun had come out and the pavement steamed in the bright sunshine. It was pleasant after the rain.

A line of cars turned slowly into the parking lot across the street, moving intermittently as those in front selected parking spots. Of those workers who had come earlier, some stood in groops in the bright sunshine conversing; others crowded around the hot-dog stands, drinking pop. In most instances the Negro workers remained by themselves. Here and there a black face stood out in a white group.

Dressed in the abandon encouraged by the climate—the women in slacks and waists, their hair tied with kerchiefs, the men in slacks and T-shirts, carrying their jackets on their arms—talking and laughing, they mirrored animation. Lee felt stuffy and over-dressed in a suit and tie. He loosened his collar and took off his coat. His was no executive's job, he thought deprecatingly.

As if the four o'clock whistle had been a starter's gun, workers erupted from the plant in a rush. They surged over the sidewalks and filled the street, swamping Lee, carrying him along. Southern dialect mingled with the melodious lilt of Spanish. Here and there came a loud Negro laugh. Pushing and running. Laughing and cursing. Giving and taking. The white and the black and the in-between. Warworkers homeward bound. Full of their self-importance. Fighting on their front. Owning the street and the air above the street and recognizing no authority but their own patriotism. Like no other workers on earth. Because they could believe it. For a dollar and more an hour, and time and a half for over time, they did not find it too hard to believe.

Now the cars came roaring from the parking lot. Hurtling toward the podestrians. Barely missing them as they jumped aside. The shrill whistle of traffic cops sounded again and again. But within a few minutes the customary day-end traffic jam had piled up. Already fenders had been dented, nerves frayed, tempers lost. T-shirted youngsters, too young for service, drove their hopped-up

Fords over the curb scattering the pedestrians, raced their motors frighteningly, and were gone. Too late were the cops' whistles screaming with futile rage.

Lee's vision sought out the Negro workers. All seemed either too loud or too sullen. Their demeanors set them apart. Lee felt an odd, unwanted embarrassment for them that they should always be so different.

Diffidence overcame him. He felt like an interloper. It required a special effort to approach them with the leaflets. Most brushed the leaflets aside and walked on. He did not blame them. Others accepted the leaflets, guiltily glancing about, and quickly stuffed them in their pockets as if they feared some sudden punishment. A very few carried them defiantly, reading as they walked. But there was some slight shade of apprehension on the faces of them all.

These misgivings were transmitted to Lee. For a moment he felt as if he was being used to embroil them in some hoax, an instrument of harm more than a bearer of good tidings. The sense of guilt was also in his manner as he grew apprehensive for his safety. Suppose the plant guards came out and attacked him? What was to stop them? The union afforded no protection. Declaring that he was within his rights as a citizen had never been of any protection to a Negro—that he could recall. The guards could say he was a Communist, agitating warworkers. The law would uphold them in anything they did to him, he told himself. Reading of it in the newspapers, the people would condemn him—even Negro people. The very same Negro workers who had accepted leaflets would turn on him in court and testify that he was agitating. It was as if by passing out union leaflets at a war plant's gates he was committing a crime for which the guards would have the right to jump on him and beat him up.

So deep was he within this morbid meditation that he had not noticed that the street had cleared. He looked up and it was empty. Nothing had happened; no one had challenged him; no plant guards were in evidence.

The trepidation left, but a distaste for the job remained. Negroes had been kicked around so much, had been told so many lies, so often betrayed, he did not relish trying to sell them on another

the one-storied, car-tracked monotony that was Los Angeles proper, the sky clouded and the day grayed.

"What you think about Joe?" Luther finally broke the silence.

"About him how?"

"Is he straight?"

"He seems straight enough to me."

"You know what I mean, man, is his thinking right?"

"His thinking seems all right to me."

Seeing that Lee was not to be drawn out, Luther changed his tactics. "Say, how much the union pay you, man?"

"Forty-two, fifty," Lee replied truthfully.

"Joe Ptak gets ninety," Luther said.

"Yes, but he works for the union. I work for the council."

"You'll get more," Luther promised. "Just stick with me."

"You can let me out anywhere on Western," Lee said.

"Aw, man, I'll take you home."

"Thanks, but that's not necessary," Lee declined. "I don't want to take you out of your way."

"It ain't no trouble, man," Luther persisted. "Gas ain't hard to git and time is all I got."

It began to rain again. "Well, okay," Lee finally accepted. "I live on 39th Place off of Western. I'll show you the house."

To anyone but a Communist he would have felt a gratefulness. He was physically exhausted and emotionally depleted, and a ride home in the rain was a godsend. But he had such an antipathy for Communists he suspected a hidden motive in anything one did for him. However, he maintained a surface cordiality. When they arrived his "Thanks, old man" contained a genuine warmth.

But Luther was not to be dismissed. "I'll come in for a minute," he said getting out behind Lee.

Fury at this unmitigated gall scalded Lee. Only an unprincipled Communist would presuppose a ride in the rain to ensure an invitation to come in, he thought. Now he would have to introduce him to Ruth. It would put him in the position of doing the thing he had objected so bitterly to her doing. But he saw no decent way he could avoid it.

"Sure, come on in," he invited, keeping his voice controlled.

The house was cold and empty for Ruth had not come home.

Lee's first emotion was a sense of relief at having escaped a scene over bringing Luther home. Then he suddenly felt a letdown.

"Where's your old lady?" Luther asked, strolling about the house. "She at work?"

Lee did not reply.

Luther wandered into the kitchen. "She didn't leave you nothing to eat, man," he called.

Lee sat in a chair with bowed head, waiting for him to finish his inspection. His nerves were raw and edged. He could only stand so much of Luther, he knew.

Returning to the living-room, Luther said cheerfully: "Now you got to eat in some hash joint."

"My wife'll be home in a minute," Lee replied defensively.

"Come on home and eat with me," Luther invited. "My old lady beats up a good scoff."

"Some other day," Lee said, then added: "Thanks, anyway."

"You're welcome, man."

"I'm sure of that. But I don't want to go out any more."

"See you tomorrow then," Luther said and took his departure.

It was dark now and Lee sat in the darkness alone. Now the hurt and disappointment came; the one hope crumbled to dust. Unconsciously he had built his entire day around his coming home. He had looked forward to painting a glowing picture of his first day at work—a picture of the white fellows and himself laughing, talking, working together in complete unison. To overwhelm her with the evidence that he could get along. To convince her again of his ability to provide a life for them—food, shelter, and some measure of happiness. And to win back her regard for him.

He had come so laden down with precious gifts of fantasy, to seek the haven of her smile. What was the line? *It is in his heart that she is queen*, he recalled.

Well—yes, Lee Gordon thought. But who wants to be queen in a Negro's heart?

He arose and walked out of the house in the darkness. For a long and bitter moment he stood on the little stone porch saying goodby to that part of their marriage which had held a hope for happiness. Then he went down the steps in the rain.

a penalty. The year before, a white boy, halfback on the football team, had been caught in the very act with a girl. Though he had been expelled, nothing had happened to his parents, his home had not been destroyed, his family had not been banished from the city overnight. What Lee Gordon could not understand was why his spying on the white girls in the gym was considered so much worse.

"Were you after one of those little girls?" his mother asked.

"I just wanted to see them," he replied fearfully.

"For why?"

"Just to see if they were different."

For a long moment she simply looked at him. Then she said in a voice of positiveness: "You're just as good as any white person. Don't you let nobody tell you no different."

"Now all you got to do is prove it," his father said, whether sincerely or satirically Lee Gordon never learned.

But his mind would not dismiss it so easily as this. He came to feel that the guilt or innocence of anything he might do would be subject wholly to the whim of white people. It stained his whole existence with a sense of sudden disaster hanging just above his head, and never afterwards could he feel at ease in the company of white people.

His parents moved to Los Angeles where his father got a job as janitor in a department store while his mother did daywork in Beverly Hills. Lee entered Jefferson High School where the enrollment was almost equally divided between Negroes and whites. Slowly he overcame his constant trepidation, but the harassing sense of deficiency still remained because just the fact of different color didn't answer it. Nor could he forget what had happened in Pasadena.

He came to wonder if there was something about white girls which grown-up white people were afraid of a Negro finding out— some secret in their make-up that once discovered would bring them shame. It made him curious about white girls, but filled him with caution too. Sometimes he watched them covertly but never made advances; he did not want to bring disaster down again. At the time of his graduation he had never said more than a dozen words to any white girl in his class.

Late one night the following summer as his father left the store where he worked, he was mistaken for a burglar by policemen and shot to death. The Negro churches organized a protest demanding that the officer be punished. But the city administration contended that it had been a natural mistake, and nothing was done about it.

Lee had never loved his father nor greatly respected him and was not deeply grieved by his death, but he felt an actual degradation by the callousness of those responsible. The fact that they called it a "natural mistake," as if all Negroes resembled criminals, only confirmed what he had learned in Pasadena. But to know that any Negro might be killed at any time a white person judged him to be a criminal filled him with a special sort of terror.

After that he was afraid to be caught after dark in white neighborhoods. Each time he left the Negro ghetto he felt a sense of imminent danger, as if any moment he might be mistaken for a thief and beaten, imprisoned, or killed. It made just walking down the street, just crossing Main Street into the poor white neighborhood beyond to buy a loaf of bread, a hazard.

A collection of twelve hundred dollars was taken up among the department-store employees and the members of the police force. The policeman who had fired the fatal shot gave one hundred dollars and got his picture in the papers. The owners of the department store gave two hundred dollars more.

And this too seemed more degrading than charitable. If this was what his father's life was worth to all these people, a Negro's life was nothing. He had once read where a pedigreed dog was worth more actual money and held in higher esteem. For the first time bitterness came into his life. He lost all ambition. Why try to be somebody in a world where he resembled a criminal and was valued at less than a pedigreed dog? But afterwards it served as a spur to his ambition. He would prove that he was worth more than that. He might never become important, but at least he would make white people give him more consideration than they had given his father. He made a vow he would pass beneath the earth no common shade.

With the fifteen hundred dollars donated for his father's death, he entered the University of California at Los Angeles. In many respects he found college but a repetition of the grammar school in Pasadena on a higher level. But he went prepared for the lack of Negro recognition in American education, and he expected no honor for himself. At home his mother was finding it difficult to

two lighted candles in a darkened church, and in them he was
seeing the end of loneliness and the faintest stir of meaning in a
meaningless world. They were together then in wonder, and in
time following they were together in each other's hearts.

One night in April as they stood in the hard, cold rain where
Skid Row crosses Main Street aching with desire for each other,
he reached for her hand and said spontaneously:

"We could get married."

She was the first girl whom he had loved, and the only one. But
he had not intended to ask her to marry him. She was a college
graduate with at least the promise of a better future than himself.

But her reply: "Yes! Yes!" had been waiting for the question.

Her mother disapproved. It was not that she disliked Lee. Only
that she could see no future for a Negro of Lee's temperament.
After all, most Negro college graduates had served an apprentice-
ship with mop and pail before they got ahead, she pointed out.
Once during a dinner party at a dentist's convention in Atlantic
City, which she and her late husband had attended, some prankster
had shouted: "Front, boy!" and all but one of the successful
dentists stood quickly to attention, she related laughingly.

Nevertheless, the following day she went with her daughter to
the Justice of the Peace where Ruth and Lee were married. And
the following day she went home.

At first their marriage was like a tale by Queen Scheherazade set
to music in a blues tempo, the bass keys sounding out a series of
shabby rooms that somehow anchored their sordid struggle for
existence—room rent when it was due and and enough food for
each meal coming up. Not once during that time did they buy any
salt, or sugar either, until each landlady in turn learned to keep
hers put away. And the treble keys sounded laughter in the night.

Marriage made him break his promise to himself. He worked
at many jobs that he had refused before—bus boy in a hotel
dining-room, porter in a downtown drugstore, laborer in a cannery
during the spinach season. And as often, he did not work at all.

For two months Ruth was seriously ill. He sat beside her bed
and nursed her back to health. He never paid the doctor who
treated her.

But they braved the hunger and the illness, and the next spring
he got a job at the country club serving drinks in the taproom. It

was the best job he had ever had, a job where all he had to do to earn fifteen dollars or more each night was just to be a nigger. But he was afraid of the members when they became drunk. They said things to him even a nigger should not be expected to take. What finally gnawed him down to a jittery wreck, however, was the fear that one might ask the price to see his wife, as one had asked another of the waiters. He simply quit.

He had thought that with Ruth he would never be afraid again. But it merely changed the pattern of his fear. Now it was the fear of being unable to support and protect his wife in a world where white men could do both. A fear that caused him to look inside of strange restaurants to see if Negroes were being served before entering with his wife.

Slowly, this changed the pattern of their relationship. For he could not contain his fear or resolve it. His only release for it was into her through sex and censure and rage.

Twice they were refused service in downtown restaurants. Each time he stood there in that blinding, fuming, helpless fury, moved by the impulse to beat the proprietor to a bloody pulp, restrained by the knowledge of the penalty. As enraged at having Ruth witness his cowardice as at being refused.

Each time having to decide before jerking her out into the street the value of his pride and how much he was prepared to spend for it.

Each time accepting Ruth's tense entreaty: "Let's go, Lee. Don't get into any trouble; it's not worth it."

Each time lying awake all night, hating her for offering him the easy and sensible way out. Tortured by the paradox of managing to live on by accepting things that afterwards made him want to die.

The first time he slapped her was not for anything she did, but for what he did not do. Preceding him between the rows of seats in a darkened theater, she requested a white man to remove his hat from an empty seat. Looking up, the man observed that she was a Negro, and snapped: "Sit some place else."

"I will not," she snapped back.

The man had moved as if to strike her when he noticed Lee and subsided.

"What's the trouble?" Lee asked, coming to her rescue.

Using the union as a lever, the Communists pried into his family life to recruit him into the ranks of isolationism. They first came uninvited, two men and a woman from his department, to ask him to head a committee to protest against the discrimination in hiring Negroes and Jews. But Lee was loath to take the leadership in such a move. He thanked them for the honor of considering him but declined.

They did not give up, however. Soon afterwards they called again. This time they requested that he join a committee to fight the discharge of a Negro clerk who had been accused of opening mail. Lee knew of the case and had thought at the time the clerk got off easily, considering the offense.

"If the guy's really guilty what do you want to do?" he asked.

"He's no more guilty than you," the woman replied.

"Then why doesn't he take his case to the Civil Service Commission?"

"They'll put him in the army," one of the men said.

"I don't see how they could do that. It's up to his draft board."

All of them shouted at him. From out of the clamor he distinguished bits of sentences. ". . . practically impregnable to attack from the Atlantic or Pacific. . . . Wall Street's dollar empire in Europe and Asia. . . . Negro in a capitalist democracy. . . . blood and agony the people would find a warless world. . . ."

"I don't get it!" he was finally able to say.

More lucidly, speaking one at a time, they explained that the time had come for all minority groups to join in the fight against discrimination and the other evils of a capitalist society. This war was but a repetition of the former World War, they claimed, instigated by capitalism for the "fool's gold" of war profits. The Negro should not be hoodwinked by it. President Roosevelt had sold out to Wall Street, betraying the trust the people had put in him to keep them out of war.

"We have a war here at home more important than the petty quarrels of the power-mad nations of Europe," the woman told him with an inclusive smile. "A war against poverty and insecurity, against the present barbarism that has blotted out civilized living for two thirds of the population. You should consider yourself a soldier in this war."

"Come, Gordon, let us fight this thing together," one of the men said as if overcome with emotion. "Let us stand side by side and fight the forces of injustice, intolerance, and prejudice. You Negroes have never had a break."

Lee was moved against his will. "Well—you know I'm for anything that's against discrimination. But I think we ought to be sure about Willie Gibson. It's just possible that he might be guilty— even if he is a Negro."

"We'll form a permanent committee to fight all cases of discrimination," the woman said. "We'll meet for weekly discussions."

"Well—all right," Lee said, "put me down as a member."

He attended the first few meetings with Ruth. But most of the discussions concerned politics. American capitalism and British Imperialism were denounced more than Nazism. The *Nation* and *New Republic* were cited to show "the pattern of liberal betrayal of liberalism in wartime." The words of Eugene Debs were recalled: "I hate, I loathe, I despise Junkers and Junkerdom. I have no earthly use for the Junkers of Germany, and not one particle more use for the Junkers in the United States." They were more concerned about the Hitlers in the United States than the Hitler in Germany.

Lee and Ruth found the meetings boring and quit attending. Although the committee grew in numbers and importance, and came to exert a certain political influence in the post office, no cases of discrimination were protested by it.

After June 1941, when Germany attacked Russia, it was disbanded. The Committee to Aid Russia took its place. The ones who had led the fight against the discrimination of minorities in America now called for unity in an all-out effort to defeat Nazism. They urged that petty racial differences and factional fights be forgotten until the Soviet Union emerged victorious over Germany. Their isolationism had changed overnight to rabid interventionism.

War seemed inevitable that summer. Huge new defense industries began mushrooming all over the city. Migrants poured into the city from the East, North, and South, each group bringing the culture of its section. Racial tensions rose and racial prejudices ran rampant.

In the departments where they composed the majority, white Southerners made life miserable for the Negro employees. Seemingly they had the encouragement and support of the superin-

of workers were being imported from every part of the country. There was something so romantic about this new growth of industry and this great influx of migrant workers that a motion-picture studio made an epic picture of it. But Lee had not yet found a job.

His savings began to run out. Each succeeding month he found it more difficult to meet the monthly payments on his house.

Then one night planes flew in from the Pacific. Shore batteries sent up a furious barrage, shaking the ground and lighting the western sky. Lee and Ruth ran out into their yard to watch. They saw the red flashes of the guns toward Santa Monica, the white lines of the tracer bullets against the black night.

"They're here!" Lee cried exultantly. "They're here! Oh, God-dammit, they're coming! Come on, you little bad bastards! Come on and take this city!"

In his excitement he expressed a secret admiration for Japan that had been slowly mounting in him over the months of his futile search for work. It was as if he reached the conviction that if Americans did not want him the Japanese did. He wanted them to come so he could join them and lead them on to victory: even though he himself knew that this was only the wishful yearning of the disinherited.

But the white residents went craven. The power was cut off and a complete blackout hid the city in darkness. Transportation was halted. Motorists were ordered to put out their lights and park on the spot until daybreak. Thousands sought air-raid shelters. Other thousands roamed the streets.

Next day raw panic reigned. People left the city in droves, by automobile, train, and on foot. The daily papers carried great black banners with conflicting reports. One stated that a squadron of Japanese carrier-based planes had carried out a reconnaissance flight over the city. Another reported that the planes had not been identified as Japanese. A reporter wrote that two of the planes had been shot down. He gave the location and a description of the wreckage.

When Lee went down to the United States Employment Service that day, he was shocked by the raw hatred in the interviewer's eyes. Even then in that extremity, with the country in its most desperate need, with all the fear and panic and the fatal unpreparedness, he discovered that white industry did not want Negro workers.

Lee said: "To hell with it!" He made a vow to himself that he would never work in a war plant. That nothing on earth could force him. That he would be taken out and shot before he did. "Never!" he said. And he meant it.

Ruth offered to get a job. She pointed out that it would be easier for her. Some of the plants that had rejected Negro men were then employing Negro women—many in skilled capacities. He wanted to jump on her and beat her for just saying it.

"We're behind in the payments on our house, Lee," she said. "We're in debt. We're on the verge of destitution."

"I don't want my wife to work," he said.

"But one of us has got to work. You've tried and can't find anything. Let me try."

"No!"

"Then what will we do?"

"I will steal," Lee said. "I'll prowl through every house in Beverly Hills. I don't have to take all this!"

The next day she went out and got a job at Western Talkie, a small plant in Hollywood making radios for the Navy. When she told Lee, he left the house and did not return until morning.

Shortly, Ruth learned that the plant was owned by Jewish Communists. Most of the employees were Communists. They were organizing a union local when Ruth went to work, and she was elected to the executive board as a demonstration of racial unity.

She became enthralled with both her job and the activities of the union. This was the first time in her life that she had worked away from home, and it kept her in a continuous state of excitement. When the other workers learned of her educational background they were impressed. Having no political convictions, she was wooed by the Communists and included in all of their activities by day and by night. They gave her books, magazines, and other literature to read, and nights when her conscience kept her home she sat up reading it.

Lee felt that the Communists were taking her away from him, and he began a slow, losing struggle for possession of her. It was then he studied Marxism to combat the Communists' arguments. But what saved her was that she got a better job. Answering an advertisement in the paper, she got the job as women's counselor

Chapter 4

SLOWED in his reflexes by a slight hangover and bowed beneath a clinging apathy, Lee dressed in the kitchen while his coffee water boiled. He had not awakened Ruth. What was the use, he thought. The importance of his job, which he had felt the previous morning, was gone. Now it was just a job and she had a better one.

When the water boiled he poured it into the percolator, but the smell of the freshly made coffee was singularly unappetizing this morning. He felt depleted, let down, cheated somewhat, as if he had spent all of his emotions and received nothing in return.

But he was not assailed by the fear of emerging from his hole, as he was the day before. For this day he would face the Negro, not the white man, and that always made a difference. It was more of a disinclination for the task and the lack of enthusiasm to pull him out of it.

There were so many more angles than just the simple job. The praising of the white Cæsar that he, as much as any one, could only wish to bury. The hawking of the white man's medicine with all the interpretations that in itself presupposed, to other Negroes who, like himself, could point out that it had not cured the white man's ills as yet. He did not want to bother. He did not have the personality for it. Nor the drive. Nor the gall. Nor the faith. He wanted merely to sit home and avoid it.

But he went doggedly ahead and dressed. Because even though his heart was not in it, he knew he had it to do.

Finished with drinking his coffee, he stopped for a moment at the bedroom doorway to say cheerio to Ruth. Without waiting to learn if she'd awakened, he went out of the house.

The rain had stopped but the dreariness of a Los Angeles winter morning remained. Out of the gray fog crouching close against the earth the cold, wet scene came hard into his sight, and the clammy chill encased him. He was the picture of dejection as he went down the walk in the gloom.

"Man, what is the matter with you?"

In his moody absorption Lee had not noticed the car parked at the curb and he started at the sound of the voice.

"What!" he snapped, then recognizing Luther, added lamely: "Oh! It's you."

"You look like you been bitten by a boa constrictor," Luther observed cheerfully, opening the door. "What's the matter, man, your wife stay out all night?"

For an instant Lee debated whether to walk on or to reply, then gave in to the comfort of a ride. "The weather's got me down," he mumbled as he got into the car.

"Better get yourself together then," Luther said. "We got a busy day."

"Doing what?" It was more of a challenge than a question.

"You heard about the boll weevil?"

"No."

"He bores from within."

"Look," Lee said harshly. "Don't include me in your plans. I appreciate your giving me a lift out to the plant but that's as far as it goes."

"We ain't gonna work at the plant today," Luther told him. "I got a list of some folks we gonna see."

"You see them then," Lee replied, opening the door to get out.

"Wait, man!" Luther clutched his arm, restraining him. "You wanna organize the union, don't you?"

Lee hesitated only because he did not wish to indulge in a tug of war. "That's my job," he replied.

"How you gonna do it?"

"I'm going to do it my way."

"He just be wasting his breath," Harold said with a grunt.

This was the moment Lee dreaded, but he did not shirk it.

Bracing himself, he asked the pedantic question: "Look, Harold, have you ever thought about the benefits of unionism?" He had been vaguely aware beforehand that it might sound a note of incongruity, but he was unprepared for the effect it produced.

One moment three Negroes were in the room, remote from the white world, bound together by the heritage of race, close to each other emotionally, unafraid of their thoughts, casually bantering to pass the time away; and the next moment the white man was there, changing the face of the day.

Slowly, both Harold and Luther turned to look at Lee. In Luther's expression was the look of startled incredulity of one who has come suddenly upon something not only unexpected, but also unbelievable.

But Harold's white-rimmed eyes shone with bitter animosity, and suspicion edged his whining voice. "I done told you niggers I don't want no white woman, so go on and leave me be."

"Aw, man, ain't nobody asking you to marry the union," Luther said, coming to Lee's aid. "All we want you to do is pass 'round a few leaflets to the guys in the warehouse. Now that ain't gonna hurt you, is it?"

"It ain't gonna hurt me 'cause I ain't gonna do it."

"You have the wrong idea of the union altogether," Lee said, trying again. "No one is urging you to socialize with the white workers. What the union offers is security, job equality—"

"Equality with who?"

"On the job, with the white people you have to work with."

It was as if Lee's words released some hidden dam in Harold's mind, for now the words came rushing out in that grating, whining voice. "With them poor white trash out there at Comstock? What you talking 'bout? I'm better'n all the poor white trash ever lived! And if you talking 'bout the rich white quality folks—if it wasn't for them you wouldn't be living. They the only friends a nigger got. All these agitating Reds and union white folks just tryin' a turn us 'gainst our friends. And what they gonna do when they get us in trouble? They gonna run off and leave us, and then we ain't gonna have no friends at all. And here you is, s'posed to be a smart man and educated and got brains and all. I done heard about you.

Went to school and all. And what you learn? Nothing! 'Cause you ain't even got sense enough to see that you is being used. You is a fool!"

Now Luther slipped in the statement that was designed to disconcert. "Man, even Roosevelt urges the workers to organize. And you know he's our friend. You know yourself if it hadn't been for Roosevelt—"

But it didn't work on Harold. "Roosevelt! Roosevelt!" he cut in. "All he ever done for the nigger was to put him on relief. If my mister hadn't just kept me and Margaret on, we'd have starved to death like you other niggers was doing. Roosevelt! You is Roosevelt-happy like the other niggers. Roosevelt! How he done it I do not know—starve you niggers and made you love 'im. Everybody know the Republicans got the money. You admit that, don't you?"

"But you can't say that the Republicans are the only people who have money," Lee said.

But Harold had been brought up in the best traditions of the freedman. "They got the money! You know they got the money! By now Roosevelt might have made hisself ten or twelve million dollars in graft but he the only Democrat got anything. You got to admit the Republicans got the money. Now if they get mad at us, what we gonna do? That's what happen before. They got mad 'cause we got to messing 'round with Roosevelt. And what happened? They leave us have Roosevelt. And then what happened? Charity! Starvation! WZA—the 'Z' is for zigaboo. Now here you is tryin' a get us mixed up with the Reds and the unions—"

"I'm going," Lee announced. "It's bad enough to be a nigger but this man is a fool."

"Call me a fool if you want!" Harold shouted. "But I'm keeping outa the army. I'm making money. When this war is over and you niggers is running 'round frantic, me and Margaret got a job."

"In the white folks' kitchen," Lee added.

"Where you gonna be eating? With Joe Stalin? Or with the poor white trash? They gonna be starving, too."

For a moment longer Lee stood there, loath to leave but caught without words. Then he followed Luther back into the street. For he could think of no argument stronger than the reality of the past. As Gertrude Stein might say, a nigger is a nigger is a nigger was a nigger and can see nothing in life to indicate that he will not

"Then how 'bout passing 'round some leaflets, Pops?" Luther asked.

"I tell you what I'll do, boys. I'll tell mah frien's and us all 'ill git ready to jine. But ef'n any trouble come I'll deny it. Dat fair 'nough, boys?"

"That's fair enough, Pops," Luther said, and Lee added: "There won't be any trouble, Mister Storey."

As they were riding along in the car once more, Luther remarked: "Man, we dug old Pops, didn't we? He'd make a revolutionist."

"The question," Lee replied acidly, "is whether he'll make a unionist."

Luther gave him an exasperated look. "What's the union but a revolutionary movement?" he asked.

Lee did not reply. But against his will he had to admire the Communists for the job they had done on Luther. They had taught him poise, restraint, the skill of adjustment, how to time a parry, the art of interviewing, and the value of retaining and restating and persisting in a contention, no matter how distasteful it might become to everyone, until it wore all opposition down. And they had taught him the subtle trick that was the trade-mark of the Communist—confusing the opposition with the disconcerting question, then holding forth the Marxist answer in all its pristine logic. All such insidious techniques of coercion were considered dangerous in the knowledge of the oppressed. The gall and the effrontery no doubt had been Luther's own, Lee conjectured, but he could see the fine hand of the Communists in the manner in which Luther now employed them.

It was wormwood to admit, but Lee realized that within the short period of time he had known Luther, he had come to lean on him for emotional support. He found Luther's company comforting even though it was annoying, and it was distinctly pleasant to ride in Luther's car.

He was recalling with faint amusement the old saw that there was nothing too good for a Communist, as they rode in silence to the home of a woman who operated a punch press on wing assembly. She was a tall, fair woman whom Lee remembered vaguely as interested in sorority activities about the university, and he wondered how she had come to be on Luther's list.

Clad in a housecoat with printed design, she invited them into a comfortable living-room and after one glance ignored Luther completely.

"So the aloof Mr. Gordon finally deigns to call," she said with a little laugh.

And although Lee tried to head it off, the conversation went rapidly to the personal, and they found themselves listening to a recital of her misfortunes, unable to utter a statement in the union's behalf. The army had taken her husband even though they had a child, which showed how perfectly unreasonable the whole system was, and she was simply bored to tears. And what was Lee Gordon, with his dreamy eyes and moody face, going to do about that?

There was a sexual overripeness that embarrassed Lee to witness in her every gesture, floating her personality in an unnatural repression. In desperation he broke into her nervous chattering with word about the union.

"Oh, I'm a member, darling," she said, smiling coquettishly. "I was one of the first who joined."

"Oh! Well in that case, maybe we could get you to pass out some union leaflets in your department," Lee said.

"I'd just love to," she answered so quickly that Lee was convinced she would do no such thing.

But they left a batch of leaflets and took their departure.

"Call me in a day or two," she called from the doorway, "and see how I'm making out."

"I'll do that," Lee said.

"That's for you, man," Luther commented as they rode along again.

"Not for me, for you," Lee replied. "Your politics permit it."

"I likes 'em transparent," Luther said.

After a silence, Lee asked: "How did you get her on your list?"

"She a worker, ain't she?"

"I know, but what made you think she would take an interest in the union?"

"She a member, ain't she?"

"I know that too. What I'm trying to find out is how you drew your list; on what basis did you select the people you thought might work for the union?"

"Them ain't the ones we want, man, them the ones we got; we gets the ones we ain't got."

"I see," Lee said. "Politics!"

"So what about it, if we gets 'em into the union first?"

"Nothing about it—only once Negroes become members of a democratic union they'll never become Communists," Lee answered, more to irritate Luther than from any high regard for his own perspicacity.

"That ain't the way it works, man. We gets the union and the niggers, too. But we just getting ready now. We don't wants either of 'em 'til we wins the war."

"I'm afraid you don't know the Negro, son," Lee said condescendingly.

"That's what we both got to learn then, man, 'cause you don't know me neither," Luther replied cryptically.

And what Lee learned, as that day wore on and ran into another and still another, was disheartening, discouraging, and depressing. First of all, he learned that not only did he know very little concerning the Negroes of America, but that he knew very few of them. As he gained in knowledge concerning them he also gained in fear. For the knowledge of them was like looking into a mirror and seeing his own fear, suspicion, resentments, frustrations, inadequacies, and the insidious anguish of his days reflected on the faces of other Negroes. It frightened him all the more because he could not divide himself from the sum total of them all. What they were, he was; and what they had been, he also had been. Their traditions were his traditions; and their identities described him too. What life held for them, it also held for him—there was no escaping.

During those days of that first week as he and Luther rode about the city interviewing Negro workers, Lee came to believe that more dissimilarities existed among Negro people than among the people of any other race on earth. They did not look alike, act alike, or think alike. Their emotions were as different as their intelligence; and their educations as different as their environments. That what was a joke to one might be an insult to another; that what one saw

as beneficial, another saw as detrimental. That each one's reaction
to an interracial union was an individual emotional process, each
reaction requiring an entire organizational campaign to itself. That
in only one reaction did they all seem to concur—all were suspicious of a "black Greek" bearing "white Greeks'" gifts.

"*I'm afraid you don't know the Negro, son,*" he had said to
Luther with jeering condescension, and many were the times in the
days that followed when he felt like kicking out his own teeth.

Yes—he was learning the Negro, Lee Gordon thought. And most
of what he learned was hurting knowledge. It brought fear and hurt
and shame to learn of the beaten, ignorant Negro laborer, so indoc-
trinated with the culture of his time that he accepted implicitly the
defamation of his own character and was more firmly convinced of
his own inferiority than were those who had charged him thus. But
it was like tearing out the heart of reason to learn of the Negro
scholar who not only was convinced, himself, of his own inferiority,
but went to great scholastic lengths to prove why it was so.

The Tuskegee graduate John Elsworth who had majored in
architecture was then bucking rivets for a white woman riveter on
the graveyard shift. For three hours Lee sat with sinking heart
listening to him propound learnedly and vehemently that the
Negro family unit was matriarchal.

Lee found all his refutations futility in themselves for the man
believed conclusively in that which he was saying.

"But even if it is true," Lee argued, "in a white society where
the family unit of the dominant group is patriarchal, doesn't that
make us something less?"

"I'm not trying to be like white people," Ellsworth said. "I'm
seeking the truth about myself and my heritage, and I don't give a
damn what it proves."

"But why accept a conclusion that in the society of your times
makes you appear inferior?" Lee asked.

"If it's the truth, it's the truth," Elsworth replied. "You can't
escape the truth—you must go on from there."

If the man had been a Communist, Lee could have understood.
For this was the Communist line. But Elsworth was not a Communist, Lee knew for he had refused at the beginning to join the
union.

"You see, I'm only a temporary employee," he had explained. "I hope shortly to become an employer, then I'll be on the other side."

The argument projected to convince him that no Negro could be on the "other side" from the worker had degenerated into a depressing sociological discussion.

What Lee rejected was not the truth of the knowledge of Negroes' inferiority, for this he was learning on each succeeding day, but its value. Why learn conclusively that you were less than other people?—it was bad enough to suspect it.

But the hurt was in the knowledge he could not reject—the voices he heard, the faces he saw, and in his own emotions that he profoundly felt. And the first knowledge was his realization of his lack of knowledge.

"The Negro! The Negro wants this— The Negro thinks this— The Negro is this—"

Obscenity! Lee Gordon thought. All who had uttered these words or had these thoughts were obscene and always had been so.

The Negro! How many times had he, Lee Gordon, used the term "The Negro" with that pompous positiveness of ignorance to describe the individual emotions and reactions, appearances and mentalities, the character and souls of fifteen million people.

But now in four short days of organizing for a union he had learned that this much was not so. He had been faced with the humiliating realization that the Negro of his knowledge represented only a few thousand people scattered here and there. That not only were ninety-five per cent of American Negroes strangers to him, but seemed as atypical to him as they appeared to whites. That not only had he never thought of them, but had never visualized them in the farthest reaches of his imagination. That not only had he never known where they lived or how they lived, but that they lived at all.

There was the one who suggested: "Why don't us get a union of our own? Just let the white folks have their union and usses have our own. Then that way we all get along and don't have no trouble."

And the other who said: "There never was a Negro got nothing but the dirty end of the stick out of any union."

Many believed that the union was a racket. Such as the two men in the bar on Sixth Street who before the war had never worked at all, and who were only working now to "dodge the draft."

Lee and Luther had dropped in for a drink and, seeing the badges the two men wore, approached them on the subject of the union.

"You know me, man, what's in it?" was the first thing one had asked.

"Well—" Lee began. "Union benefits are more of a security than—"

"I mean on the line, man, what's on the line?"

"Nothing, if you're talking about a handout," Lee answered with a snap.

"We with you, daddy-o, you know that. But the union got plenty dough, you know that. Give a man a ride, man. I seen you drive up here in your fine chariot—"

Luther gave them a dollar apiece and some leaflets to pass out. "Now don't leave us come back in a half hour and find these all over the street," he said.

"Man, you know that ain't gonna happen. You know us, man."

The leaflets did not get as far as the street; they left them on the bar.

And the three teen-age boys holed up in a pad on Crocker Street, high off of marijuana weed—

"Oh, what does the wenches buy one half so good as the stuff they sells?"

"The men is talkin' 'bout the union, man!"

"Who is talkin' 'bout the union, man? I am reciting poetry. Oh, what does the wenches buy—"

"The lady said 'venchas,' man, not 'wenches.' "

"What's a vencha, man?"

"A vencha is a cat what makes venches."

"That's what I mean, man. What does the wenches buy just one third so fine as the stuff they sells—"

They bent double with laughter.

"Man, you is crazy."

"The beginning of the Negro," Lee Gordon thought.

Vera O'Neal who paid her initiation fee right then, thinking of the white men she would meet.

And Mrs. Lucinda Williams who promised to join if they'd have someone say a prayer before each meeting.

"I ain't gonna have nothin' to do with no Godless Communism.

If you don't believe in the Lawd God A'mighty, nothin' good gonna ever come to it. 'On this rock I'll build My Church,' sayeth the Lawd. 'And I am the rock—' "

There were some who knew the union, who had relatives who were members of the union in Detroit, Cleveland, Chicago. These would join but few would help organize.

Others who were "white folks' niggers," such as Harold, who would do whatever they thought their bosses wanted.

Those who would follow the majority, who would be on the popular side.

And those who did not care about the union or the bosses. Who would work the hours out the days side by side with any white man, grin in his face and laugh at his jokes, be his butt and take his dirt, and come night, would cut his throat from ear to ear if ever they thought they could get away with it.

Lee Gordon learned that what these people wanted and did not want was an individual process, different in each one. To have and to be and to do to the limits of their visions were the most that any of them could hope for. All would want more as time brought enlightenment, Lee could foresee. And the more they would want, the greater the benefit they would be to themselves, the community, and the nation. Only the simple fact of being Negroes bound them all together.

But in the spring of 1943 few were thinking of the future, Lee also came to know. Few had ever thought about it and few ever would. They were making money, trying to enjoy it then and there, trying to live in that eternal present where they had always been the safest. They knew the past had been against them. They expected the future to be the same— "What is the union going to do for me now? Next year, man, I might be dead. You might as well say next century—"

These were some of the Negro workers at Comstock whom Lee Gordon interviewed. In each he saw the signs of what they were, and what the past three hundred years had made of them, reflected in himself.

Old man Lem Saunders with his parchment-colored skin and white kinky hair, looking like any Uncle Tom and talking like any Texas cracker. "Aye God, yuh boogers, yuh, 'round heah talkin' 'bout that confound union. Aye God, Ah thought you wuz mah pals, yuh boogers, yuh. Buy the ol' man uh quart bottle 'n Ah'll jine eny confound union that comes erlong."

And Proctor Carpathian Johnson whom most people called "Posie." He was a small, nappy-headed black man with delusions of grandeur. He had small, knotty muscles, reddish eyes, bad teeth, and one of those big wide mouths that droops at the edges like that of a cat fish. But as soon as he had three drinks he thought he was the best-looking man ever put a foot in a shoe; he thought that he was six feet tall and that women fell down and worshiped him.

He had had three drinks when Lee saw him. "Sure, man, gimme some of those leaflets," he said eagerly. "I'll pass 'em 'round. There's a couple pink tits been tryin' a say something to me all week and this'll give 'em a chance." He was the first enthusiastic volunteer they had yet recruited—for all of Luther's Marxist training.

Well—yes, Lee Gordon thought. Why not? Wasn't this opportunity, too? And wasn't opportunity what the union also offered?

This growing tendency toward dangerous thinking also frightened Lee, for it was as if he had suddenly come upon himself and was shocked by the sight of himself.

Now homeward bound that Friday evening, he struggled to put it from his mind. Fear and discouragement had been the harvest of the days. "But please, God, let there be some consolation in the nights. Let Ruth be home," he prayed. "Let her have dinner ready and for one time smile a welcome even if she didn't mean it."

The telephone was ringing as he arrived and he let himself into the empty house in time to catch it.

"I will be working late, darling," Ruth's voice came over the wire, faint, distant, remote.

"Okay," he said, cradling the receiver before she could add the rest.

Shedding his raincoat as he headed toward the kitchen, he felt a sense of unreality envelop him. No one but himself would live a life so devoid of meaning; would suffer such depressing emotions or go through such aimless actions without honor, love, or purpose, he thought. No one but himself would suffer such prolonged agony, going forth into it daily to tramp its bitter trails, seeking what he did not know; nor was there any promise that he would know it if he could find it. Surcease? Surcease? he asked himself. Was it only surcease that he sought and did not know it?

He opened a can of sardines and made sandwiches with crackers, and as he sat in the cold kitchen at the bare table eating in solitude, the loneliness came like greedy swine rooting in the rottenness that might have been his soul, all the more terrible because he was afraid of it. Could you just curse God and die, he thought. What an easy out!

The ringing of the telephone sounded a warning. He got up to answer it.

"Mr. Gordon?"

"Yes."

"This is Lester McKinley. Will it be convenient for you to call on me?"

"This evening?"

"At eight."

"I'll be there."

"Thank you, Mr. Gordon."

How he had forgotten McKinley he did not know. He was exactly the fellow Lee wanted, and he had already offered to help. For one full, futile week he had been following Communist leads. Lee Gordon shook his head, but the first sign of enthusiasm showed in his general attitude.

Chapter 5

$\mathbf{A}$LL that day Lester McKinley had been absorbed in brooding. A black mood was upon him, affecting his entire family like a blighting plague and changing the usually gay atmosphere of his home into a sinister silence.

His wife Sylvia, a buxom blond white woman, had seen it in his face that morning upon his arrival from work. The limpid brown of his eyes had changed to smoky agate, and a restrained violence kept flashing like summer lightning across the tautness of his mouth. She had moved warily and remained apart, taking care not to vex him in the slightest, for out of these moods his rages struck abruptly and left destruction in their wake. She believed him capable of killing her and their three children and himself in one of his fits of fury—from nothing she had seen him do, however; it was just a feeling. But she respected it.

Now she prepared the breakfast and set the table while he bathed and shaved. While they ate she kept the children quiet. She hustled the eldest two off to school, then took the baby into the nursery and remained with it. She was not curious to know what had happened to him. She could tell from his expression that it had something to do with race. It was such a terrible business and he suffered so much because of it. She always wanted to do more for him than she ever could. Her heart hurt for him and her sympathy knew no bounds. But she never liked to hear the details. It was always so stupid that she could never clearly understand just what had happened or why he should be so furious, and her inability to understand enraged him so. He would call her when he was ready and tell her what had happened, and this time she hoped that she would understand. Until then she waited.

While in the living-room with the Venetian blinds drawn against the world and the door closed against his wife, McKinley sat in a deep armchair beneath a floor lamp and let his blind gaze fall on the worn pages of his Vergil. But his thoughts were far removed from the Roman poet. He was plotting murder with deep concentration.

That morning near the end of the graveyard shift he had seen Louis Foster walking alone through his department, and had stopped him to apply for a job as inspector.

Foster had neither accepted nor rejected the application. With a grin he had asked: "Where'd y'all get that Harvard accent, Mistah McKinley?"

McKinley had kept his voice on level keel. "I am a graduate of Atlanta University for Negroes, sir." But blind white fury had scalded him.

"Georgia, eh? What did you do in Georgia?" Foster had asked.

"I taught school—I am professor of Latin," McKinley had replied.

"Latin!" Foster had said with a laugh. "This is a little different from teaching Latin, isn't it?" Without waiting for McKinley's reply, he had walked away.

Now McKinley sat devising a plan whereby he could murder Foster and escape punishment. But his attempt at concentration required a strenuous effort. For the blood-red lust to go to Foster's home, break into his room, and cut his throat from ear to ear pulled at his mind and stirred a violence within his body that he could hardly control.

But he restrained himself. He had to do this in such a way that his wife and children would not suffer. Perhaps he could make it appear an accident, or at least so that he would be absolved from blame. Only the two of them must know that it was murder— Foster and himself. Foster must know. In that interval before death he must realize that he was being murdered. McKinley told himself that if Foster did not know that he was being murdered by the man he had ridiculed, he, Lester McKinley, would become a maniac. He might commit a violence on those he loved—his wife and children—and they should not have to suffer any more for what white people had done to him. They had suffered enough for his abrupt flights from place to place over the past ten years.

For Louis Foster was not the first white man whom McKinley had felt compelled to kill. Sixteen years before at the age of thirty, Lester McKinley had fled from Atlanta for fear of killing some white man—any white man—and being lynched for it. Even before then he had felt the overwhelming compulsion to kill white men. At the age of twelve he had lain in ambush and had seen a Negro lynched. And ever since he had felt the urge to kill white men.

Following his escape from Georgia, he had settled in Albany and had changed his name to Lester McKinley. But his homicidal compulsion had not changed. He had felt the same urge to kill white men in Albany as he had in Atlanta. It was then he had visited a psychoanalyst in Rochester.

Sitting there in the silence of his living-room, it all came back. The talks, cagey at first, rose on a slow scale of intimacy until the bursting crescendo where everything had seemed to whirl in blackness and he had emerged standing forth in unashamed nakedness. Talking! Talking as if the very dam of his soul had burst.

He had related in a steady breathless flow how he visualized taking his pocketknife and cutting a white man's throat, drawing the blade from beneath the ear in a clean, swift stroke underneath the chin. He saw himself stabbing the blade into the chest and lungs, cutting out the genitals—slashing the face until the white was obscured by blood. He had even studied advanced anatomy to learn more about the vital organs of the human body so that no knife stroke would be wasted.

How deep within this homicidal mania, and seemingly unrelated, was a desire to possess a delicate, fragile, sensitive, highly cultured blond white woman, bred to centuries of aristocracy—not rape her, possess her. Possess her body and her soul; her breasts to feel the emotion of his hands; her mouth to seek the communion of his lips; her whiteness to blend with his blackness in a symphony of sex, rejecting all that had come before and would come after.

How he would look at white women on the street and wonder at the exact shade of their nipples, the texture and coloring of their bodily hair, the flexibility and passion of their sexual responses, their underarm odors, the sharpness of their teeth, the positions of their sleep, their reactions to everything imaginable.

How race had come to be within him not a designation of a people, but a real and live emotion, stronger than love or hate or fear, containing the compulsion for self-identity so urgent at times he felt that nothing less than murder would create the acceptance of his humanity in this living world.

Listening, probing, the analyst had drawn it out of him like some malignant cancer and had prescribed a cure. First, to overcome the fixation of racial inferiority, McKinley must possess a white woman. He must marry her and have children by her— this to overcome the psychosis of race. But within the society where he lived, he might never overcome class. So he must marry a white peasant girl because he was of peasant stock himself.

McKinley had married Sylvia, a second-generation Russian Jew from New York's lower East Side. He had possessed her body and soul, fathered her first child, Miriam, and had felt secure. They had been happy and contented, and for a time his life had seemed normal. They had moved to Chicago and had prospered.

But within the very cure had been the germ of its recurrence. For in time McKinley came to interpret the very prescription as an acknowledgment by the analyst of the fact of Negroes' inferiority. He had sought cure from the fear and had been presented with the fact.

He had become convinced that the analyst, even while prescribing for his cure, had known that in this society there was no cure. He became certain that the analyst had known beyond all doubt that over the centuries of oppression—an oppression of body, spirit, and soul so complete that no one had ever plumbed its depths; an oppression composed of abuses that had completely destroyed the moral fiber of an entire people, abuses to the innate structure and character and spirit so brutal that their effect was inheritable like syphilis—the Negroes of America had actually become an inferior people.

This conviction had tortured him, had driven him from job to job, from city to city, and more than ever he felt the urge to kill white men. Finally he convinced himself that there were many people in the world—perhaps all intelligent people—who, like the analyst, knew beyond all doubt that the Negroes were mentally ill from this oppression—ill beyond the circumstances of their present lives. People who knew that these products of oppression would be ill in any environment under any conditions, and that only centuries of equality—the mixing of blood and race and culture—would ever effect a cure.

Now, sitting in his living-room, plotting the murder of Louis Foster, McKinley knew that he was insane. But the knowledge did not terrify him, because he was through fighting against it. He had accepted it. He would kill this white man, he resolved. And if that did not do any good he would kill himself.

Now that he had settled that he gave his whole attention to the planning of the murder. An accident would be next to impossible—he discarded that. There were too many safety devices, the safety inspectors were always on the alert, and Foster did not take unnecessary risks.

But there were other ways. He knew of two frailties in Foster's character he felt certain could be put to use—Foster's lightning temper, giving vent to uncontrollable rages, especially at being thwarted by a Negro, and his deep, gouging hatred for the union, which he could scarcely contain. Few others suspected such foibles in Foster's make-up, but McKinley had the faculty of seeing first the evil in all white men.

Once he had seen Foster move as if to slap a Negro who had brushed him with a hand truck. Watching him ride out his rage McKinley had thought to himself: "If he would slap me I would kill him."

And from that quite suddenly came the plan, simple in its formulation and foolproof in its execution. He would begin working for the union as a volunteer organizer, passing out literature in the shop. This would enrage Foster on two counts and would strike at both of his weaknesses. It would be very easy to stage an incident that would send Foster into a rage. Perhaps he would need do no more than let Foster see him reading union literature on the job. Then he would have a weapon within easy reach—perhaps a ball-peen hammer. He would wait until Foster had slapped him, and then as if he had gone out of his senses, he would snatch the hammer and bash out Foster's brains with a single blow. It would be an open-and-shut case of temporary insanity, Public opinion would condemn him, yes, but no court would convict him. And what was more, he would have the support of the union for he would have become a martyr to a cause.

Now for a moment his thoughts lingered on Lee Gordon as he had first seen him sitting there in the union shack ringed in by hostile whites, and he said to himself: "I'll call him and offer my aid; by the time I have killed Foster they will have made him into a perfect witness."

But first he called to his stolid blond wife: "Sylvia! Sylvia!" When she appeared in the doorway he asked with sharp suspicion: "Where have you been all day, dear?"

Chapter 6

L ESTER McKINLEY opened the door and said in his softly modulated voice: "Come in, Mr. Gordon, come in; we are awaiting you." He appeared stiffly formal in collar and tie and a blue-bordered, gray flannel smoking jacket.

Lee turned his thin, gaunt face to the brightness of the scene and was suddenly cheered. "Thank you, sir," he said.

After taking his coat and hat McKinley introduced him to his wife: "Mr. Gordon, Mrs. McKinley."

"I'm happy to meet you, Mr. Gordon." She came forward and extended her hand. "My husband speaks so well of you."

"Oh—how do you do?" Lee stammered, belatedly accepting her hand. "I didn't know Mr. McKinley had given me a thought."

"But he has," she assured him with a smile. "You made a good impression on him."

"Oh—well I'm glad of that," Lee said.

It was not so much the fact of her being white, as it was the unexpected that caught him off his balance. McKinley had certainly not impressed him as being a Communist, and among Negro workers he expected only Communists to have white wives. But it was a pleasant surprise, for he liked her immediately.

"And now I would like you to meet my children," McKinley said, putting his arms about the two children who had materialized by his sides. "This is Miriam—she is nine years old and in the fourth grade; and this is Lester Junior, who is six and in the first grade."

They greeted Lee seriously and he spoke to them seriously in return. Then Sylvia brought the baby in her arms for him to see. They were all beautiful children with brown wavy hair and complexions of sepia and rose, alert but well mannered. Lee was profoundly impressed by their appearance of intelligence.

"Mr. Gordon is organizing a union in our plant," McKinley explained. "In that way our rights will be better protected."

Miriam nodded solemnly and Lester Junior looked at Lee with childish awe. But Lee felt like an intruder, bringing such a controversial topic as the union into that perfect family scene. He was relieved when Sylvia took them off to bed.

"It's an hour past Junior's bedtime, but we wanted you to meet them," McKinley explained.

"It was a pleasure to meet them," Lee replied.

"Be seated," McKinley said, for Lee was still standing. "May I fix you a highball?"

"That will be fine," Lee said, and a few minutes later they were settled comfortably for their discussion of the union.

"What is Foster's official position on the union?" McKinley asked.

"No one seems to know. Joe Ptak—he's the white organizer—takes it for granted that Foster is opposed to the union."

"That would be my opinion."

"I don't know. From all I hear he seems to be very shrewd. And after all the union won't cause any trouble for management."

The poor boy doesn't know, McKinley thought as he sat calmly studying the haggard lines in Lee's thin face. "However, I would say that Foster will fight the union with an unrestrained viciousness," he finally said.

"Oh, I doubt that," Lee replied. "He doesn't seem that sort of man."

"Are you acquainted with him?" McKinley asked.

"Well, no. I'm just going on what I've heard."

"It does seem a bit far-fetched," McKinley said with a smile, "but I am acquainted with the man."

"Oh, is that so? Then of course you know much more about it than I."

"Much more than you will ever know," McKinley thought with an outward air of attentiveness. "For I know what this bastard thinks of both you and me, therefore I do not have to strive for fairness in my talk of him." "Foster is a bitter and ill-tempered man given to violent rages," he said aloud. "And he hates the union in a deadly manner—that much I know."

Lee showed his amazement, for McKinley quickly added: "He keeps his feelings well concealed, I will admit, but I think that I am right about him, Mr. Gordon."

"Oh, well—" Incredulity struggled with concession in Lee's revealing face. "I was going to ask your help, but if it's dangerous—" He broke off lamely.

Insanity? Of course it was insanity, McKinley told himself, looking at the tired, dull hurt in Lee Gordon's eyes. This thin, too intense, tightly hurting boy across from him was also insane, but did not know it yet, as were all Negroes, he told himself. But aloud he said pleasantly: "I will be glad to help you, Mr. Gordon, regardless of the danger. That is why I sent for you tonight." And with a sudden smile he added: "Perhaps I've grossly exaggerated the danger of Louis Foster—he's just a human being after all."

Lee returned his smile and said: "I think so too; not that I was going to charge you with gross exaggeration."

"The worst that could happen would be for him to lose his temper and strike me," McKinley conjectured. "And if I kept my temper there would be no great harm done."

"Oh, I don't think he would do that," Lee said. "At least I hope not."

"You need have no fear of me: I have a pretty level head," McKinley reassured him.

"Thank God that some of us do," Lee said. "Now as to what you will have to do, all I want at the present is for you to distribute a few leaflets announcing the time of the meetings."

"You have only to give them to me, Mr. Gordon, and I will distribute them not only to the workers in my department but to all the workers I meet," McKinley said.

"Thank you," Lee said, arising. "It has really been a pleasure to meet a man of your intelligence among the workers at Comstock."

"I strive more for sanity than for intelligence," McKinley replied enigmatically, helping Lee into his coat.

"Well, I certainly thank you, and good night."

"Good night, Mr. Gordon."

Walking through the dark night to catch the streetcar home, Lee's thoughts lingered long on McKinley and his family. His was certainly a favorable example of the mixing of the races. Maybe it was the salvation of the Negro, after all, for McKinley seemed as calm and sensible and sane as a man could wish to be. Lee wondered what would be his own reaction to a white wife. It was hard to imagine. Yet he deeply envied McKinley his.

Chapter 7

AT the end of the working day that Saturday, Luther invited Lee to a party at his house. "Bring your old lady, man, we gonna have a time."

"Oh, we seldom go out any more—" Lee broke off because he could not bring himself to add "together."

"I tells you what, you brings your old lady to dinner and just stay on," Luther said persistently. "The party begins right after anyway."

"Well—I'll see what Ruth has to say." It would be a change, he thought.

Leaving Luther in the car parked before his house, he went in alone to speak to Ruth. But she did not want to come.

"You always objected when I wanted to go to some Communist affair," she reminded him.

"But that was different," he said. "I'm using them."

"So was I."

"No you weren't! You weren't doing anything but running around with them, agitating and having a fine time."

"Why, Lee, that isn't so. You know, yourself—"

"Oh, let's don't argue," he cut in. "Do you want to go or don't you?"

"You make everything so hard," she answered, but when he turned and started off, she reluctantly said: "Oh, all right, I'll go."

But the spontaneity was gone. Standing there a moment before replying, his head seemed to swell almost to bursting with a resentment underscored with bitter fury. Why couldn't she just say yes for once without always pointing out his inconsistencies? Why did his slightest request have to bring on this bickering? Did she think he was an idiot, incapable of judgment? But to her he merely said: "Never mind, I'll go alone," and went out of the house and left her.

On the long drive out to Hollywood the fury left but the resentment kept riding him. With a stumbling preoccupation he followed Luther up the stairway over a garage into an incredibly disarranged room of lush, low divans, loud-colored sofas, and oil paintings. In opposite corners sat a black-faced doll with huge red lips and a white-faced doll with golden hair, facing across a white brick fireplace that smoked lazily. Four shaded lamps turned on against the early dusk shed a diffused green light over the Bohemian scene, stirring within Lee's mind the first faint traces of aversion.

"Caliban?" A voice throaty with sex greeted them from the kitchen along with the smell of cooking food.

"Me, baby," Luther called.

A middle-aged, horse-faced woman with burning eyes and a thin, wide mouth came into the room.

"Mollie, Lee," Luther introduced. "This my old lady, man. Ain't she fine?"

In the queer green light her hair was bright orange and her skin an embalmed white. Her short, chubby feet, white on top and blackish on the bottom with purple painted nails, were bare. And her soft, sagging body, which seemingly had reached satiety in years long past, was clad only in dirty green satin pajamas. There was an abandon in both her manner and appearance that was slightly obscene. She looked at Lee and began laughing.

"So this is Lee?"

"Oh—you've heard of me?" Lee stammered self-consciously.

"Should I have?" she asked, laughing with her lips while her bright blue eyes appraised him with a predacious stare.

"Oh, well no, that is— Well, you said: 'So this is Lee,' and I thought—"

Now her laughter came in gales. "It's the Continental manner."

Luther sat on a divan, took off his shoes and sox, and flexed his big, splayed feet which were black on top and whitish on the bottom. "What you got to eat, old lady?" he asked.

"I call him Caliban," she said to Lee. "Don't you think he's marvelous?"

"Well, er, I don't know what—"

"Oh, don't bother," she cut him off.

"As Marx would say," Luther said, "a misdirected intent."

Laughingly Mollie returned to the kitchen, her buttocks jiggling loosely in the pajamas.

Kicking a sofa to one side, Luther crossed the room and stacked Sibelius's First Symphony on the record player. Against the symphonic music, he was grotesque, with his long, black, muscle-roped arms swinging from the white, T-shirted, convex slope of his shoulders like an ape's. The impulse to laugh welled up in Lee but Luther's appearance of absorption in the music quelled it.

"You like that?" Lee asked.

"I likes it," Luther replied solemnly. "No culture too high for the proletariat."

Lee could not decide whether he was being kidded or not. Luther continued to appear absorbed. Then Mollie returned to the room with a tray of vodka highballs and turned off the record player.

"Enough culture for one day, my Caliban," she said, then lifted her glass. "To F. D. R."

"To Joe Stalin," Luther said.

"To the three component parts of Marxism," Lee said slyly. He caught the quick glances exchanged between Mollie and Luther and grinned to himself.

But Mollie only said: "This calls for another," and when she had refilled the glasses, moved Lee's coat and pulled Lee down on the divan beside her.

"Well, what do you think about it?" she asked brightly, looking him slowly over with a disrobing, half-laughing interest.

"Er, about what?"

"Oh, anything. The war, politics, Marx, or Freud."

"Oh, well—I'm not distinguished for my thinking."

"Nor is my Caliban. But he doesn't let that stop him from ex-pounding on Marx and other of his gods."

"I'm not a parlor pink," Luther said, giving her a flat, muddy look. "Sucking around the party 'cause I'm scared there might be a revolution and I'll lose my little income."

"You're converted," she jibed.

"Not converted—convinced! After the war people like you'll be running back to your fascist friends."

"I was a Marxist abroad long before it became popular over here."

"You don't act like it."

Sitting erect, she took the pins from her hair, plied her fingers through it, and let it cascade down about her neck and shoulders. Then she cooed: "Come to me, my intellectual Caliban, my strong, black apostle with the pygmy brain; come to me and make love to me, my dark, designing commissar."

"Body Marxist!" Luther said, turning his back to her.

"Then be an American Negro," she said laughingly, "and refill our glasses while I talk to Lee."

"And make love to 'im too," he muttered.

"At least give us time," she murmured. "Lee might prefer women of his own race."

"Well—yes," he said.

"Such insolence! Such bourgeois puritanism! Let's eat and forget it."

Holding to an arm of each, she steered them into the kitchen. When they had seated themselves, Luther said to Mollie: "Say the blessing."

"She knows I'm not a Communist," Lee said.

Mollie laughed. They washed down the meat balls and spaghetti with a concoction of Rhine wine and vodka, which enhanced the taste of garlic in the sauce. Luther took off his T-shirt and suggested to Lee: "Take off your coat and tie, man. Your shirt, too. It's hot in here."

"What are we to have, a wrestling match between my two dark gladiators?" Mollie asked delightedly.

"I just b'lieves in being comfortable," Luther said.

"Oh, I'm quite comfortable," Lee declared.

"You are so beautiful, my Caliban, so unsullied and undomesticated. You remind me of a baboon I saw in the Paris zoo." She was laughing outside and all down inside where the effect of the drinks was concentrating the heat of passion in her.

"That's why you likes me."

"I like you because you are black."

"I know you likes me 'cause I'm black."

"Why else do I like you?"

"Now, Mama, we got company."

She turned to Lee. "Isn't he marvelous?" Then she began feeling the muscles in Lee's arms as if she had just discovered them. "You are marvelous, too. A man of thin, dark tempered steel."

"All dark mens is tempered steel to you," Luther said sarcastically.

"You, my darling Caliban, are more than just steel. You are bone and steel. You are fire and bone and steel. What do you call those things that make all the noise in the street?"

"A garbage truck," Lee suggested helpfully.

"Aw, man, she mean an air hammer," Luther said sheepishly.

"You know what I mean, you air hammer, you."

"We're shocking Lee, Mama. He don't go for all this stuff."

"Oh, I'm doing fine," Lee averred drunkenly.

"Do you see that nigger?" Mollie finally asked. "That nigger does something to me."

"You drunk, Mama," Luther said levelly. "If you warn't I'd slap you 'way from this table."

"I'm a white woman, and you're a nigger from Mississippi. You wouldn't dare touch me. You lived in Mississippi too long."

"Now quit showing off, Mama," he warned. "You know I lived in Frisco too. That's the sheet you gots to bleach."

"What did you do in Frisco, as you call it, that was so important?"

"I had a fine time and you know it."

She turned to Lee, laughing. "Let me tell you about my Caliban in San Francisco—"

Lee remembered only the part about Luther sunning on the beach, exercising his right as an American citizen and a member of the Communist Party, when a blond, skinny, predatory, oversexed white woman stopped to admire him, picked him up, took him home, fed him, and slept with him.

After that day, Luther quit his job on WPA and moved into her mansion, Mollie related, and under her supervision he began writing illiterate stories about his boyhood in Mississippi. She joined the Communist Party to be near him always, and informed the party officials about Luther's beautiful soul. How exquisitely sensitive he was underneath his Negroid exterior, how noble and courageous, yet retaining the purity of the primitive, the unspoiled, uncluttered originality of the aboriginal—

"Now, Mama, you laying it on too thick," Luther interrupted her.

"And didn't I take you away from her?" she asked.

"Must have. You got me."

She took him by the hand and led him from the table. Without excuse or apology, they crossed the green-lighted living-room into the bedroom beyond and closed the door. Presently the sound of laughter came from within. Lee served himself another drink, speculating as to the cause for laughter now.

From unionism to Communism to sensualism, he thought with drunken cleverness. But was that not man's spiral to man's own humanism? For were not these two the appointed apostles of Marx and macrogenitals? And who was he, Lee Gordon, to make fun? What did he, Lee Gordon, believe in? Nothing! Lee Gordon did not even believe in salaciousness, which would have at least procured him a white woman in the last stages of debauchery and a green-lighted living-room on the Roman order, he told himself.

He awoke to find himself stretched upon the bedroom couch, dressed except for coat and shoes. From the other room came the sound of many voices. Jumping to his feet, he fought down the impulse to escape through the window and began a frantic search for his coat and shoes, throwing aside the bedding and disarranging the room. He could not tell how long he had slept or what had happened during the interim, which was the thing that worried him. Finally finding the missing garments before his eyes, he fled to the bathroom where he sloshed cold water over his face until his sense of panic left.

A swift, engulfing fear of self-abasement sobered him. He scoured his memory until he had provided himself with a fragile absolution. But it was with considerable aversion that he put on his coat and went hesitatingly into the living-room.

In the weird green light, frantic people in defiant garb created the illusion of a costume ball. But the workers had come as workers

—proudly, the Negroes as Negroes—apologetically, the Jews as Jews—defiantly. Only the two Mexican girls had come in costume —they had come as Castilian Spanish.

The self-styled Marxists of Los Angeles were having their hour. Each drink served across the table blocking the kitchen doorway meant another dollar for Russian aid. Russia was being aided while the guests were becoming hilarious, argumentative, indignant, or belligerent, as was their bent.

Nothing said in the babbling flow of words was intelligible. And had it been so, had each shouted word presented the answer to man's eternal seeking, the import would have been lost on Lee Gordon. For Lee was troubled in mind and heavy in heart, hot but he could not sweat. His thoughts were on his wife now, and he was but little short of hating her. If she had come, her presence would have maintained some semblance of decorum, for not even a white woman as depraved as Mollie would want a Negro woman to witness her abandon with Negro men, he told himself. He would not have become drunk. And even if he had, he could have at least retained his self-respect so he would not now feel as depraved as those other two.

Seeing him, Mollie came over quickly and asked with an air of concern: "How do you feel now?"

"Oh, all right," he muttered, avoiding her gaze.

Now debonair in a dramatic red dress, she seemed to have forgotten the episode. She laughed and felt the muscles of his arms.

"And you will do your bit for Russia too," she said sardonically.

"Well—yes—"

"I'm sure you will." She patted him on the cheek, laughing, and moved on.

And later Luther came over, his snow-white, turtle-neck sweater accenting the blackness of his skin. "Hey, man, how you doing?"

"Oh, all right. Have a drink."

"You have one on me, man."

They had their drink. Someone called Luther away. The girl on the other side of the table said precisely: "That will be two dollars."

"Well I— Well yes—"

He wondered if they knew that he was not a Communist. Maybe

a Communist had some way of identifying another Communist—
as a Jew can identify another Jew, or a Negro, another Negro.
Maybe a Communist could smell another Communist—the prole-
tarian pungency or the Stalinist scent. The thought stirred a laugh
in him.

A white girl passing turned a brightly painted smile. "Is it personal or can we all share in it?"

"Oh, it's for the masses," he assured her. "I was just thinking
about the Stalinist scent."

"What?"

"If a Communist could smell another Communist."

The smile went off. She looked at him a moment longer with
hostile curiosity, then went to the table, jerking her head toward
him. "Where did they find that?"

The girl selling the drinks shook her head.

After that no one said anything to him or included him in what
they were saying. And he had thought Communists were supposed
to pounce on a single male Negro. But times had changed, he told
himself. Now, there's a war, didn't you know? Or rather the Communist twist, there's a war against fascism.

A defensiveness grew within him. They could not reject him any
more than he could reject them. He bought another drink, staring
into its amber depths as into a crystal ball, listening to the tinkle of
the ice. And his thoughts went back to where for eight long years
they had always ended and begun—Ruth!

During the time she had worked at Western Talkie, he had spent
a week in San Francisco looking for a job. While he was there he
had received a letter from her. He did not know how many times
he had read that letter since, because it was the only letter he had
ever received from her, and now the words of it came easily to his
memory,

"A little while ago a book entitled, *You Might Like Socialism*,
fell into my hands and I read it to the delight of all my Leftist
socialist-minded friends, who had persistently not given me up in
spite of the fact that they labeled me as an ignoramus who dares
live in America as a member of the most oppressed group without
joining forces with them in their fight for freedom. My own efforts
they say are silly, ineffectual, and even a bit ridiculous. They tell

me that unless I awaken very soon I will be living in a world bowed
down in slavery forevermore by international fascism.

"Realizing my ignorance I admitted that I would like to learn
more about this international fascism and I am greeted with sneers
and shouts. They all speak at once denouncing everything.

"They point out eagerly that I am a social worker trained for my
job and have to accept work for a time as an industrial worker. They
become very bitter and accuse me of trying to evade the issue. They
ask me what I know of the Marxian Scientific Formula and want
to know sarcastically if I am not aware of a great class struggle
going on of which I am a part and parcel. They look quite wild and
apoplectic.

"They point their fingers in my face and ask me, answering their
own questions: 'You are black, aren't you?' Sometimes, when I am
worn out mentally and physically, I say facetiously: 'I'm brown,'
and they pounce wildly on me with: 'If you have one per cent
black blood you're a nigger.' They sit back triumphantly after such
a statement as though to say: 'There you are.'

"What they apparently can't see is that I like being a Negro
regardless of what color I am; that I like being an American even
more so and that I wouldn't exchange this democracy I live in for
all the Utopias they can possibly picture—"

That was crazy, silly, contradictory! he thought. But so like her.
For a moment he felt a smother of tenderness for her, remembering
all the pleasant passionate things that had happened between them.
All of a sudden from some passing woman he caught a faint essence
of perfume that reminded him of her standing in her black lace
nightgown on their wedding night, rubbing lotion over her face
and arms and spraying perfume on her lips and ear lobes and over
her firm young breasts and all down her round slender body so
she would smell sweet when she came to him in bed. He filled with
a compelling desire for her. His eyes clouded with a film of tears
and he remained rigid for a long time, his hand grasping the empty
glass in a death grip. His love for her was so intense he could feel
it like a separate life throughout his body.

A voice in front of him said: "If we don't get a second front the
worst is yet to come."

When Lee Gordon came out of it, he did not see the stubby,

bald-headed man in front of him. He saw Ruth as he had left her, critical, cold, apart, a long way off. Still without seeing the man, he said evenly: "Goddamn a second front!"

And then he stepped over to the table and said: "Make it a double this time."

A big white man in a dark gray suit, also buying a drink, braved Lee's tight, black scowl. "I'm Ed Jones, I work for a newspaper."

It required a moment for Lee to get the handle to his voice. "I'm Lee Gordon, I work for a union." Then suddenly he grinned and felt better.

"Good. I belong to a union—and work for it, too."

"Well, I—" He started to say that he was not a member of the union but said instead: "I am strictly for the union men."

Ed looked at him curiously. "At least we don't say grace to the wrong people."

Now Lee looked at Ed curiously. But before he could reply, a pleasant-faced young man with a Boston accent and crew haircut, dressed as a college student, spoke up with a smile: "We don't say grace—period."

"Why?" Lee asked, yielding to the impulse to bait the both of them.

"There is no one to say grace to," Ed replied seriously.

"We have not yet discarded the great god Money."

"But we are discarding it."

"And quickly at this moment," Lee said, noting his empty glass.

The young man laughed and bought them drinks. "What is money but a means for its own discard?" he stated more than asked.

"I might point out that religion and materialism are much the same," Lee said.

"How is that?"

"There is no proof for either unless one believes. I wonder how many of you Marxists realize that it is your belief, and not Marx's proof, that has established the truth of materialism."

"But Marx did not establish the truth of materialism, no more than did we," a fourth voice said. "He merely employed the dialectical conception of it to demonstrate the cycle of capitalism."

Lee looked down at the stubby, bald-headed Jew who had made the remark concerning the second front. "To me the two are the same—Marx and materialism," he replied.

"To you, yes. But you will admit the danger of drawing any conclusion from a lack of information?" the stubby Jew asked equably.

"I admit nothing," Lee snapped. "I said—"

"By the way, my name's Don Cabot," the young man with the Boston accent interrupted quickly.

"Lee Gordon," Lee replied shortly.

"I'm Abe Rosenberg," the stubby Jew said. "But they all call me Rosie."

"Lee, dialectical materialism proves itself," Ed argued doggedly. "Which religion does not do. We see the truth of dialectical materialism in our daily lives, in each step of progress we make. Man discovers nothing, learns nothing—he reflects. Matter changes, develops, progresses, but we think only of the change, the development, the progress of man. But every scientist knows that man could not develop if matter were unchangeable.

"While on the other hand, religion is static. We can not see the truth of religion; we can only believe it. And we can only believe it so long as it serves its purpose. Man is not embodied in religion—religion is embodied in man. There is no religion that man, in his reflection of materialistic progression, can not outgrow and overthrow—in fact, has not already outgrown."

"You make it sound as logical as Lenin did, I admit," Lee replied. "But you can not convince me that the masses in Russia are converted to the philosophy of dialectics, or that they know themselves to be reflections of materialistic change. I say the majority of the peasants in Russia have just swapped the Greek Orthodox faith for the Communist faith."

"To be sure," Rosie agreed, spreading his hands. "That only illustrates the truth of dialectical materialism. Are not the masses of Russia reflecting change? Do they have to know it? Or even believe it?"

"As long as they are *it*, eh?" Lee asked.

"What have you against the Soviet Union?" Rosie challenged.

"The people have no freedom."

"The people have more freedom than any people in the world. Do you have freedom here?"

"We have more than they."

"Pfui! There can be no such thing as freedom in a capitalistic society. They say we have a free press. Pfui! We have the most controlled press in the world today. First of all, it takes a million dollars to buy a small newspaper. Is that free?"

"It is freer than having a big newspaper and having what goes into it dictated to you."

"Are you so naïve as to believe that the contents of an American newspaper are not dictated by the overlords?"

"Not to the extent the contents of the Russian newspapers are dictated by Joe Stalin."

"Pfui! There are no dictators in Russia. The people dictate— all the people. Do all the people in America vote?"

"Why ask me that?"

"Because you, of all people, should know. Freedom! What is freedom?"

"According to Martin Dies it is anti-people," some one said.

"According to Father Coughlin it is anti-Semitism."

"To Hitler, it is anti-everything."

Several laughed.

Lee quoted with drunken memory: "According to Karl Marx, 'Freedom is the appreciation of necessity.'"

There was a moment of startled silence.

"Hear! Hear!" a broad-shouldered man with coarse, lumpy features called from the center of the room. "May I have your attention, please."

"Mike! . . . Mike! . . ." The name ran through the crowd.

"The young man is right," Mike stated. "Freedom is the appreciation of necessity. That is why I am here. We must be informed of the necessities. The necessity of aiding our great ally Russia, who is now valiantly fighting our battles for us—"

From one side of the room came a spontaneous cheer.

"You don't have to cheer me," Mike declared. "All of you know what I am saying. You all know it is the truth. What I am talking about is the necessity of knowledge, the necessity of news from the battle fronts that is not falsified to serve imperialistic ends, the necessity of a free press bringing you true and correct information. I am referring to the *Daily World*. We need money to bring you news coverage of the world during this most important period in the history of mankind. You know that. We need money to compete with the imperialistic press. Our goal is to raise three hundred and fifty thousand dollars. Now I am going to ask for a collection of ten dollar bills. I want nothing but tens—" He smiled indulgently. "Last night I was to a party in Beverly Hills where I collected nothing but hundreds. Now come on, folks. Don't rush. Nothing but tens—"

Several people went forward with ingratiating smiles. Next Mike called for fives, then ones. Then he passed his hat around and took a silver collection.

No sooner had he departed than someone else appeared and took up a collection for a second front.

"I don't mind so much being pressured out of my money," Lee complained to Rosie, "but what good can it do? You can't force the United States to open a second front."

"But we can let the people know the necessity of it. And the people will know who are their enemies and who are their friends."

"Well, what is the necessity of it? Let me know."

"Our frontiers are no longer on the Atlantic Ocean. They are in Russia."

Another Jew joined the conversation. "Russia must be saved!"

"For who? You Jews?" Lee asked harshly.

"You a Negro and you say that?"

"I say that because I am a Negro. Russia is no haven for me. Not even an ideological defense."

"How is it any more an ideological defense to the Jew than to you. You are human too, aren't you?"

"Not in this country. And this is where I have to live and die. I don't see any collection being taken up to fight the Negro problem."

"The Negro problem is indivisible from the problem of the masses. You have no special problem. And Russia is the only nation in the world where human rights are placed above property rights. As long as Russia stands the masses will have hope."

"Not the Negro in America. Our only hope is here where Russian influence will never mean a thing."

"You know nothing of the international implications of this war—"

"And I don't care!"

"If it were not for Russia this would be an imperialistic war—"

"All I know is that now is the time to fight the Negro problem and what are you Communists doing but—" Lee broke off to stare at the label on the package of tobacco from which Rosie filled his pipe. "Nigger Hair," it read.

"Good tobacco?" Lee asked.

Rosie's expression did not change. "Cheap. We got the U. S. Tobacco Company to stop using this label, then we bought up the stock at a discount for personal use."

"You shouldn't feel badly about your hair," consoled a woman who had noticed the label. "We can't all have beautiful hair. And it doesn't take a thing away from your character."

"After all, it's what dialectical materialism gave to me," Lee said evenly.

"There's a great deal of anti-Semitism going on right now too," the woman continued.

"Well—yes. How many Jews were there lynched in America last year?"

"Why, I never heard of any Jew being lynched in America."

"There were six Negroes lynched last year in the first year of this war against fascism." He turned to Rosie. "And no Jews. Yet you say the problem is indivisible from the problem of the masses. Lynching alone would divide it."

Rosie shook his head. "I'm worried about you, Lee."

"Oh, sure," Lee drawled. "Now I suppose I'm confused—which is the next charge you Communists make."

"Confused, yes. But that's not what worries me."

"What worries you is that you don't have the answer—"

Someone tugged at his arm. He turned and scowled down at a small, elderly Jewish man with a tired, seamed face and kindly eyes.

"I have something to show you," the old man said.

"Some other time—"

"No, now," the old man insisted. "You must see this now."

"But what is it? I don't want to read anything—"

"Come, let us go into the other room where—"

"No!"

"Yes, you must!" The old man gripped him by the sleeve.

Lee allowed himself to be ushered into the bedroom where he was forced gently but firmly into the chair while the old man extracted the small precious package from his inside pocket and began unwrapping it.

"Look!" he commanded.

It was a vague, blurred picture of a naked Negro but Lee's drunken vision would not focus immediately upon it. "Look, Pops —Mister—"

"Goldman."

"Look, Mr. Goldman, what is it? A Negro ballet dancer?" Was that what this old man wanted him to see.

Leaning close, the old man whispered in his ear, "It is the picture of a lynching."

Shock went through Lee like veins of gall. He struggled to his feet, fighting down the taste of nausea. "No!" he shouted. "No, goddamnit! You goddamned fool!" He was moving toward the door. It was like escaping.

The discussion had now touched upon the double standard. Lee headed toward it with a sense of seeking cover. Someone was saying: "There are no such things as male and female personalities. There is only one personality—the human personality."

He swerved toward the bar. But Don called him back: "What do you think, Lee?"

"What do I think about what?"

"The equality of sexes that exists today in the Soviet Union?"

"Where they have community nurseries with competent instructors for the children," a woman supplemented.

"I like the home," Lee said.

"We all like the home. The home still exists. But the old patriarchal institution of home life where it is regarded as the center of culture is outdated."

"I like women who are women," Lee went on. "I like to sleep with them and take care of them. I don't want any woman taking care of me or even competing with me." He realized suddenly that he was getting very drunk.

"My, my, such a big strong man," the woman murmured.

"Let's have some music, Luther!" some one called.

Lee found himself at the bar again. A jive record filled the room with a boogie beat and some of the younger Marxists began jitterbugging. Soon an argument ensued as to the correct manner of executing the steps. A young man stated authoritatively that it was done by the entire body.

"It's not! It's in the knees!" shrieked a young woman's excited voice.

Lee turned to look at the speaker. She was a medium-sized girl showing small, pointed breasts in a tight yellow sweater. Her hips were too broad even in the dark blue skirt. And the saddle-leather loafers made her legs seem too large and her ankles too thick. From the neck down she was any girl Lee might see anywhere. But there was something in her face, the zestful mobility of finely cut, sensitive features framed by brown wind-blown hair, that was arresting—more than just the vitality of large brown eyes, the irresistible challenge of a candid mouth. There was an unconscious maternalism that seemed to come from within, as if she not only mothered the meek, but had given birth to them.

Lee was at that stage of drunkenness where the mind is a tricky thing. For he did not realize how long he had stared at her with an intense concentration until the recording had played to the end and, surprisingly, he found himself crossing the room to light the cigarette in her hand.

"Thank you," she said courteously, without coyness, and seemingly without curiosity.

Erskine Hawkins blew the room full of high trumpet notes and they found themselves doing something like a jitterbug waltz to the beat of *Don't Cry Baby*. Lee found her young in his arms but stiff with what seemed an inner reserve.

"If you ride out the beats, the breaks will catch you," he told her.

"I do it from the knees," she persisted.

He laughed indulgently. "That's as good a way as any."

The dance finished and she went to someone else. Then Mollie took Lee for a dance and they did her special crawl. Between laughs she said: "Everybody is for you, dear."

"In what way?"

"In every way."

"They don't act like it."

"You must co-operate."

"I am co-operating."

"That is what I am saying. They are all for you."

He shook his head to clear it. "I must be getting drunk."

Next he danced with a tall, willowy, dark-haired woman who seemed inexpressibly beautiful.

"Last year at this time I weighed two hundred pounds," she informed him.

"You did? What do you weigh now?"

"One hundred and twenty-two pounds."

"That's remarkable."

"You shouldn't worry so about the Negro problem. The Negro is a nation, you know."

"No, I didn't know."

"It is. Are you familiar with Marx's scientific formula?"

"Not very."

"You should read it. I'm one of Smitty's secretaries, you know."

"You are? Maybe I'll be seeing you."

"Watch out for Mollie. She's a fink. They won't have her in the Party."

"No? Why?"

"Oh, she's a capitalist stooge. And she doesn't work. Don't you know who she is?"

"No, I don't."

"Her husband is a big Hollywood producer."

"Oh, is that so?"

His next dance was with Mollie again.

"What was Sophia saying about me?"

"Who is Sophia?"

"The cow you were dancing with."

"She said you were rich."

Mollie laughed. "They're a jealous bunch of bitches."

"What's the pretty girl's name?"

"You can't mean Jackie?"

"Maybe not. The girl in the yellow sweater."

"That's Jackie. Stay away from her. She's bait."

"That's kinda hard to believe."

"Then take her home. But we may as well be realistic about it. Use a prophylactic."

"Thank you. But I will use dialectics instead."

When he went to buy another drink he was told the whisky was all gone and there was only rum left. Behind him someone proposed a toast to Stalin.

"I will take a shot of rum to drink to Stalin," Lee said to the girl selling drinks.

Several others came up and bought rum to drink to Stalin. Then someone proposed a toast to Roosevelt. Lee and the others refilled to drink to Roosevelt. Twelve Russian heroes were toasted next by name, but Lee could not toast more than three of them, whose names he soon forgot.

After that he found himself out in the kitchen solemnly telling Don that when a Negro raped a white woman, that was a crime, but when a white man raped a Negro woman, that was a joke.

"Speaking of jokes, I will bet you that I can give a dirtier toast than you, Lee," Don challenged.

"Go ahead, it's a bet."

"Here's to two old whores out on the block—"

"One white and one colored," Lee cut in.

"An interracial meeting," Don laughed.

Lee started to say "a Communist get-together" but thought better of it.

Ed came into the kitchen on the tail end of it and remarked seriously: "You know, I will be happy when the day comes when a white man can kick a Negro in the ass without being called a nigger-hater."

"I agree with you," Lee replied solemnly. "And I will be glad when the day comes when a Negro can kick a white man in the ass without being called a frustrated homicidal maniac."

"I will buy you comrades a drink," Don said.

"The man's a capitalist," Ed observed.

"Don't call me a capitalist. A capitalist is a man who panders for his mother, rapes his children, and buys bonds. I'm a Communist."

"Then what is a Communist?" Lee asked.

"A Communist is a person with the head of a capitalist, the heart of a capitalist, the soul of a capitalist, and no money," Ed replied.

Silently they turned to the girl selling drinks and had three rounds of rum. Then Lee staggered into the bathroom and was sick for a long time. When he turned to leave he found that he could not stand. On his hands and knees he crawled through the back hall and out onto the back stoop.

It was raining. He sat in the rain and the water soaked through his clothes and felt cool and clean on his head and face and refreshing to the heat of his skin. Lights in the movie stars' mansions way up in the Hollywood Hills looked like little stars in the darkness— "And the stars shone down over the lot of man—" Some half-remembered line from some forgotten book.

In the cold, clean rain his thoughts cleared and his mind took him back to a party in New York. He had run into an old Los Angeles acquaintence, Al Roberts, in the Hotel Theresa. Al had said: "Let's go up to Mamie's."

"Where's that?"

"Up at 940."

"Is she having a party?"

"She's always having a party."

"Oh, like that. Look, Al, I'm broke."

"You don't need any money. She gives her liquor away. Got an old man making good money and she spends it."

They went up to St. Nicholas Avenue on the bus and climbed to the top floor of an apartment house. A fat, light-complexioned woman with black hair and sleepy eyes, clad in flaming red lounging pajamas, let them into an apartment filled with people getting drunk.

"Mamie, this is Lee. He's a home boy."

She had murmured something incoherently. As Lee was to learn before he left, incoherence was her only charm. He had wandered about and met the people. There had been as many white persons present as there had Negroes, but the whites were inconsequential while most of the Negroes were people of importance who held high positions and were known throughout the nation as leaders of their race. But he had listened in vain for anyone, white or Negro, to make a single statement that had any meaning whatsoever. The Negroes were being niggers in a very sophisticated manner as tribute to their white liberal friends. And the whites were enjoying the Negroes' tribute as only white liberals can.

It would have had some meaning to Lee if the purpose of the party had been sex. A prelude for adultery, or even suicide. But there at Mamie's, sex had been but a vulgar joke. And drinking for drinking only, like tonight—as it had always been, it seemed.

Now as he began to sober up, before the dull aching remorse of hangover settled in, he wondered about this drunkenness. As an aphrodisiac, it would have meaning, yes—or for digestion, as he had heard the Italians drank—or for verve, as the French did. But everywhere he had ever been in America, drinking was for getting drunk, as an anodyne for some great hurt, or for oblivion.

And this was one thing they could not hang on the nigger, he thought with sharp disdain. The nigger loved his watermelon, even though the white folks ate most of them. And the nigger loved his chicken—what little the white folks left. But everybody got drunk —nigger, white man, gentile, Jew.

Maybe the Communists knew something after all. In a nation where so many millions of people kept getting drunk for drunkenness, there must be something deeply wrong. Some gnawing dissatisfaction was too great to endure, because they were not only Negroes and they were not only Communists.

And then he thought, as his sharp sardonic thoughts turned inward: "I ought to go back and have another drink."

Chapter 8

NOW everybody was drunk. Many had reverted to what they had been before they had become Communists. And Mollie had reached that twilight stage of self-deceit where there was no longer need to clown. The laugh was off and in its place the small-eyed glitter of predaciousness. Mind, body, and spirit were given to uninhibited speculation upon the hard, vibrant quality of virility. A growing, almost uncontrollable warmth crept slowly up her thighs and was actually seizing her.

"Where is Lee?" Ed asked.

"Lee has gone home," she replied shortly.

"Well, where is Jackie? Has she gone, too?"

"With Lee? No. She is hiding in the bathroom."

Ed stumbled to the bathroom and banged on the door. "Jackie, let me in."

There was no answer.

He stepped back and hit the door with his shoulder. Luther came up and restrained him. "Don't break down my house, man."

Ed drew erect with aggrieved dignity. "Where is my hat? I am leaving."

"Well, leave then."

Mollie went to the bathroom and knocked on the door. "Ed is leaving."

She received no answer. "Everybody is leaving," she continued.

"The party is breaking up." Though her voice was gentle and sweet, her face was marked with an angry malevolence. "Are you ill, dear?"

Still there came no reply.

"He has gone too."

"I am a little sick, Mollie, dear," Jackie finally replied. "I hope you won't mind too much if I use your bathroom a little longer."

"You are welcome to spend the night, darling."

Now all were leaving and Mollie's impatience for them to be gone was scarcely civil. She was tired of them, tired of stifling her frenzy, tired of this sneaking little slut in her bathroom. When all the others had gone she called to Jackie again: "Dear, you are the only one left—and I am occupying Luther, if that is what you are waiting for."

Jackie unlocked the door and came out. "All I can say to you is that you are a dirty-minded, vulgar old bitch."

"Not in my own house, darling."

"Then I will get out of your house. I would have gone a long time ago if I hadn't been ill."

"If you had known he had gone so soon. You should have been watching instead of pretending."

"I was not waiting for anyone."

"The liquor is all gone too."

"Oh! Oh! You are—"

"Not in my house."

Observing a hat and coat bundled on a chair, Jackie remarked: "Oh, someone left their coat and hat."

"It's Luther's."

"I wonder if it's raining," Jackie said, and walked to the kitchen door. "Oh, someone's out on the back porch!" she exclaimed. "It's Lee! He's sitting in the rain." Her voice was accusing.

"Now that you have found him, you can have him," Mollie mocked.

"You are vicious," Jackie said, and went outside.

When Lee heard the door opening, he knew it would be Jackie. For now he realized that underneath all of his other thoughts had been the thought of her, not lustfully or even curiously—just there.

"It's in the mind, Jackie."

"No, Lee, it's in the knees."

They laughed together.

"I was waiting for you to come in and take me home." In the rain her face was a blurred white pattern. But her voice was velvety.

"I didn't think about it."

"Didn't you?"

"Yes, I did. But I didn't know I was thinking about it until you came out."

They were silent, sitting in the rain.

"I believe in being honest with myself," she finally said. "Are you married, Lee?"

"Yes."

A cat came hurrying up the stairs, saw them, and scampered back. "Kitty-kitty-kitty," she called. But the cat did not return.

"Are you?" he asked.

"No."

"I would like to ask you something. Will you answer it?"

"I think so."

"Did they send you out?"

"They?"

"The party. Someone in the party?"

"No, we don't do that."

He let the silence run on.

"Not now—not since the war. We're not interested in recruiting colored people. It causes disunity—"

After a time she added: "I never did."

"I don't think I like Communists," he said.

"I don't particularly like them either. But I believe in Communism. That comes from being honest with myself. If you were honest with yourself, you would believe in it too."

"Perhaps." The silence between them was nice.

"The lights look like stars, don't they?" he asked.

"The wild grass will be coming up soon and late afternoon in the sunshine the hills will look like emeralds. Have you been up there and looked over the Pacific?"

"Where's your home, Jackie?"

"Everybody asks me that."

"Well—you look different."

She told him that she was from the state of Washington. In 1940 she had come to San Francisco to look for work and had become interested in the movement. From there she had come down to Los Angeles.

"I work at Comstock, you know."

"You do? Well, well! In what department?"

"In Foster's office."

"Is that so? For Foster, eh? Say, what kind of a guy is he?"

"Oh, as a man he's swell. He's so good-looking—really handsome —and considerate too. I don't think he gets along well with his wife, though."

"Does he favor the union?"

"Oh, no, he's a capitalist, of course."

Suddenly he began to shudder. "Are you cold too?" he asked.

"No."

"Well, I am. I'm getting a chill."

"Oh, we better go inside."

The lights were still turned on in the kitchen and living-room but the bedroom door was closed and the sound of laughter came from within.

"I wonder what they do that Mollie finds so funny," he said.

Jackie giggled. "Probably tickle each other's feet."

She found half a bottle of brandy and they drank all of it straight.

"May I kiss you?"

"I want you to."

He pulled her close to him and kissed her. When they looked up Mollie was standing in the bedroom doorway, a green crepe negligee draped carelessly about her, watching them. Then suddenly she began to laugh.

"Let's go," Jackie said.

They slipped on their wraps and went outside and down the stairs. The rain had thinned to a misty fog, which lay in the streets like a wet gray blanket. They walked with their arms about each other and once he stopped and pulled her to him and kissed her. Their lips clung, seeking, and then she broke away. Her eyes seemed large and bright and her blurred white face seemed fragile.

"You're cute," he said.

"You're not so bad, yourself."

"Then kiss me again."

She smiled. "You'll ruin my reputation."

"I like you when you smile. You're cute."

She put her arms about him and they fused together in a long passionate kiss. When they had separated and were walking along again, she said: "I've never kissed a Negro before."

Everything went. A slow, crazy hurt ran all through him—tart, brackish, bitter. And though he did not move his arm from around her waist, he moved away, across the city, across the gulf. And where between them there had been a young and stolen sex attraction, now there was race.

"Is there any difference?" There was belligerence in his voice.

"I didn't mean it like that. I just stated it as a fact."

"I don't like the racial facts of life."

"I know, Lee, and neither do I." Now the maternalism was back in her voice. "But they are here and you have to learn to face them."

"Do I?" He felt nothing but a cold, dispassionate resentment.

She turned unexpectedly into the entrance of a Hollywood apartment house, and he experienced a moment of trepidation. She noticed it in the sudden movement of his arm from about her waist and took him by the hand and led him as one leads a little child. But at the appearance of the elevator operator she released his hand. It was as if she had left him standing there alone.

"Step inside, please," the elevator operator said.

He gave a start and beneath Jackie's searching glance felt inexpressibly stupid. "Oh, I didn't notice it was an elevator," he said as stupidly.

She merely smiled at him, squeezing his arm encouragingly. But after they had alighted and passed beyond the hearing of the operator, she asked gently: "You didn't think I would live any place you couldn't come?"

"Well—" Goddamn her soul to hell, he thought. Why couldn't she let him alone? "No."

She unlocked the door marked "3-C" and ushered him into a cosy three-room apartment.

"I live with another girl," she informed him, lighting the gas logs in the fireplace.

"Oh! Is she here now?" He had put his hat back on as if to prepare for flight.

"No. She went down to San Diego last night. But she'll be back any time now. You can't stay but a minute."

"Oh, that's all right. Do you have anything to drink?"

"Only some wine. And take your things off to dry. I'll bring you a robe."

"Oh, that's not necessary." In the sudden misgiving that seized him, he failed to notice the inconsistency of her words.

"Don't be silly, you're wet."

She brought him a robe and retired to the bedroom. Finally he overcame his reluctance and undressed and put on the robe. It was much too small, too tight across his chest and shoulders, and his arms and legs stuck out like poles. She came back, looking girlish in a light-blue robe, and at sight of him began laughing.

"Kathy would just love to see you in her robe."

But quickly she discerned that he did not like her laughing and stopped. "I'll make some coffee," she said and went into the kitchen.

Alone, he began to worry; not only this crazy, senseless fear of being disrobed in a white woman's house in a white neighborhood, one lost Negro in a white world—a fear he could not help; but the fear that Ruth might divine, by some strange intuition, that he had spent the night with some stray Communist woman. Suddenly as apprehension overwhelmed him, he began to tremble.

"Coffee's ready," she called.

He arose as if obeying a command and went to her. She stood with her face slightly lifted as if expecting him to kiss her. But he felt too uncomfortable and ill at ease to notice, and pulling out a chair, sat down as if to hide. Behind him she smiled to herself and rubbed her hand across his hair. Then silently she sat opposite to him and poured the coffee.

She had prepared sandwiches of liver pâté and saltine crackers. But he could not eat them—his throat was too tight. He could barely drink the coffee.

And she knew this. She let her mouth become soiled and ate sensually, licking her lips with the darting red tip of her tongue. If there had not been this crazy restraint of race, he would have become so excited by the sensual way she ate that he would not

have been able to restrain himself. But now he could only stare
at her in rigid fascination.

"I shouldn't be eating so much," she finally said, breaking the
silence between them. "I'm getting awfully stout."

"Oh, I don't think so," he forced himself to say, swallowing.

"Well, not so much here," she gestured, forcing his gaze to her
breasts. "But my hips are getting horrid." And standing, she
turned slowly before him, the tight blue robe revealing every line
of her body.

"Oh, well—" He could not think of another single word. His
gaze clung to her body and the strength poured from his eyes until
he became physically sick and could no longer support the weight
of his body. He slumped down in his seat, staring at her.

She sat down again, torn between shame and disappointment.
"At least they sit comfortably," she murmured, moving from side
to side on them.

"Oh, I think they're very interesting," he stammered as if mes-
merized.

Now cupping her chin in her palms, she drowned him in her
eyes. She could not help her shame. She did not care, she told herself. While her inhibitions drew her back, her passion pushed her
on.

"They're fat."

"Oh, no," he contradicted with an effort at gallantry.
"They're—"

"Exciting?"

"Oh, yes—exciting."

But he sounded more hypnotized than excited. Abruptly, she
turned out the light and taking him by the hand led him into the
living-room to sit by her side on the sofa. The flickering light from
the gas logs in the fireplace bound them in breathless intimacy,
making of her a picture of remote loveliness, something ethereal,
not quite real, an oil by an old master seen at the first break of day.
When she spoke, her voice was as startling as if the night had
spoken: "I feel so lazy! So sleepy! Just like a little cuddly kitten!"
And as human as a woman's.

It was the human quality in her voice that let him down again.
"Oh, you do?" His own voice came out raspy and tense.

He could smell her, a soft perfume like tiny fingers in the nose, and the strong musk scent of sex—a woman scent, more telling than a voice could ever be. His gaze touched her face, the marvel of her eyes and the glisten of her moistened lips.

So now it came, she thought, resting her head back on the sofa and closing her eyes to the world. Now she could recite to him because culture was only sex-deep after all:

> Send me some token, that my hope may live,
>   Or that my easeless thoughts may sleep and rest;
> Send me some honey to make sweet my hive,
>   That in my passion I may hope the best.
>
> I lie noe ribbond wrought with thine owne hands,
>   To knit our loves in the fantastick straine
> Of new-toucht youth; nor Ring to shew the stands
>   Of our affection; that as that's round and plaine,
> So should our loves meet in simplicity,
>   No, nor the Coralls which thy wrist infold,
> Lac'd up together in congruity,
>   To shew our thoughts should rest in the same hold;
> No, nor thy picture, though most gracious,
>   And most desir'd, because best like the best;
> Nor witty lines, which are most copious,
>   Within the Writing which thou has addrest.
>
> Send me nor this, nor that, t' increase my store,
>   But swear thou thinkst I love thee, and no more.

For a long time after she had finished she let the words linger in the mind, then murmured, "Isn't that beautiful?"

"Yes, it is. You make it sound more so." Now, slowly, the strain was leaving him. "I like to hear you recite poetry," he added.

"I love John Donne."

"I love you." Though he could say the words, he could not get the feeling. The vaunted burning lust Negroes are supposed to have for white women would not assert itself. He felt impotent and a fool and took his hand from her thigh.

With the abruptness of a curse she snapped on the light.

But he kept trying, because he thought it was expected of him, and sooner or later it would have to come. For after all, he was a male.

"Kiss me," he demanded, putting his arm about her shoulders.

She looked at him in the glare of light and sighed. "No, let's be sensible," she said. But for the ragged edges, her voice was level now. "Tell me about the union. How is it coming? Are the Negro workers joining up?"

"I don't want to talk about the union. I want to kiss you."

"No you don't."

So she knew, he thought. Well, let her know. He had felt nothing for her since the remark that he was the first Negro she had kissed, as if it was some kind of special honor she bestowed.

But he could not leave it. "I can make you kiss me," he said. Deep within him was the faint desire to hurt her.

"Don't, darling. Some other time when we both feel more like it."

"You know I want—"

"No, Lee!" She stood quickly up and went across the room. "I want to read you something."

"I don't want to hear it."

She returned with a copy of the *Crisis* magazine and turned to the editorial page. "This is the farewell speech of Lieutenant Colonel Noel F. Parrish, a white Southern officer, to the men of the 99th Pursuit Squadron," she related as if he had not spoken. "Listen, darling, these are some excerpts:

> You have a double responsibility. As a squadron of the Air Corps, you are responsible to the army of your comrades and to the nation which shelters those you love. As the first flying Negro fighting unit in history, you are responsible to all the darker people of America who look upon you with pride. . . . Whatever you do badly will encourage those who hate you, and that includes the Germans and the Japanese who hate you most of all because your mere existence is some proof of the sincerity of this nation in trying to provide opportunity for all people. Whatever you do well will encourage those who have fought for a square deal for you, who have insisted, sometimes against great odds, that the chance you are given should be a fair chance. . . .
>
> I must face you with the fact that you, as Negroes, have not been particularly encouraged to be heroic in the past. You have been more often taught to be patient and to endure misfortune. Those are excellent abilities and I hope you can continue to cultivate them and keep them. But there is a time to keep quiet and a time to fight, and the time for you to fight may come soon. Not

to fight for me, for the Air Corps, for Negroes, or even for yourselves. I hope you will think of yourselves as fighting, first of all,
for this nation, not because it is a perfect nation, from your stand-
point, but it is our nation, an improving nation, and the best nation of all.

I hope you will think of yourselves as fighting for more, even,
than a nation. I hope you will remember that you are fighting for
all mankind. . . . It is your privilege, for the first time as Negroes, to play a part that is by no means a low or subservient part.
You now have a top role. And you must win in that role just as
any other group of men must win, by unselfish, vigorous effort
and determination. . . .

You can not expect to be one hundred per cent successful. Air
Corps squadrons have run into serious trouble before and will do
so again. For this squadron to fail in any mission would be doubly
unfortunate, but it could happen through no particular fault of
your own. . . .

I can only remind you in the midst of these problems of race
that seem so serious now . . . that we must not forget the human race, to which we all belong and which is the major problem
after all. The fate of all of us is bound up with the fate of humanity, and the most important of all—men. No one can ask
more than that you acquit yourselves like men. Each of you, and
all of us, must prove first of all that we are capable of the dignity
and nobility of manhood; that we can, when the occasion calls for
it, fight and die for a cause that is greater than any one life, or
any one man, or any one group of men.

At the end of her voice there came a profound silence. She
reached up and snapped off the reading light. Outside it was dawn.

One line above all remained etched on Lee Gordon's mind. Not
the line about the nation: ". . . fighting . . . for this nation . . .
an improving nation. . . ." Nor the line about the top role: ". . . a
part that is by no means a low or subservient part." Nor even the
reference to the price of failure. The first thing that Lee Gordon
learned about failure was that when he failed, it was not the failure
of a person, but the failure of a race.

The line that etched itself on Lee Gordon's mind and crucified
him to his seat was: ". . . that you, as Negroes, have not been
particularly encouraged to be heroic in the past." In this nation
rooted in heroism, built on heroism; where this one virtue runs

through the pages of its history like a living flame, where its people worship heroism before they do their God! It was a hurting thing to hear a white man's admission that this exalting and redeeming virtue had been denied a people because of race; that instead, they ". . . have been more often taught to be patient and to endure misfortune." In a nation where patience and fortitude are viewed with subtle contempt!

Finally Jackie said: "Don't you think that is an inspiring speech? And from a Southerner."

"No."

"Well, encouraging?"

"No. It is depressing. To fight and die for one's country in time of war is the privilege of any citizen. Why should it become such a great honor when a Negro does it?"

"Because you've never before been allowed to play such a part."

"Should I be grateful now? For what? Do you feel grateful when you vote? Or when—"

"Yes, I do."

"When a Communist begins agreeing with a Southerner it's time for me to leave."

"You are not being fair—and perhaps you had better go."

"I don't think I will. I think I will stay here and argue with you since you invited me."

She became abruptly angry and showed it. Jumping to her feet, she said: "Good night! I'm going to bed!"

He reached up and caught her wrist and pulled her back. "If you go to bed I'm going with you. Who do you think you are that you can dismiss me at your will?"

"I think you're stupid and hypersensitive and have absolutely no understanding of historical progress."

"I don't think you're so smart, either. And since you've been trying all night to get me—on orders, I suppose—now you can have me."

"Now who do you think you are?"

"Just a man. Just the man you've been tempting with your body since we came inside the house, that's all."

"Well, now that I'm bored with you, you can go."

"It's not going to be that easy," he threatened hoarsely.

But inside of him was that crazy, tearing sense of desperation—

the knowledge that he was again being a fool, that he had always been a fool, and was unable to restrain himself from being so. He was furious with himself for this sense of confusion, and angry at her for confusing him with the words of a white Southerner. For there was that part of his mentality that rejected anything a white Southerner might say, and another part that, against his will, found the words of Lieutenant Colonel Parrish as inspiring as Jackie had said they were. It was this awful necessity of facing his dilemma in reality, instead of blindly revolting against it, that provoked in him the impulse to hurt her, dominate her, subdue her and bend her to his will. She was here, and she was white, and there was no one else to take it out on but himself.

"I think I'll make you kiss me," he said harshly, and took her in his arms.

"Don't!" She tried to free herself without giving the impression of struggling. "I don't want to kiss you now."

"I can hurt you and make you kiss me."

Now she began struggling slightly.

"Don't you believe it?" he persisted.

"Please go home, Lee."

He clutched her wrists and began bending back her arms.

"You're hurting me!" she cried angrily.

"I'm going to make you kiss me!"

"Don't hurt me!" And now she became alarmed.

"Kiss me then!"

He pushed her back on the sofa while she fought wildly. "Goddamnit, kiss me!"

"Don't do this to me!" she pleaded. "Don't, Lee! For your sake!"

"Kiss me then, if it's for my sake."

She began crying, thoroughly frightened. "Don't! Please don't! You don't know what you're doing!"

"I will hurt you as sure as hell if you don't kiss me."

"Oh, don't! Please don't! You *know* I wouldn't do anything to hurt you! You *know* I wouldn't! You *know* it!"

He forced her roughly down on the seat. "I'm tired of your fighting!"

"Why do you take advantage of me like this? You *know* if you were white, all I'd have to do would be to scream. You *know* it! The doorman and the elevator operator could hear me. They could hear me on the street. You know I wouldn't cry that you were raping me." She began sobbing hysterically. "You know I couldn't do that to you!"

He released her and got slowly to his feet. "I wasn't trying to rape you," he said.

"Oh, what are you trying to do to me then?" she asked. "You know I wouldn't hurt you even if you raped me."

His face creased with a tight groping frown, because in his mind he actually was not trying to rape her. There was no desire in him for sex—just a deep sterile hurt he had sought to release. But he did not know himself how he had sought to release it or what he had intended to do. And the fact that he did not know frightened him.

"I thought you wanted me to hurt you," he said, as shocked by his own words as she was.

"Why, in heaven's name? Why would I want you to attack me?"

Now in his own mind it took the shape of truth. Welling from some deep subconscious source within him came the strange bewildering knowledge of his attitude toward her. From the very first he must have thought she wanted him to hurt her.

"Well—" he groped for the words to explain. "Well—because you're a Communist for one thing—" That didn't make any sense so he tried again: "Well—you must have expected something like that when you didn't respond—"

"Please go home." She stood up. For the first time he saw the fear in her eyes. "Please go." He watched her lips flatten, widen, swelling at the edges, and her face begin to quiver, breaking up as she began to cry again, her eyes pinned on him with the deepest look of pity that he had ever seen.

"Well—" In all the world there were no words to tell her that he had not wanted to rape her. "Okay— All I can say is that I'm sorry—"

She went into the bathroom and brought his still-damp clothes. Then she gave him one last bewildered look and crossed quickly into the bedroom and closed the door.

He dressed and went out and walked through the fog to catch a Sunset bus. He felt lost and depraved and horrified by his own emotions and his own reactions, which were as strange to him as to anyone.

Chapter 9

$\mathbf{A}$ MOMENT back, when he had boarded the bus, searching in his raincoat pocket for change to pay his fare, his hand had encountered a folded sheaf of papers. But at the time he had been so immersed in mortification he had thought nothing of it. Now it came back into his consciousness with the grim review of other things, and he drew it from his pocket. It was some sort of document. Frowning, he unfolded the clipped typed pages and began to read:

EXCERPTS FROM THE RASMUS JOHNSON CASE TRANSCRIPT

The excerpts have been selected to show the following points:
1. The prejudiced remarks of the judge;
2. The improbable story told by the prosecution to explain the fight; the contradictory testimony of the prosecution witnesses;
3. Johnson's own story;
4. The failure of the defense attorney to prepare a case for his client;

Just some more Communist propaganda, Lee thought. He vaguely recalled the case—it had been in the daily papers several years back. And the Communists had picked it up as they had done with the "Scottsboro Case" to inflame Negroes to revolutionary fervor.

But what concerned him at the moment was that he could not

recall who had given it to him. He searched his memory for a clue. Rosie? No, he hadn't seen Rosie since the conversation about the Jews. Don? Ed? The old man, Goldman? That memory made him shudder.

It was in his raincoat pocket. Now who did he talk to while he had been wearing his raincoat? Jackie? He dismissed Jackie; he did not want to think of her in any way.

What worried him was not the possession of the document, but the discovery that he had blank spots in his memory. What he could remember—the episode at Mollie's and all this mess at Jackie's—was depressing to the core. Now the possibility that he might have done things he could not remember at all unnerved him.

Against his will his thoughts came back to Jackie. But why? Had she thought she could convert him to the cause with this sort of cut-rate agitation? No, she had not been interested in his philosophy, he was certain.

But someone had wanted him to read it, and now he began to read again, curious as to the reason:

5. The biased instruction to the jury which precipitated the conviction of Rasmus Johnson and caused his subsequent sentence to prison for sixty-five years;
6. The mockery of justice when a Negro is tried in any American court on the charge of raping a white woman . . .

So! His eyes stopped seeing and his body tensed as from some sixth sense of danger. In the wake of realization emotions surged through him so violently that he trembled in his seat. So! What more could any Georgia woman do? he thought.

Now he forced himself to read with controlled concentration, holding his body rigid to clamp his screaming nerves; because he had to see each typed word to know, and when he knew—

THE COURT: I thought all the spectators were excluded.
MR. BROWN: (defense attorney) They are relatives and close friends of the defendant. You have no objection to their staying, Mr. Loesser?
MR. LOESSER: (prosecuting attorney) I haven't, no.
THE COURT: Pardon me, I still think, gentlemen, either we exclude them all or none. If the young lady is going to take the

stand, the very purpose of it is to save embarrassment. I don't
know why one row should remain here. I feel that all should be
excluded.

MR. BROWN: Very well, Your Honor. . . .

(*Lieutenant Gregory is on the stand*)

MR. LOESSER: When you left the car, where, if anywhere, did
you go with the young lady?

LT. GREGORY: We went for a walk through the park.

Q. Did you encounter anyone on the way?

A. We saw that man (*indicating the defendant*) hiding in the
bushes. I believed he might be a Peeping Tom or something like
that. I was slightly angered and I made some remark to him to the
effect— No, I didn't make a remark. I thought—

Q. Never mind what you thought, Lieutenant, what did you
say or do?

A. I hesitated and stood and looked at him.

Q. I see.

A. Then he came closer and stepped through the bushes. I
realized he had a mask and a hat on and he had a gun in his hand.

Q. Then what happened, Lieutenant?

A. Then he told me to walk over a short distance, about five
feet north and kneel down with my face in the bushes.

Q. Yes.

A. I did so. And he had me move up a little farther. Then he
said he was going to—well— I had never heard the expression before and I asked him what it meant. Well—he said—he told me
what he was going to do. He said that was all he was going to do.
He said for her not to be frightened. Then he made the young
lady lie down. . . .

Lee Gordon lifted sick eyes from the defiling words and almost
vomited at the repulsive insinuation. Was she trying to tell him
that this was what she thought of him, that this was what she had
expected from the first and all else had been insolence? Because if
it was, he would have to go back and rape her to prove it wasn't so.
And he knew he could not do that. He would rather kill himself,
because that would prove something else to her that wasn't so—
that he desired her body above his freedom.

But he refused to believe that she had thought of this. He put it
from his mind and told himself that she could not have thought

of it—that there had been nothing in his words or actions to give
her cause to think of it.

So now he began to read again from urgency:

Q. Could you see, Lieutenant, from where you were?

A. I could not. From time to time I tried to turn around, but
he was evidently watching me closely and every time I turned he
made me turn with my face in the bushes again.

Q. Do you know how approximately long you remained there
in that position and at that place?

A. I haven't the slightest idea. It could have been a year or ten
minutes.

Q. Then what occurred, Lieutenant, or what, if anything,
caused you to change your position?

A. Why, I heard a movement back there, cloth moving and
elastic snapping.

Q. You come from Alabama?

A. I come from Rhode Island. I was stationed in Alabama for
a while.

Q. Go ahead, Lieutenant.

A. Then just shortly afterward I heard the young lady cry out.

Q. Yes? Then what did you do, if anything?

A. Well, I don't know. Something snapped, and I just turned
around and jumped on him. . . .

MR. BROWN: (*questioning the witness*) When was the first
time that you observed the defendant was a colored man?

LT. GREGORY: Immediately after I attacked him.

Q. Up to that time you didn't know he was a colored man?

A. That is correct.

Q. Did you observe a gun during the time he was committing
these acts you described to the ladies and gentlemen of the jury?

A. No. I may explain I tried to look around several times and
he wouldn't let me. He turned me around again.

Q. Did the young lady make any exclamation to you or to your
brother officer or to the young lady who was in the automobile,
that is, in your presence, that the defendant had raped her?

A. She did when we were driving to the station. I asked her
definitely and she answered me definitely.

Q. Well, at any rate, is it true that you and the police officers
went to the hospital?

A. The emergency station, whatever that is.

Q. Do you remember what emergency hospital you went to?

A. No, sir, I don't.

Q. After leaving this hospital where were you taken?

A. They took us—they took both young ladies from the emergency station to another hospital for further examination and treatment for shock.

Q. You didn't accompany them to that hospital?

A. No. At the time they left us to go there, we left to go to the scene.

Q. Was there anything said when they left as to what hospital they were going to?

A. I believe they did say. I believe they also told me the name of the doctor but I don't remember. . . .

(Lieutenant Roberts takes the stand)

Mr. Loesser: What did you see, if anything, when you appeared on the scene?

Lt. Roberts: Well, the nig—the defendant and Lieutenant Gregory were wrestling on the ground and Johnson was on top so I jumped on his back, pulling him off. I pulled him off and he started to strike at me with what appeared to be a knife.

Q. You saw that, did you?

A. Yes, sir.

Q. Then what happened?

A. We took what later turned out to be a broken drinking glass away from him and subdued him. . . .

Mr. Brown: Was there any particular reason why you were looking for a knife at that time?

Lt. Roberts: Well, sir, the defendant started to strike at me with something Lieutenant Gregory said he thought was a knife.

Q. Did he have something in both hands?

A. No, sir.

Q. Did you know when you were subduing the defendant that he was a colored man?

A. Yes, sir, I did know it, but I can't say how I knew it.

Q. Well, did you observe that he was a colored man?

A. There was a full moon, sir, but you couldn't naturally tell— I mean by the time I got there everything was so mixed up— Lieutenant Gregory said, "He has a knife."

Mr. Brown: Thank you very much. . . .

(Mary Lou Haskell takes the stand)

Mr. Loesser: Did the defendant say anything before he made you lie down?

MISS HASKELL: Yes, sir. He said—oh, Lieutenant Gregory said: "What are you going to do?" and the fellow says: "I am going to tickle your girl friend." And Lieutenant Gregory says: "Listen, fellow, you can kill me or anything you want to, but please let my girl alone." The fellow says: "It isn't you I want, it's the girl." So he made—every time Lieutenant Gregory would start to say something, he would put the gun in his back, and he told him to be sure and not make a move or it would be too bad for him. And so then he made me lie down. He made me put the blouse up over the top of my head so I couldn't see anything. And then he—well, Chuck started to move and he made him be still then. And then— just—well, I guess that took place about five minutes. Five or ten minutes. And then he attacked—he started to rape.

Q. Then what did you do?

A. Well, I started to cry just as he started and then Lieutenant Gregory jumped on him. . . .

MR. BROWN: When was the first time if at all that you learned he was a colored man—the defendant?

MISS HASKELL: Well, when he attacked me, I kind of thought he was but I didn't know for sure, and I didn't know for sure until the boys got him in the car.

Q. When he told Lieutenant Gregory to turn around the other way and bend down on his knees and keep his hands up, was Lieutenant Gregory facing him?

A. No, sir, he never did face him.

Q. Now you testified, I believe, on direct examination that it took some five or ten minutes while the defendant was committing this bad act upon you, is that true?

A. Yes, sir.

Q. Then subsequent to that time he raped you, is that true?

A. Well, just as I felt it, Lieutenant Gregory realized that he had gone that far and jumped on him.

Q. Do you remember what hospital you went to, Miss Haskell?

A. No, sir.

Q. Were you examined by a lady doctor?

A. Yes, sir.

Q. Do you remember the name of the lady doctor who examined you?

A. No, sir. . . .

As in slowly mounting horror, Lee Gordon saw revealed before his eyes the ease with which a Negro could be convicted of rape when the white woman was willing to take the stand and confess that he had raped her. The first motive he had attributed to Jackie passed from mind. Now he was torn between accepting it as a warning or a threat. But he could not stop reading until the gristly revelation came to its inevitable end:

(*John O'Shaunessey, Police Officer, takes stand*)

MR. BROWN: Was any statement made by the defendant ever reduced to writing?

OFFICER: To writing? A written statement? We took no written statement. . . .

(*Inspector Kelly takes stand*)

MR. BROWN: Isn't it the custom of the police department in a case of such a serious nature as this, when the defendant gives a statement, to reduce it to writing?

INSPECTOR: Not particularly so. And in this case for the simple reason that the man was caught right in the act.

Q. Was the defendant in this case asked to give a written statement?

A. Yes, he was.

Q. What was his reply?

A. He denied that he had done anything. . . .

(*Rasmus Henry Johnson (the defendant) takes stand*)

(*He testified that he had received his check, cashed it, had some drinks, played pool, gone to the theater, gone to the beach, walked along the beach, and then walked across the park to catch the Geary Street car to go home.*)

MR. BROWN: How far did you go along the beach?

JOHNSON: I imagine two or three block farther down to the old diner there.

COURT: Was that lit up that night?

J.: No, sir, I don't think it was.

COURT: It has been closed for a year.

MR. B.: When did you see Lieutenant Gregory that evening for the first time?

J.: I saw Lieutenant and this young lady lying on the ground.

MR. B.: What was he doing?

J.: Well, he was on top of her, and I came near walked on them and I jumped back. Because it is a pass there.

MR. LOESSER: What is that?

COURT: There is none on the picture here.

J.: On the picture right in the back over there if you would go out to the space out there you can see it. There is numerous passes between those bushes six and seven and eight foot wide.

Mr. B.: Your Honor, I submit there is.

Court: Not where he is showing, no.

J.: In the back over here, Your Honor.

Court: That is not on the picture.

Mr. B.: No, if the Court pleases I submit that is—

Court: That is not on the picture. I am talking about the picture.

Mr. B.: I think we ought to be fair.

Court: Show me on the picture. Show me the path on the picture.

J.: I can't see the pass on the picture.

Court: No, that is what I am saying. There is no path on the picture.

J.: That is full of passes all through the bushes. There is passes enough to drive a truck through.

Mr. B.: How do you know that?

J.: Because I worked out there in the park.

Court: When?

J.: I worked out in the park in 1936. I worked on WPA.

Court: That shovel-leaners' paradise! So you're an expert now —working for the government. How long have you lived in San Francisco?

J.: I came here in 1923.

Mr. B.: Tell the court in your own words what happened.

J.: When I walked up and I saw him, I stepped back and he jumped up and pulled his trousers up. He said to me: "Why don't you get out of this park where you belong, nigger?" I looked at him and I said: "I think I got as much right in this park as you have." I told him: "I am minding my own business." He said: "Do you know who I am?" I told him: "I don't know who you are and I don't care." He says: "Why, I am a lieutenant in the U. S. Army Air Corps." I told him: "That don't make any difference to me." I said: "I am just a poor fellow minding my own business." He said to me: "Do you know what they do to you, to guys like you, where I come from?" I said: "That don't make no difference." He takes a poke at me and, I struck him and knocked him down. When I knocked him down he hollered for this other guy, and the girl started yelling and hollering for the other guy. And then they both got me down and started kicking me. Then they took me by my arms and twisted my arms up and carried me about one hundred and fifty or two hundred feet away and jumped on me again. When they carried me to the police station, Lieutenant Gregory told the police officers there that I held him up and attempted to rape his girl.

MR. LOESSER: When you came home you changed from the old rusty boots to these here?

J.: No, I did not.

MR. B.: If the Court pleases, I object to the manner of examining the witness, holding a paper in front of the jury.

MR. L.: Of course, you know as well as I that I can't call his wife as a witness against him. I have got a statement from the wife where she said he had an old rusty pair of boots on that laced up the front when he came home—

MR. B.: Just a moment. I object to that and I assign it as a prejudicial misconduct on the part of the District Attorney. He knows he can't prove indirectly what he can't prove directly.

COURT: You have to have two suits on to work?

J.: Yes, sir. A pair of extra trousers—and every tree topper out there wears the same. You can send a man out there and investigate the project.

COURT: I don't care about the project at all. I want to know why you were sneaking around with boots and rubbers on and two suits of clothes.

J.: I wasn't sneaking. I was walking.

MR. B.: I object to that question as improper. There is nothing in the evidence that he was sneaking around.

COURT: There certainly is— All right, we will take out the word "sneaking." . . .

COURT: (*instructing the jury*) This has been a short case, ladies and gentlemen of the jury. We started it yesterday and we heard the testimony— This is a case in which the witnesses on one side, five of them, testify one way, and the defendant testifies another way. It is for you to determine on which side lies the truth, and who has reason not to tell the truth. . . .

(*Foreman and jury come back for further instructions*)

FOREMAN: Is there any difference between attempted rape and rape, whatever it is?

COURT: Yes, two different offenses.

FOREMAN: And the bill of information calls for what charge?

COURT: Rape, yes. . . .

Rasmus Henry Johnson was found guilty of rape, robbery, and violating section 288A of the California Penal Code.

After the verdict and before the sentence, Judge Gleason told representatives of the N.A.A.C.P. that he would drop the rape charge if Johnson would plead guilty to robbery and not ask to appeal the case. Johnson said he would rather serve ten thousand years than plead guilty to something he did not do. . . .

For further information relative to the case of Rasmus Henry Johnson, write to:

MRS. MARY EMMERSON, SECRETARY,
LOS ANGELES JOHNSON DEFENSE COMMITTEE.

When Lee Gordon came to the end he did not want to stop, for now he would have to determine the reason Jackie had given him this, and he did not feel up to hating anyone that morning. He felt only a sickening dread, akin to nausea, and the tremendous, overwhelming desire to be safely in Ruth's arms.

So engrossed had he become that he had ridden to the end of the line at Pershing Square, and wearily he alighted. For a time he sat slumped on a park bench in the early morning fog. Aside from the usual coterie of homeless bums, the square was deserted so early on a Sunday morning, and Lee did not see the bums. He felt lost, alone, the one remaining inhabitant of a lost world with only this conviction that he had to reach—was it a threat or a warning?

His mind kept rebeling against the thought that she would threaten him, although it would be just like a Communist to employ revolutionary propaganda as a personal means of threatening. But if she did not mean it as a threat, why should she feel impelled to warn him, and against what? Did she think he ran about the city attacking white women at will? Or was she just trying to illustrate for his own benefit how easily the case of Rasmus Johnson might have become the case of Lee Gordon, had she screamed?

Could this be what Jackie was trying to tell him by the document, that only her pity for him had saved him from a prison sentence, to impress him with the quality of her soul? If she was being noble at his expense, he told himself, he would hate her just as much as for the other.

Whatever had been her motive, she had succeeded only in frightening him, he reflected as he started doggedly for home. Could this then be what she had intended after all?

Chapter 10

SHE was sitting on the top step when she saw him turn into the walk. Her heart gave one great leap of pure relief and the cold wet air gushed into her lungs. And as suddenly it sank again. He looked so bowed and beaten. Everything down inside of her began to cry.

"Lee!" It was a prayer.

At the sound of her voice he saw her. He had not seen her before and now he stopped and did not move. Every fiber of his being went defensive.

"Well, say what you got to say and get it over with!" he said.

"Is it that bad?" she asked gently.

"Is what that bad? What are you talking about?"

"Nothing, Lee." Now only despondency was in her voice.

For a moment longer he stood with his lips slightly parted. Inside of him were all these things he wanted her to know—the whole abhorrent story of the evening—dammed at the very tip of his tongue by the fear she wouldn't understand. He felt like crying over this, for once they could have laughed at everything, at least discussed it, even the episode at Jackie's. For together they had seen the nude white women in the burlesque shows on Main Street, holding nothing back. His curiosity had been no secret then, and often, with her knowledge, an aphrodisiac. Now with the conviction that this would never be again, he closed his mouth and went inside the house and shut the door behind him. After a moment of dull regret he began undressing.

She came in and asked him quietly: "Do you want breakfast now?"

"No."

"Coffee? It's already made."

"Nothing."

"I think I will have some coffee," she said and went into the kitchen.

He put on his robe and came out and stood in the kitchen doorway. A place was set for him but he did not take it. Finally he said: "Everybody got drunk and just kept staying, that's all."

She did not reply and nervously he lit a cigarette. If she had made the opening then, he would have told her all. It was bursting in his heart to tell her. And if she had known that this was so, she would have made the opening if it killed her. For at this moment, more than anything in all the world, she wanted him to talk to her, lean on her, confide in her, as once he had always done. For in his distress she was his haven, wouldn't he remember that? For to be his haven gave her the strength to be his slave, and that was what he wanted, wasn't it? And that was the road to happiness again, she knew. But like Lee, she did not know the words to make the opening, and there they stopped, two people with the one desire separated by perhaps no more than a single little gesture.

As the silence ran on, weighted with this yearning, he could not stand it. "Goddamnit, what are you mad about?" he said defensively. "You stay out all hours of night on your job."

"I'm not angry, Lee." She too was defensive. "I was just worried."

"Worried about what?"

"Oh, I don't know. About everything. I thought maybe something had happened to you."

"What could happen to me at a party of Jewish Communists?"

"I thought maybe you had been run over by an automobile, or had been arrested, or gotten beaten up or something." Her face contained an odd expression of guilt, as if she had committed a sin by worrying. "I can't help but worry when you stay out like that."

Now his defensiveness ran out into soft contrition. "You shouldn't worry like that, Ruth. Nothing's going to happen to me. Damn! I just went to a party."

And then he thought of Jackie and his breath caught up short. "I know it sounds silly," she said, "but I can't help it. You worry too. Just worrying—about anything, everything!" She took a sighing breath. "I never know, Lee. I just can't ever tell—anything might happen. I don't want to worry, but with you keyed up and tense all the time—" And suddenly she was crying; tears streamed down her face into her coffee and her quivering lips looked swollen.

She touched him then. He went over and put his arm about her shoulder. "I'm sorry, baby doll."

She buried her face against his stomach and beneath his hand her body shook with sobbing. "I suppose there're a lot of people afraid in the world, but I don't want to be afraid." She beat her clenched fists spasmodically on the table top. "I don't want to be afraid! I don't want ever to be afraid, Lee."

"You don't have to be afraid, baby doll," he said, trying to console her.

"I'm always afraid," she sobbed. "You make me afraid, Lee."

"How?"

"Oh, I don't know. I've just always been afraid with you and I wasn't afraid before." She sobbed hysterically. "I don't want to be afraid, Lee."

"What do I do?"

"Nothing, Lee; it's nothing you do, it's nothing at all. It's just me, it's all in me."

"Are you afraid without me?"

"I'm not afraid on my job." And she looked up as if in wonder. "No, I'm not. And when I'm around other people, I'm not afraid. What is it, Lee? What's wrong with us?"

He took a long, deep breath to steady the hurt in him, and when he spoke there was only the lie in his voice: "I don't know, Ruth." Because he knew what was wrong with them was only what was wrong with himself.

"I don't want to be such a cry baby." Her voice came muffled through his robe. "But I get so scared, Lee. And when you're scared too I can tell it, and that makes me worse. I never told you, Lee, but I didn't sleep a wink all the time we stayed at old man Harding's. Remember how we both used to get—you did too, I knew—just that sort of crazy trepidation. I feel that always now with you."

"Don't cry, baby doll, don't cry," he said. The sobbing of her body beneath his hand was like his own requiem. "Don't cry." After a silence he added: "I didn't sleep either."

"What is it, Lee? Do you know?"

"I wish I did," Lee said, gone now down the bitter road of memory.

They had gone to live in old man Harding's house the second year of their marriage before he began work on WPA. The old man had been one of several dishwashers at a hotel where he was bussing dishes. At the first tray of dishes he had lugged in from the dining-room, the old man had snapped at him: "Don't put those dishes there!"

He had put down the tray and from it picked a heavy salt-cellar. "If you say another word to me, I'll knock out your brains!" he had threatened.

Several days later old man Harding had reproached him, "You shouldn't talk to an old man like you did, son."

"Well, let an old man tend to his own business."

"You don't like this work?"

"No, I don't."

"I didn't like it either when I first started. I'm a watchmaker by profession," he had added proudly.

"Why aren't you working at it?"

"My hands." The old man had spread his gnarled and twisted fingers. "Oh, I don't mind it now. As soon as I get enough money, I'm going home to see my boy."

From that had grown a strange friendship. Between trays they had talked a little, and Lee had told him of his hopes and ambitions and had listened to the old man talk of the man he once had been. After a week they had begun eating together in the dining-room for the help off from the kitchen, and Lee had told the old man of his wonderful wife and the places where they had had to live.

Old man Harding had felt sorry for him, but he did not discover it until Harding was about to leave for Altoona, Pennsylvania, to visit his son. He had offered Lee the use of his house while he was gone.

"Leastways, you and your wife can have a place of your own till I get back."

"Your home?"

"It's not much, but it's mine."

"Well—" Lee had not known just how to thank him.

But the old man had not wanted thanks. "Young married people ought to have a place to themselves," was the way he had put it.

Lee had never thought of the old man as being white—probably because he had been a dishwasher—until he and Ruth moved into the old man's house and felt lost in a strange neighborhood, fifteen minutes from the streetcar line, an hour and a half from downtown, and cut off from the black world.

It was a run-down, unpainted shack overgrown with crawling rose vines, weeds, and wild geraniums, located in City Terrace, far out in the northeast section of the city. Outside, the underbrush teemed with garter snakes, gophers, lizards, and lice, and inside through the dry, faded wallpaper, cracked and peeling from the walls, and in and out the crumbling cupboards and dilapidated furnishings, rats played a slithering cacophony.

In his twenty years of ownership, old man Harding had never installed gas or electricity and had depended for water on a spigot in the backyard. There was a small coal stove in the kitchen and a tumble-down outhouse in the weeds at the back of the lot.

On both sides were vacant lots also overgrown with weeds. Beyond, going up the hill toward the reservoir, lived Mexicans, and going down toward City Terrace Drive, lived Jews. Several families of white Southern migrants lived on the cutoff circling down behind.

Ruth had hated the place on sight—the filth and the lack of sanitation and modern conveniences, and all the hard, drudging work that had to be done to make it livable. But they could save rent, she had reasoned, and the cheap Jewish markets were near by, so they had prepared to make the best of it.

At first it had been the creaking, ghostly noises in the middle of the night, the slithering of lizards across the roof, the horrible gnawing of rats as if any minute they would come through the walls and devour them both alive.

Then she had almost stepped on a snake on the back porch that first Monday morning. After that she had refused to venture through the dense undergrowth as far as the backhouse, and before they could find a diaper pot she had contracted constipation.

The second night one of the white women who lived behind them had frightened Ruth terribly by picking her way down the front walk with a flashlight. Ruth had seen the light and had come screaming to him: "Somebody's coming! Somebody's coming!"

The woman had heard her. "It's only me, a neighbor," she had called.

Lee had welcomed her in, but Ruth, in the reaction from her fright, had been hostile. But the woman had merely called, she said, to warn them that the Jewish people down below were trying to get the white people to drive them from the neighborhood.

"That Mrs. Friedman called to tell me some colored people had moved in here and if we didn't get 'em out the price of our property would go down. I told her: 'So what, the price of our property ain't worth nothing nohow and the colored people got to live somewhere.'"

Then Tuesday afternoon before Lee had returned from work, Mrs. Finklestein had caught Ruth alone and had warned her that the white people in back were planning to do something to them.

That night they lay awake as they had lain awake the night before. Now in addition to their fear of the dark and the noises, the rats and the snakes, had come the fear of white people scheming against them. But they did not want each other to know they were awake—lying there in a dry sweat, each simulating sleep, lying rigid until their bodies ached. At the slightest sound carefully raising their heads on aching necks to free both ears for listening, their breath catching in their lungs, hurting in their diaphragms.

For seven nights they did not sleep—taut and rigid from dusk to dawn, afraid to turn over to relieve aching muscles lest the other know, afraid to get up to relieve their urges.

"Are you asleep, baby doll?"

"Ho-hum! I was but I just woke up."

"I was, too. But since I woke up I can't go back to sleep."

"Did you hear something?"

"No, just the noises of this old broken-down house. What?"

"I thought I heard somebody."

"There's nobody around, go back to sleep."

Or they had quarreled.

"Why don't you go to sleep, Ruth?"

"I can't help it if I can't sleep."

"You're keeping me awake."

"I don't see how I'm keeping you awake just because I can't sleep."

"You keep twisting and turning and shaking the bed."

"The rats were gnawing. And I heard something."

"There isn't anything to be afraid of."

"I'm not exactly afraid."

"Well, if you're not afraid why don't you go to sleep?"

"I keep hearing something."

"Goddamnit, there isn't anything to hear!"

Hearing it, himself. Hearing it in his mind and in his aching chest and in his hurting diaphragm. Hearing it in his breathless trepidation, in his waiting for it to happen. Lying there waiting for the white people to come and do something to him.

Hearing them coming every night, every moment of the night. Crouching at his door. Tiptoeing across his porch. Putting dynamite underneath his room. Setting fire to his kitchen. Throwing a snake through his window.

He didn't believe that anyone was going to bother them. This was Los Angeles, California, where the police answered a call for help in three minutes, he had told himself. It was senseless to think anyone was going to bother them. He did not believe it. But he had feared it.

If you have never lain sleepless for seven straight nights, your navel drawing into your spine at the slightest sound, your throat muscles contracting into painful stricture, terrified by the thought of people whom you have never seen and might never see, then you would not understand. Living in the world, outnumbered and outpowered by a race whom you think wants to hurt you at every opportunity—

During that time no one else spoke to them, no one had harmed them in any way. No notes had been left in the mailbox. No letters had been scrawled on the door. No rocks had been hurled through the window. There had been no necessity for it. On the eighth day they had left. Just the simple suggestion in their minds, and it had driven them away.

Now holding her sobbing face against his flattened stomach, he was scared all over again. The fear of white people wanting to do something to him came back to lurk in the corners of his mind. Because what was Jackie's motive, after all? Were the Communists planning to frame him in some sort of way?

"Don't cry, baby doll," he said consolingly. "Nothing's going to happen to us. I'm not taking any chances on anything."

She stopped sobbing and looked up at him. "I don't want anything to happen to us, Lee."

He patted her on the head. "Now fix me some coffee."

When she had poured the cup, she asked again: "Are you sure you don't want anything to eat?"

"No, baby, and please don't worry." He started to add: "I love you so much, baby doll, I don't want you to ever have to worry," but she spoke first.

"I'll have to hurry then, or I'll be late for work."

"Today?" he asked incredulously. "Today is Sunday."

"The plant has gone on a seven-day week now."

"Does that mean you'll work every Sunday now?"

"Only every other Sunday."

"But why any Sunday? What's so important about what you do that—"

"You have your work too Lee," she interrupted. "If you were asked to work on Sunday you'd go, wouldn't you?"

"Yes, I would, since you put it that way," he replied, but the closeness had gone from between them and he did not feel affectionate toward her any more.

For a long time after she had gone he sat there nursing his empty cup. When he discovered that he was thinking of Jackie again he got up and went to bed. Outside the gray was thinning and the sun was struggling through.

He could not go to sleep. The lines kept running through his thoughts: ". . . only remind you in the midst of these problems of race that seem so serious now . . . that we must not forget the human race, to which we all belong and which is the major problem after all . . . and most important of all—men. No one can ask more than that you acquit yourselves like men."

Well—yes, Lee Gordon thought, Lieutenant Colonel Noel F. Parrish, a white Southern officer. The white Southerners had always known it. And had always been the first to deny it—

That Jackie. Just what was her story?

Chapter 11

T HE Avalon streetcar was crowded with servicemen and workers, all in the uniform of their participation—the navy's blue woolen and the workers' blue denim, the army's khaki and the workers' tan.

Soldiers for democracy, for an eighty-dollar check or death on some distant isle; the home front and the battle-front; relief clients of yesterday and of tomorrow too—who knows? Lee Gordon asked himself as he shouldered down the aisle. But soldiers today—important, necessary, expendable.

That they felt their importance was a tangible thing that could not be overlooked. Lee observed it in their stances, in their loud, positive voices, their hard, unhesitating steps, their bold, challenging stares, in their high-shouldered arrogance.

From one point of view—say, from Jackie's point of view—it was inspiring, he thought. Great things could be accomplished by this mass consciousness of self-importance, great progress could be made, great change could be brought about. With the guidance of the union— He stopped it there, aware that he was thinking in terms of union propaganda, not because he disputed the logic of his thoughts, but because he rebelled at their regimentation.

Now his mood became sardonic— Ah, the great unwashed masses of the world. The people and their stink— But underneath there was still a defensiveness in his attitude, and he cursed himself

for a fool. Why couldn't he ever think straight? Yes, important people; they were important people, because people were important. They were born with importance. Negroes—yes, Negroes— From some forgotten poem the stanza trickled back:
"Nigger, white man, gentile, Jew,
"Stepping in a smart review . . ."
The streetcar stopped at Forty-Second Street to let off four Negro girls who were hostesses for the Avalon USO. Not a segregated center, Lee Gordon thought cynically, just a center in a Negro community, staffed by Negroes, served by Negroes, and serving Negroes. But not segregated, no. Across the street the gaunt outline of the Wrigley baseball field loomed ghostly in the dark. The rain fell with a soft, sobbing sound. Now the car began to move again, past Vernon through the half-black and half-white neighborhood.

The line kept going over and over in Lee Gordon's mind, like a broken record:
"Nigger, white man, gentile, Jew . . ."
Mexicans, Europeans, Orientals, South Americans—and Filipinos, he added to the quartet. Southerners, Northerners, Easterners, Westerners—and Indians—this was manpower.

With the curious blend of native and migrant, racial and religious, current and traditional hatreds—this was culture.

Living in overcrowded houses and dilapidated shacks, deserted stores and trailer camps, four beds in the bedroom and two beds in the hallway—this was housing.

Sugar shortages and black-market meat, double prices for half values—this was food.

Overcrowded hospitals and brutal police, idle streetcars and hustling criminals, and bewildered administration and prejudiced lawmakers—this was welfare.

Twelve-year-old prostitutes and seventy-year-old degenerates, lesbianism supplanting conjugation, adultery for pleasure and perversion for relief—this was sex.

The cultists and the faddists, the Christian Jews and the Great I Am's, the holy rollers and Aimee Semple McPherson—this was religion.

Niggers alongside nigger-haters. Jews bucking rivets for Jew-

baiters. Native daughters lunching with Orientals. Lumped together in the war plants. Soldiers on the home-front now. For this
was a war-production city. The birthplace of the P-48. Womb of
the Liberty Ship. Week end of the armed forces. The bloated,
hysterical, frantic, rushing city that was Los Angeles in the spring
of 1943. And these were the people who made it go, Lee Gordon
thought.

Now into the pattern of his roving reflections came thought of
all the pretenders of the world who had asked him, as a Negro, to
be reasonable and understand that the thing could not be done;
the "friends of the Negro" who always had some mush-mouthed
theory of patience for him to take instead. "My friends! My
friends!" Lee Gordon thought. "While I am ducking my enemies
you are cutting my throat. At least please be honest for just this one
time and do not tell me what can not be done. Do not tell me
whose feelings might be hurt and who won't stand for this and
who won't put up with that and who will start another civil war.
Because I am seeing it done, here with these people, and now at
this time. So please do not tell me all that stuff again because I am
tired of hearing it," Lee Gordon thought. "Say aloud for this one
time that you do not do it because you do not want to do it. Give
me a choice, if nothing more."

The streetcar arrived at his stop just as he was beginning to enjoy the eloquence of his thoughts, and he had to cut it short. Immediately upon entering the union hall he was approached by five
Negro workers, four men and one woman, who appeared to be lost.

"There he is now," the woman said.

"Hey, man, this the union hall, ain't it?" one of the men asked.

It required an effort to adjust his thoughts, but he said heartily:
"You bet it is, and I'm glad to see you people out."

"Ain't they gonna be no meeting?"

"Sure, the meeting's upstairs in the assembly hall."

"We was up there."

"Why didn't you stay?"

"Warn't nobody there."

"That doesn't make any difference. You could have sat down
and waited. Others will be coming in."

"We warn't sure we was in the right place."

"You're always in the right place," Lee assured them with a forced smile.

The woman laughed. "Hey-hey-hey, we just didn't wanna be the fust. Ain't no need of rushin' these white folks."

They were dressed differently. The woman wore a rose-beige slack suit that fitted tightly across her bucket-shaped hips, one of the men wore a striped, brown suit, two wore draped slacks and sport shirts, and the fourth wore starched overall trousers and a white shirt. And they looked differently. They were of different color, different physiognomy, different build. One of the men wore a mustache, another's hair was conked, a third had two prominent gold crowns that Lee suspected had been placed over sound teeth for decorative purposes, while the woman was pungent with rare and expensive perfume. But all were wearing their Sunday best, and in the faces of them all was a look of apprehension, and in their attitudes the sameness of Negro migrant laborers.

Lee had been afraid that the others wouldn't come—the educated ones, the slick ones, and the ones who felt that industrial employment was only temporary anyway. But if enough of these came the others would have to come, he thought, and he gave his attention to putting these at ease.

Several white workers upon entering had heard the woman's last remark and looked at the group derisively.

"Now are all of you members?" Lee asked loudly to avoid a scene.

"How come you think we's here?" one answered for them all.

But the white workers passed without comment. Instead of following them upstairs, the Negro workers turned from the hallway into the ground-floor bar.

"Better come on up, it's about time for the meeting to start," Lee called after them as he turned away.

"Hey, wait, man, you with us, ain't you?" one of the fellows halted him again.

"Why, sure."

"You for us, ain't you?"

"Sure, I'm for you."

"You our buddy, ain't you?"

Lee was becoming annoyed. "Say, look—"

"Then have a drink with us," the man interrupted with a wide, sudden grin.

Lee had to laugh. "Okay."

They went into the taproom and lined against the bar. Seeing them there, three other Negroes, two women and a man, came immediately to join them. Now in the bar the eight Negroes posed a problem. The white workers who had been there before them resented their presence. One Negro in a bar seating fifty could be ignored, but eight Negroes in a bar seating twenty comprised a black uprising.

The bartender remained studiously impersonal. "What'll you folks have?"

"Whatcha got?"

"Lucky Lager, Acme, Pabst—"

"Just beer?"

"Wine also. Port, Muscatel—"

"I'll take some wine," the woman ordered. "Beer makes me go too much."

"Mus-I-tell for me, too," a man said, and the others said the same. Lee ordered beer.

After her second glass of wine the woman remarked: "I see ri' now I'se gonna like this here union."

"You ain't even been to no meeting yet."

"What I care 'bout the meetings?"

Soon the sound of their voices drowned out all else. Their speech was in dialect sprinkled with casual, unthinking vulgarisms, and their manners were uncouth. In a few short minutes they had taken over the bar and changed it into a rowdy gin mill. They had become objects of scorn, derision, and resentment, yet they had done nothing they would not have done at home.

Patting Lee on the shoulder, nudging him in the ribs, they accepted him as their leader.

"Now don't you be scared," one expressed the general sentiment. "You git ri' up and tell 'em what we wants."

"Tell 'em we wants some colored leadmens an' some colored foremens."

Try as he would to overcome it, Lee felt a shame for them, ashamed of being one of them. But he met the derisive stares of the whites with a level challenge and did not look away. When Joe Ptak put his head through the doorway and shouted: "Time for the meeting!" it came as a relief.

"Hey, Joe!" he called and caught up with him. "How's it going?"

"I don't see any colored workers upstairs."

"They haven't gone up yet."

Joe looked about at the group that trailed along behind them. "Are these all?"

"The rain's keeping many away," Lee began to alibi.

"It shouldn't. If they won't come to union meeting in the rain, they don't give a damn about their union."

"Oh, I don't know."

When they entered the assembly hall Lee noticed that it was less than half filled, and started to remark to Joe that this was a poor showing for the whites too. But Joe had continued forward to the platform where Smitty and the local's officials were already seated. As he was about to follow, Lee noticed Lester McKinley beckoning to him from where he sat at one side with several other Negroes. For an instant he hesitated, debating the importance of his sitting on the platform too, then turned in McKinley's direction.

The Negro workers who had followed him upstairs stood grouped about the doorway, as if trying to decide where to sit among the scores of empty seats. When they saw Lee turned in the direction of McKinley's seat, they followed and filled the empty bench behind. Too late Lee noticed that no white workers sat beyond the aisle and realized that they had segregated themselves. But there was nothing to be done about it now.

He put it from his mind and turned to McKinley. "Hello, Lester, what's new?"

"I have been working assiduously distributing leaflets to one and all in my department," McKinley reported in his pleasant voice. "But there is underhanded opposition being raised against me."

"In what way?" Lee wanted to know.

"Foster."

Lee frowned involuntarily, experiencing his first doubt about McKinley's judgment. "How so?"

"If I know Foster correctly, and I think I do, I am certain he has bought out one of our leaders."

Lee looked around to see if any of the others had heard. No one appeared to have been listening but Lee was not convinced for he had known Negroes who were past masters in the art of expressing disinterest. But when he replied to McKinley he pointedly lowered his voice. "Do you know this for certain?"

"I can not prove it," McKinley said. "But I am as certain of it," he added, "as I am of sitting here."

"Well—" Lee did not believe it. But his concern at the moment was that some of the others might overhear and would believe it and start some sort of groundless rumor to the effect. "Keep it under your hat," he finally advised. "We'll get to work on it and find out who it is."

"I am already at work on it," McKinley informed him.

Lee was relieved when Marvin Todd called the meeting to order. Todd outlined the structure of the local and informed them· that when the membership was large enough there would be a general election of officers. Then Smitty spoke on the history of the union and the importance of unionism. Joe Ptak defined in detail the organizational procedure, peppering his talk with anecdotes of his organizational activities elsewhere. Then Benny Stone reported that there were five hundred and sixty-five paid members to date.

In the lull that followed one of the Negro workers on the bench behind touched Lee on the shoulder. "Why ain't you up there with them other organizers, man?"

In turning around to reply, Lee noticed that all the Negroes within earshot had leaned forward to hear his answer. "Well, it's not really necessary," he said. "It doesn't make much difference where I sit."

"You just as big as they is, ain't you? You got as much to say 'bout all this as they is, ain't you?" another persisted.

"I suppose so, yes."

They let it drop and Lee thought that it was over with. But later when the meeting was opened for questions, the man who had first questioned him immediately gained the floor.

"What I wanna know is why-come our organizer ain't sitting up there on the pulpit with the rest of y'all?"

A sudden laugh arose from the white side.

"Aw, man, hush yo' mouth an' set down!" came a shamed out-cry from another of the Negro workers.

"He has the right to ask the question," McKinley stated quietly.

Todd ruled the question out of order. A din arose as many tried to speak at once. But heard above the din was a white Southern voice. "Well now, by God, that's a fair question."

"What's fair about it?" a similar voice demanded.

Lester McKinley was suddenly on the floor. "I'll have a word to say to that."

Both Joe and Smitty had sprung to their feet but Smitty was the first to speak. "Lee, come on up here where you belong."

"Damnit, the man can sit where he pleases," Joe said in rebuttal. "This is a democratic union. Everybody can sit where they please. That ain't no problem. As an organizer Gordon can sit on the platform, sit in the audience, or stand on his feet."

"The meeting's adjourned!" Smitty shouted. "Everybody come back next Saturday night at the same time and bring two new members each!"

Lee had not moved. Now he stood up and tried to talk to the Negro workers who had suddenly ganged about him. "You shouldn't have raised that issue, men. I could have sat on the platform—it's my prerogative. But I chose to sit with you fellows because I wanted to."

"Well, if all that's so, what they doin' jim-crowin' us over here on one side?"

Smitty appeared just in time to catch the question. "Who told you fellows to sit over here? We'll get to the bottom of this right here and now. We're not going to have any kind of segregation of any kind. I want you fellows to know that from the bottom of my heart."

"No one directed us over here," Lee explained. "It was just an unfortunate choice of seats."

"You come over here and I followed you," one of the women said. "I thought that's where we was supposed to sit."

"You people can sit where you want to. You're members just like anyone else," Smitty assured them, then turned to Lee. "You should have told them that, Gordon."

Lee felt the blood rush to his face. "I didn't see any need to tell them. They should know that."

Smitty turned back to the workers. "Now, fellows, I want you to know, and I want you to tell all the other colored workers in the plant, that we are not having any segregation in this union. You can come here and sit where you want. You'll vote just like everyone else. You can hold office just like everyone else."

"Can us be president?" one wanted to know.

"If you get enough votes you can be president of the local just like anyone else."

"If us get enough votes. I knew there was a catch."

"We don't want to be president. What we want are some colored leadmen out in the plant. We want some colored foremen too. And we want a square deal."

"I'll promise you that. You folks will get a square deal out of this union." Smitty spoke with deep sincerity.

Satisfied, the group began breaking up. Joe Ptak, along with most of the white workers, had already gone, but several groups of whites had remained to see the outcome of the discussion. Now Benny Stone detached himself from one such group and came over to speak to Lee.

"It'll smooth out, kid, as soon as they learn a little more about the union," he said. "We have a lot of educating to do yet. Get Luther to tell you—"

"There's nothing to smooth out," Lee cut him off, resenting his sympathy and reference to Luther equally. "They understand and if they don't, let me handle it. It's my job."

"Sure, pal, sure. Take it easy," Benny murmured and scampered off.

McKinley had not taken part in the discussion, but now as he prepared to leave, he tapped Lee on the shoulder and said solemnly: "Beware."

Lee gave a start. Then Smitty called him to one side and they sat down at the end of a bench.

"Lee, this is all your fault," he said bluntly. "You shouldn't have let it happen." He was angry and disturbed.

"How was it my fault?" Lee snapped, the resentment at being jacked up riding him into a rage. "Nobody told me to sit on the platform."

"You should have known your place was on the platform."

"How was I to know that?"

"Because you're an organizer."

"Then why didn't you tell me it was part of my job to sit on the platform?"

But Smitty was through with it. "Now this segregation business —you shouldn't have let them bunch themselves together like that."

"It had happened before I noticed it, and then the meeting had started."

"But you have to notice things like that. There's no telling how much harm was done tonight, both with the whites and the colored. You have to impress the fact upon new members that the union is democratic."

The very fact that Smitty was right impelled Lee on to argument. "You can't just tell them, Smitty. You have to show them."

"Well, let's show them then. Let's get them in here and scatter them about among the white people and make them know it's democratic."

"You can't do that, either, because they want to sit by themselves."

"Well, by God, Lee, you're talking in riddles now. They don't want to be segregated and they do want to be segregated. What kind of business is that?"

Now Lee was in the position of either having to explain what was nearly unexplainable or appearing a consummate fool. It had taken him some time to realize the scope of the Negro worker's attitude toward unionism. At once it was a curious mixture of logical antipathy and great expectation. For while their cold racial logic told them that the union also was another racial barrier, their deep yearning for democracy caused them to expect from it not only the opportunity for full-fledged participation but in addition special consideration and privileges. They did not want to be just members; they wanted to be special members with rights and privileges above all other members.

This had been hard enough for Lee to understand, and now before opening his mouth he realized the futility of hoping that Smitty could. The thought processes of Smitty would not be the same as those of any Negro; they had been planted in a different soil and cultivated differently. And Lee knew this, but he attempted the explanation because it was congesting within him and had to come out.

First, he argued that no more discrimination existed then in the plant than there would be after it had been organized; that the lack of Negro leadmen and foremen, both before and after organization, would be attributed to seniority. By seniority white workers would be promoted to higher paid jobs and Negroes employed to fill the lower paid ones. And what had the union to offer that would relieve this? Nothing! For the basis of unionism was also seniority, which seemed right and just. The union would always press for the establishment of the rigid rule that the first to be hired should be the last to be fired and that promotions to higher ratings should also be based on length of service.

But Negro workers read it the other way, Lee doggedly insisted —that the last to be hired would be the first to be fired. And they would always be the last to be hired—first, because of prejudice, and second, because of their lack of experience, for how could a man get experience at a trade without ever having had a chance to work at it?

Under the company merit system Negroes could at least hope that by application and hard work, superior acumen and Uncle-Toming, they might get a better job than they would by the process of seniority. They would accept discrimination because without unionism they would expect discrimination.

Lee Gordon struggled earnestly to explain the Negro workers' attitude toward discrimination—the fact that discrimination had become a way of life. They had accepted it as a part of the role they lived, as a condition of existence, beginning with the ability to think—and never ending. They had resigned themselves to expect no better.

It was this acceptance of theirs that kept them living, Lee Gordon contended. This state of believing said they must stay in their place, expecting only a Negro's due. It was this that kept them alive in a nation where equal opportunity was a hallowed legend and civil equality the law. For whenever a Negro came to believe that full equality was his just due, he would have to die for it, as would any other man.

And this was what the union meant to them, Lee Gordon painstakingly propounded. Equality! They did not expect it from the company. They did not think about it. And as long as they did not think about it they were all right. But the union made them think about it. The union preached it. The union promised it. They did expect it from the union.

"And face it, Smitty, face it!" Lee broke into a shout. "The union can't give the Negro worker equality!"

"What's to stop us?"

"You haven't got equality to give. Look, man, let's face it. The union could be very wonderful for Negroes if it first took into consideration that you can not have equality in the plant and inequality on the street. Look, you should be able to see that there can be no equality on the job unless it first exists in the employment office."

"We know that, Gordon; that's why political action is the first duty of the union council."

"What political action? Where? This union's never made a promise to see that fair employment is carried out."

"Gordon, what are you trying to say? Do you believe in unionism?"

"Yes, I believe in it," Lee Gordon said. "But I am trying to explain a problem you don't seem to understand."

"Are you trying to explain it or confuse it?"

"I am trying to explain it if you will listen."

"I am listening. Goddamnit, that's all I've been doing!"

"Well—fine. Because you're telling me what to tell the Negro workers to get them to believe in the democratic equality offered by the union. But what you don't understand is that equality to the Negro worker who has never known equality is more than equality. To us equality is not a chance to participate equally. To us equality is special privilege. Is that so hard to understand? A Negro must earn twenty thousand dollars to feel as secure as a white man who earns five thousand. Why? You know why! Because it's part of a Negro's conviction that he has to be twice as good to be considered at all. There is no way to get around it. The Negro's confidence, or his ego, or whatever in the hell you want to call it, has to be built up to where he can feel equality without having to first achieve superiority. Therefore at the beginning of any democratic movement the Negro will always be a special problem."

"Well, Lee, there's one thing you ought to know. We can't have unity and special problems at the same time. They just don't go together. And we must have unity to have an organization."

"Look, Smitty, you can't have unity without having equality, either."

"Lee, I'm tired of talking about it. You're just trying to complicate the issue. If we make a special problem out of the Negro workers then we have to make a special problem out of the white Southern workers, the Chinese workers, or the Jewish workers. The Negro is a worker just like anyone else. Why in the hell should the goddamn Negroes always want special consideration?" In his earnestness he had forgotten he was also talking to a Negro.

"It's not so much that they want special consideration as that they must have it," Lee argued stubbornly.

"You folks don't know when people like you," Smitty said.

Now Lee had that sudden sickening sense of being crazy in a crazy world—an idiot among idiots, all speaking in an unknown tongue. No one understood anyone else—only listening to the sound of the other's words, and then mouthing the sounds of insanities in their own meaningless tongues.

"Is it necessary that we know?" Lee Gordon asked.

Smitty looked profoundly shocked.

"If we don't know," Lee continued, "does that mean you will do less for us? Does what you do for us have on it the price that we recognize it and feel grateful? Is it a personal favor you are doing us?"

Now Smitty became defensive. "Hell no! I'm asking no gratitude for what I do. I believe in what I do. I don't ask any Negro to like me because I like Negroes. That's ridiculous. I like Negroes just as I like any other people—because I've been around them and grown to know them."

Smitty then told the story of how in kindergarten he and a little Negro girl had become so enamored of each other that they cried each day when the time came for them to separate.

"Well—yes," Lee Gordon said.

It was one of his most disheartening experiences—listening to Smitty tell of his personal regard for Negroes while having no understanding whatsoever of the issues involved. Realizing that no matter what Smitty might do to harm Negroes, destroy their objectives, or deter them from their aims, he would want them to understand that he did not do it because he hated them.

Lee had met this kind of liberal on WPA, in the post office, and during his short stay in New York City, and had always been frightened by them. They were the kind of white people who were honest and sincere in their regard for Negroes, who would eat and sleep with them, marry them and live with them on a social level, who might fight ceaselessly and valiantly to bring about a solution for their oppression, who might even become martyrs for their cause and bleed and die for them—as did "the brave men, living and dead who struggled here. . . ." But from beginning to end they could not accept the proposition for which they died, and could never live in equality with those for whom they had fought so heroically to have considered equal—simply because deep inside of them inequality was a fact.

"Anyway, I'm glad you like us," Lee Gordon finally said.

"I do like you," Smitty insisted. "I have confidence in you, Lee. I believe in you."

Lee could not find the words to say how ironical he thought this was. Because by the very statement, Smitty was insisting that he, Lee Gordon, mug, and did not even know it—in fact, would not have believed it if Lee had tried to explain. For like many other white people whom Lee had met, Smitty mistook the mugging of a Negro for integrity. And if he, Lee Gordon, had any sense, Lee said to himself, he should have learned, as had the great Negro leaders who always mugged, that white people preferred the mugging to the honesty.

"Look, Smitty," he promised, "I'll get this straightened out and see that it doesn't happen again." And then he added: "Forget all this stuff I've been saying. You're right as hell, the union does offer democracy."

And now he, Lee Gordon, was mugging, and could not help himself—because something inside of him impelled him to.

"Sure, Lee, goddamnit! We all have to blow off sometime."

Chapter 12

NOW he was wound up, entangled in his own con-
fusion, chagrined by his inability to make Smitty understand what
he did not quite understand himself. It was important, urgent,
that someone understand him if for no more than to ensure him
that he could be understood. His own thoughts had never before
taken him quite this far and it was too far to be alone.

He thought of talking it over with Ruth, trying to make her
understand. But that was hopeless, he told himself. She could not
even understand his necessity for dominance, or anything at all
about his ego—his warped ego, his sickly, dwarfed, cowardly, cringing ego that his fear had given him. An ego that made a man beat
his wife just to prove that he was stronger.

So what if he did want in a wife a sycophant and a slave? A wife
who, if she could not think of him as great, could at least tell him
he was right—a wife who would always be beneath him, who would
have to look up to him to look at him at all? So what if he did need
such a wife to know that he was not the lowest person in the world?
And what if it did make her the lowest instead of himself? It would
just be her unfortunate predicament of being married to a Negro
man. It was not fair—of course it was not fair. It was a mean, dirty
thought, of course, of course, he admitted to himself. But, Lord
God, a man had to stand on somebody, because this was the way
it was.

No, not Ruth. If she could not understand his antipathy to a hard, critical, competitive wife, she certainly could not understand that to a Negro equality meant special privilege.

Then he thought of Jackie—not that he expected her to be any more understanding than Ruth, or understanding at all. She could not even understand how he, a Negro, might interpret her loss of interest as a subtle invitation for him to overpower her, since in his limited experience he had seen nothing barred in the frantic search for strange sensations from interracial sex.

But he could better bear the thought of her not understanding, since there was no reason why she should. She had no interest in him beyond the physical and he was not expected to marry her. In the place of understanding she offered sympathy. And even though he knew it to be false, no more than a preparatory step to sensualism, it was better than facing the lack of understanding in his wife.

For at least Jackie could be a woman with breasts and limbs and flesh, and not always a condescending counselor like his wife. And to him, a Negro, she could be more than just a woman—a white woman enshrined in the fatal allure of the forbidden, and veiled in the mystery surrounding white women as seen by some young Negro men. And now she had a greater attraction, for she had threatened him.

So it was to Jackie that his hurt pride sent him, for what he did not know. But after he had entered the telephone booth in the downstairs hallway to call her he discovered that he did not know her name. So he had to call Mollie first to get her telephone number, and when finally he called her, the build-up was intense.

"It's Lee, Jackie—Lee Gordon. Remember me?"

"Of course, Lee," but her voice was noncommittal.

"I didn't realize it was so late until after I had dialed."

"We haven't gone to bed. Kathy and I were playing records."

"I thought maybe I could stop by for a few minutes," and when she answered this with silence, he felt impelled to add: "I want to apologize." No sooner had he said the words than he regretted them.

She let the silence run a moment longer, and then said cordially: "Please do," allowing him to breathe once more.

"In about a half an hour," he said, but now the thrill had gone from it.

After he had hung up he was assailed by a feeling of strangeness, as if he was wandering outside the scope of his own known world. Then a sense of guilt engulfed him as he thought of Ruth. She would be worried again, would probably wait up for him. He began hurrying from his pursuing conscience.

Jackie again looked girlish in the light-blue robe, with her wind-blown hair falling in a brown cascade about her neck and shoulders. Her face had a scrubbed, tinted look and beneath her hairline a tiny scar, which he had not noticed before, glowed whitely. Only her lips were painted freshly carmine, and her eyes were full of friendly interest, no more.

"Kathy's turned in," she said, and led him to the sofa where they had sat before.

It had been Lee's intention to challenge her about the Rasmus Johnson document but in her presence he felt a tongue-tied diffidence, and the memory of the previous meeting chastened him. He found himself again apologizing. "I'm sorry about the other night. I really didn't mean—"

"We were both a little drunk."

"I know, but—"

"Forget it, Lee. It doesn't count when you're drunk."

"Well, I—well—yes."

She gave a fresh, wholesome laugh. "Where did you pick up that?"

"Pick up what?"

"That 'well—yes.' It's quite an accomplishment."

"Oh, I don't know. Sometimes I just can't find the words."

"How was the meeting?" she asked, channeling the conversation into another course.

"Oh, fine. The rain kept some away."

"It was unfortunate you had to run into difficulty at your first meeting. But don't look so downcast, it's not fatal."

"Oh, were you there?"

"No, but I heard about it."

"Oh!" And then doggedly, he came back to it, "What Smitty can't seem to understand is—" He broke off. Couldn't he ever let it go? he asked himself.

When it became apparent that he was not going to continue, she asked: "What is it that Smitty can't understand?"

"Oh, nothing much. We had a little argument about how the Negro workers feel."

"How do they feel?"

"I was trying to tell him that the Negro workers presented a special problem."

"Do they?"

He looked sharply at her and then, remembering that she was a Communist, let the question pass, "Oh, I don't know. I'd rather not talk about it now, anyway."

She did not press him for an answer, but instead asked pleasantly, "What shall we talk about, then?" She appeared serene and amicable but not overly interested; and he had the slightly disturbing sensation that she was laughing at him.

Again he braced himself to challenge her about the Rasmus Johnson thing, but could not bring himself to put it into words. "You talk about something," he suggested. "I like to listen to you." And then spontaneously he said: "Recite some poetry, won't you?"

A bright, pleased look swept across her face, but she said: "I'm not in the mood for it tonight. Tell me about yourself, Lee. What sort of person are you?"

"Oh, I'm just another guy—an amateur union organizer."

"Do you like it?"

"It's a job."

"Is that all?"

"Well—no. I believe in unionism too even if I do argue with Smitty."

"You'll like it better when the results begin to show."

"I like it all right now."

"Don't you think Luther's a great help?"

"Not necessarily, no."

"Perhaps you don't listen to him. He's had a lot of experience in organizing, you know?"

"No, I didn't know."

"How do you like Benny Stone?" she asked, again channeling the conversation.

"I don't like him, why?"

"You don't know him well." It was more a statement than a question.

"No, I don't."

"He's a marvelous person once you get to know him. We want him for the president of the local, you know?"

"Oh, are you a member?"

"Certainly."

"At least he would be better than Todd," Lee admitted.

"Marvin is useful, too," she said. "He has quite a following."

Lee was tired of it now. "What is your last name, Jackie?" he asked, channeling the conversation himself.

"Forks. Just remember kitchen utensils. And it's not knives."

"Or spoons."

They laughed perfunctorily.

"Would you like coffee?" she asked.

"No, thanks."

"I'll turn the fire off under the water," she said, arising.

He watched the lithe sway of her hips as she walked into the kitchen but experienced no desire. It was enough to be in her presence, to lean on her impersonal strength. When she returned, he said: "I have been thinking of the colonel's speech you read to me. I find it inspiring—much to my surprise, in fact."

"I thought you would. The very fact that he is a Southerner shows a sense of awakening."

"What I mean is, well, you need encouragement sometimes from any source." At that moment he felt receptive to anything that she might have to say.

Her face leveled under the slow spread of maternalism and when she spoke her voice was beckoning as to a little child. "Communism is the answer to that."

It caught him like a blow into his stomach and his mind closed rapidly again. He felt only aversion and now he had the nerve to challenge her.

"Why did you put those excerpts from the Rasmus Johnson case transcript into my raincoat pocket the other night, Jackie? Was it to threaten me?"

Her eyes widened as if in complete bewilderment and she looked at him as if fearing that he had gone out of his mind.

"You know what I mean," he went on determinedly. "Those typed excerpts from the Rasmus Johnson rape trial that you Communists used to pass around."

"Oh, I remember. That was years ago. I was in San Francisco at the time. What about them?"

"When I got home I found a copy in my raincoat pocket. I wondered if you had put it there."

"No, why should I?" Her eyes were the essence of pure candor but coldness had come into her voice.

"I don't know. That's why I asked."

"If I had felt that way about you I would not have let you come tonight."

"I was wondering about that. You know now that I had no intention of—well, you know what I mean?" He couldn't say the word.

A sudden show of anger brought her quickly to her feet, but she moved slightly to one side so that the light from below delicately shaded the exquisite lines of her features and gave the illusion of height and slenderness to her sturdy peasant's body.

"Lee, look at me!" she said, the sharpness of outrage in her voice. "Do I look like a whore—a cheap tramp who would get a thrill out of your raping me?"

Now he became defensive in the face of her indignation. "Jackie, I didn't think that, honestly. I don't think of you in that way at all."

"But you think I'm a pushover!"

"No, no I don't. I don't even want you in that way."

She turned slightly, showing the curve of her hips and the light caught brightly in her hair. "I am a Communist because I believe in it," she said evenly, "but that doesn't make me want to hop into bed with you at your least desire as you seem to think."

"I don't think that at all. If you mean you think that's why I called you tonight, you're wrong. I just wanted to talk to you."

Now she wore a wounded look. "I understand so much more about you than you realize, Lee. You're so confused, so mixed up in your thinking. But you don't understand me at all. If I have anything to tell you, I won't tell you in that way."

"That's what has been puzzling me. What could you be trying to tell me?"

"I want to help you, Lee." She thawed slightly and into her voice came a note of genuine sincerity. "Don't you realize that? I want to help you because you're important to the union—and because as a person you're so—so lost."

The antagonism ran out of him beneath her candid gaze, and he wanted to tell her everything, to confess his fear and his weakness and nurse at the breast of her sympathy.

"I know you do, Jackie. In a way you're strangely good. That's why I'm so attracted to you, I suppose."

Now she sat again and patted the back of his hand, glowing all inside from a sense of triumph. But the longing for him to desire her began riding her again and it showed in her voice as she tried to take her thoughts away from it, "Lee, you can't solve the Negro problem by yourself. All you can do is work with others, darling."

"I'm not trying to solve the Negro problem, Jackie. I'm trying to solve my own problem."

"What kind of person is your wife, Lee?"

The question startled him. "Why, she's all right. How do you mean?"

"Is she intelligent?"

"Why—certainly. She's a women's counselor at the Jay Company." He said it with a sense of pride.

"Do you get along?"

"Well—yes. We get along all right."

"I'm glad you didn't say you were one of those misunderstood husbands."

"No, we get along all right most of the time."

"I'm glad for your sake. You need an understanding wife." And now that she had gotten past her sudden swell of passion, she glanced covertly at her wrist watch with just enough of a gesture to be noticeable but not obvious.

Lee noticed it and jumped to his feet. "Oh, I must go; it must be awfully late."

She stood beside him and lightly touched his arm. "You'll be all right," she said, smiling into his eyes.

He stood for a moment looking at her, searching for the words to express his sense of satisfaction. "I want to thank you for letting me drop by, Jackie," he finally said. "I enjoyed talking to you."

Her voice was pleasant as she said: "I enjoyed talking to you also, Lee," and then she put the three hundred years in between them, "but I would rather you didn't come to see me again."

"Jackie!" A sudden breathless hurt was in his voice. "But I want to see you again. I—we're just getting to know each other."

"I don't think we're good for each other. And I know your wife must be wondering where you are."

"I don't care if she is. I like you more than you can realize. Please, Jackie, let me call you anyway."

Into her eyes came a sudden winning look. But her voice remained noncommittal. "We'll see."

He braced himself and said: "I'd like to kiss you, if I may."

For just a moment she hesitated before she said: "I want you to."

Beneath his lips hers were cool and unresponsive, and what he got from it was the simple knowledge that he had kissed a white girl while both of them were sober. And yet on the way home he experienced a sense of having gained something. Ruth had gone to bed, and when he climbed in beside her he felt a strange forgiveness—for she knew not what she did, he thought.

Chapter 13

AND how is it going with my fine anti-Semitic friend?"

The words reached out and stopped Lee as he came down the walk from the union shack. Hearing the delayed cadence ending on a question mark, he thought, "Jew," before he jerked a look down at Abe Rosenberg's bald head in the sunshine. Sitting on a disbanded wooden casing, feet dangling and his froglike body wrapped in a wrinkled tan cotton slack suit, Rosie looked the picture of the historic Semite. Lee's reaction was an alerting, a quickening of defensives, a sharpening of caution.

"Not so fine," he muttered in reply. "And you?"

"What is the problem?" Rosie asked.

"Does there have to be a problem?"

"With you, yes."

"Then how is the second front, Karl Marx, Joseph Stalin, Leon Trotsky, and other friends of yours? I have no problem there."

"Not so good the second front. Karl Marx okay. Joseph Stalin is still standing. He'll still be standing, that fellow." He tapped his pipe and began to fill it from a pouch. "The traitor Trotsky is no friend of mine. He is what happens to a man who hates the people."

"Sure," Lee agreed half laughingly. "He was a dirty, stinking, double-crossing rat." He paused to watch Rosie fill his pipe. "Still smoking Nigger Hair?"

Rosie laughed, unabashed. "It's good tobacco—and cheap. But now I carry it in a pouch, you observe."

"I observe."

"You think I shouldn't smoke it?"

"No, I don't think you shouldn't smoke it. I think you ought to give up one of them, however—your Nigger Hair or your Communism."

Rosie shook his head. "That shows how wrong you are. To be a Communist in a capitalistic nation you must use every resource of capitalism."

"To fight capitalism?"

"How else? Communism is the acceptance of reality. We're not dealing in religious mysticism."

"Even to the Nigger Hair?"

"Why not? It's cheap and I have it. Better for me, whom it can not indoctrinate with anti-Negro sentiment, to smoke it than for others whose prejudices it might feed."

"You know, Rosie, you always have the answer. Is it the Jew in you or the Communist?"

"Of all the rotten results of racial prejudice," Rosie said, "anti-Semitism in a Negro is the worst."

"I think the same thing about anti-Negroism in a Jew," Lee retorted. "With Jews being slaughtered in Europe by the hundreds of thousands, brutalized beyond comprehension, you Jews here in America are more prejudiced against Negroes than the gentiles."

"That's silly. Have you ever heard of a Jew in a lynch mob?"

"Only because the white lynchers discriminate against him. He does everything to the Negro short of lynching."

"Now that we have exhausted our stupidity, let's go to lunch."

"I'm not going to lunch."

"I came to take you to lunch—all of the way from Boyle's Heights."

"Oh, so that's why you're here. I suppose to boost Benny Stone for president of the local?"

"He's the best man for the job, isn't he?"

"I don't know."

"But I came to take you to lunch."

"Then why didn't you come inside?"

"Inside is for the members of your union. I'm just a kibitzer from the clothing workers' union."

"And from the Communist Party."

"Lee, I'm worried about you, boy."

The edges of Lee's face drew down in a sudden frown. "You're not the only one. Every one is worried about me, it seems. Even my wife," he added bitterly.

"So? And don't you think you're worth worrying about?"

"Not to the extent that it becomes obnoxious."

"Come, let us eat then before we reach that point," Rosie said, sliding from his seat. Noticing Lee hesitate, he added: "I'm paying for it."

"Well, okay," Lee had to laugh. "I'd better not miss this opportunity. It'll probably be the only time a Jew will ever buy a lunch for me."

"I don't understand it," Rosie said, turning along the pleasant street that went to San Fernando Valley. "A young man like you talking such stupidity. What's happening to the Negro people?"

"We're just getting tired, that's all," Lee replied as he shortened his steps to keep pace with Rosie. "Just getting tired."

"That I can understand. But why take it out on the Jew? What has the Jew done to you?"

"What hasn't the Jew done?—cornered us off into squalid ghettos and beat us out of our money—"

"Oh, stop it!" Rosie snapped. "Such nonsense should never be spoken." Coming to a halt, he asked: "Where do you usually eat?"

Lee had gone a step ahead and turned to look at Rosie. "You're taking me to lunch, I thought."

Chuckling, Rosie walked on ahead. "Come on; at least you are consistent in not co-operating."

Lee caught up, pacing his steps again. "If you could open your mind a little and see beyond that Communistic rote you would realize that what you call my lack of co-operation is consistency itself."

"At least I know the place to eat," Rosie said. "And it won't be what you can call a Communist hash house, although most of the people you see there will be Communists."

"You make it seem as if I am hypercritical of everything," Lee said. "I don't think I am."

"No?"

"No."

They walked the remaining block in silence and turned into the palm-shaded grounds of a roadhouse not far from a motion picture studio, where few but the officials from Comstock dared adventure.

"So this is where the big-shot Hollywood Communists come?" Lee asked interestedly.

"Why not? Communism is for everyone."

Inside was a cool dim oasis filled with a well-dressed crowd. Only Rosie, because of his slack suit, and Lee, because of his color, seemed out of place. But Rosie gave no indication that he was aware of this. In his bright-eyed look furtively recording the reactions of this tall, thin Negro youth was the wisdom of five thousand years and his hard insouciance was eternal. And by his studied refusal to acknowledge their obvious difference, he helped put Lee at ease.

Unable to obtain seats immediately, Rosie squeezed Lee into the bar and ordered Martinis. And for once Lee did not feel the tearing microscopy of white eyes or the sexual calculations of white women, whether because the people gathered there were Communists, he could not determine. But he felt grateful for it, and a strange sense of detachment from his former self came over him.

"This is a nice place, Rosie."

"I like the Martinis here," Rosie replied.

Shortly the headwaiter beckoned and they followed him to a table in the corner near the pantry door. When the waiter had taken their orders, Lee remarked: "My customary seat in a white restaurant."

"You don't like it?" Rosie questioned.

"Oh, it's fine. But I look forward to eating in a white restaurant and sitting up front."

"I don't think this has anything to do with you," Rosie declared. "It's on account of my having on a slack suit."

"You keep your answers ready, don't you?"

"Lee, doesn't it ever occur to you that all the people in the world are not trying to humiliate you? People have other things to think of. Most of the time they're not even thinking about you."

"Rosie, I wish I could believe that. But in America, it is not so. People give more thought to ways and means of humiliating the Negro than to any other single endeavor—white people, I mean."

"No! No!" Rosie objected.

The waiter appeared with their soup and Rosie ordered Martinis again. Then to Lee he said: "You disconcert me, Lee. You don't act like a Southern Negro, but you have the Southern Negro's basic animosity for all things white, it seems."

"Well, frankly, Rosie, you don't act like the average Jew, either," Lee replied. "You don't have the Jewish allergy to being a Jew. When we came in, the average Jew would have tried to establish the impression that I was a servant or the like."

"I doubt that."

"Do you call yourself an average Jew?"

"There is no such thing as an average anybody, or a typical anybody. Those are terms employed to hide reality. As to myself, I am a Communist besides being a Jew. Therefore I can accept the fact that it is not the accident of birth, but the mark of history that makes me a Jew. But don't forget that as a group Jews are also oppressed, and to accept the fact of being Jewish in a society dominated by gentiles is not an easy thing to do."

"Maybe not, but it doesn't make it any easier to deny it. And that's what gets me down with Jews. It seems to me like the Jew should be the first to help the Negro for the simple reason that he too is oppressed."

"That is logic but not reality. In a bourgeois society all groups make an effort to be identified with the dominant group. Naturally there are Jews who seek to disidentify themselves from their people. And in so doing they must rationalize this action. By escaping Jewish life and culture they feel they can become integrated into the rest of society and solve their own problem, so what better way than to absorb or emulate the national prejudices? And there are other Jews, many among the progressives, cardholders in the Communist Party, who regard acceptance of their identity as Jews as a narrow nationalism—"

"Now you're talking as a Communist," Lee cut in.

"And also as a Jew," Rosie said, but after a moment's thought added: "Perhaps more as a Communist, after all; for the progressive Jews are the ones with whom I am personally concerned—and with whom you've probably had most of your contacts. They are the ones who feel that to be a Jew might subtract something from their stature as Communists. As concerned as they are, and genuinely so, with minority group problems, even their own, they still retain many of the prejudices of the land—perhaps as some sort of defense. But for all the faults that Jews might have, you will have to admit that they do more to help the Negro than any other group."

"Help the Negro be a nigger, I would say," Lee muttered.

Their lunch was served but they barely noticed.

"Lee, let me put it like this. In this nation Jews are usually the first to give Negroes a chance to progress—that's a fact. Perhaps what you object to is their motive. They are not afraid to tap the great reservoir of Negro potentiality—but they make a profit by it. Is that what you object to?"

"What I object to this moment," Lee replied, "is your Communist trick of trying to disconcert me with the loaded question. Why not talk about some Jewish faults?"

"Okay, I will proceed without question. Jews are the first to open up new housing for the Negro. I'll admit that what they do is turn over their ghettos to make Negro ghettos—yes, and at a profit. But if they didn't do that, where would the Negroes go? Jews have opened, and still own and operate, most business establishments in Negro communities all over the country. Many exploit Negroes, I'll grant that. But the gentiles wouldn't even open the businesses. They didn't even want the Negroes' money. At least Jewish business serves the Negro community. And Jewish business people don't exploit Negroes any more than Negroes exploit each other. Just what is back of all this growing anti-Semitism among the Negro people, anyway? It worries me."

"Now I can answer you," Lee replied, "and frankly, Rosie, just two things—contact and attitude. Most of the Negro contact with the business world is with the Jew. He buys from the Jew, rents from the Jew, most of his earnings wind up, it seems, in the Jew's pocket. He doesn't see where he's getting value in return. He pays too much rent, too much for food, and in return can't do anything for the Jew but work as a domestic or the like."

"That is only in cities and—"

"That is only where anti-Semitism exists among Negroes, also."

"And it's not true," Rosie continued. "Only the brashly uninformed would make such a statement. Jews have opened practically every field of endeavor, in which they themselves are engaged, to worthy Negroes."

"Rosie, it might not be true, but most Negroes think that it's true."

"Do they object to Jews making profit? The Jew is going to make a profit like anyone else."

"And the Negro is going to hate him for it."

"Do they think gentiles would give them more?"

"No, but they do not expect any more from gentiles. Look, we accept the fact that gentiles hate us; we've always thought they hated us ever since they brought us over here as slaves. We expect them to exploit us and segregate us. We don't like it, no, but we expect it. That's the picture we have of them—"

"And your picture of the Jew?"

"We don't expect it from the Jew. We see the Jew as oppressed also—despised and restricted and segregated by the gentiles who do the same to us. So we expect him to be the first to give us a square deal."

"Is that what you mean by 'attitude'?"

"No, by 'attitude' I mean that most Negroes feel that most Jews are anti-Negro."

"Anti-Negro in what way?"

"Well, whatever the Jew might do to help the Negro—as you contend he does—it appears that he is also the first to oppose Negro equality. It seems that he can't bear the thought of Negroes being considered equal by the gentiles. Then, too, the average— well, not average, but many Jews treat Negroes with contempt and condescension. It seems that they often go out of their way to humiliate Negroes. I can't exactly explain it, but Negroes feel that the Jew will hold them up for ridicule by the gentile—that in instances where the gentile is not thinking of the Negro, the Jew will call his attention to the Negro as to an object of scorn."

"Do you know this to be so?"

"Well—"

"Is this what you dislike about the Jew?"

"Well—I dislike many things about the Jew—manners and personal habits—"

"Be specific."

"Well—for one thing, I dislike the manner in which Jews bring up their children, the repulsive manner in which Jewish mothers worship sons, making little beasts of them. I've sat on a streetcar and seen Jewish tots beat their mothers in the face until—"

"Many people dislike the color of black skin; they find the formation of Negro features personally abhorrent—would you consider this a valid reason for them to be anti-Negro?"

"Well, no, but there are certain customs in a land—"

"Must we acquire them to keep from being hated? Isn't it the best society that provides cultural autonomy for all the racial and religious groups?"

"That's not what I mean. There is a certain repulsiveness in the Jew's basic approach toward life—"

"In what way, Lee, in what way?"

"Well, take money, for instance. It seems that Jews put the value of money above all the common courtesies of life. I won't say Jews are all for themselves as many people think, but Jews can do some pretty harsh things where money is concerned. Look, one time my wife and I were invited to a Jewish doctor's home to see some moving pictures his wife had taken of the family at a summer resort. It was during the winter and there was an epidemic of colds in the city. After they had finished showing the picture the doctor called all of his guests into the kitchen and gave us cold shots. I thought at the time it was just a favor he was doing us, and although I didn't want to take the shot, I didn't see how I could refuse without appearing boorish. But a couple of weeks later we received a bill for the shots."

"For how much?"

"Three dollars for each of us."

"That was cheap enough. Even a Negro doctor would have charged you five."

"But that's not what I'm talking about. You don't invite people to your home and force them to become your patients."

"You were not forced, were you? You didn't have to accept the shots, did you?"

"Well, practically."

"Lee, you try to escape realism. The doctor was doing you a favor to give you the shots for three dollars when the customary price is five or more. Perhaps he could not afford to give them to you for nothing. Do you think that all Jews are rich?"

"I don't, no, but many Negroes do, and that's another thing. They think that Jews control all the money in the world. We Negroes in America know that money has power. We feel that because of their money, the Jews have the power to do more for us than anyone else."

"But you, Lee, know that's foolish, don't you?"

"Well—yes, some of it—about the Jews having all the money. But I believe, like other Negroes, that Jews fight, and underhandedly, our struggle for equality."

"Lee, let me tell you this. There are few great Jewish capitalists in this nation. Historically, there is a reason for this. Most Jews who emigrated to this country did not have money to buy land. The gentile landowners, merchants, and manufacturers would not employ them for any but the most menial of tasks. Therefore many went into business in self-defense. The same condition exists today. There has been a concerted effort on the part of gentile capitalists to keep Jews out of big business. That's why Jews—a very small percentage, actually—entered the virgin field of Negro business. The gentile didn't want it, as the gentile has never wanted any of the dirty, low-profit businesses. You see few Jewish names in the auto industry, the steel industry, aluminum, coal, petroleum, utilities, or building. These are the American big businesses. The Jews have had to grub, Lee; they've been discriminated against, oppressed, and segregated right here in this nation. It's not as obvious or as brutal as Negro oppression, but in many ways it has been more terrifying. Until the Russian revolution this was the last nation on earth where the Jew could feel safe from physical violence. He had nowhere to go and no way to get there. But the Negro American is an American. No matter what happens to him he is still an American. That's something even Bilbo can't take from him. He might be pressed down but he can never be liquidated."

"That's all fine, Rosie. But answer me this: why don't Jews want Negroes to have equality?"

"With that I don't agree."

"Then you say the Jew is fighting for Negro equality."

"Let me answer that in this way. I think you will discover that most Jews are disturbed by the problems of all oppressed groups, and most social-minded Jews take pride in fighting against all racial and religious discriminations."

"Against all but the Negroes'."

"Perhaps it can best be explained by saying that Jews think in terms of self-preservation. Most of their manifestations of both prejudice and progressiveness are directed toward that end. The Jew has been oppressed, not only today, but for nineteen hundred years; he has been oppressed in practically every nation where he has wandered, in every historical era through which he has passed. The fact that he has survived is not an accident. The Jew has survived by developing habits of survival. He bears the stamp of his oppression—just as the Negro bears the stamp of his oppression. If this is what you dislike in the Jew, you must also dislike it in yourself."

"I do," Lee Gordon said.

"And that is where you cease to think," Rosie pointed out. "For out of the people's oppression has come every new way of life. This is not accident, but one of the processes of materialism. As Marx wrote in the preface to his *Contribution to the Critique of Political Economy*, 'It is not the consciousness of men that determines their being, but, on the contrary, their social being that determines their consciousness.' This is the source of most of our Western culture, civilization, religion, ethics; the source of American democracy, Russian socialism. The Mosaic laws came out of a people who had been enslaved; Christianity was the haven for the Jewish forgotten man when he was being persecuted by the Rabbis and the Cæsars; democracy grew from colonial subjugation; Marxism out of industrial exploitation—"

"Therefore out of Negro oppression—"

"Might come Communism to America. Why not? The Negroes are no more separated from the masses in search for a satisfactory way of life than are the Jews."

"So all the answers lie in Communism?"

"What else? The ideal existence of mankind is where property is vested in the state and human values are the highest values."

"Look, Rosie, suppose we don't want to be Communists? Suppose we want first to be capitalists as do most other people of America?"

"But you can never become bourgeois. To become workers is the Negroes' millennium. Do you think the Negro people can become bourgeois when they have not yet been accepted by the proletariat."

"Perhaps not, but we can give it the old American try."

"That is the pity of it."

Now the waiter approached. "Are you finished?"

Neither of them had more than touched their food. "I am," Rosie replied. "How about you, Lee?"

"Yes, I'm finished also."

"Will you have dessert?" the waiter asked.

Rosie glanced at his watch. "No, I don't have time; I have a three o'clock appointment." Turning to Lee, he said, "But you stay and have your dessert."

"No, thanks, but I've had enough also. I filled up on conversation."

Rosie chuckled and said to the waiter: "Just bring the check."

While they were waiting Lee said laughingly: "You still have not given me one really valid reason why the Negro should not be anti-Semitic."

"Then I will give you one. Because the Negro has greater enemies than the Jew can ever be."

Now Lee laughed aloud. "You always have the answer, Rosie."

The check came and Rosie paid it. As they arose Lee said: "I can really say truthfully I enjoyed this lunch, Rosie."

"I'm glad you did, Lee. Call me up some time." Rosie gave him the telephone number. "And when you have a free evening come out and see me—and bring your wife. If you forget the number I'm in the book, the only Abraham Rosenberg on Pomeroy."

"Pomeroy? That's in City Terrace, isn't it?"

"Yes, you know it?"

Following Rosie to the street, Lee blinked his eyes against the afternoon sun. "I lived in City Terrace once."

"You did?"

"Yes, for a week."

"For only a week?"

"That's right, but that's another story."

Rosie halted at the bus stop and Lee waited with him until the bus came.

"See you, Rosie, and thanks again."

"Don't mention it, Lee. It was a pleasure."

A funny Jew, Lee Gordon thought, walking back toward the union shack. And how much of what he said was true? And how much was Communist propaganda? And how much just plain Rosie? But it softened Lee's tendency toward anti-Semitism to know that the Jew also was afraid.

Chapter 14

L EE GORDON lay on the davenport, his head cushioned on the arm rest, reading "Lil Abner" in the Sunday comic section. Ruth sat across from him, curled in the deep armchair, musing over the pictures in the society section. Along with the faint perfume of freshly cut grass and flowers, a pleasant warmth stole in through the open windows and filled the room with the soft, wonderful glow of a lazy day. The serenity of a Sunday had enchanted them.

At her slight exclamation over something she had seen, he turned his head to look at her and thought how lovely she was in the pale-green robe with her hair down and her professional demeanor relaxed for a change. The impulse stirred in him to kiss her, but he was too lazy to move.

Just as his eyelids were about to close, the sharp sound of laughter from next door opened them. He raised himself on his elbows to watch the Morrows' teen-age daughter Yvonne, clad in printed shorts, scamper across the lawn with her Scotty, Zulu, at her heels. The muscles of her long brown legs rippled in the midday sunshine.

Sight of their well-trimmed lawn reminded Lee that his needed cutting but he put it quickly from his mind as a horrible thought and settled in complete relaxation. If life could be like this, just one long lazy day—he was thinking when the telephone rang.

"I'll answer it," he finally said.

"You're welcome," she smiled.

He struggled to his feet and went into the bedroom. During the few short minutes of conversation the pleasantness had gone from the day. For a long moment after cradling the receiver, he stood beside the night stand wondering what it was that Foster wanted of him as uneasiness settled in his mind. Then he went back into the living-room and announced to Ruth: "Foster wants us to come to dinner this afternoon. Would you like to go?"

She looked quickly up, frowning at the constraint now in his voice. "What's the matter, what's happened?"

"We have an invitation to Foster's for dinner this afternoon."

"Foster? Who are the Fosters?" She made it sound as distasteful as if she had spoken of filth.

"Foster," he said, "is vice-president of the board of directors of Comstock Aircraft Corporation, one of the major stockholders, and general manager in charge of production in the plant."

"Oh, Foster!" Her voice had a sudden singing quality. "Of course. For dinner?"

He gave her a sighing look as if torn between tears and laughter. She had gained her feet and was moving quickly toward the bath when suspicion overtook her. "What does he want, did he say?" she questioned sharply.

"It was his secretary who called. He only said that Foster wanted us for dinner."

But she would allow no stray doubts to dim her enthusiasm. "Oh, he probably has a job for you."

"I doubt it," he replied.

And then he recalled what Joe Ptak had said to him his first day on the job: "There is a man named Foster. If you want a job making twice as much as you do, go over and tell him you're working for me."

But if it was just concerning a job, why would Foster invite them both to dinner on a Sunday afternoon? his reason asked him. Was it to exert some kind of pressure on him, to put the fear of God in him, or have him slugged by goons? He thrust this from his thoughts as foolish. But then McKinley had said that Foster was "a bitter and ill-tempered man, given to violent rages," who "hated the union in a deadly manner." Afterward, at the meeting the week before last, McKinley had stated further that Foster had bought out one of the union leaders. Lee had thought it silly at the time but now it took the shape of credence. And then that "Beware!" McKinley had whispered just as he was leaving; had it been a warning that Foster would also try to buy him out? McKinley had been absent from the meeting the night before and only eight Negro workers had put in an appearance. Did that mean that something had already happened to him?

He checked his galloping imagination and took himself in hand. Just because Foster had asked them to dinner he was seeing goblins in the land. What harm could possibly come to them? As Rosie had said the other day, people had other things to think about besides dreaming up tortures for poor Negroes.

It was, no doubt, as Joe had stated and Ruth had guessed, that Foster wanted them out to dinner to offer him a job. After all, Jackie thought he was all right—swell, she had said—and she should know since she worked right in his office.

But his uneasiness would not relax and it kept him wondering just the same.

"What shall I wear, Lee?" Ruth called from the bathroom.

"Wear? Oh, just a dress. I don't suppose it's anything elaborate."

"You're a lot of help," she cried. "I mean what type of dress? Will there be sports, tennis or riding—"

"Oh, I don't know. He just said dinner."

"Do you think my black satin will be too flashy? It's for afternoon."

"Any dress. What difference does it make?"

"It makes a lot of difference if you're looking for a job. I don't want to appear too prosperous and still I want to make a nice appearance—"

"I'm not looking for a job," he growled.

"Oh, don't be so pessimistic, he might offer both of us a job."

Lee Gordon did not reply to that because he hoped it was not so. But it rooted in his uneasiness, and by the time he had combed and brushed his hair and changed his clothes he was of half a mind to call the whole thing off. Before he could reach a decision he looked out the window and saw the long green convertible pull up before the house.

"The car's here," he called, catching some of Ruth's excitement.

"I'm ready," she replied, and came dashing into the bedroom fresh from her bath.

Looking up again, Lee saw a short dark Negro in chauffeur's livery alight from the car and saunter toward the house, and he went to the door to meet him.

"You Lee Gordon?" the chauffeur asked.

"Yes, I am. We'll be right out."

"Mr. Foster wants you to come and see him. He sent me after you."

"Yes, I know. His secretary called."

The chauffeur gave a sheepish grin. "He been double-checking on me. He told me to call but I was going to surprise you."

"I can imagine." Lee started to withdraw but the chauffeur stopped him,

"This your house?"

"My wife's and mine," Lee replied.

"Partners, eh?"

"Well—yes."

"Nice place. Me and my old lady been thinking of buying a little place like this, but Mr. Foster says he's going to build us a house on his grounds and we just going to wait and let him do it."

Turning indoors, Lee called: "Ruth—"

She came quickly beside him, serene and svelte in a chic black ensemble, wearing the tiny professional smile she had developed for the working class.

But the chauffeur was not to be awed by people of his own race. "My name's Roy," he announced, letting them know that they were Negroes too. "This your wife?"

Lee felt a slight resentment at his familiarity. "Mrs. Gordon," he said.

But Roy mistook it for something else for he grinned engagingly at Ruth and said: "Lee's scared, but it ain't nothing bad. Mr. Foster ain't going to hurt him."

Now he permitted them to follow him to the expensive car Climbing beneath the wheel, he left the front door open for them. "There's plenty room in front."

Ruth hesitated, but at Lee's nod she took the middle seat and he climbed in beside her. As the long low car moved into fluid motion, Roy asked as proudly as if it was his own: "How do you like it?"

"Oh, fine," Lee replied absently.

"Cost eight thousand dollars," Roy informed.

"Does Mr. Foster own many cars like this?" Ruth asked.

"Only seven," Roy grinned.

"How does he get along?" Lee murmured.

But Roy had given his attention to the traffic as they swept along Sunset out toward the Pasadena speedway and did not hear. On the wide, winding turnpike the long car flowed along at sixty, curving effortlessly past the green lush countryside. It was pleasant with the wind in their faces and the bright sun overhead. Life could be so simple, just floating along, Lee thought—no movement of the masses, no racial problems, no workers' unions, just relaxation and enjoyment.

But Lee could not relax. This crossing into the domain of wealthy white seclusion was never a casual thing, and to Lee Gordon it was something more. For now after seventeen years he was going back to the city where he had been born and he did not relish seeing it again. He had no pleasant memories of Pasadena; he had been born in the backyard and in his unhappiness had known only the back door. He and his parents had been driven away like thieves in the night.

Now he was going back to dine at the master's table, but without honor it seemed from their treatment by the chauffeur. He would be on his mettle, required to act a part that life had never given him a chance to rehearse, and now his thoughts concerned themselves with minor things. How should he act in Foster's presence? —like the timid Negro son of domestic servant parents; or the reserved and quiet Negro college graduate, picking his chances to speak, weighing his words for the impression they might make; or as the blustering unioneer, walking hard and talking loud and trying to give the appearance of being unafraid? He wondered how Ruth felt in this situation, how she would react, whether she would have any emotional advantage in being a woman. But Foster would expect more out of him, he knew.

And with this thought all of his senses tightened and panic overwhelmed him. It was as if the unseen gatekeepers of the white overlords demanded of him a toll to enter—an incredible toll in disquiet, anxiety, trepidation, and, greatest of all, in fear. He could not help his fear, he knew, and waited for it to strike.

But from somewhere deep inside of him came the reassuring thought, he was not returning to Pasadena as a Negro begging opportunity or as a worker seeking a raise in pay, but as a representative of many people. And that made quite a difference, for when they turned into the private driveway and circled through the landscaped woods to draw to a stop before a huge colonial mansion and Lee looked up to see the tall, gangling man in a plaid woolen shirt and old corduroy trousers whom he knew immediately to be Foster, strangely he was not afraid. It was amazing what just the realization of the other people in the world could do for him, Lee Gordon thought, as he alighted from the car and helped Ruth to alight.

Foster came down the flagstone walk and met them by the two cast iron statuettes of pickaninnies that served as decorative hitching posts. His face was deeply seamed yet mobile with vitality, and his gray streaked hair still retained youthful cowlicks.

"Mrs. Gordon," he greeted first, touching her with a glance that was at once appraising and admiring from deep-set eyes of the youngest, brightest blue. Then turning to Lee he tapped him lightly on the chest in a friendly gesture. "Lee Gordon, I've seen you before."

"How do you do, sir," Lee mumbled stiffly, offering his hand.

Foster gave Lee's hand one quick, firm grasp and quickly let it go as his gaze raked Lee with bright penetration. And then to both he said with a sudden fascinating smile: "I'm delighted that you could come on such short notice." His voice was richly cordial without condescension or constraint, and in his slow enunciation was the hint of infinite patience.

"Oh, we think it grand of you to ask us," Ruth was the first to reply, looking up at him in feminine wonder and finding him completely charming.

"That rascal Roy didn't frighten you with his wild driving, did he?" he spoke again to Ruth.

"Oh, no, I enjoyed it," she replied.

"He must be lazy today; the sun's got him. He likes to rip and tear up and down the highways."

Roy stood to one side with a grin of ecstasy on his flat, black features. "Now you know I don't do that, Mr. Louie. You know I'm just like a lamb."

"A wolf, you rascal. You know you're a rascal." He turned his attention back to Lee and Ruth. "Roy's a great man with the ladies," adding dryly: "especially with my cars."

Roy turned to Lee and gave a companionable grin, different in both essence and execution from the one he had used on Foster. "Have a good time, Lee. Don't let Mr. Louie get you balled up in no argument. He likes to get people out there and then drop 'em."

"Lee is not like you," Foster said with a faint touch of sarcasm. "He's an arguer by profession."

"Well—by necessity more than by profession," Lee demurred.

Foster gave him another quick glance.

When they turned toward the house, Ruth exclaimed as if she had just noticed it: "Oh, what a magnificent place!—and so American."

She could have said nothing to please Foster more. He had erected this mansion of twenty-one rooms, each feature of which was an exact replica of features in the homes of early American patriots, upon his return from a war-crazy Europe in 1939, and had dedicated it in solemn thankfulness to the fact that he was an American. For Louis Foster considered being an American the greatest thing of all. He was an American-first-to-hell-with-all-others American. The difference between him and other American-Firsters being not that he loved his country less, but not so rhetorically.

"Would you like to see through it?" he asked.

"Oh, we'd love to," Ruth replied.

"We like it and we think everyone else should like it too," he smiled. "That's terribly presumptuous of us, isn't it?"

"Oh, not at all," Lee said.

Foster restrained from looking at him again, but the urge showed plainly in his gesture for them to walk ahead. From the outside the wide, rambling structure, with glass-enclosed verandas flanking the center section, seemed imposing, but inside the arrangement gave a sense of intimacy. They entered a tiny foyer, flanked by a powder room done in pale print and a tile-lined washroom, and then came into a wide, paneled hallway, at the end of which red-carpeted stairs, converging at a landing, led above. To the left, three steps led up to a small, book-lined living-room, beyond which were the bedrooms of Mr. and Mrs. Foster separated by a bathroom, hers furnished simply in a period style and his, in dark-toned, rugged, he-man fashion, smelling of horses and dogs. Returning through a flower room with a concrete floor and drain, they re-entered the hall through a door beneath the landing, and crossed into the huge living-room that extended the depth of the house. An immense fireplace surrounded by mirrors occupied the center of the back wall. It was flanked by French doors looking out upon a patio, beyond which was the swimming pool. To the front, similar doors led to one of the enclosed verandas. Through an archway they entered the dining-room, which contained a mammoth banquet table, beyond each end of which grew an indoor hanging flower garden.

Until then they had met no other occupants of the house and Lee thought cynically: "Now we will go in and meet the servants," whose voices he could hear beyond the kitchen door. But with a curious realization of his misgivings, Foster did not take them through the kitchen as he did all other guests, and by not doing so earned Lee's eternal gratefulness.

"On Sundays the servants prepare a little buffet snack and take the remainder of the day off," he explained.

Neither Lee nor Ruth cared to comment on this, and Foster was afforded a faint amusement by their silence. All along he had been covertly appraising both of them, for although he prided himself on his knowledge of Negroes, these were of a type he had rarely seen, and he was curious to know all that went on behind the lean, dark features of this boy. That they were laboring under an emotional strain, he had no doubt, for he could fully comprehend the delicacy involved in any situation that put the three of them together on a social plane. He knew that he held in his power their peace of mind, and this brought forth a greater effort to put them at their ease than he would have made for any white persons, rich or poor.

Now he led them back through the living-room out into the patio. "We call this our 'WPA Project,'" he informed with a sweeping gesture toward the terraced landscape of which the swimming pool was but a tiny part.

"Oh, how beautiful!" Ruth involuntarily exclaimed, and Foster laughed delightedly.

"I think we must have built it just to startle people," he confessed with engaging candor.

"And named it after Roosevelt's relief program," Lee commented curiously.

Foster turned and looked at Lee until he drew his gaze, and then he smiled inclusively, "We discovered it to be a waste of time and money—also." But in his voice beyond control was the indication of his hatred.

For he abhorred Roosevelt with an intensity that he could not contain. Not only did he detest Roosevelt as a President, considering him a meddler, a socialist, and a stooge of Stalin, but he despised him as a man, a traitor to his heritage and profaner of tradition, "a cripple bastard with a cripple bastard's spitefulness and lack of honor," as he was wont to say.

So incensed had he become with the Roosevelt Administration that in 1934, at the age of forty-six, he had retired from active business, shut down the steel plant he had inherited, and spent the next five years abroad. For every subsequent event and occurrence detrimental to his personal prosperity and well-being and opposed to his personal convictions, he blamed Roosevelt; for Communism and unionism, as if Roosevelt had sired the one and given birth to the other; for the raise in taxes, which he considered more Marx than Morgenthau—as if one had a choice, he thought; for the entrance of the United States into the war. By God, with any other President under the sun the yellow-bellied Japs would have been afraid to breathe in America's direction! It took a war in Europe to send him back to a Rooseveltian America. And now just the thought of Roosevelt was riding him again.

But Lee did not know this and he was inclined to argue. "I always thought that WPA saved the country from revolution," he contended.

"I have more faith in America than that," Foster quickly challenged.

But by now Lee had sensed the danger signs. "Well—yes," he said and let the matter be.

Seizing the opportunity, Ruth came quickly to his aid, bringing the conversation to safer matters. "Oh, there're the stables."

But Foster was also willing to let it pass, for he wanted no psychological barriers in between them when it came time to broach his proposition. So he became the charming squire again. "I imagine my daughters are down there. They're at the horsy age."

"Oh, do you have daughters?" Ruth asked.

"Three," Foster replied. "They're my pets"—which was an untrue statement, for of them, he liked only Hortense, slim, blond, and boy-crazy at sixteen. Martha, his oldest, who was nineteen and feeble-minded, he wished had never been born, and he resented Abigail, who at nine was the most serenely sensible of the lot, because Hortense did not have her mind. As an afterthought he asked: "Do you have children?"

It was Lee who answered: "No, we never could afford them."

Ruth wished he hadn't used the word "afford"; it sounded too much like a bid for sympathy, and now she sought to cover it. "Everything has been so—well—indefinite. The depression and now the war."

Foster did not want to dwell on it. "Would you like to take a dip? We keep the water tepid."

"Yes, we would!" they both replied in unison, and Lee thought: "Well at least we agree on one thing."

"But we don't have suits," Ruth added.

"I'm sure you'll find something here to fit," Foster said as he escorted them to the dressing-rooms in the tiny cottage called the "Dolly House" at the end of the pool. "I'll join you shortly."

The first to change, Lee came out alone, and suddenly was overwhelmed by the immensity of the place. For a moment it seemed that he stood naked in the windows of the house, and he walked quickly to the edge and dove beneath the water to escape the accusing eyes. When he came up for air a big bass laugh soared above him. Looking up he saw a grotesque woman with a bloated stomach, tall in the angle of his vision.

"I'm Mrs. Foster and you're Mr. Gordon," she said, laughing.

Thinking that she was laughing at him and hoping she was not, Lee became so painfully embarrassed he could not find his voice.

"No one introduced us; that's the way we do things around here," she said, dragging a canvas chair to the shade of a parasol. "Go right ahead and swim. I'll sit here and watch."

Lee mutely nodded and dove again to escape the sight of her.
What Foster had done to his wife, and why, no outsiders ever
knew. At that time she was a fifty-year-old Ophelia, not so much
an idiot as uncaring. Signs that once she had been beautiful were
still visible in her full, florid face; but she had deliberately let her
body go to seed as a defense against her husband's brutal passion.
Now she wandered vacantly about the house, bemused with the
cheap sherry she drank against reality, her deep pointless laughter
echoing from room to room. Despised by Hortense, unknown to
Martha, and ignored by Abigail—her daughters paid allegiance
only to their father and obeyed only their nurse—she was not so
much a mother as a stranger in the house. Denied voice in its management and forbidden the kitchen, on occasion, however, when
Foster was absent and Charles his secretary elsewhere occupied,
she would slip into the kitchen and ask the Negro cook: "If it's
not too much trouble, if it doesn't upset your routine, if you don't
mind, would you bake me a small chocolate cake? And just leave
it in the pantry, I'll find it."

Now suddenly and without sound, Foster stood behind her,
brown and muscular in blue swim trunks.

"I see you've met Mr. Gordon," he said blandly, and as Ruth
came from the bathhouse, he added: "This is Mrs. Gordon. Mrs.
Gordon, Mrs. Foster."

"Welcome to our swimming pool," Mrs. Foster greeted, boom-
ing out her laugh. "I don't swim in there myself. Louis keeps his
snakes in there and I let them have it."

"Snakes!" Ruth almost screamed, and Lee echoed: "In here!"
swimming for the ladder.

"Dear, you know those little snakes have been gone for months,"
Foster said, giving his wife a slow imperturbable look.

"Well, they were there once and that's enough for me," she said,
making herself more comfortable in the chair.

Foster turned to Ruth with an ingenuous smile. "They were just
a pair of tiny water moccasins, pets of Martha's. They were perfectly harmless; she used to carry them around with her."

But the swimming pool had lost its attraction. Ruth went in
for a few minutes out of courtesy but she did not enjoy it. Later,
after they had showered, Foster mixed and served cocktails on the

dining-room veranda. One by one the other members of the household—the three daughters, the secretary Charles Houston, a bachelor who had no other home and seemingly no other friends or relatives, and the middle-aged, motherly-appearing nursemaid Miss Martin, whom he had employed in London for the sole purpose, it sometimes seemed, to vent his spleen for the English, whom he loathed—drifted in and were introduced.

The conversation reverted to the house again, and Mrs. Foster commented that she did not like the automatic lights in all the closets. "Whenever I open one of those doors absent-mindedly, the light pops on and frightens me to death."

"Oh, I think that's a good feature," Ruth said. "I mean when you get used to it," she added lamely.

To cover her embarrassment, Lee said politely that he enjoyed the swim. "The water was just right."

"Louis often invites Negro couples out to swim in his pool," Mrs. Foster informed them, and Lee wondered if the snakes had been there. "Our friends are horrified," she added frankly.

"Are you familiar with Pasadena?" Foster inquired.

"I was born here," Lee replied.

"Then you know of its narrow-minded traditions?"

"In a way."

"Are you a native also?" he inquired of Ruth.

"No, my home is in St. Louis. I came here on a visit with my mother eight years ago, and Lee and I were married."

"Oh, a real love match!" Mrs. Foster exclaimed.

Ruth smiled. "When I saw that guy I knew that he was mine."

"How wonderful!" Mrs. Foster said.

"Were your parents in business here, Lee?" Foster asked.

"No sir, they were domestic servants." Just the recollection of his background had compelled him to give the title of respect.

"And you completed college?"

"Yes sir—U. C. L. A. My mother helped and I worked also."

"There is no place like America," Foster said, and the emotion in his voice was genuine because the opportunity for betterment afforded by America was his special love. He was convinced that any American (except women, whom he did not consider men's equal; Negroes, whom he did not consider as men; Jews, whom he did not consider as Americans; and the foreign born, whom he did not consider at all), possessed of ingenuity, aggressiveness, and blessed with good fortune, could pull himself up by his bootstraps to become one of the most wealthy and influential men in the nation—even President. The fact that neither he nor any of his associates had been faced with this necessity had no bearing on his conviction. Like other fables of the American legend, the truth made little difference—as long as he believed, just as he now believed that there was no other place on earth where a Negro son of servant parents could achieve a college education. "No place like America," he repeated.

"No place!" Lee echoed, and he meant something else again.

"And this is the challenge which lies ahead," Foster continued as if Lee had not spoken, "whether we shall retain these principles of democracy or lose them to a handful of crackpots and Communists."

Now once again Lee Gordon felt the compulsion to agree, flatter, serve the vanity of this great white man, but he could not show such base˜servility in the eyes of his wife and expect her to still respect him. So he forced himself to offer a contradiction, "I don't believe that there are enough Communists in the United States to form any real danger."

"There is no danger in the Communists themselves," Foster said. "They're nothing but a bunch of malcontents, individual failures, and professional agitators. The danger lies in the people who are influenced by them."

"I doubt if many people are influenced by the Communists," Lee said. "Most people I've met are as opposed to Communism as I am."

This drew a smile of commendation from Foster and now his voice became inclusive again. "No, but they are influenced by the President who sanctions Communism, and they are influenced by the President's wife, who associates with Communists. Each time Mrs. Roosevelt attends a Communist demonstration it has a direct bearing on public opinion—and she knows this."

"Oh, but I don't think Mrs. Roosevelt is a Communist," Ruth protested.

Foster's face went completely still. "I've often wondered how colored people felt toward Mrs. Roosevelt," he slowly said. "I've always thought her patronizing friendliness toward colored people was a cheap political trick."

"I think she's a great woman," Mrs. Foster interposed with calm defiance.

Foster did not look at her, but when Ruth echoed: "Oh, I think so, too," he chose to answer.

"I know nothing of her greatness," he said, "but I doubt her sincerity. And I don't feel that the daredevil escapades in which she indulges are benefiting the colored people."

"I've never particularly been a fan of either of the Roosevelts," Lee ventured. "But I think we have to give Roosevelt credit for the way he's handling the war effort."

Foster appeared thoughtful. "Lee, I wonder if the war effort would not have gained impetus and cohesion without so much governmental interference."

"Well—big business has its own way of doing things—"

"But don't you think it's an effective way?" —this alchemy of turning human effort into profit, which was always to Foster not only the zenith of a system, but the zenith of man—to become the maker of men, and with profit— "Look at what it's done for America."

"Well—yes. But I thought production was sort of slow getting under way after war was declared," Lee said.

"There has been so much governmental interference and red tape it is a miracle that production has reached its present peak," Foster insisted. "Take the President's fair employment directive, for instance. Before my retirement I employed colored workers in all of my plants on the same basis as others. Here at Comstock I have made no distinctions. Americans are inherently fair-minded, and many of us find such a dictatorial order unnecessary and offensive. I know of several instances where the results were actually adverse."

"You mean that it influenced firms against hiring Negroes?"

"Exactly. We Americans hate dictatorship. We are engaged in a war against it. And it appears as if that is what our President is endeavoring to establish."

"Oh, I don't think so," Ruth said. "The President must have

extraordinary powers in time of war. Otherwise he could never get anything accomplished."

"But we have won quite a few wars and accomplished a great deal without the benefit of Franklin Roosevelt," Foster said, smiling at her.

Charles came in and interrupted the conversation with the announcement that it was time for dinner. They went into the dining-room and served themselves from the sliced rib roast and array of vegetables arranged on the buffet. During the meal the children dominated the conversation. Lee's experience with young white girls was a tragic memory and he felt stiff and ill at ease. With the unconscious cruelty of youth, the girls did nothing to allay his uneasiness. Hortense asked him if he had seen Roy's baby since she began to teethe, assuming that the two of them were old acquaintences, and Martha said witlessly: "She's the blackest little thing to be a baby," and blushed a moment afterwards.

And now that the sharp focus of his interest had become diffused, Lee began to wonder again what it was that Foster wanted. A slow resentment against Foster, inspired by no particular incident, began building in his mind.

Dessert was a peach mousse which momentarily held the center of attraction, and afterward the grownups went into the living-room for Scotch-and-soda highballs.

Charles, acting as Foster's straight man, a role which was the major part of all his duties, said to Lee: "So you're the young man from the union? How do the workers react to being organized in time of war?"

"Well, we're making a little progress," Lee replied.

"Don't you think that during a war is a pretty bad time to be trying to organize workers in essential industry?" Charles asked bluntly.

"No, I don't," Lee replied. "I think it's the best time. We have full employment now and after the war there might be a great deal of unemployment. You know a union only organizes the employed; we can't organize the unemployed."

"That's what I mean," Charles said. "These people are working for the war and it's not fair to the boys at the front that they should be agitated by a union."

Foster had come up with a drink for Lee and he gave Charles an indulgent smile. "Charles is antiunion," he commented. "I can't do a thing with him."

"So I see," Lee said quietly.

"Yes, I am," Charles said. "I'm not blaming you, Gordon, but most of these fellows who run these unions are nothing but crooks. I know, I've been a member."

"All unions are not the same," Lee pointed out. "There are good unions and bad unions. Perhaps you belonged to a bad union. But our union is different. You can't condemn unionism itself because there are a few unions run by unscrupulous men." He turned to Foster. "What do you think, sir?"

The three of them were standing by the unlighted fireplace while across the room Ruth and Mrs. Foster were engaged in conversation. Outside, a soft golden twilight filled the patio with a burnished luminescence and turned the swimming pool to molten metal.

"The privilege of collective bargaining is the democratic right of all workers," Foster solemnly replied.

"I don't think they have the right to be carping at production in time of war," Charles said.

Foster made a slight gesture of annoyance. "I have never considered an honest union as an obstruction to management," he continued as if Charles had not spoken. "In fact, I think of it as an ally of management, both working together for the benefit of the employees and of the employers—"

"The trouble with the unions is their leaders," Charles interrupted. "Communists and opportunists have gained control of the unions and now they're only out to fleece the workers."

"There's not so much of that now," Lee said. "The way most unions—our union, for instance—are organized, the structure of the union, I mean, makes such corruption impossible."

"My boy, I have been dealing with unions and union men for thirty years," Charles said. "I know them pretty well, what they will do and what they will not do, those that are honest and those that are not. And I will tell you frankly there are very few, if any, top union men who are not thieves and liars by the clock. Your own union will not touch the problem of colored workers."

Caught off guard by the last remark, Lee could only stammer: "Well—but that's just during the war."

"But you just said that during a war was the best time to organize," Charles said insistently. "You know, as well as I, that colored people in industry pose a special problem that must be faced forthrightly by those who would claim to be their friends."

"Well—that's true," Lee had to admit, since not long before he had advanced the same argument to Smitty.

"No doubt your union leaders call Mr. Foster a dirty capitalist, but he has faced your people's problem squarely at Comstock. He has employed colored workers in all departments at the same rating and doing the same work as all others. Does that sound like a friend or an enemy?"

"Oh, I don't think Mr. Foster's an enemy." He appeared so embarrassed that Foster gave him a reassuring smile. "But that's all the union wants. How would it interfere?"

"That's where I disagree with you," Charles said. "The union is controlled by Communists, and you must know where you colored people stand with the Communists by now."

"Well—" Cornered, Lee did not know what to say.

And there Charles left him. "I must run!" he exclaimed glancing at his watch. "It's been a pleasure talking with you, Gordon, but you're on the wrong team, boy."

"Glad to have met you too," Lee said.

Both he and Foster turned and watched Charles as he crossed the room and went from sight, and then Foster took the ball. "Of course, Charles' experience with unions has been pretty bitter. He is a highly qualified journalist, but because of political differences with the officials of the Newspaper Guild, he is not allowed to work."

"But he shouldn't condemn unionism as a whole," Lee said stubbornly.

"His bitterness impairs his judgment and gives rise to his silly bias," Foster commented dryly, and Lee looked up in sharp surprise, taking the bait as offered.

For this was the way it worked in all things concerning Negroes: Charles playing the perfect stooge, mouthing the maledictions while the master retained his dignity sacrosanct in the halo of impartiality and denounced Charles as the offensive ogre of the lot. This was the way it worked both on the Negroes whom Foster had to dinner and the Negro servants who served the dinner. For

instance, the management of household affairs was ostensibly dele-
gated to Charles but actually directed by Foster with picayunish
attention to detail, even to the reprimanding of the servants and
the more subtle punishment of arranging the meals so as to keep
them late on their half-days off. While Foster, for himself, maintained a seemingly frank and good-humored relationship with the
servants, kidding them, making humorous allusions to Charles's
"choleric" disposition, and passing out the rewards, which were
sometimes money and other times a day off. And though they
were underpaid and overworked, the former to satisfy a vanity that
they liked to work for him, and the latter because the work was
there, they truly loved Foster and hated Charles. Foster appeared
amused by this but actually it was a matter of great pride.

Now with this criterion, he went to work on Lee with complete
confidence in its efficacy. "As for myself, I don't see the union in
such awesome aspect. It has its faults, yes, but what large organization doesn't?"

"I am certainly glad to hear you say that, sir," Lee said, breathing
a sigh of relief. "I thought perhaps the reason you had us to dinner
today was something concerning the union."

"No, I am more concerned with people than with unions,"
Foster said with inspirational intensity, "with what affects them,
their lives, and their futures, with the things that influence them,
the courses they may take. It is always my most optimistic hope
that I may be able to point out to them what will be beneficial and
what may be detrimental. Only in this way may we preserve the
spirit of our democracy—our American way of life. Are you proud
to be an American, Lee?" he asked with sudden sharpness.

Taken aback by the suddenness of the question, Lee could only
stammer: "Why—yes, sir."

"Your people have had a long hard struggle to attain their present position," Foster went on, "and it would grieve me to see you
at this point alienate the good will of us who have your problem at
heart and are not trying to use you to foster our own selfish ends."

"I'm sure we wouldn't want to do that," Lee Gordon said, and
Foster smiled.

Now he would inject a little fun into this game the union played,
Foster thought with a sense of secret satisfaction. For his object
was not to break the union. He had not the slightest doubt but

that he would squelch the union's campaign by simply continuing his present policy. The workers liked him; they were satisfied. He had them in his control and there was nothing to be feared. He wanted only to annoy the unionists by taking their favorite colored boy away from them. He could already see himself telling it as a joke at a board of directors' meeting.

"I'm sure you wouldn't," Foster said, "and that is the reason, I must confess, that I am concerned with your people, with your thoughts and ambitions and political convictions—and with you, boy. I am concerned with you as a man."

Drawn by the quality of sincerity in Foster's voice, Ruth and Mrs. Foster had come over to join them and were there in time to hear Foster's last remark. Ruth looked sharply to see how Lee was taking it, whether he had kept his mind receptive to anything that Foster might have to offer.

But Lee experienced a slight withdrawing, a vague repudiation of the sincerity of this white millionaire who thought of him as a boy yet claimed to be concerned with him as a man. He knew that Foster was going to make him an offer and hoped that he would have the strength of will to refuse, because whatever Foster offered to a man whom he thought of as a boy would be a handout with condescension, like old clothes given to a servant.

Watching Lee's every expression with clinical appraisal, Foster was immediately aware of Lee's changed attitude, and he made a better offer than he had at first intended.

"For some time now," he said, "I've been considering employing a colored man in the personnel department at Comstock. I think you are the man for that job, Lee. I'll start you off at five thousand a year and you can report to work at eight o'clock tomorrow morning."

Foster could not bear to have a Negro, any Negro, dislike him. And before he would allow a Negro to really hate him, he would make the Negro rich.

Ruth gasped audibly at the offer, and Mrs. Foster's eyes went wide in amazement. Lee's breath turned rock-hard in his chest and his heart seemed caught in his throat. For he was not prepared to withstand such an offer as this—Lord God! Five thousand to start! He could have Ruth home—home! And he'd never have to be afraid anymore—

"You have a streak of stubborn integrity in you, boy, that I like," Foster said, smiling across at him, already gloating inwardly at putting this one over. "I'll see that you get the breaks."

And it was this that gave Lee Gordon the courage to refuse; because if he had integrity that could be bought, he had no integrity at all. And if one man held it in his power to make the breaks for him, he held it in his power to make the breaks against him. He would feel alone, lost in a white office, afraid, his destiny subject to the whims of this one man—better to be with the union where there would be others who were lost, lonely, and afraid. So he said: "Well—thank you, sir. I want you to know, sir, I certainly appreciate your considering me for the job. But I can't quit the union now. The union is depending on me."

Admiration was first in the eyes of both Ruth and Mrs. Foster, and it remained in the eyes of the older woman. But Ruth's next reaction was a sharp, deep hurt, because she thought that he had only been thinking of himself; if he had been thinking of her, or of them together, he could never have refused.

But it was shock that showed in Foster's face, stronger than his control. In the sudden fury that raced through his mind he thought with deadly venom: "You goddamn black bastard, you'll pay for this—" And then he composed his features to a stillness and kept his voice on an even keel: "I won't try to persuade you, boy, for I can understand your loyalty even though I know it to be misplaced."

It was the end of the afternoon and now Lee and Ruth awaited their dismissal. But Foster was not ready to dismiss them quite yet— This was the second colored boy, he was thinking. First a worker at the plant, the Lester McKinley boy, and now this boy. Either he was losing his touch or they were having too much war prosperity. But he would see, he would see. It goaded him to say: "I'd like to give you a bit of advice, boy, keep an eye on your fellow organizers. They're not as honest as you seem to think. Less than a week ago one of them came to me with an offer to break the back of the organizing campaign. I chased him from my office but there are other executives in the company who do not have my impartiality toward the union at this time."

But now that Lee had had the strength to refuse his offer, he could resist this scare of union treachery Foster sought to throw into him, and it was only out of politeness that he asked: "I don't suppose you want to tell me who it was?"

"I don't mind telling you; I would like to tell you. But it wouldn't do you any good; it would just get you into trouble. This man is too big for you to tackle; he is one of your big boys. I'm not telling you this to make you lose confidence in the union, or through any desire to undermine your loyalty. I am just advising you to watch your step."

"Well—thank you, sir," Lee Gordon said.

And now the silence dismissed them, and Ruth spoke the words of departure: "We've had such a wonderful time! I don't know how to express it, but I've enjoyed every minute."

"I have enjoyed it very much also," Lee echoed.

While waiting for the car to come and take them home, as at the beginning, they discussed for a moment the beautiful house. Foster was his charming self again, and when Roy sounded the horn, he gave Lee his quick, firm clasp and turned his devastating smile on Ruth.

But it was Mrs. Foster who walked to the door with them. She shook Lee's hand with added pressure and said with genuine emotion: "I wish you luck, both of you." And her parting smile to Ruth was completely wistful.

It was this memory they both carried as they walked down to the car unaccompanied, and now separated from each other by Ruth's reproachful silence.

Chapter 15

ON INTO the night her silence ran like a river down from a hill of memories into the rapids of change. This was too hurting to talk about, too much of a final repudiation to probe into with words. After all the privation she had been through during their eight years of marriage, all she had done for him, had taken from him, if he couldn't do this for her, if his honor was so great and his pride so priceless—

"Do you love me, Lee?" Her thoughts had found their first words since they had left the Foster's.

He raised his head wearily from where he sat hunched in bewilderment on the davenport, thinking that now it was coming and he would catch it for whatever it was that he had done to hurt her.

"Yes, I love you, Ruth." There was only a dull resignation in his voice.

"Do you ever think of me?" As during that wonderful, peaceful noon, many centuries ago it now seemed, she sat curled in the deep arm chair. But where then she had been lazily relaxed, now she was tense with a poignant ache.

"Yes, I think of you. I always think of you, Ruth."

"Do you ever remember that we are married, that you are not just one person in the world?"

"I do."

"But you couldn't have been thinking of me this afternoon, or of us and our marriage."

"I was."

"Then how could you have turned down Foster's offer without at least talking it over with me?"

"I was thinking of us," he doggedly defended. "I thought of what the salary would mean to us, what we could do with it. I thought perhaps if I accepted it you would be willing to quit—"

"If you had been, Lee," she interrupted—"if you had actually been thinking of me, that only makes it worse, because it proves that you don't care anything at all about me anymore."

"I couldn't sell out the union, Ruth. Is that what you expected me to do?"

"Would you be selling out the union to accept a better job?" she questioned bitterly. "That's the same as saying that I'd be selling out the Jay Company if I went to work for Comstock."

"Is that all the union means to you, Ruth? You used to make me think that you believed in unionism."

"I do believe in unionism; but I wouldn't put it above you, above our welfare, Lee."

"You don't understand. I don't put it above you, but—"

"Then what is it, Lee?" she cut him off again. "For God's sake, tell me what it is? Are you deliberately trying to hurt me?"

"I've got to be true to myself, Ruth. Can't you understand that?"

And though she did understand the quality within him that had made him refuse the job—a quality that once she had been so proud of him for having—now she felt excluded by it and resentful of it, as though she wanted him to be honorable and courageous, but only for herself. It was this that kept her tearing at him.

"At the expense of me, Lee? Is that how you have to be true to yourself, by having us live in poverty and fear all of our lives?"

Her face came suddenly, and with a stab, into the focus of his vision. Now he saw the harshness in features he had always thought so inexpressibly feminine. He saw frowning lines around glazed brown eyes that had seemed like lighted candles in a darkened church when he had first looked into them. He saw ravages in her mouth, as if the smiles had come with too much pain. Had just so short a period of working in the world done this to her? Or was it hurt? Had he hurt her so much in their eight years of marriage?

"Ruth," he said slowly, "I've always wanted you to have the best of everything."

And now she looked at him, at his tight, gaunt face with too much blankness in his eyes hiding all his fear and torment and sense of inadequacy that she could feel hard and constricted inside of him. She opened her mouth to say: "I know it, darling. Please forgive me for being so cruel to you." But in her state of discontentment she could find no voice for words as these. So instead she continued to reprove him. "How can I believe it, Lee, when you just refused an opportunity for us to live as decent human beings?" And now each hurting thing she said led her on to say another. "Is it that you are trying to evade the responsibility of marriage? Is that it? Ever since you left the post office you've acted as if you wanted to get out of supporting me. Is that why you ran off to New York City and left me? You don't have to support me, Lee, if that's what you're afraid of."

"I do want to support you," he contended.

"But how? By sticking to your little union job where you can hide from life? Lee, I'm not asking for the best, God knows! but I want more than just bare poverty. I want a few pretty clothes and enough money not to feel strapped all the time. I don't want to be a drudge all of my life. For five years I made excuses to keep Mother from visiting us because we were so poor. Don't you think I love my mother and want her with us sometimes? I'd like to be able to have her live with us; she's not rich, you know. I should be helping Ronnie to support her."

"I'm sorry, Ruth. But that was all I had to offer—that was the very best. If you didn't want that, you didn't want me."

"But you can't say that now, Lee. Other people are making money on jobs you've refused in the past. And now this job— where can you ever beat it?"

"Would you want me to work on a job where I'll be unhappy all the time?"

"Do you think I'm any more happy on my job than you would be? I suffer from all the racial strains and tensions you do. I die from some humiliation or other almost every day. I always have, ever since I took my first job. But I don't try to take them out on you. I keep them to myself so as not to worry you. Perhaps that's what makes me appear the superficial person I must appear to you."

"What do you want me to do, Ruth?" he asked, running the flat of his hand hard down his face. "Go back to Foster and beg him for the job?"

"I only want you to think of me sometimes, Lee, instead of always thinking of yourself. I can't stand it much longer. It's only because I've always hoped that some day you might think of me that has kept us together this long."

Because as her husband, Lee Gordon had been the greatest disappointment in her disappointing life. Not so much for what he had failed to do, to offer, and provide, as for what he had failed to be—a greater, braver, stronger man. Nor so much that he had failed, because any man could fail, but the way that he had failed, as if failure was his destiny. It was within the man that she saw the failure.

And this hurt her more than he could ever know. For all of her life she had dreamed of this one man who would come into her heart. Her years before their marriage had been one long odyssey of books, and from all the stories she had ever read she spun these dreams of him. A tall, strong, handsome Negro, as brave as any knight, who would come to her and take her and love her and cherish her and protect her; who would make his way through the world with her always at his side and never be afraid of white people.

At first he had been the star halfback for Sumner High School the year they played Wendell Phillips from Chicago. Then he had been the erect, distinguished, middle-aged man whom she would see from time to time alighting from a Rolls-Royce limousine in front of Poro College. For one brief interlude he had been the turbaned East Indian visiting down the street from them. The last of these was her sociology professor at Lincoln University in Jefferson City, Missouri. —Only in her dreams.

It had remained for Lee Gordon to bring reality. She had seen him then as a tall, proud Negro youth with hurt eyes and a tormented smile and a touch of Byron in his make-up. And when she discovered after she had married him that he was afraid of white people, that this fear from which he did not hope ever to escape had beaten his life into a weird infirmity, it was a disappointment, as it would have been to any Negro girl with dreams.

Even now after eight dreary years of marriage this romance in her heart was too un-dead, too filled with eternal yearning, too much like just lying down and crying like a baby.

And now this man whom she had married and who had disappointed her was saying: "I don't know how I could think of you any more than I do, Ruth. But you don't make it easy for me."

"I don't make it easy. How could I make it any easier? I am working like a slave every day. What more can I do?"

What she could not understand, Lee Gordon thought, was that he could not be the man she wanted him to be without first being honorable. If she wanted him to be more than the Negro he was, she would first have to think of him as more than the Negro he was made to be. She would have to believe that he wanted to do all the things for her she wanted him to do—support her in comfort, idolize her, cherish her, give her everything in the world. And she would have to understand that he could not do so without honor; that he had reached the point in life where if he could not have the respect of men he did not want the rest. And if this entailed her having to work for what he would not give her in dishonor, she should at least understand that there was nothing noble in her doing so; it was only the white man's desire to deride the Negro man that had started all the lies and propaganda about the nobility and sacrifices of Negro women in the first place.

Perhaps once he could have said this to her, but not now. For the years in between them, shaped by his inadequacies, his helplessness, confusion, and fear, had brought a change in their relationship. That was progress, he thought with searing cynicism—the movement of materialism. Time will bring the change—dialectics. Johnson P. Time, the Great Leveler, who would make all people equal, black, white, brown, and yellow. If He could not do it with the flesh, He would do it with the dust. And in the dust Lee Gordon would find his honor, Lee Gordon thought with bitterness.

He took a deep breath and said aloud: "You can quit your job, Ruth. Will you do that? I'll make you a promise that you'll never regret it."

No, not eventful, like the winning of a war, or dramatic, like the dying of a hero; but to Lee Gordon who found it hard to make any decision, it was the most important decision that he had ever made. For he had hit that height within himself. He had been trying for it, never really believing that he would make it; and then suddenly he had made it.

If she had said okay, he might have gotten everything he had ever needed—reassurance, courage, even honor. He might have taken that feeling and gone on and never looked back.

And if she had known that all she had to do to give him that feeling was say okay, and mean it, she would have said it over and over again. It would have been a pleasure for her to quit her job. But she did not know that he had hit that height. She had lost faith in him to the point where she no longer believed that he could hit it.

So she cried as if he had wounded her: "Is that it, Lee? Is that what you're waiting for? Is that why you refused the job today—to have me at your mercy again? Is that it?"

So he lost it— The quality of human courage is a fleeting thing, God knows. To some it comes again and again. To some it never comes. To him it might never come again, Lee Gordon thought. And he knew that no degree of reason, no purity of logic, no amount of common sense—nothing!—would suffice for his having lost it.

"Ruth, I refused the job today simply because I did not want to take Foster's goddamned handout."

"Don't you see!" she exclaimed. "I couldn't quit with you feeling like you do. I couldn't face the uncertainty again of not knowing whether you would have your job from one day to the next."

"I didn't think that you would quit, Ruth," he said dully.

"Lee, please believe me. I do want to quit. But it would be foolish now after you've refused the job that Foster offered."

"Ruth, if you think that it'd be foolish, there is nothing more that I can say."

"But your own job will be over with as soon as Comstock is organized, won't it?"

"Why keep on bothering, Ruth? Why not just let it go?"

"Answer me, Lee, won't it?"

"It doesn't make any difference. I don't feel like talking about it."

"Lee, I'll quit," she suddenly relented. "I'll quit tomorrow, if it's that important. All I've ever wanted was just to be your wife."

But it was too late—J. P. Time had had His moment.

"No, Ruth, you keep your job."

"But I'll quit if you want me to."

"I don't want you to now."

"Lee, what's the matter, darling?"

She arose and crossing to him tried to put her arm about him, but he pulled away and went into the bedroom. A moment later he returned clad in his hat and outer coat.

"Where are you going?" she asked.

"I'm going out," he snapped.

"Lee, please, Lee—" She began crying.

"Ruth, there isn't any goddamn need of crying," he said bitterly. "You want to keep your job. And I want you to keep it too. That's settled. Now you can be happy that I won't have you at my mercy. And I'm going out and take a walk."

"May I go with you?" she asked, dabbing at her eyes.

"I'm just going for a walk, and I don't want you with me."

And now she tried a smile. "I'll make some waffles while you're gone. Will you be back in time?"

"I don't know. But I don't want any waffles."

"I'll make some anyway."

"That's fine. You make them and eat them too," he told her, and went out of the door into the darkness.

But she made no waffles. When she could no longer see his figure in the darkness down the street, she turned slowly and sat down, biting the back of her hand in an unconscious gesture. It was not that she suspected him of going to see a woman, she told herself, but her intuition troubled her because if he was going to see another woman in his state of mind, there would be nothing left for her.

Suddenly she began crying again, because she felt sorry for herself. And then slowly as the long night ran its course, her vague suspicions passed, and she was overwhelmed by such a sense of guilt that he could imagine him doing all manner of desperate things—murder, robbery, suicide. For in the end, it was not to another woman she ascribed his staying out all night, but to an unbearable frustration inspired by her refusal to quit her job—because she knew that she had failed him.

And yet in this hour of her complete self-condemnation, she could not see how she could have sensibly done otherwise, for what would become of both of them if she did quit her job?

Chapter 16

L EE GORDON walked west on Sunset now, his raincoat buttoned and belted and the collar turned up against the world. The twelve o'clock curfew had long since closed the bars, but still the people filled the streets—servicemen and working women—in their frantic search. But Lee Gordon did not notice them. His face was set in slanting lines and his eyes were luminous with brooding.

It was not so much that she had refused to quit, he thought, as that she had not wanted to. That made the difference. And yet, in this rare lucid moment, he could not really blame her for not wanting to give up the lot she had gained for the little he had to offer. She had no way of knowing what this particular job of hers did to him, that for each development of her own personality he paid a price in loss of self-esteem.

But what really made it hopeless, he thought, was the character of her intentions. He knew that concern for his own welfare was a part of everything she ever did. She was not only convinced of this herself—it was true. So it was doubly unfortunate that the effects she struggled so ardently to achieve never served her purpose. Instead of his being benefited by what she intended to be benefiting, he was injured. Words of encouragement became blows to his pride, actions aimed to inspire his courage nursed his fear, and logic offered to a point the goal for him so often confused his purpose. And this was due to the fact that these intentions, while good and noble, grew out of her ignorance of the essential character of his frustrations and became destructive condescensions instead of constructive assistance to the need they were to serve. She deserved credit for trying, he thought, even though her motives were not always unselfish. It was not her fault that in all the things she tried to do for him, she was the one to benefit. And this, he felt, was just. This was right. Yet that did not keep it from being ironic also.

Well—yes, Lee Gordon thought, looking up.

He was at Jackie's. He had walked the seven miles without realizing where he was going. And for an instant he was touched by a sense of omnipresence.

> Then of the THEE IN ME who works behind
> The Veil, I lifted up my hands to find
> A Lamp amid the Darkness; and I heard,
> As from Without—"THE ME WITHIN THEE BLIND!"

The involution of a mystic, yes, and the actions of a fool, Lee Gordon thought.

"Who is it?" Jackie asked when he knocked upon her door.

"Lee."

She opened the door and stood aside to let him enter, her face showing neither pleasure nor surprise, only a composed complacence as if she had always known that he would come in the night like this.

"Is Kathy asleep?"

She closed the door and locked it. "She's away."

He turned and looked at her ethereal face with open-mouthed wonder and could not breathe at all. Emotions burned through him like flame, and all the things he had always wanted to say to her came clearly worded to his lips. But he said only: "You're beautiful, Jackie," because that said it all.

Now it was in her eyes again, that winning look. Without replying she turned quickly away from him and crossed to close the bedroom door. Watching the natural unaccented pulsing of her hips, he went sick with desire for her and began stripping off his rain coat, tearing at the buttons.

She turned and came back. "What happened, Lee?"

"I'm just tired, Jackie."

"Would you like to go to bed?"

Their gazes hung: his questioning, hers level and unreadable.

"With you?"

She smiled for the first time, friendly, motherly. "Don't be so old-fashioned, Lee. I'm a Communist. If you're tired you may sleep with me. I've slept with many men—" and just before she opened the bedroom door she completed: "who didn't have me." Now matter-of-factly she asked: "Would you like some coffee or something to eat?"

"Well—no. No thanks."

And then he began to undress, excitement beating at his heart and fear throttling him as with a garrote. His common sense tried to inform him that this was no uncommon thing, but his body jerked with a thousand alarms. Jackie had already returned to bed, and when he entered the room without night clothes, she simply turned over and put out the light.

For a moment he lay there away from her, not touching her, and then he said: "Jackie—" in a tone that made it clear.

When she did not immediately reply, he turned, groping, and her breast came alive in his hand. She waited a moment longer, then pushed him gently away.

"You can't have me, Lee."

It went tart, bitter, brackish, and went through him like bile. And suddenly it stilled to a quiet resolution and he said to himself: Yes, yes, I'll do it. I'll sleep naked with this young, beautiful, desirable white woman. And I will not touch her.

When finally he spoke aloud his voice was apologetic. "I might not be able to sleep, but I'll try not to keep you awake."

"You can get so tired you can't go to sleep," she murmured.

"Mine is more mental."

"Would you like for me to play you something?"

"Play me something?"

"Music."

"Oh!—Well—"

"Yes," she finished with a little laugh, snapping on the light and slipping out of bed.

He had the sudden crazy feeling of being hurled through life by the emotions of others, by idiocies and insanities and false values in which he had no part.

And then the opening movement of some unfamiliar symphony sounded with arresting tone. His mind opened and deepened, absorbing the music. Strained and cleared and soared and trod the notes to fantasy in a darkness rocked by Jackie's gentle breathing.

One moment, it was a morning in spring, taking his breath in a burst of newness. And another, taps for the dead, tearing out his heart. It was the merciless cruelty of people, bruising his soul. And then a pastoral scene beside a waterfall, anointing his wounds. It was the majestic march of mountains through his heart, the laughter of the ages in his throat, the roll of man-made thunder in his stomach, a softly played organ in an empty church, and a baby crying in the night.

And his thoughts were like tongueless words, like his black skin trying to speak, like the mute prayers of the dark scared night, like life itself trying to tell him of its mystery in a language never heard, only felt.

It helped more than he could ever say.

Suddenly he began to cry. He buried his face between her breasts and she stroked his kinky hair. He wanted to tell her how much it had helped, but the words still had no tongue.

After a time he stopped crying and turned over away from her looking up into the darkness. "It got me for a moment," he whispered.

She put her arms about him and drew him back to her.

Never so violently responsive, so flagrantly wanton, so completely consuming, but it was not the same. In it was a defiance of the forbidden, shaping it in a way he could not tell.

For a long time afterward they were silent, then she asked: "What's the matter, darling?"

"I'm just unhappy."

"I knew it when I first saw you. You're just frustrated, darling."

"Perhaps I am."

"Frustration always begins with sex, the lack of gratification—"

"But not with you."

And for a long time again they were silent.

"What are you thinking about, darling?" she finally asked.

"You."

"What are you thinking about me, darling?"

"I was wondering how you would be as my wife."

"I would be a wonderful wife to you, darling."

"I bet you would."

"Would you like for me to get up and fix something to eat?" she offered.

"No, kiss me—"

"You're sweet," he said afterward. And a moment later mused: "I wonder why white women are so much more affectionate to Negro men than our own women are."

"It's only in your mind," she said.

"How in my mind?"

"In your mind we are the ultimate."

Lee Gordon vaguely wondered whether to be flattered or insulted, and to avoid deciding, smothered her in his arms.

"And we can give you happiness," she thought triumphantly, offering her body with warm, passionate surrender to another ecstasy.

She could give him this illusion of manhood even while denying that he possessed it, for to her he was the recipient of her grace. But Ruth could give him nothing that to her he did not have. So with Jackie he had these moments that rightfully belonged to Ruth. It could have been wonderful with Ruth, for she had all that Jackie feigned. But he could never be for her what Jackie could make of him for her own designs.

And yet in the morning when they parted, he had given Jackie infinitely more than she had given him. But he did not know it.

Chapter 17

U PON awakening that Monday at noon, a sense of drifting seized Lee Gordon as if he were a bloated and forgotten corpse whirling aimlessly in a sea of dead remembrance.

Nothing seemed real—the lateness of the hour, the familiar room with its dotted-Swiss criss-crossed curtains, the view of the neighbor's yard etched in the vertical sunlight, the smiling face of Ruth from the photograph on the chiffonier, the night before, or the day preceding. And Lee did not seem as real as any of the rest.

Nothing seemed real.

But slowly the hard and pointed memories brought reality again, giving to the torpid emotions of a poignant yesterday a new and bitter life. And the fingers of all things personal began pulling at his mind.

What did he, Lee Gordon, have that so many people wanted? he asked himself. And why did they all deny him the one small thing he needed? What was happening in this world that he did not seem to know?

What was the union's angle? Did they really need him to organize the plant? Or was his job just another form of Negro charity?

And why would Foster go to the trouble of making a job for him? Surely Foster did not think that by so doing he could hurt the union. But what else could one lone, dark Negro boy, haunted by fears and weakened by uncertainties, mean to a man as **Foster?**

Rosie? What did Rosie want of him?—giving him that long lecture on the psychology of the Jew. What did Rosie expect him to do about the Jew's oppression?

And Jackie? It tortured him to think of her, for only the night was made for believing. The sharp sunshine brought the rigid question: what did she, an attractive, single, white girl, want with him? Surely she could not consider him such an asset to the Communist party as to win him with her body. No, this was something more—a frightening thing, exciting, bewitching, and deadly. For it only offered him the fruit of one forbidden tree in a forbidden garden, and after he had tasted it, what then—an unforgettable aftertaste of bitterness, corroding in the society wherein he lived, or something else? For a moment he hoped wistfully that she really liked him more than just sexually—liked him as a person. No one but his wife had ever truly liked him, and she didn't like him anymore.

And so at last his thoughts came back to where they always ended and began—his wife. He could understand her devotion to security, for it was consistent with the times. But what more did she want of him? Was it merely happiness? But how could they have happiness without having all the rest? And if he had the choice to make, would he choose happiness?

So now the question asked itself: what did he, Lee Gordon, want of Lee Gordon? Viewed in the light of one day hence, his bitter stand of yesterday for honor seemed an insensate thing. Who but a fool in 1943 would have refused the job that Foster offered for so inconsequential a thing as one's integrity? But if he did not want honor or integrity, what then did he want? What was he looking for—purpose, motive, wealth, fame, or just a long easy ride to a painless death and oblivion? He did not know what he wanted, but it was none of these. It was more—something more.

Now in the slow beginning of despondency, only the union held forth hope—not that it needed him, but that he needed it. For if he could not be important to anyone else in the world, perhaps through the union he could be important to himself. And when his wife referred to his job as a "little union job" he would not have to believe it so.

He reached for the telephone and called a number. At the previous union meeting, Buster Boy had offered the use of his house for small midweekly gatherings. Aware that Buster Boy's chief aim was to fill a gambling game, he had turned the offer down; but now he decided to accept it. He would use any means to gain his end, he resolved, and if the workers could not protect themselves, it was not his prerogative to protect them, their money, or their morals.

"This is Lee Gordon the union organizer," he said in answer to a woman's voice. "May I speak to Buster Boy?"

"He ain't here," the voice came loudly to his ear. "He say if you ring him to tell you that he can't do what he say."

Taken aback, he tried to make it clear. "He offered to let me hold meetings of the Negro workers in his house—"

"He say for me to tell you that you can't hold 'em here."

Perplexed but unalarmed, he did not let it aggravate him. Perhaps the police were on to Buster Boy, he thought, and quickly put it from his mind. Next he tried to call McKinley but was informed that the line had been disconnected, so he stopped there on his way to the plant. But Lester was out, and his wife said he would not be home all evening.

Arriving at the union shack, he found Joe Ptak also absent, so he gathered an armful of leaflets and went down to help Luther work the gates during the change of shift. But Luther was not there either, and a slow presentiment of trouble began forming in his mind. Were the Communists holding a secret meeting? But then Lester would not attend. Was it a meeting at the union council hall? No one had given him notice of it, he tried to reassure himself. But still he was beset by worry that something was happening of which he did not know.

The first concrete indication came from the Negro workers' manner when they surged from the gates. It was in their eyes when he hailed them, in the drab, repressed tones of their replies, in the way their faces blanked up at sight of him and they looked away.

Certain now that trouble was afoot, he hastened to the little café where he and Luther had made a habit of meeting various workers to buy them beers and talk about the union. Finding only three present, two men and a woman, instead of the dozen or more who usually appeared, he asked sharply: "Say, what's going on? Where is everybody?"

They looked at him and looked away without replying.

"Say, what's the matter?" His voice was rough from alarm.

"Matter with us?" the man called Play Safe countered with that defensive circumlocution at which some Negroes are perfect. "Look like anything the matter with us?"

"Well, where are all the others? Where's Scotty and Sugar and Mary Lou? Where's Shortdrawers, he's always here."

"Maybe they had somp'n else to do."

"You're here, you didn't have anything else to do."

"Maybe we's the bravest."

Lee Gordon turned with a quick gesture to hide his irritation and ordered drinks for all, wondering vaguely as he did so why only the most ignorant of Negroes participated in such militant movements as unionism. Was it just in Los Angeles where the migrant Negro workers were in predominance? But even so, there were scores of Negro college graduates in war industries; he knew seven of them employed by Comstock who had never signed a union card or attended a union meeting. Did they feel it in some way beneath their dignity? Only Lester McKinley had shown any signs of active interest in the union. Was it that the others had been bought out like island natives with a few glass trinkets of education and a few bright baubles of wealth? Was this all the educated Negro wanted, or did they expect to some day earn their wings and fly to high heaven with their Cæsars?

The procession of his thoughts was interrupted by the woman's voice, "We earning our little money same as usual."

Calmer now, he turned to her. "Look, Susie, for God's sake cut out the clowning! What's happened?"

"Course ain't nobody we can sell out so we just naturally has to be honest," the man named Johnson interposed.

"What?" Lee asked with a sinking of his stomach. "What did you say?"

"Well, to tell you the truth," Play Safe confessed, "we heard you folks was selling out."

First into Lee's memory came McKinley's parting admonition, "Beware!" and then the voice of Foster speaking spitefully of betrayal. Foster, of course, would know since it was likely he would be the one to supply the purveyor with the Judas gold. But how could Lester? Yet he must have known from the beginning. Did he have powers of mysticism, or was it just as he had hinted—given Foster for the man and the union for the object, the betrayal of a leader would be the inevitable result?

Who then was the Judas? He could not believe it was Joe or Smitty. Both seemed fanatical in their zealous unionism—Communists, perhaps, but never traitors. And then the mocking voice of introspection asked, were the two so far apart? But what could the Communists seek to gain? he now asked himself. Control of the union? That's what they wanted, of course. But how could they hope to gain this by breaking the campaign down? Benny Stone? But he was a Communist, too. And that left Marvin Todd. But Foster had said it was a "big boy." And who would be so foolish as to buy the treachery of Todd? But then, Jackie had said he had a following. The rebels had been known to elect a president, of course, but only of the Confederate states. Was this to be another Dixie rebellion?

Aloud he said: "That's foolish! Who told you that?"

Even as the denial came rushing from his lips, he recalled that at their first union meeting Lester had been talking too loudly concerning someone selling out. Was this then just the repetition of his words mushroomed into rumor?

"We heard it," Susie said.

And Johnson elaborated: "I got it straight from high up."

"High up where?" Lee asked.

"High up," Johnson repeated.

"Look," Lee started to explain with a patience that was alien, "no one can sell out the union. The union is too big. The union does not belong to anyone for them to sell it out. It's your union. If an organizer tried to sell it out, you could go right ahead and organize it yourself and then apply to the national union for a charter. And after that you could ask for an NLRB election in the plant just as we intend to do. The company is well aware that we are organizing the union. You workers have a right by law to organize and join a union—it is the law that you may do this. The company can not stop you. If they take any reprisals or try to harm you in any way for joining the union, the company has broken the law and can be convicted in court—"

"You say it's the law," Play Safe asked seriously.

"I say it's the law. A law called the National Labor Relations

Act." Now he said to Johnson: "You go to the person 'high up' and ask them if they have ever heard of the National Labor Relations Act, commonly known as the Wagner Act, and they will tell you yes."

"They will, eh?"

"They have to."

"They ain't tol' me yet and they tol' me you was sellin' out."

"He don't mean you," Susie said quickly with a nervous laugh. "He means one of y'all."

"An' we got our s'picions who," Johnson said.

Luther had come up to the group in time to hear the statement. "S'picions 'bout what?" he asked.

When Lee had informed him of the rumor, he brushed it off as a gag. "You go back 'n tell Foster he got to come again," he said to the workers.

"You go tell 'im!" Play Safe said. "You the bigges'."

Luther chuckled. "You tell 'im, Lee, you the smartes'."

Lee caught the spirit of the thing since it seemed to be incredibly effective. "I'll let Joe Ptak tell him, he's the baddest."

They all laughed. "He the lion, eh," Luther remarked. "We just the ol' signifying monkeys."

"Who dat, man?" Play Safe asked.

"You never heard 'bout the signifying monkey?"

Play Safe shook his head.

"It was thissaway," Luther prefaced, leaning against the bar to order drinks for the lot, and then began to recite:

> It was one bright sunny day
> The Monkey an' the Lion met across the way.
> The Monkey said to the Lion
> Leo I know you're king
> An' you can 'bout beat mos' any ol' thing,
> But there's a big motherforyou across the way
> Says he'll whip yo' ass mos' any ol' day.
> Now he talked 'bout your mother
> An' your grandma too,
> An' it was a downright dirty shame
> The way he talked 'bout you.
>
> Now this made the Lion mad
> An' he got all in a rage.

He took off through the jungle
Like some frantic 4-F jodie
Who's high off'n gage
Like the swift of the breeze
Knockin' down gorillas
An' bringing giraffes to their knees.

Now he ran up on the Elephant
Under an old shady tree.
He says up you big motherforyou,
It's either you or me.
But the Elephant just rolled over
An' looked out the sides of his eyes.
He said you better go on
You little motherforyou
An' mess with somebody yo' own shrimp size.

Just then the Lion made a pass:
That's when he tore his ass.
The Elephant kicked him in the face,
Broke his two front legs,
An' knocked his eyesight out of place.
Now they fit all that night
An˙ half the next day,
An' I can't see how in the hell
That Lion got away,
Now dragging through the jungles
Mo' dead than alive.
That's when the ol' Monkey
Started his signifyin' jive.

He said Oh Oh Oh Leo,
You have sure caught hell.
That Elephant have whipped yo' ass
To a form frazzle-well.
Now you say you're the king of the jungles.
Ain't you a bitch?
Why yo' face looks like you done broke out
With the seven year's itch.
Now every morning when I'm trying
To sleep just a wee bit mo',
Here you come with some of that who-shot-Joe.
Now you big motherforyou,

Don't you dast ro'
'Cause I'll get down from this tree
An' whip yo' ass some mo'.

So the Monkey got frantic
An' began jumpin' up an' down.
He broke off the limb
An' come tumblin' to the groun'.
It was like a streak of lightnin'
And a bolt of white heat
That Lion was on 'im
With his las' two feet.
But the Monkey lay there
With tears in his eyes.
He says Oh King Leo,
I apologize.
Leo says no you little motherforyou,
Don't you dass shed a tear,
'Cause right here is where
I'm gonna end yo' jungle signifyin' career.

Now the Monkey pleaded and he pleaded
Until he got hisself free
And he jumped right back
Into that same cocoanut tree.
He says now you big motherforyou,
You needn't get so so'
'Cause I'll go get that Elephant
An' have him whip yo' ass some mo'.
So the Lion walked off
With tears in his eyes.
He said I'd rather be dead
Than alive
So I wouldn't have to lissen to
That ol' Monkey's signifyin' jive.

Luther looked at his audience with a grin. "Thass me," he said.
"Man, thass you, ain't it?" Play Safe echoed, roaring with laugh-
ter.
"Thass me, man."
"Got that ol' lion cryin' out his eyes."
"Mos' beat to death."

Despite the fact that the suspicions of these workers seemed momentarily allayed, Lee continued to worry. At home he was restless, uneasy, disturbed by a sense of negligence. If he had reported McKinley's charges to Smitty, perhaps all of this could have been averted. Finally he called Smitty at the union council hall, but Smitty had heard nothing of the rumor and attached no significance to it.

"Take a drink and forget it," he advised. "By tomorrow it will have blown over."

But while they slept the rumor spread like an insidious plague. It moved down the assembly lines, hovered in the latrines, found voice at the lunch hours. Possessed of no actual facts, it fed on the instinctive fear of double cross and was kept alive by minds escaping the realities of war, change, and strangeness in a strange land. And during the dull, endless hours before dawn when foremen and workers alike were wont to "ride the dog," it flourished and became fantastic. By noon of the next day it had touched them all, leaving its imprint of anger, apprehension, and resentment.

When Lee finally came upon Joe Ptak in the union shack he found him in an angry mood.

"If it made any goddamn sense we could refute it easily," Joe said angrily. "But it's one of those things without reason. And that's where we're at fault."

"How so?" Lee wanted to know.

"If we had really sold the union, a crazy lie like this would make no difference."

"There must be something we can do."

"If I knew it, I'd have done it. I'm an organizer, not a goddamned mealy-mouthed evangelist! That's what's needed here. Give me something definite to work on, a strike or a raise, and I'll organize anybody. But this goddamn campaign is driving me nuts! What the hell do these goddamned sharecropping patriots want with a union? All they want is to make a little money and go back to the farm and starve to death. They ain't never been able to see from one goddamned crop to another, so how the hell do you expect them to see a couple or so years ahead!"

But he called a conference for that night. Marvin Todd, Benny Stone, Joe Ptak, Smitty, and Lee were present. Now how could a rumor be stopped that the workers were willing to believe? If the workers had confidence in the organizers' integrity there would be no rumor. And if they could be made to listen to reason they would have listened to the reason of themselves.

Plain words of refutation would be of no avail, they knew. A concrete plan was needed—something visual, actual, a sign, a token, some definite symbol of good faith, if not more credible than the rumor, at least more exciting to believe. Marvin Todd, with the gristly humor of a Montressor drawing a trowel from beneath his robe, suggested that they frame someone and put the blame on him. Lee violently objected to this with his deep abhorrence of any form of lynching, and the two almost came to blows.

"Men! Men!" Smitty exclaimed. "We came here to achieve unity."

Benny Stone then suggested that they pay someone to confess and vanish. "You can get one of these Okies to take a rap like that and never be seen again," he said, looking obliquely at Todd.

"Men! Men!" Smitty exclaimed again.

Lee suggested offering a reward for information pointing out the traitor, but Joe was opposed to that. "The instant we give any credence to the goddamn rumor, these scatterbrained workers will begin suspecting everyone."

Nothing was accomplished but ill will and a vague suspicion of each other. So again Lee tried to see McKinley.

"Do you think you should keep bothering him?" Mrs. McKinley asked.

"Why, it's about the union," Lee replied, perplexed.

"Well—" she hesitated. "You come back again and maybe he will see you." And she closed the door gently in his face.

Now Lee was positive that Lester knew the truth, and he became increasingly fearful of the traitor's being Smitty or Joe. Why then would Lester hesitate to reveal the truth to him? It was as if he was slowly becoming embroiled in some sinister conspiracy of which he knew nothing. He felt the need of someone sympathetic to get another point of view. The night before, Ruth had been solicitous, trying to draw his confidence, but he had repulsed her, his pride still rankling from the hurt she had inflicted. Now it was to Jackie he turned again.

"I was hoping you would call," she said. "Can you come up?"

"Now?"

"Yes."

"Of course." And then: "I love you."

"I want you to."

It was not the answer he had expected and it left a funny taste. So he bought the daily papers to read on the bus to rid himself of the feeling of always being a fool. And reading them, he learned of the growing racial tensions throughout the city— A Negro had cut a white worker's throat in a dice game at another of the aircraft companies and was being held without bail; and a white woman in a shipyard had accused a Negro worker of raping her. A group of white sailors had stripped a Mexican lad of his zoot suit on Main Street before a host of male and female onlookers. Mistaken for Japanese, a Chinese girl had been slapped on a crowded streetcar by a white mother whose son had been killed in the Pacific. And down on the bottom of page thirteen there was a one-line filler, "Negro Kills Self. Charles Bolden, known to intimates as 'Fatso,' an unemployed diemaker, took his life this morning by slashing his wrists with a razor."

Well—yes, Lee Gordon thought and laid the paper down. A Negro called "Fatso" could have hurts too that would make life unendurable—

Arriving at Jackie's, he found that Luther and Mollie had preceded him. But before he could ascertain the purpose of their presence, Jackie admitted another caller, "Oh, come right in, Bart, we're waiting for you," fawning upon him with a deference only befitting a district commissar.

To Lee's surprise even Luther jumped to his feet, although there seemed to be a pretense in his effusiveness; but when Mollie replaced her sardonic attitude with a polite attentiveness, Lee turned again to view the man.

Elderly, his heavy-set body clad in a dark-blue suit, he had coal-black, African features and a longish head as smooth as a billiard ball. "Good evening, comrades," he greeted in a high, precise voice, startling from a man of so stolid an appearance.

Lee had often heard the name even as far back as when he had attended the meetings of the antidiscrimination committee during his employment in the post office. But this was the first he had seen of the man who was West Coast Chairman of the Communist

Party. He was amazed to find him so blatantly a worker and so black.

Selecting the most comfortable chair, which was conveniently vacant at the time, Bart surveyed each of his sycophants in turn, then addressed himself to Lee, his cold, brown eyes devoid of all emotion.

"How do you like the job of selling people a democratic ideology, Gordon?"

"The job's okay."

"It has its compensations."

"That's true."

"And it also presents its challenges."

"Well—yes," Lee replied uncertainly, resentful at being grilled by this Communist official.

"Don't become discouraged, Gordon," Bart propounded in his high, colorless voice. "For twenty-seven years, three months, and thirteen days, I worked in a fertilizer factory. I started off at eight dollars a week and when I quit I was making twenty-two. Somewhere something was wrong, I knew. But I did not set out to solve it by myself. I reasoned that there must be others who knew that something was wrong. So I set out to find them. The problem of humanity is indivisible. That is why you find a bourgeois nation such as ours fighting on the side of the Russian proletariat. Do you read John Pittman in the *People's World?*" he asked abruptly.

"No, I don't," Lee replied defiantly.

Bart dismissed him without another glance. "Well, Jackie, how do you like Los Angeles by this time?"

"Oh, I like it fine."

"Since you've been working?"

"Yes. The job gives me a chance to do something. I don't like to sit around and watch the others do all the work."

"There must be followers too."

"I don't mind following but I want to help too."

"You are of great help in the job you now have."

"I hope so."

Now he turned to Mollie. "You're looking in fit condition."

She broke suddenly into laughter. "I am fit as a fiddle, Bart— as Heifetz's fiddle."

"It would naturally be a bourgeois fiddle," he commented dryly. "Is Luther making you a good husband?"

She laughed again. "From anyone else that would be impertinence."

"To ask about your husband?"

"To ask about his excellence."

"Have you been working for a second front? Or is that impertinence also?"

"I love you, Bart," she laughed.

"It is more important that you love the people."

"I love the people too."

Finally he asked Luther: "What's this about the union?"

"Foster bought a boy," Luther drawled laconically.

Lee looked up with quick concentration, his mouth opening to ask a question but Bart was the first to speak.

"Is this just a rumor?"

"If it is it sho got feet," Luther declared.

Now Bart turned again to Jackie. "Is this what you discovered, too?"

"I found a memo of a payment for five hundred dollars in the file marked 'Miscellaneous' which was not accounted for," she told him.

"Is that unusual—such payments?" Bart asked.

"No," she said. "But this is of a recent date."

"Did you tell this also to Smitty?"

"I didn't think it wise before I talked to you."

So she was a spy for both the union and the party, Lee Gordon learned to his surprise, and his regard for her became unsettled, hung between approbation and disgust.

"And you can not discover who wears the feet?" Bart turned back to Luther.

"It ain't a matter of discovering," Luther said slowly. "We know who it is—"

"Who?" Lee interrupted.

"Wait, darling," Jackie said gently. "Let's hear what Bart has to say."

Lee jerked a look of reproof at her, not only resenting her giving Bart precedence in matters of the union, but annoyed by her use of the affectionate term in public. However, his emotion was quickly lost in the deep-brown candor of her eyes.

But Bart continued with his interrogation as if he had not been interrupted. "You have some evidence?"

"Oh, sure," Luther said. "Benny's been working on it right 'long with Jackie."

"Don't you know how to take care of such a thing?" Bart remonstrated more than asked. "An old organizer like you should need no help of me."

"You know how Joe Ptak and Smitty are," Luther pointed out. "Even if we took 'em the proof wrapped and sealed, they wouldn't wanna use it if it came from us."

"I see," Bart said. And now as if in accord all turned to look at Lee. "You want to know if Gordon will co-operate with the Communist Party to expose this evil traitor?"

Feeling obliged to say yes and impelled to say no, Lee hesitated on the answer and Jackie spoke for him, "I'm sure that Lee will co-operate where the union is concerned. If you give him the proof he will present it to Joe and Smitty."

"I—" he began, looking quickly to Jackie again for some sign of reassurance. But she gave him only a level uncompromising glance and released him from her vision to give his answer without promise of future favor or regard. "Well—" His mind rebelled against believing that she would front him for a fool, for then he would have to accept that this was all that she had ever wanted of it, but caution restrained him from stepping onto the stand. "If you know the person who's selling out the union and you have the proof," he finally said, "I don't see why Smitty and Joe wouldn't accept it from you as well as from me."

Now they turned to look at Jackie as if she had misplayed her cue. "It's politics, darling," she hastened to explain. "They don't have our politics—"

"Neither do I," he stubbornly answered.

"But you believe in the union, don't you?"

"Certainly."

"And you want to expose the traitor and save the campaign from failure, don't you?" She spoke as to a child.

"Of course, Jackie," he replied with an increasing irritation.

"Then you shouldn't object to accepting this evidence and presenting it to Joe and Smitty," she concluded uncontradictably.

"Well—" If she had asked him this in private, he would have objected, he knew; but to object now would be tantamount to impugning her integrity, destroying their affection for each other. He would not only lose Jackie but would not save himself, since by his presence he had become a party to the action anyway. And it was more gallant to assume that she would not ask this of him unless she was convinced that it was honorable. "Okay," he said. "But I have to be convinced first of the person's guilt."

"It must be done from the floor," Bart said.

Lee turned to look at him. "I don't understand."

"You must denounce this traitor from the floor at the union meeting before all the rank-and-file members. This is no private thing."

"Lee won't object to doing that," Jackie said quickly, "if he's convinced of the person's guilt."

"Well—" He gave her a stricken look as if to say: "For you!"

"The point is, Gordon," Bart said, "we are trying to avoid ejecting politics into this organizing campaign. By your working with us in this the objective is achieved and we do not have to show our hand."

"Well—that's fair enough," Lee Gordon said. "I'm willing to help on that basis." And now at last: "Who is the person?"

"We don't want to name him until we have all the evidence in," Luther replied. "But I'll let you know, man."

"Well—yes." Lee Gordon wanted to laugh hysterically—all this build-up, this awful strain, this Communist hammering, and then to say they couldn't name the man. Were all these Communists crazy? Now it was imperative that he see McKinley and get the facts, and though Jackie asked him to stay, he left soon after with the others. If it was Joe Ptak or Smitty they named, he would not believe it unless McKinley named him first. And he was so afraid that Jackie might say something that would turn him away from her.

Through the wide front window of McKinley's house Lee Gordon looked into the softly lighted living-room and saw Lester McKinley sitting in a gray upholstered armchair beneath a reading lamp, his dark head bent with immobile absorption to an open book, and to one side Mrs. McKinley knitting with comfortable serenity, her hands moving with tiny methodic motion in the spill of light. For a moment he hesitated, loath to break into this tranquil scene with the disturbing business of betrayal.

But Lester, sensing an alien presence, looked up and saw him outlined against the night. Although he could not recognize Lee, he knew instantly it was he, and through him raced the murderous fury he had been struggling so long to control—ever since early Saturday morning when Foster, arriving early, had sent for him just before the change of shift.

"Lester, some time ago you spoke to me about an inspector's job," Foster had said.

"Yes, I did," he had replied. "But now I have changed my mind. I will be satisfied with the job I have."

"It's not teaching Latin," Foster said.

"No, but I will be more satisfied with it than I would be teaching Latin," he said, looking forward with keen anticipation to murdering this white-faced man.

"How would you like to work with Lee?" Foster had then asked.

"Lee?"

"Gordon, the colored boy employed by the union. He's going to work for me now—in the personnel department. And you could work with him. The two of you should make a good team. And I will stick a few hundred dollars extra into your pay envelope."

He could have killed Foster then. He had the red-raw urge, and it would not have mattered what they did to him afterwards. Now he bitterly regretted that he had not. But instead he had maintained his iron composure, replying in a level voice: "You can not buy me, Foster, as you have bought this feeble boy. You can not buy me with all the wealth that white men own. You can not buy me."

"Then I can fire you."

"You can not fire me. For when you made the offer I had already quit."

And what had all his cool composure meant? he now thought with bitter scalding chagrin as he opened the door for Lee Gordon to enter. It had not made a dent in Foster's ruthless nigger-hatred and Foster lived. But there was no indication of this in his quiet manner as he said cordially: "Come in, Lee, come in, I was expecting you." And now he would look into this traitor's eyes and study his Judas face and listen to his lying voice and then be through with him, he thought. Through with all of them, lying, cowardly, traitorous, depraved, bastards who were the Negro men, and through with their white overlords who not only spat into their open mouths but fed them their own genitals to eat.

"Hello, Lester," Lee said, pumping McKinley's hand with a heartiness he did not feel. "At least I'm glad to see you're still among the living."

"Come into the living-room and sit down," Lester said, his softly modulated voice pleasing to Lee's ears. "I am very glad that you stopped by."

Mrs. McKinley had quietly disappeared, and taking the chair she had vacated, Lee said seriously: "Lester, remember at the meeting before last you said that Foster had bought out someone connected with the union. It seems that all the workers know about it now."

Does he want me to kill him? Lester wondered. Or is he trying to test me to see if I know, or force me to deny that I know? If I thought that, I'd kill him now. But when he spoke his voice had not changed. "And what are you working on now?"

"Working on?" Lee looked at him with a puzzled frown, aware of some deep misunderstanding, but totally in ignorance of the murderous chaos of McKinley's thoughts. "I don't understand."

You bald-faced bastard, Lester thought, scarcely able to control his savage fury. Traitor! Nigger! You white man's bootlicker! . . . But his voice was still contained. "You are not working in the personel department of Comstock?"

"Oh!" Lee laughed with relief. "Foster did offer me the job but I refused it," he said, wondering how Lester knew, but he did not want to ask. "Did you think I had accepted it?"

So he just took the money and will continue to betray the union, Lester thought, studying Lee's thin, serious face. And yet he is very smooth with it; did all weak people have this ability to lie? "No doubt it was a better job," he said aloud.

"Yes, he offered a handsome salary."

"But you prefer to continue with the union?"

"Well—yes. I suppose I'm something like you. At first it was just another job, but now I believe in it."

"I see. And now what do you want of me?"

"Well, since you were the first one to know of the traitor, I was hoping you'd give me his name."

For a long moment Lester did not speak, his tautly leashed body rooted in rigidity. The urge to charge Lee with his guilt almost overwhelmed him and frightened him to nausea, for to draw a denial would impel him to certain murder, he knew. Trembling in cold sweat as the compulsion threatened him, he hung to sanity by one thin thought. For finally, with gristly irony—the ultimate poetic madness of racial prejudice—only his concern for his white wife and half-breed children restrained him from murdering Lee as he sat there. And now, hoping Lee would leave, he quietly said: "I did not really know of an actual traitor then," and slowly added: "And do not now. I only know that as long as there are men like Foster who possess the wealth to buy, there will be other men corrupt enough to sell."

So that was all he knew, Lee thought, feeling a sense of letdown. "Well—" he hesitated for a moment before revealing it, "the Communists are getting prepared to denounce someone as the traitor and I just wanted to be sure they denounced the right one. I don't exactly trust them."

So he is a Communist too, Lester now thought wearily. I might have known . . .

"Anyway," Lee said in conclusion as he arose to leave, "we can keep working on it until we find the one. That's about all we can do."

Now McKinley also stood. "I should have told you before, Lee," he said in his soft, scholarly voice. "I am not working at Comstock anymore."

"Not working?" Lee stared stupidly at him.

"I quit Saturday morning at the end of my shift," McKinley informed him.

"You—quit—" For a moment he could only stare blankly at McKinley as all manner of fantastic conjectures soared wildly through his mind. But just before he asked: "Why, for God's sake?" the answer exploded in his brain— It's Lester! He's the traitor! He was profoundly shocked.

"We are leaving for Denver tomorrow." McKinley's voice finally penetrated the dull, glazed torture of his thoughts.

"Well—" he said in that light, weightless voice that follows shock. "I guess I'll be getting on. I've taken up enough of your time as it is, seeing as you're not with us any more."

"Good night," McKinley said, his urge to violence burned to ashes now, but his hatred for this haggard, traitorous boy a gruesome stain that would remain forever on his consciousness. "And I hope you a full measure of all that you deserve."

"Good night, and the same to you," Lee replied, hurt more deeply than he realized. For he had liked Lester McKinley and had trusted him all the way.

Outside Lee Gordon breathed deeply of the pure fresh air. So it was Lester—good old black loyal Lester. His legs were rapidly carrying him to the nearest telephone when suddenly he stopped. For he could not tell a white man that a Negro was a traitor—he just couldn't do it, that was all. And after a moment he added in his thought—nor a white woman.

Then it struck him that he did not have to tell her—she knew. So Lester was the one whom Luther would not name. And now he understood, all the pieces fitted. Lee Gordon the Negro would denounce his friend Lester McKinley the Negro as the traitor. And by so doing he would not only place unity above friendship and the union above the race, but would proclaim himself a Communist for only a Communist would do such a thing.

The very clever Communists, Lee Gordon thought. And then again he wondered about Jackie.

Chapter 18

LEE GORDON dreaded reporting for work and dreaded facing Joe Ptak, having to feign and lie because he could not reveal that Lester McKinley, a black man, was a traitor. For the first time he felt dishonorable—as if he had the power to halt the onrushing chaos, knowing he would not use it and could not use it, because it would kill a race.

But Joe Ptak greeted him with a plan. "I'm going down to the gates with a sound truck and talk to these ignorant bastards," he announced. "Since your boy has a car he could drive you out to San Pedro to pick up the truck." To disclaim official recognition of Luther's assistance, Joe Ptak only referred to him when it was unavoidable, and never by name. "The longshoremen are lending us theirs."

"Fine!" Lee said, relieved to get away.

Luther did not mention the conference at Jackie's the night before, for which Lee was profoundly thankful. After a cautious greeting on the part of both, they drove out of the city in silence.

And then Luther grinned. "The boys wanna race," he said and stepped on the gas.

Lee looked up startled and Luther thumbed to the rear. Looking back, Lee saw the car. "It's not the law?" he asked.

"Naw, I know their cars."

"Whoever it is, they're really highballing."

"Yeah, but they ain't gonna catch this baby 'less they got wings. I got a supercharger in this baby."

But the car hung on, and when they came into a lonesome stretch flanked by fields of new-grown corn, it closed up and the siren sounded.

"Not the law, eh?"

"Ain't the state patrol," Luther still contended, pulling to a stop just ahead of a culvert over a deep, twisting ravine. "Least ain't the cars they been using."

A long, black county car drew up ahead and four deputy sheriffs walked back.

"Speeding, eh?" a hard cracker voice raked Lee with antagonism.

"Hey, Luther," the second one took it up. "You know this boy, Ed?"

"Sure, I know that boy. He's a chauffeur out in Hollywood. One of your boys, ain't he, Paul?" He winked at the second speaker.

"He's a good boy most of the time. Got his lady's car out though. She know you drive her car around like this?"

"Why not?" Luther said.

"Did you hear that?" Ed ejaculated. "He said why not!"

"Okay, step out," Paul ordered. Now his voice was harsh.

Two of the deputies had approached on Lee's side along the edge of the gully, and one commanded: "This way, boys."

Ed stood on the road, motioning the cars of the curious on ahead. Paul came around the car to aid in the frisking of Luther and Lee.

"Ray, can you tell these boys are Reds?" it began.

"One is black and the other is off-black." Paul offered with a laugh. "The reddest thing about them is their eyes."

"Walter knows. Ask Walter. How do you tell a Red, Walter?"

"I can usually smell 'em," Walter declared. "A Red and a Jew smell just alike. But there's so much nigger smell here I can't smell nothing else. Are you boys Reds?"

Neither replied.

"Speak up! Speak up when you're spoke to! Are you Reds? I asked you."

Lee's tight, hot gaze searched the speaker's face for signs of levity but found only a blunt bestiality that frightened him.

But Luther's voice was level, only slightly thickened. "Just plain American."

"You hear that!" Walter feigned indignation. "Just plain American! How 'bout you, boy?" he turned to Lee. "You just plain American, too?"

Lee looked into his piggish eyes, debating whether to reply civilly or tell him to go to hell. "Yes, I am," he finally said.

Walter nodded with satisfaction. "They Reds all right. Any time you hear a nigger say he's an American, then you know he's a Red. The Jewish Communists teach 'em that. Ain't no other nigger that impudent. I got a good mind to beat you til you're red sure enough, you—"

"Aw, they're good boys," Paul intervened.

"That's right, this black one here is one of your boys, ain't he?"

Paul grinned. "I'm looking out for you, Luther." When Luther failed to reply, his smile came off.

"How's you boys' grandfather Stalin?" Walter taunted. "I always knew that kike had nigger blood. Now here's the proof—two black grandchildren. Confidentially," he leered, "I want to ask you is there any truth in the Communists making you boys turn pansy after you become members of the Party?"

Failing to get a rise out of either of them in this manner, they reverted to the traditional barbarism of racial abuse.

"Did you ever see a nigger who looked as much like an ape as this nigger?"

"These two are getting all the apes together to start a second front. It'll be what they call the baboon brigade."

"Nigger, goddamnit, why don't you say something!" Walter roared with rage.

"Aw, let him alone," Paul cautioned. "You see the nigger's scared."

"Who was your father, boy?" Walter spoke to Lee.

"How does he know? His mother was a whore," Ray said. "How does he know who his father was?"

A tiny hammer began tapping at the base of Lee's brain, but he kept his body under control, his voice under wraps. "I wouldn't talk about your mother," he said.

"By God, if I thought you even thought about it—" Ray made a threatening motion and again Paul intervened,

"Aw, let the boys alone. These are good boys. They're the two organizers for the union."

Ray grinned at this. "What you say we run 'em in for rape, Paul. You can see they're dirty nigger rapists."

"Not these boys; they're my boys."

"Why the hell didn't you say so?"

"I was just letting you get yourself off."

"Why, you son of a bitch! Just for that I oughta beat the hell out of both of 'em!"

Though realizing that the deputy was in deadly earnest, there were such tones of a bloody humoresque within this blatant baiting that Lee felt the creepy impulse to laugh, as at an idiot attempting to milk a fly. But the voice of Paul quelled the impulse and drew him back to the urgent danger.

"How much do you want, Gordon?"

For a moment Lee made no reply, then his curiosity got the better of him. "I don't understand?"

"You understand, all right! For selling out the union!"

"Give him twenty-five dollars," Ray said, then turned to Lee, "That'll be fine, won't it, fellow?"

Lee laughed aloud.

"Well, fifty then," Paul offered, his face getting red.

"That's enough to buy his mother," Walter said.

"I've asked you fellows once before not to talk about my mother," Lee Gordon said. "Now I've had enough of this!"

"Did you hear that!" Ray exclaimed. "He's had enough!"

"Okay, a hundred then," Paul said. "And that's the top."

Lee looked Paul in the eyes and said: "I wouldn't sell out the union for a hundred thousand dollars."

For an instant Paul was impressed by the sincerity in his voice, and then he laughed it off. "Your buddy did and all he got is what I'm offering you."

And now Lee Gordon could not say a word, for if all McKinley got was a lousy hundred dollars to quit his job and leave the city, it was an awful thing to be a Negro.

Thinking that Lee was about to succumb, Paul became confidential. "This boy here got his little piece of dough. What are you waiting for?"

Lee turned and looked at the stolid face of Luther and laughed for the second time. "Nuts!" he said, because now he was convinced that they were only taunting him.

Paul also turned to look at Luther. "Tell this boy what Mr. Foster gave you," he demanded.

Luther gave no sign that he had heard.

Thwarted and enraged, Paul drew his service revolver and dug the barrel deep into Luther's belly. "I will blow out your guts, you black son of a bitch!" he threatened in a murderous voice. "What did Mr. Foster give you?"

"Five hunnered dollahs," Luther replied, and now his voice was flat.

"You're a goddamned liar!" Paul accused. "He gave you a hundred."

"Have it yo' way," Luther conceded in that flat black voice. "Uh hunnered then."

"Now that's more like it," Paul crowed triumphantly, swinging the pistol at his side.

Lee's first emotion was one of thankfulness to know that it was not Lester, after all. And then looking from the black defeatism of Luther's face to the red exultation of Paul's, he went sick and utterly afraid. This was one time he hated being a Negro.

Paul extended a folded hundred-dollar bill. "Mr. Foster wants you boys to break up the next meeting."

So deep were Lee's thoughts in racial torment that he did not see the money.

"Here, here's your money!" Paul snapped. "Take it!"

"Take de money, man!" Luther muttered. "Doan be no fool!"

"You goddamned rat!" Lee cried, as tears came into his eyes.

Paul slapped him across the face with the pistol barrel, catching him unawares. He reeled back, stepped beyond the edge of the shallow gully, and fell. Landing on his right side and forearm, he rolled over and started up on his hands and knees. The deputy Walter jumped flatfooted into the gully and kicked him on the shoulder.

"Son of a bitch!" Lee growled and got to his feet. A sixth sense caused him to duck. Paul's pistol barrel landed on his shoulder bone where Walter had kicked him. The sharp, acid ache ran down into his groin. He fell forward into Walter, wrapped both arms about his waist, and carried him back, falling down the steep embankment into the muddy ravine. Lee got one arm loose and hit him twice in the face.

By then Ray had scrambled down from the ledge, taking care of his shined shoes. He leaned forward and gripped Lee's coat tail. Lee kicked back, striking him in the chest.

"Get aside, goddamnit, and let me shoot the nigger!" Paul screamed, sliding down the steep embankment in a shower of gravel and dust.

Terror brought Lee to his feet and he broke away from Walter's grip. Turning with the wild sheer strength of panic, he closed with Ray. They spun, clawing, twisting, gasping, and butted into Paul. The three of them went down in a biting, kicking, cursing melee. Walter came out of the stream, dripping mud like a deep-sea ghoul, and pointed his pistol at the squirming fray. Murder was in his face, not the intent but the deed, he had already killed the black bastard in his mind before his finger could squeeze the trigger.

"Walter!" Ed screamed from above.

The raw, rasping urgency in his voice stilled them all. In the sudden tableau of suspended fury, Lee's gaze went above. He saw Luther standing there looking down at them, the flat black features of his face set in Negroid negativism. The next instant he was on his feet fighting again. What had he to fear from these four incidental white men, he thought, that Luther McGregor had not already done to him.

Then Walter closed in and struck him across the head like a man hammering down a nail. Lee reeled back from the force of the blow, stunned but not down. Then Ray and Paul got to their feet. The three of them beat Lee Gordon twenty yards back down through the twisting ravine, pistol-whipped him until he didn't have the strength to raise his hands. Once he moaned but he did not cry. And then he just started going away.

As he lay unconscious, face down in the muddy water, Walter kicked him twice in the body with sadistic savagery.

"Don't kill him," Paul cautioned. "There'd be hell to pay."

Ray reached down and clutched him by the coat collar, dragged his inert body from the water so he would not drown. Then

leaving him there, they started up the steep embankment. Muddy
and disheveled, all bearing marks of the conflict, their tempers
were at murderous pitch.

Walter stalked toward Luther and growled in his face: "Did
you like what we did to your buddy?"

Luther's set expression did not waver and his muddy eyes did
not blink. "Yassuh."

"You know your place, don't you, boy?" Ray closed in from the
side.

"Yassuh."

Paul returned from the official car with a pint bottle. Taking a
swallow, he passed it around. Ed took the last drink and passed it
to Luther.

"Drown your troubles, Luther, boy. We're not going to hurt
you."

Luther took the bottle and tilted it to his mouth. Then he
passed it back to Ed.

"Goddamnit, keep it! Who the hell you think wants to drink
after you!"

Luther held the bottle in his hand.

"Luther's a good boy," Paul taunted. "Aren't you a good boy,
Luther?"

"Dass ri'."

"What'd you do with that hundred you got from Mr. Foster?
Spend it on the little nigger gals?"

"Sho did."

"You didn't give it to those Communists, did you?" Walter
asked.

"No suh."

The four deputies started off. Then Paul stopped and turned
again. "Maybe your buddy's got some sense now. Bring him
'round to see me."

"Yassuh."

When they had driven off, Luther got his own pistol from the
glove compartment of his car and stuck it into his pocket. Then
he went down into the ravine where Lee lay, with the bottle of
whisky in his hand.

Lee was moaning slightly. Luther raised his head and forced

some whisky down his throat. Lee strangled and coughed, but did not regain consciousness. Lifting him easily, Luther carried him up the embankment and laid him gently on the back seat. Then he turned the car around and drove back to the union council hall. Leaving him in the car, he went in search of Smitty. But Smitty had gone out to Comstock to work in a sound truck, the secretary informed Luther, and she did not know when he would return. Luther said nothing to her about Lee, but instead looked into the regional offices of the various unions for fellows he knew.

It was the noon hour and most of the union representatives were at lunch. Luther returned to the main floor and telephoned Bart for instructions. Bart directed him to take Lee to an emergency hospital that served all of the unions, and he arrived there himself in time to help Luther carry Lee inside.

After putting Lee in the charge of a young staff doctor, they returned to the lobby. Bart pulled Luther down onto one of the hard wooden benches and demanded, "Let's have it, son."

"Four deputies waylaid us on the road to Pedro and sapped Lee up a little," Luther said. "That's all."

Bart massaged his jaw. "About the union?"

Luther hesitated for a moment and then replied, "Yeah. One of 'em tried to buy him out."

"But he told them off?"

"Somp'n like that."

"What did they expect with you present?"

"Well, that's it. I may as well tell you, old-timer. I took five yards from Foster a coupla weeks back."

"Luther, confound it! What did you do that for?"

"Hell! the son of a bitch stopped me one day as I was going out to help Lee at the gates and ast me how much I wanted to double-cross the union and I said five hundred, thinking that'd discourage him. So he pulls out his wallet and hands me five C notes. What else could I do? It was like finding money in the street."

"Luther, you are an incorrigible thief," Bart reprimanded, but there was a twinkle in his usually cold eyes. "Did you tell anyone else?"

"No."

"Mollie?"

"Hell no. I have a hard enough time getting a little money out of that bitch as it is."

"Is this how the rumor started?"

"Aw hell, Bart, you know better'n that. Foster's had his shop foremen priming it since the first day of the campaign. It just all of a sudden took hold, that's all."

"How does all this figure with Gordon? How did he know?"

"One of the bastards went and told him I got a hundred from Foster, then put his gun on me and made me admit it."

"How did Gordon take it?"

"Well now, that's the trouble, old-timer. He took it as hard as a man takes a hanging. You see, when they jumped on him and started sapping him there wasn't nothing I could do. So he thinks I'm up with all of it."

"Why didn't you help the boy, Luther?"

"Bart, you know me. If he didn't have sense enough to take their rotten money then spit in their face afterwards, he didn't need no help."

"That's not the point. You should have denied it and then helped him fight and he'd be convinced then that it wasn't true. Now he's probably convinced that you've been selling out the union straight along."

"Sure as hell is. But lemme tell you one thing, old-timer. The first white man ever hits me loses sight on the world. And that's final. No need of me killing four white men no matter what the punk might believe."

"Well, now we have to deny it straight through. Smitty isn't going to like this."

"Lee ain't either, far as that goes."

"What about your other plan?"

"McKinley's gone."

"And Gordon is not going to help."

"Don't give 'im up. That l'il pink frau can make a monkey eat cay'n pepper."

"Well, you let it alone," Bart said. "And now I had better call Smitty." They stood to their feet, two thick black men who were always looked upon as strangers in their native land. "And let me warn you, Luther. This is the last time."

"You know me, old-timer. I always learns the first time."

Bart entered the telephone booth and Luther went down the hallway toward Minor Surgery and halted respectfully in the doorway.

"Hi do, Dr. Greenbaum," he addressed the young staff doctor. " 'Member me?"

"Hello, Luther," the doctor replied cheerfully, looking up from the hand he was dressing. "How could I ever forget you, boy? You had a sprained back from lifting a sack of cement. Did you get your compensation?"

"They didn't believe it."

The doctor laughed. "We did the best we could."

"I know, doc." Then he asked: "How's the fellow we just brought in?"

"The colored fellow? He's fine, just bruised up a little. I gave him a sedative and want him to rest for a while. You can take him home this evening. What happened, anyway?"

"He ran into some cops."

"Oh! He seems pretty upset. They beat him up, eh?"

"Yeah."

"Well, we'll have to make a report. Who's taking care of it?"

"The union. Smitty'll be here after a while. What I wanna know is can I talk to him 'fore he goes to sleep?"

"Oh, sure. Just go right in; he's in room four."

Lee lay on a small white cot in the tiny room looking at the ceiling. His face was splotched with mercurochrome and bandaged in one spot, and his body was rigid in a rough cotton gown. What puzzled him now was the Communists' angle. Did they know what Luther had done? And if so, had they planned to frame McKinley to cover up for him? Was that the reason for McKinley quitting and leaving town? He wondered if McKinley had thought he was in with them.

Turning his head, he saw Luther in the doorway and for a moment just looked at him with cold contempt. "You're a god-damned rotten nigger," he said at last.

"Lissen, man, ain't no need of being mad at me." Luther came into the room with his hands spread wide. "Lemme hip you to the jive."

"I don't want to hear anything you've got to say," Lee said.

"You wanna hear this, man. It's for your own good. I took the dough from Foster but I ain't no rat, man. I'll take any peckerwood's money but I ain't gonna—"

"Get out and let me alone! You've done enough harm as it is."

"Okay, pal, but you oughta keep me out of it for your own good."

"I'm going to tell everybody what kind of rat you are," Lee stated.

"Okay," Luther warned, turning to go. "But remember I'm a Communist. An' de proof, pal, I'm de proof."

Lee drew his gaze back from the closed door to the white, unbroken ceiling. What hurt him most at this time was his doubting Lester. And Lester had been the only honorable one of them all. But he would get those deputies and Luther too, he resolved. He'd tell Smitty the whole story and they'd blow it wide open. The rotten, lousy, stinking, double-crossing Communists! And Jackie, too! Then he drifted off to sleep.

Chapter 19

J OE PTAK and Smitty were the first to arrive. Bart had departed. Luther was waiting alone in the lobby.

"What happened to Lee?" Smitty asked as soon as he caught sight of Luther.

"Some deputy sheriffs jumped on him."

"Where?"

"On the road to Pedro."

"Well, what in the hell did they do that for?"

"They flagged us down for speeding and started cussing us out. Lee cussed 'em back and they jumped him."

"How many?"

"Four."

"Where were you?" Joe Ptak asked.

Luther looked at him. "I was there."

"Well, when in the hell did deputy sheriffs begin patrolling the highway?" Smitty wanted to know.

"These the first I ever seen," Luther admitted.

"Let's go in and see Lee," Joe said.

But Lee had not awakened. They went back to the lobby to wait. Steve Hannegan the attorney for the union and one of his assistants, Carl Dawson, arrived while they sat there.

"What's it all about, Smitty?" Hannegan asked.

"We don't know yet. One of our boys got hurt."

"Goons?"

"No, police."

"All the same," Hannegan said.

Joe caught sight of Dr. Greenbaum and called: "Hey, doc, just a minute."

Dr. Greenbaum walked over.

"You got one of our organizers here. How 'bout seeing him?"

"I suppose so," Dr. Greenbaum replied, looking over the assemblage with open curiosity. "Come this way."

He led them into the tiny room, snapped on the light, and awakened Lee.

"Some friends of yours, young man." Then to the others: "I'm sorry, there're no seats. You can use my office if you like."

"No, this'll do," Joe Ptak replied.

Lee sat up, looking gaunt and battered. "I want a lawyer," he said.

"We have our union lawyers right here," Smitty replied. "Hannegan, Dawson, this is Lee Gordon."

Both shook hands with Lee and Hannegan said: "How are you, Lee?"

"Not so hot."

"So I see. Just tell us what happened."

"Well, we were driving out to San Pedro to get a sound truck when four deputy sheriffs in a county car pulled up and ordered us to stop. They made us get out the car and after they'd searched us they began calling us Reds and abusing us in the worst way. I didn't mind that so much because you expect that from these ignorant bastards. But then one of them, Paul was his name, offered me twenty-five dollars to double-cross the union—"

"Prodigal bastard," Dawson murmured.

"—then he raised it to one hundred," Lee continued. "When I told him I couldn't sell out the union, he said that Luther had sold it out and why couldn't I—"

All eyes turned toward Luther for an instant then back to Lee.

"Luther didn't say anything, and then Paul put his gun on him and said: 'How much did Foster give you?' Luther said that Foster had given him five hundred dollars. Paul didn't believe that Foster had given him that much, so Luther said one hundred. Then I said something, I forget now what it was. And they jumped on me. I remember Luther standing there not helping me in any way, and the next thing I remember I was here in the hospital."

In the silence following the sound of his voice, Dawson said nervously to break the strain: "There wasn't much else he could do, was there?"

"I didn't expect him to do anything else. I'm just telling it like it was."

"You said Luther, who is Luther?" Hannegan asked.

"I'm Luther."

Hannegan looked around. "You!" Then he turned back to Lee, "You said Luther admitted to the deputy name Paul that Foster had given him five hundred dollars to sell out the union?"

"That's right," Lee said.

"Aw, man, goddamnit, you know that ain't so!" Luther denied. "Why don't you tell the truth? You cussed the mens and they jumped on you."

Hannegan looked at Smitty. But it was Joe Ptak who spoke. "Let's get one story at a time."

"You said one of the deputies was named Paul. Do you recall the names of any of the others?"

"Yes, all of them: Ed, Paul, Walter, and Ray. I didn't hear any of the last names."

Hannegan turned to Dawson. "You can check that now, can't you?"

Dawson nodded and went out. Smitty blew air into his cheeks, then said slowly to Lee: "Are you certain you remember what this guy Paul asked Luther, and what Luther said in reply?"

"I'm certain," Lee replied.

"It could have been a gag to work on you, couldn't it?"

"No, it couldn't."

"Aw, Smitty, goddamnit, ain't nothing like that happened at all," Luther again denied.

Joe turned toward him. "Keep quiet."

Luther looked at him again but made no reply. Smitty's face set in a deep, troubled frown. "But Luther brought you to the hospital? He took care of you after you were beaten up? Does that sound as if he was your enemy?"

"Maybe not."

"It's hard to believe that about Luther, Lee. That's why I want you to be certain."

"I am certain."

"Well, it doesn't sound like Luther. He's been out there in the field working for the union for a long time and no one's ever charged him with anything like this. We've always considered him very reliable. A few years back he was up at Bakersfield trying to organize the agricultural workers almost singlehanded, and he could have sold out then to the owners for plenty."

"Listen, Smitty, I'm telling it just like it happened."

Hannegan turned to Smitty and asked: "What's Luther's official connection with the union."

But it was Joe who replied: "He has none. The Commies sent him out to work on Lee."

"Well, he's a sort of volunteer," Smitty said, trying to soften it. "While he hasn't any official connection, we've always appreciated his assistance."

"That's what's the trouble with this goddamned drive now," Joe said. "We got too many unofficial assistants."

"Well, we need more than we have," Smitty said, turning on him angrily.

"If we didn't have this one we wouldn't be fighting the goddamned sellout story," Joe snapped back.

Hannegan looked up inquiringly at this, but Dawson entered at the moment and interrupted what might have been an argument. "There's an Edward Gillespie, Paul Dixon, Walter Thomas, and Ray Young listed as deputy sheriffs," he announced.

"Is that the Paul you know?" Hannegan hurled at Luther, trying to catch him unawares.

But Luther was not to be caught unawares. "I don't know nobody by the name of Paul."

"Did you hear any of their names called?" Hannegan persisted.

"Naw, I didn't."

"That's odd. Lee hears all four names correctly and you hear none."

"He was listening better than I was."

"No doubt of it."

"Shall we make·a charge against them?" Smitty asked Hannegan.

"Smitty, it's tough—there's that business of false arrest." He turned back to Luther. "Can you identify the four deputies by sight."

"Sure."

"But not by the names of Ed, Paul, Walter, and Ray?"

"Not by no names 'cause I didn't hear no names."

"I see." Hannegan turned back to Smitty. "Without this boy testifying, we don't have much to go on. We wouldn't have much even if he testified, but this way we don't have anything."

"I believe Luther will identify the deputies if he sees them."

"He ain't done it," Joe Ptak put in.

"He hasn't seen them, either."

"He heard their names."

"But he doesn't know their names."

"It's hardly conceivable that Lee heard the names of all four and Luther did not hear the name of any," Hannegan said.

"Lee could be mistaken," Smitty said persistently. "Luther's always been honest to the letter 't'."

"Well, what we can do is give the sheriff a little call and put some political pressure on him," Hannegan suggested.

"When?"

"Now, if he's at his office. And if he isn't, we can call his home and have him meet us at his office."

But Hannegan could not locate the sheriff, either at his office or at his home. The chief deputy suggested that Hannegan try to contact the sheriff at his office at eleven o'clock the next morning.

So Smitty called a taxi to take Lee home. "I know how you must feel, Lee," he began as soon as they were seated.

"I don't think you do, Smitty."

"You feel pretty badly over this now, and you want to get even with Luther—"

"No, Smitty, that's not it. You see, I know Luther is the person who sold the union out. I know that this was what started all the stories. Smitty, I know this beyond all doubt. Not just by what happened today, but by many things. And if we hope to save the campaign, he should be exposed. The workers should know who's guilty, then all this talk will stop."

Now Smitty was stumped. He did not doubt that Lee wanted to save the campaign. But he felt that what Lee wanted more at just the moment was simply to be believed. The bitter part about it was that he did implicitly believe him. But if he admitted this to Lee, he would have to join him in a battle royal against the Communists. And while such a battle would hurt himself, he felt that it would hurt Lee immeasurably more.

He believed that Lee Gordon could be hurt more easily than the average person. Since the night of their discussion, which was memorable for him, he had come to believe that to be hurt was Lee Gordon's destiny. Though at the time he had been annoyed by most of what Lee had said, now he was just beginning to understand what Lee had been trying to say. And while he still did not accept the logic of all Lee's conclusions, he was profoundly touched by their undercurrent of longing. He was especially moved by Lee's confession that whenever a Negro came to believe that full equality was his just due, he would have to die for it, as would any other man. It was as if Lee Gordon was searching for this moment when he would have to die, and at the same time fearing its discovery. And yet he felt that Lee would be hurt terribly before he discovered it, if he ever did.

It was partly this that made him want to protect Lee from the almost certain hurt of fighting with the Communists. And another statement from the same discussion that restrained him from revealing it: "Is it necessary that we know? . . . Does what you do for us have on it the price that we recognize it and feel grateful?"

No, he would have to do it and brave Lee's displeasure. For it was almost a certainty that Lee would not understand.

"One thing you must remember, Lee," he said, "is that the organization of the plant is the main objective. It's bigger than any one person, bigger than personal differences, bigger than us all."

"So you don't believe me."

"It's not a question of whether I believe you or not, Lee. It's not even important. But I believe in you, and I want you to stay with us and fight this thing through. But to do that you'll have to rise above your personal emotions. I am exceedingly sorry this happened, and I say this sincerely. But you'll have to forget about it, about your injuries. And you will have to forget about Luther also. Luther's not important, but you are."

"Well, Smitty, I'll tell you. I'll go ahead and do my best if you want me to—"

"We do want you to, Lee."

"But that's all."

Chapter 20

O H, LEE! Lee! You're hurt!" Ruth exclaimed, rushing forward to help him as he came into the house.

He turned to look at her, his bruised, bandaged face set in somberness, and his stare passed through her into nothing. In that moment the motion ran out of her and she stopped as if turned to stone, for more terrible than a Gorgon's head was the hurt in Lee Gordon's eyes.

"Lee! Oh, Lee!" she cried, and now it was a prayer as her first shocked concern for his physical condition gave way to a gripping fear.

Without removing his hat he went to the davenport and sat down. His face held that naked look of protest seen in the face of a young girl just ravished trying to absorb the effects of the brutality, and his body looked more beaten than by guns alone.

Across the room where she had stopped Ruth Gordon stood helplessly, her heart mobile with the impulse to hold him in her arms but her body crucified by the fear of his repulsing her.

"Lee, is there anything I can do?" she finally asked across a distance far greater than the room.

As if her words released the motion, he slowly raised a hand and removed his hat. "No thanks, Ruth, I'm fine," he said, and in his voice there were only the words.

She started toward the bedroom, turned toward the kitchen,

came back to stand hesitantly in the room again. "Would you like your dinner now?"

"No thanks, Ruth, I'm not hungry now," he said in that same dead voice.

Her hand came up in a lost gesture and dropped to her side in defeat. As silence held the tableau imprisoned in a hopelessness, she fought against his closed mind with all her might and will. Gone now was her rigid resolution of the past that she was through with worrying about Lee Gordon, through with abasing herself for his ego, through with absorbing his hurts. For in this tearing urgency she would have sacrificed all that she held dear in life to alleviate his hurt.

"Would you like a drink?" she continued to try. "I bought a bottle of whisky today."

He looked up, slightly frowning as if trying to interpret her meaning, and for the first time sight of her came into the focus of his vision. "Yes, I would like a drink, Ruth. Thank you." There was the slow, groping falter in his voice now as if he found it difficult to enunciate the words.

"With soda?" she asked, her voice singing with a gratefulness that this much she could do.

Again he seemed to consider his reply. "Yes, I would like soda—fine."

Turning quickly toward the kitchen, she halted with the thought. "Oh, do you think a drink would be good for you? I mean—"

"If you thought it wouldn't be good for me," he asked in his slow, faltering voice, "why did you mention it, Ruth?"

"Oh, I just mean—I thought—" She turned quickly away from his fixed, blank stare and hurried into the kitchen.

But as she mixed the drinks she began crying softly, feeling shut off from him by the days of apprehension, the row of frightened years. For a long time—ever since she had first learned a little of the fear inside of him—she had expected Lee to be hurt, dreading it and yet convinced that it would happen, because she did not see how Lee Gordon could live in the society of America and escape being hurt. And she had feared that when it happened, there would be nothing she could do; that he would be hurt and that he would be alone with it.

Yet, somehow she had still retained a faith in him even while disclaiming it; perhaps because she loved him, she thought with self-effacing bitterness. And the hope that he would find himself had never died. For paradoxically she saw within him a quality of belief in human nature that kept this hope alive; a slender thread of integrity between him and his God that she had seen conditions bend but had never thought would break.

But what she now saw in his eyes made her so terribly afraid that his belief was lost and his integrity broken, she hoped against hope not irremediably. And she knew that whatever there was to be salvaged it was hers to save. The occasion was here, hers to rise or fall to it.

She brought two drinks and sat quietly across from him, sipping hers, until the slight sound seemed to widen the distance between her heart and his hurt, and then she put it down.

"That son of a bitch!" he said as if the words tore loose from the bottom of his stomach.

She sat perfectly still, fearful that the slightest motion might profane him. After a time he asked for another drink, and when she brought it, he told her what had happened, covering the nakedness of his hurt with a hard, brutal indifference.

"Now you may as well say you don't believe me either and make it a perfect day," he concluded.

"I believe you, Lee," she said from behind a look of faith.

"Then you're the only one," he muttered disbelievingly, without even seeing it.

"But Smitty believes you, doesn't he?"

"No."

"He's not a Communist, is he, Lee?"

"I don't know."

"Doesn't Joe Ptak believe you?"

"He didn't say he did."

"You've spoken rather well of Smitty in the past. You always said that he tried to be fair about most things."

"That's what I thought then."

"Maybe he was just upset and didn't know what he was saying. I feel almost certain, without even knowing him, that he must believe you."

"You're more certain than I am," he said.

"Luther's not important, is he?" she asked. "I thought you said that he was just flunkying around for you."

"That's where I was a fool. I was just flunkying around for him, it seems like now."

"Unless all of them as dishonest, some of them must believe in you, Lee."

"I don't understand it, myself. They ought to know I wouldn't tell a lie on the bastard. What the hell would I get out of lying on him?"

"It was just that they wanted time to think it over, Lee. They're like that in all organizations—afraid to take any immediate action on one person's accusation of another even though they are absolutely convinced of its truth."

"But they didn't even say anything to the son of a bitch." And now she knew that this was what rankled him.

She arose to refill his glass and when she returned sat beside him, timidly resting her head on his chest. Absently he put his arm about her shoulders and she looked up at him, hoping he would kiss her. But his gaze was focused on the wall across the room and his thoughts were gone.

"You can beat me, darling, if that will make you feel any better," she said half seriously, trying to make him smile.

But when his gaze came back to her it was laden with resentment. "At least you were sensible in keeping your job," he said bitterly. "The way it looks now, I might be out of mine any day."

"Lee, please try not to think about it," she begged.

"What the hell do you expect me to think about?" he asked harshly.

She put her hand on his thigh and willed its gentle pressure into his consciousness. "Remember how we used to get drunk on wine," she recalled, moving her hand to make him conscious of it. "You'd be angry at someone and then we'd quarrel, and afterwards we'd make love and you were always so passionately—"

But he cried: "Ruth, goddamnit, no!" out of other memories.

In his desire for revenge against white men who denied his honor and doubted his integrity, there was nothing Ruth Gordon could give him, no incentive or release. And now since she had sold her own honor and integrity to these same people, he thought con-

demningly, he did not even want her body since that also, she was
sooner or later to learn, was included in the bargain with the rest.
And even though he suspected that this was a lying thought, he
did not care since she had nothing for him anyway.

She got slowly to her feet, giving him a chance to say he didn't
mean it, and when he did not do so, she went into the bedroom
and to bed. But not to sleep. She heard him go back to get another drink, straining her ears to catch the sound of his slightest
motion, holding her breath in suspended fear until he had returned
and was seated again, tortured by the aching of her lungs. And
when she could no longer hear the sound of any motion, she could
hear the silence of his brooding and she wondered at his thoughts,
so hurt by his loneliness that she could feel but could not help.

Lee Gordon reached a conclusion sitting there: that the one
rigid rule in human behavior was to be for yourself and to hell
with everyone else; that within all human beings, himself included, were propensities for every evil, each waiting its moment of
fulfillment; that honor never was and never would be for the
Negro, and integrity was only for a fool; that from then on he
would believe in the almighty dollar, the cowardice of Negroes,
and the hypocrisy of whites, and he would never go wrong.

And because all these fine conclusions were so dissatisfying, he
arose and went to bed with Ruth. And she could have been any
woman with two legs and a stomach.

After his rejection of her a few short minutes earlier, this was
the most brutal thing that he had ever done to her. And the only
reason she accepted it was because she loved him.

The following morning she remained home from work and prepared him a wonderful breakfast. And when he had finished she
said: "Let's go away, Lee—to another city and find some new
people and do some new things."

He looked up, startled. "But what would you do?"

"I would be your wife."

She touched him then, because that was all that he had ever
wanted. Rising, he went around the table and took her in his arms.
"I love you, baby doll."

She began to cry, the soft sobbing of her body filling his arms
with despair. He kissed her lips and eyes, the warm salt taste of

her tears like blood on his emotions, but his mind opened eagerly to the idea.

"We could go to San Francisco," he thought aloud, and then smiling down at her he added: "You'd like it there. On clear days the city's like a jewel in the sunshine, and the people are pleasant. You'd like it, Ruth."

He felt her draw away from him as her sobbing stopped, but his enthusiasm had carried him away. "I know a house on Vallejo high up on the hill overlooking the bay. Look, baby doll, it's got a great big attic room paneled in mahogany with three wide windows across the front, and you can sit there and see the ships come underneath the Golden Gate Bridge just like they were in your lap. When the sun's shining—" He broke off as he caught sight of the fear that was in her face. "What's the matter, baby doll?"

"We couldn't go now, we'd have to wait—" she began, but he cut her off:

"Why? You mean I shouldn't quit the union now?" He damned it with a gesture. "To hell with the union!"

"But what would you do, Lee? Neither one of us would have a job and—"

"Oh, there're plenty jobs in San Francisco. I'd get a job." And then he looked at her again. "We'll make it, baby doll. We've always made it, and we always will."

She saw the past strung out behind them like a line of tattered banners of things that never were—dreams that had been shattered and hopes now crumbled into dust, fear and apprehension, poverty and abuse. And now he wanted them to do it over again, to give up everything that they had gained and start from scratch. And it would be the same, she thought—Lee refusing to accept the jobs offered to him and taking out his hurts on her. And insecurity would always be their lot, even in this time when everyone else was making money. She could not go through with it again; she could not do it, that was all.

"Lee—"

His soaring thoughts were brought back by the quality in her voice. "What, Ruth?"

"You won't be angry?"

"Angry at what?"

"Thinking it over, Lee, I don't see how we can do it now."

"We can if—" he broke off. "Then you didn't mean it?" There was accusation in his voice.

"I did, Lee, I did mean it. Please believe me, Lee."

"But what is it, Ruth? What's the matter?"

"I wanted to say something to help you, Lee. Don't you see? I thought if I—"

"But you didn't think that I would do it?"

"I— You haven't given it any thought, darling. You're just going headstrong—"

As his mind closed to the sound of her voice, the wide scope of his conjecturing narrowed to the single thought, and in all the world there was only her smooth brown face, unbeautiful now, again doubting him.

"Well—yes," Lee Gordon said, bitterness hardening about him like a shell. He should have known that whatever he had been to her just this past Sunday, he was even less today.

"Lee, listen, Lee—"

Without again looking at her, he turned and went into the living-room.

Chapter 21

AT TEN THIRTY that morning Smitty and Hannegan called for Lee and drove him to the sheriff's office.

After listening to Lee's story with a fidgety impatience, the
sheriff said: "It couldn't have been any of my deputies, Hannegan.
None of my deputies would do a thing like that."

He was a large, loose-jointed man of Spanish extraction with a
hatred for Negroes second only to his hatred for Mexicans. He was
often mistaken for a Mexican by persons who did not know him.

"May we have Gordon see these four deputies whom he has
named?" Hannegan requested.

"No, by God!" the sheriff refused. "I'll not have my deputies
subjected to any such tommyrot because of the wild story this boy
tells."

"But you have pictures of them in your files," Hannegan said.

"I do, yes."

"May we see the pictures?"

"No, by God, you may not!"

"Then we will have to file charges against the lot of them for
assault and battery."

"Then, by God, you are a bigger goddamned fool than I think
you are! Because what this boy says is impossible. Paul Dixon was
off yesterday. He's on duty Sundays, and Wednesday is his regular
day off. Ed Gillepsie and Ray Young were working on a case in

Whittier and were there all day with a dozen witnesses to prove it. By God, I can testify to it myself. I stopped there and talked to both of them. And Walter Thomas was here on jail duty. And I've got the records to prove it."

"May we see your records?"

"No, you may not see my records. But I will show them to you quickly enough in court if you make a charge against my men."

"You're not co-operating, Sheriff," Smitty said. "We're not after any of your deputies. We want to get at the truth."

"I'm telling you the truth, Smith. And I've given you more time now than this cock-and-bull story is worth." But he took a little more time to appear thoughtful. "There is a possibility that there could have been four men impersonating deputy sheriffs—"

"No, that's out," Smitty interrupted. "There could be nothing they'd want from these boys to warrant such impersonation. No, if they were not deputy sheriffs, then there was no one."

"There was no one," the sheriff said. "I'm always glad to help you fellows with your unions when you have some reasonable request, but I wish you wouldn't bother me with these colored boys' nightmares. Every time something happens to a nigger he says a deputy sheriff did it."

"You know, Sheriff, a large number of Negroes are migrating to Los Angeles," Hannegan reminded him. "It is possible that within a few years the Negro vote will have much to do with the election of sheriffs."

The sheriff's face reddened as he came abruptly to his feet. "I don't like threats, gentlemen."

"Nor do we like to have our union organizers pushed around," Smitty replied.

"Good day, gentlemen," the sheriff said.

When they were again seated in Smitty's coupé, Hannegan turned to Lee. "Well, Gordon, that's it. You can file charges against the four deputies if you wish, but you will lay yourself open to be prosecuted for false arrest. I advise you against it."

"Well—" Lee said. "If that's it, that's it."

"Lee, I want you to know that we are with you," Smitty said sincerely. "But let this business drop, won't you? Luther won't be around anymore, and we are going to check the Communists too."

"Well—I won't make any more fuss about Luther and I won't file any charges," Lee promised. "But I won't forget it."

"That Luther!" Hannegan commented. "He's some boy, it seems."

"I don't understand him," Smitty confessed.

Instead of taking Lee home, they dropped him at the hospital to have his bandages changed. It was past two o'clock when he arrived home.

Abe Rosenberg was sitting in the living-room, reading the morning paper. Looking up with those bright, wise eyes, he said: "You shouldn't try to fight four men at one time. A Jew would never have done that."

Lee laughed for the first time in two days. "A Jew would have taken the money and said nothing about it, I suppose."

"Why not? It's not like as if they could buy me."

"That's probably what Luther thought."

"That Luther! He shouldn't have done a thing like that. An old Jew like me, I would take their money and deny it to their faces. But that Luther, he's a crook."

For a moment Lee looked at Rosie, grateful to be believed. Then he started toward the bedroom door.

"Your wife told me to tell you that she had to go to work," Rosie said, stopping him.

"Oh!" He looked inquiringly at Rosie. "When did she leave?"

"Around noon."

"And you have been here since?"

"I have no other place to go that's any more important."

"What's important here, Rosie?" Lee asked from curiosity as he crossed to the davenport and sat down.

"You are, Lee," Rosie stated. "You are important. And what's happened to you is important. And how you feel about it is important. So for that reason I want for you to go with me to the headquarters of the Communist Party to see Bart."

"Rosie, what good will that do? Bart knows what Luther did. They all know; they've known all along. I'm the only sucker of the lot."

"Not the only one, Lee—I didn't know."

"No, I'm convinced you didn't, but the others did." For an

instant his thoughts touched Jackie and he added bitterly: "All of them!"

"As a favor then, Lee—as a favor for an old Jew who wishes you well. Perhaps some day I may be able to do as much for you."

"Well—okay," Lee consented, rising to his feet. "You have a way of putting things that makes it hard to refuse."

During the long streetcar ride downtown they avoided discussion of all union matters and Lee related to Rosie his experiences in old man Harding's house. Once Rosie interrupted to say: "Lee, you have a wonderful wife."

"That's what everybody says," Lee replied, and caught Rosie looking at him.

Entering a dilapidated office building on Spring Street, they rode a creaking elevator to the fifth floor and turned down a dimly lit, narrow corridor toward offices in the rear. They found Bart seated behind a battered, flat-topped desk, conversing with a one-armed, mannish-appearing Jewish woman who had been pointed out to Lee several years before as one of the Communist party executives.

"Well, Rosie and Gordon, this is a surprise," Bart said in his high, precise voice. "What brings you comrades here today?"

"Business!" Rosie replied in his most Jewish voice. "Always it is business—party business. And how are you, Maud?"

"Hello, Rosie," she greeted in a rasping voice, looking at the two of them with brazen curiosity.

"You know Lee Gordon, Maud?" Bart asked. "Maud Himmelstein," he said to Lee.

"I've heard of Lee but I've never seen him," she rasped. "Hello, Lee."

Lee nodded briefly to them both. "Hello."

"I have a report of a confidential nature to make," Rosie said. "It is a matter of serious business and I wish to present a formal charge."

Sudden suspicion flared in Maud's hard face but Bart remained impassive.

"Well, what is it, Rosie?" he demanded.

"Yesterday Lee was beaten by four deputy sheriffs—"

"Yes, we know that," Bart interrupted.

"And he was with Luther McGregor—"

"We know that too."

"And he heard Luther confess to accepting a bribe from Foster, the manager of Comstock, for betraying the union—"

Maud's look turned from suspicion to malevolence, but Bart raised his hand, silencing her.

"You don't believe that, do you?" he asked Rosie, but underneath the question lay a subtle threat.

"I believe it," Rosie said defiantly. "And I wish to state formally that I do not think Luther is fit to be a member of the Communist Party and should be expelled."

"What kind of Communist are you?" Maud said, but again Bart silenced her.

"That is a serious charge to make against a fellow member," he said to Rosie in his precise level voice. "You have only Gordon's word—"

"And for me that is enough," Rosie interrupted.

Without looking up, Bart continued in the same tone of voice, "—and you are putting it above the word of one of our most militant members, Luther McGregor, a tried and true Communist. No one can seriously believe that Comrade Luther, with all of his burning revolutionary zeal, would sell out the proletariat."

"Lee heard him confess to it—"

"At the point of a gun, he claims. Yes, we've heard Gordon's story and it's doing incalculable harm to the union's organizing campaign. But the true story, as Luther reports it, is that Gordon's temper led him into the fight. As to his charge against Luther, we can see no purpose in it unless it is Gordon himself who is guilty of selling out the union and by this means is bringing confusion into the ranks."

"That's a goddam lie!" Lee shouted, no longer able to restrain himself. "And you know it's a lie. You knew it was Luther all the time, even night before last when you were plotting to frame Lester McKinley to cover for him. And you were going to front me to do it for you, weren't you?"

"Don't you come down here and try to start trouble," Bart warned, rising to his feet.

"You don't scare me," Lee said in a contained voice, starting around the desk to meet him, but Rosie clutched him from behind.

"Lee!—Bart!" he cried. "Are we Nazis that we can not talk like comrades?"

"And you do not frighten me," Bart said to Lee, ignoring Rosie. "You have caused trouble enough."

Lee ceased to struggle but his voice was harsh with rage. "Not nearly as much trouble as I'm going to cause all you dirty rotten Communists."

"Lee! Lee! Don't judge all Communists by Luther," Rosie entreated. "I'm a Communist. Bart's a Communist—"

"I told you it wouldn't do any good, Rosie," Lee said as he turned toward the door. "And I've had enough."

"Wait, Lee, wait, let's be men about this thing—"

"No, Rosie, I am through," Lee said over his shoulder and went through the doorway and down the corridor. Disdaining the elevator, he went down the stairs. Rosie started to rush after him but was halted by Bart's harsh voice, "Rosie, I am going to hold you responsible for this."

"For what?" Rosie asked, turning back again.

"You have made a serious and unsupported charge against a comrade of high dependability, one of our most dynamic working-class leaders."

"Then I wish to make it formal," Rosie replied, undaunted. "I wish to present my charge before the executive committee and demand Luther McGregor's expulsion from the Communist Party."

"You dirty little Jew!" Maud rasped.

But Bart merely uttered: "As you wish, Rosie, as you wish!"

On the way home Lee stopped at a bar and had a couple of drinks to get the tightness from his mind, but the whisky fed his aversion to them all. But long after his thoughts had contemplated and condemned all others, they remained on Jackie inconclusively. His logic lumped her with the rest, but his heart held her apart. Or was it vanity? he asked himself. Was he trying to acquit her of guilt or himself of folly? He felt more chagrined by the esteem he had given her than by the fool she had played him for, since the latter was the usual risk, but the former a tribute above the price demanded. What worried him now was the fear he had given it to her race instead of to herself. And after he had another couple of drinks it became urgent that he find out.

He called her from the booth beyond the bar. Kathy answered and he asked to speak to Jackie. He could hear her calling: "It's for you, Jackie. I think it's the colored fellow."

And then Jackie's voice: "Lee—darling."

"May I come up?"

"Of course, I want you to."

"Can you get rid of Kathy."

"Oh, sure, she's good as gone for the night."

After hanging up, he stood for a moment pondering over the affection in her voice. Could it be that she was so happy to hear from him? Or had she received further instructions from Bart? It was with an impelling sense of urgency that he hastened to the bus. The late sunset was fading into darkness when he arrived.

Her bright-carmine smile was already fashioned when she opened the door for him, and there was a Hollywood abandon in her sensuous attire, from her loosely flowing hair and tight white sweater, to her pleated blue slacks. But shock showed sharply in her face when she looked into his eyes and saw the grinding hurt. It confused the attitude of three-fourths sex and one-fourth understanding she had so carefully rehearsed, and brought dismay.

"Oh, Lee!" she exclaimed with involuntary irritation. "What all did happen to you?"

"Well, *I* didn't do it," he snapped, coming in and closing the door behind him. "I took a sapping, what more do you want?"

Now in her eyes there was acute vexation. The bargain she had made on the telephone was for a hurt no greater than sex could cure, around which she could attitudinize until the flesh was hot. In showed in the delicate mold of her features, cramping them, and in the inflection of her voice, leveling it.

"Oh, Lee, you're so tight. Can I fix you some dinner?"

"All you can do is kiss me," he said, roughly taking her in his arms. For to him in that moment of seeing her eyes go disappointed came the necessity for taking her as a woman, shorn of race, brutally if required, or ever be denied his physical masculinity.

His lips sought hers, searching, feverishly demanding, until he could feel all of her flowing up to him. And she could not stop herself. She became like a river running up a hill, spreading her ardor on the warm plateau of his passion. He shook her then, to the core of her reserve, struck her loose in a strange, remote, terrifying wilderness of sensuality. Now she became a woman in all of the contradictions it entailed. Her body cried out to him for love while her mind whirled in racial chaos. But once, before the breath had left them both, she closed her mind and was lost in the great black interdiction. And when she opened it, their mouths were apart, gasping, while their bodies clung and she trembled from head to foot.

"I'll make coffee," she said, tearing herself from him. But so weak had she become she could scarcely make the distance to the kitchen.

Lee went over and sat on the divan, stretching out his legs toward the cold fireplace. Well, he had finally scratched her cool, white surface, he thought, and it was disillusioning to discover that she was just another woman underneath. And now he knew without having to go any further that whatever it was he was looking for, she didn't have it either. In a way he wished he hadn't come.

By the time she had made coffee she had regained an outer composure although inside she still tingled with an unceasing warmth. And when she appeared with the two steaming cups, she said: "I love you, darling," soulfully, coming over to sit beside him on the divan.

Although that night before as they had lain naked in each others arms she had said the same: "I love you, I love you, I love you," reaching the culmination of ardor, her saying it now as she stood in the light and fully robed startled him—not the words, for the words were trite. It wasn't the proclamation of an emotion, for this he did not believe, but her naïve assumption that the knowledge that he was loved by a white woman should be of so much help.

He gave an abrupt burst of laughter.

It shocked her but it did not hurt her, for she was white enough to take it. That he was rejecting her race would never occur to her, and that at this time he would repulse her body was no less inconceivable. She attributed it to his distraught condition further aggravated by his desire for her, and was actually sincere in wanting to help him.

"Tell me what happened, Lee."

"Haven't you heard? I thought all the Communists would know by now that I've been maligning their favorite comrade."

"There has been a little talk, of course—" The telephone wires had buzzed and telegrams had gone from coast to coast and every party member knew all there was to know concerning Lee's accusation against Luther and were waiting breathlessly for instructions from the national committee— "But I haven't heard your side."

"Why hear my story, Jackie? You know the truth—you and Bart and all the rest of you," he said. "You knew the other night when we sat here and you fronted me off to—"

"No, Lee darling," she interrupted. "Don't say it, please." She put her palm across his mouth. "You're so confused, Lee darling, don't make it any worse."

He removed her hand and held it in his own as he continued: "You knew then while you were offering me on a platter to your fellow traitors as the Judas to put Lester McKinley on the spot. And you thought that because—"

"You know I wouldn't do that to you, Lee. You know I wouldn't—" The sound of the tears in her voice drawing his gaze to the pure, open innocence of her eyes. "You know I wouldn't, Lee, you know it!"

"Why wouldn't you?" he asked, and from this she should have known that he had changed.

But she said: "Because I love you, Lee," as ardently as ever, and reached up and drew him down to the full benediction of her lips. It was not the same as before but she did not know it, and rising in her glory she stood looking down at him.

"I believe Luther accepted the money from Foster, darling," she conceded. "But you are giving the incident a bourgeois interpretation, and it was conceived with Marxist intent. You see—" And now as to a little child. "—we don't have the same set of ethics as the bourgeoisie, or rather, we do most of our fighting with the ethics of the upper class, and in a bourgeois society these are denied the working class. Honesty to the employer, for instance, is in no way like the kind of honesty he demands from his employee. You know that, darling—"

"Jackie baby, you have a wonderful body but your ankles are too thick," he taunted.

She swirled with a motion of frustration, blushing furiously. "You go to hell!"

It was then that Mollie knocked. Taking one look at Jackie's blushing fury and Lee's hurt cynicism, she began laughing. "The course of true love is overrun with ashes, as the poets say."

"Do you have your car?" Jackie asked tensely.

"Yes, dear," Mollie said. "I shall take other means to prove my militant communistic zeal than walking myself to death."

"Then you can take Lee with you."

"No, dear. You would only lather yourself to frustration and wouldn't sleep a wink. And you would curse me all night for it."

"You are a dirty bitch!" Jackie said with insulting deliberation.

"Of course," Mollie said, laughingly. "But I'm not drowning myself with warm douches every night."

Jackie gave her one last furious look and went into the kitchen. Crossing the room to sit beside Lee on the divan, Mollie laid her hand caressingly on his knee.

"What's all this between you and my ardent Caliban?"

"He's just a rat, that's all."

"Of course he's a rat," she said. "And aren't we all?"

"At least I'm not the kind of a rat who sells his buddies out."

"Now, Lee darling, that doesn't sound like you. Leave the nobility to the Hearst editorial writers."

"I don't want to talk about it. I'm tired of talking about it. If Luther sent you, go back and tell him I say he's a rat and always will be a rat."

"No one in the Communist Party believes Luther took a bribe from Foster," Mollie said.

"What do I care? I know he took it. He wouldn't have stood up there and lied like that."

"You don't know Luther, darling. He'd do anything to save his skin."

"I was there and I know he wasn't lying."

"Don't be silly, darling." She caressed his leg. "If Luther needed five hundred dollars he wouldn't have to sell out the union; he could always get that much from me."

"He's probably got that much from you anyway—"

"Of course."

"But I still say he sold out the union."

"Oh, don't be so damn honest," she snapped. "You know Luther took the money and I know he took it. He's just a black incorrigible rascal, and what're you going to do about it? The party is going to back him and you can't beat the party—why don't you make him divide it with you," she suggested.

"Why don't you?"

"I have tried, darling; don't think I haven't."

From the kitchen doorway, Jackie said: "You are the most unscrupulous, disloyal, despicable bitch I've ever seen! I suppose it makes no difference to you what sort of person you sleep with."

"If he isn't tired. I'm past the stage of warm baths and sleepless nights for virtue's sake. Why don't you get married, dear? Your nerves are shot."

"An Arizona wedding like yours?"

Mollie began laughing again. "What's a wedding to a Communist? All ceremony is performed in bed."

"I'm sure Lee doesn't appreciate your vulgarity."

"Oh, Lee is nursing his honor now." She squeezed Lee's thigh. "But I bet he isn't tired."

"I appreciate neither your corny wit nor Luther's dirty advice," Lee said.

Mollie arose and prepared to leave. "The Communists liked you, Lee. They thought you and Luther made a good pair." Laughingly she added: "Two big strong dark men of purpose." At the door she turned and smiled toward Jackie. "You'll sleep well tonight, I'm sure. Then you'll see what I mean."

For a perceptible time after Mollie had closed the door behind her, Jackie was too embarrassed to look at Lee. But Lee was lost in brooding again. Even an old lecherous bitch like Mollie had to feel sorry for him, he thought. He was tired of it. Tired of everyone taking him for a sniveling brat—a lying, vicious weakling. Even his own wife—

When Jackie finally looked at him, she saw the change and crossed quickly to his side. "What's the matter, darling?"

Slowly he rose to his feet. "Jackie," he said, looking down at her, "once you mentioned that we were no good for each other." Now there was again that slow falter in his speech.

"But we hardly knew each other then, darling," she said softly. "You know I don't think so now."

"Well—we're not," Lee Gordon said, and turning away without seeing the pity that came instantly into her face, went unhesitatingly across the room, out of the apartment, down the stairs, into the night. At least he felt a satisfaction.

Chapter 22

Bart sat behind his battered desk, his broad, muscular shoulders drooping, and his tired, black face set in solid melancholy. It was late. Save for himself, the offices of the Communist Party were deserted. There was no longer any need for him to pretend, and his emotions had seeped through his mask.

Deep, disturbing thoughts were settling slowly over the hard crust of communistic rationale, and doubts flared momentarily in the dark blind line of obedience. Before him lay the directive from the national committee ordering the state committee to kill the rumors of betrayal at Comstock and issue a memorandum concerning Luther's innocence. He knew fully the implication of this order and what it entailed. In the Soviet Union someone would be taken out and shot. Here they executed in another way.

Bart had been thinking of this business since the incident occurred. And he had known the irrefutable answer before the directive had been received. There was only this answer to know, for to the politically initiate the logic of such a position was elementary Marxism.

And Bart was a good Marxist. He fully understood that in a revolutionary movement the objective must be attained by any means. As set forth in the *Communist Manifesto*, "In this struggle —a veritable civil war—are united and developed all the elements necessary for a coming battle."

Therefore guilt and innocence were inapplicable in the moral sense. Revolutionary tactics were not to be interpreted in the light of bourgeois concepts, or defined by bourgeois terminology, but considered only in terms of preparation for the coming battle.

Did not Marx write: "Law, morality, religion, are . . . so many bourgeois prejudices, behind which lurk in ambush just as many bourgeois interests."

The guilty were those who hindered, obstructed, opposed, or were indifferent to the rise of the proletariat. In revolutionary terminology there was no such thing as neutrality. Those who were not for, were against. And those were also guilty who had to be spent, for in this continuous warfare of the proletariat no individual was beyond sacrifice for the ultimate aim. Had not the Soviets often found it necessary to execute the most loyal Communist to achieve an objective? he reminded himself. And this was as it should be, for materialism was a fact, and loyalty simply a virtue. Materialism embodied loyalty but did not rely on it, for revolution was the order of the day and would ripen like the grain in the field, because this was the rise of the proletariat and could not be stopped.

And yet there were times such as this when he was more Negro than Communist, and his American instincts were diametrically opposed to the ruthless nonconformity of revolutionary maneuvering; when the long list of his acts as an executive of the Communist Party judged themselves in the light of Christian reason; when the voice of his Baptist mother could be heard in the night of his soul; when virtues such as honesty, loyalty, courage, and kindness, charity, and fair play had meaning and value; when his mind rebelled and could not follow the merciless contradictions of reality; when he no longer wanted to face the fact of his own inferiority in a bourgeois world, but just wanted to be a nigger and forget about it.

At these times he did not admire himself. He felt no pride in the things he had done. For he had done so many things against his innate convictions. His Protestant, puritanical, Negro inheritance rose to torture him. And that severe division deep in his mind between right and wrong, vice and virtue, complicated his adherence to revolutionary tactics and made it extremely difficult for him to rationalize what seemed at first to be political contradictions.

He had found it hard to follow the Soviets in their pact with Nazi Germany, and harder still to follow the American Communist Party line through its rejection of minority-group problems and into its coalition with capitalism.

Vivid in his memory, even then, was that classic thesis in the May 21, 1940, issue of *New Masses*: "Mr. President: This Is Not Our War—An Open Letter." And those burning lines: "*New Masses* calls for the organization of this peace party. The trade unions must be the backbone of this movement and John L. Lewis has pointed the way by suggesting a conference of representatives of labor, the farmers, the youth movement, the Negro people, and the old-age pension groups. . . ." For he had believed it. "To the mothers and sons of America living under the shadow of a terrible fear we bring the vision of a different life . . ." had been written on his mind.

As a consequence, it was increasingly necessary for him to return to the Marxist conception of materialistic reality to revive his faith. Just as he had often faced the necessity of convincing himself that there was no such thing as integrity, he now had to convince himself of the reality of this move. It was not that the Communist Party lacked integrity; it simply did not recognize it. For integrity was the virtue imposed by the *bourgeoisie* upon the proletariat to stabilize oppression. And materialism not only embodied flexibility, but in itself was change, breaking the bonds of all oppression. The field where once gay picnickers lounged in laughing leisure would tomorrow be planted to wheat. And where once there were rock mountains, now there were sand pits. The world changed, moved, progressed. "Motion is the mode of existence of matter," he quoted in his thoughts. Nothing could stop this. The minds of people, which were but the reflections of matter, reflected this change and were changed by their own reflections. As distances became smaller, ideas became larger. Where once there was religion, now there was reality. Mysticism became lost in materialism. Emotions retained no permanent formation but were shaped by historical necessity.

By such a process he had arrived at the conclusion that Luther was indispensable long before the national committee had. It was not that Luther was a Marxist—for he was not—or even a believer in communism. What made him so valuable to a revolutionary movement was his simple antagonism toward authority and his deep vicious hatred of white people. He would be a rebel in a socialist state also, Bart knew. Here in America, during what Lenin once described as a "historical development of such magnitude twenty years are no more than a day," Luther would often embarrass the party, Bart firmly believed. But, "later," as Marx wrote to Engels, "there may come days in which twenty years are concentrated." And it was for such days that such men as Luther would be needed.

Yet even as he arrived at this conclusion, Bart knew that it had not been his power of reasoning—which was but memory of his Marxist studies—but his ability to dissemble that had formulated it for him. Just as it had taken him far up the ladder in the Communist Party. This was his racial compensation in a nation where he had known but an inferior role.

For within Bart, as within many Negroes, there had developed a defense mechanism similar to a sixth sense whereby he could reach agreement with his masters with greater accuracy and rapidity than by logic—for delay or disagreement would bring the blow, the kick, the curse. As a dog trotting along in front of his master will instinctively choose the right path at the fork, such Negroes divine the right way to turn in an argument. Thus Bart had risen in the party more rapidly than any intellectual, for while the intellectual was plodding the devious paths of logic, Bart had made the short cut of instinct, leaping to the decision before it had been reached by others, giving color to the legend of his brilliance as a leader.

But self-revulsion was often the price he paid—such as now. For he knew what he had to do. And the following day he did it. Calling a special meeting of the state committee, he read the directive and pointed out that a sacrifice must be made.

Then he offered the name of Jackie Forks. Though she had served as a spy for both the party and the union, her service was not indispensable. The party had another spy in the offices of Comstock, Vera Slagel, confidential secretary to the company's president and assistant to the secretary of the board of directors. Unknown to the union organizers, she kept in direct contact only with party executives. Therefore the loss of Jackie would be no great hindrance to the movement.

On the other hand, the shop workers would be more prone to believe an office worker was the traitor than another shop worker whom they might know. Many shop workers had an innate antagonism toward office workers that would make the discovery of Jackie as a traitor a matter of jubilation. Also of importance was the fact that Jackie had no influential friends within the party, and she did not know any party secrets with which she could oppose her sacrifice.

But most important of all, Bart pointed out, was her friendship with Lee Gordon. The very fact of her exposure as the traitor would destroy any lingering credence given to Lee's accusation of Luther and instead cast suspicion on Lee.

While many distrusted Luther and some even suspected that he had not only sold out the union but the party also, not once but many times, still, he was a Negro. He symbolized the Negro problem. To accuse him of betrayal or deceit would be to accuse the the Negro race. To publicly doubt his loyalty would be to doubt the finest quality of the Negro people—their undying loyalty. Luther was known within the party and liked by all the Negro members. To expel him at this time might sever a vital link with the race. The effect it might have on the Negro workers at Comstock could be disastrous. For it might band them together not only against the Communist Party and the union, but against all the white workers. They would not believe him disloyal since most Negroes believed in the myth of their own loyalty as much as did others. They would have interpreted his expulsion as another manifestation of Communist racial prejudice. Therefore Luther was untouchable.

"But above all things," Bart concluded, "we must consider the effect of any act in our relation with the union. Our objective now is control of the union, and all things must work toward this end. 'Of all the classes that stand face to face with the bourgeoisie today, the proletariat alone is a really revolutionary class,' Marx wrote in his *Communist Manifesto*, and we must keep it so."

The committee supported this tactic unanimously, for the decision had been Bart's from the first and theirs had been only the duty of substantiation. One of the women workers on the assembly line, Jane Weaver, was selected to make the denunciation.

At the union meeting the following night Jane gained the floor and loosed a tirade against Jackie, reading a long list of charges. She accused Jackie of accepting a bribe of five hundred dollars from Foster for reporting union secrets; of having union members transferred to unpleasant jobs; of discriminatory practices against Negro workers. At the end she recited with parrotlike rapidity, the inflection of her voice having no relation to the meaning of the words, a conclusion written by a party strategist: "Now that the traitor is discovered and pointed out, we must be vigilant to preserve and strengthen the unity of our union, and equip ourselves to more effectively perform our vanguard role in the great economic and political struggles which lie ahead. In this way we will strengthen our union ideologically, politically, and organizationally."

The Communists in the audience identified themselves by their applause. But the others maintained a shocked, stony silence.

Finally Smitty rose to his feet, his face bearing a stricken look. "To my knowledge, sister Forks has been a sincere, loyal, conscientious worker for the union," he said in a hollow voice, "and we can not allow her to be maligned by any such unsubstantiated charges as these."

"I have proof!" Jane cried, jumping to her feet again. "I have a statement here from her own roommate who saw her with the money—five one-hundred-dollar bills. She told Kathy—that's her roommate—that Foster had given her the money to keep him informed about what we do in the union, and offered Kathy fifty dollars to keep her mouth shut. And I got statements from other workers in the office who have heard her talking to Foster about union members and suggesting how he could segregate Negro workers in the plant."

"Let me see them," Smitty demanded.

"I'll read them aloud," Jane retorted.

"That's not necessary."

"Everybody's got a right to hear," she argued. "This is a matter for the rank and file."

"Read them! Read them!" the Communists shouted.

Smitty turned to Joe Ptak. "Do something to stop her, Joe, you're the organizer."

"Let her read 'em!" Joe said, the rocklike set of his expression unchanged.

Sitting, listening to the damning affidavits of Jackie's guilt, knowing they were false, seeing the fine hand of the party behind them as clearly as if the words had issued from Bart's own lips, Lee went sick at heart. In his lifetime he had seen many persons, mostly Negroes, victimized with cold-blooded premeditation. He, Lee Gordon, had been so victimized, not once or twice, but many times. Always it roused in him a deep sense of protest. But this was the first time he had seen a person lynched, and his reason found it intolerable and his heart, unbearable. Not because she was Jackie Forks—a white girl whom he had once held in his arms —for he had sworn to himself with a sense of satisfaction that he was through with Jackie Forks, but because she was another human being.

When Jane sat down again, Smitty slowly said: "I do not believe it."

And in the following silence, Lee Gordon rose—knowing that he was being a fool, knowing that the sensible thing for him to do was keep quiet, and knowing also that his first word would forge the link of suspicion against himself. But he could not help it. For deep inside of him was a sense of justice that could not accept the rotten deal.

"Union members! Men and women!" he cried for their attention. "This whole thing is a frame-up on the girl by the Communist Party. I know the person who is guilty of betraying the union. That person is Luther McGregor—"

"No, Lee!" Smitty shouted. "Let's not have any more of these insane accusations!"

Lee turned on him and cried: "Smitty, you know that this is a dirty frame-up and I'm going—"

He was shouted down by the Communists in the audience.

"Maybe he's in on it too!" one cried.

"She's his little girl friend!"

"He's been accusing Brother McGregor for too long now. I move that we give Brother McGregor a vote of confidence. Brother McGregor's a true, tried worker for the masses."

"McGregor isn't a member of the union," Smitty pointed out.

"He's a better organizer than the one you got."

"I move we expel Sister Forks from the union and fire Gordon at the same time!" a Mexican woman screamed. "He's just as guilty as she is."

"Gordon's not mixed up in this business at all!" Smitty shouted. "Keep his name out of it."

"Who says he isn't mixed up in it?" the same woman contended. "How do we know?"

"We don't know any of it," Smitty said, trying to reason with them. "This business has no place on the floor. It should be taken up in executive meeting."

"No! No! No!" the agitators shouted in unison. And then a voice above the others shrieked: "I move we vote to expel Jackie Forks from the union right here and now."

"Someone make a motion for adjournment," Smitty pleaded.

"No, let 'em vote," Joe said.

"Joe, you don't believe that the girl is guilty of all this, do you?" Smitty asked him.

"Let 'em vote! Let 'em vote!"

"All in favor of expelling sister Forks from the union let it be known—" Marvin Todd chanted like an auctioneer.

And when she had been expelled from the union by a show of hands, Lee Gordon turned to Smitty and said: "Here's where I'm quitting."

"Lee, for heaven's sake," he cried, "we need you more than ever now."

"But you could have stopped that," Lee accused.

"Lee, before God, I—" He broke off to turn on Joe. "Joe, what the hell has come over you?"

"They wanted a victim," Joe said in the same hard, uncompromising voice. "Now they got a victim. Now maybe, goddamnit, we can get some organizing done!"

"Well—yes," Lee Gordon said and walked away.

But at the door leading out into the street, he turned and went back. Because he could not let it go like that—he just couldn't do it, that was all. Smitty and Joe were still in the assembly room, arguing heatedly.

"Joe, I'm going to see Foster," Lee announced, breaking in on them. "I'm going to get a sworn affidavit from him stating that he did not give Jackie the money but gave it to Luther instead."

"Lee, you say Luther's guilty?" Joe asked.

"I know he's guilty."

"So what? Lee, brother, get some goddamn sense. I know the black bastard's guilty too—"

"I wouldn't go that far," Smitty interposed.

"I would!" Joe declared. "But that hasn't got anything to do with this."

"Why the hell hasn't it!" Lee argued. "They're sacrificing Jackie just to clear him."

"That's them! What do I care what the Communists do—so long as it doesn't hurt the union?"

"You don't think this will hurt the union?"

"Lee, listen. They framed one goddamn Communist to clear another one. All right. Who the hell cares? It'll stop those stories about some bastard selling out and we'll be able to get something done."

"But, Joe, the girl is innocent!"

"Well, she's innocent then. She's a Communist. She oughta known what she was getting into before she joined their stinking party."

"We haven't got anything to do with that," Smitty argued.

"It was the Communists who framed her—her own goddamn bedmates! Let her fight it out with them."

"But it's the union that expelled her," Lee said.

"Look, Lee! The Communists have done us a favor. If they want to cut the throats of their own members, let 'em! But let us take the favor and say no more about it. I want to get this plant organized and get the hell out of this screwy town."

"I agree with Lee," Smitty said.

"What's done is done!" Joe said. "And I'm through talking about it. I'll see you out at the plant tomorrow, Lee."

But Lee Gordon could not let it go like that.

He went down to the telephone booth and called the Communist Party headquarters. Receiving no reply, he thought of Rosie but decided against calling him because Rosie had already done all he could. Then he looked up the telephone number of

Bart's home, but before calling he realized that Bart might not talk to him over the phone. He decided to ride out to Bart's home and call on him in person.

An hour later he arrived at the little white stucco house in Watts where Bart lived, and saw a gathering of people through the living-room window. Bart answered his ring and stepped out on the porch and closed the door behind him.

"Well, Gordon, what brings you here at this late hour?"

"You know why I'm here, Bart," Lee said.

"I can't imagine," Bart said blandly.

"You folks are framing Jackie Forks and I just wanted you to know that I'm going to fight it. I'm going to Foster first."

"I had nothing to do with the expulsion of the Forks woman from the union," Bart said in his high, precise voice. "In fact, I have just learned of it. But I understand that proof of her guilt was presented before the membership and her expulsion was voted by the rank and file."

"Listen, Bart, I'm not as big a fool as you seem to think. I have been around you Communists for some time and I know what you have done. Just the other night you were trying to get me to denounce Lester McKinley when he quit and you had to change your plans. And now you get some woman to do the same to the Forks girl. If I didn't know she was innocent—"

"How do you know?" Bart interrupted. "As I understand it, overwhelming proof of her guilt was presented—"

"Lies made up by you dirty Communists—"

"You are at my house, Gordon—"

"To hell with your house!" Lee cried as he turned away. "But I'm warning you—remember that! I'm warning you!"

Now as he walked rapidly down the dimly lit street of Watts he felt that sick sense of frustration again. Wasn't there anything he could do—nothing? Did he have to see a person lynched and know that she was lynched and be able to do nothing about it? Now the old sense of his inadequacy began riding him again.

While he was returning on the interurban train, the impulse came to him to go in search of Luther and force him to write a confession at the point of a gun. But he did not have a gun. And at that hour of night he did not know where he could find one. So engrossed was he in thoughts of striking back, that the slightly humorous idiocy of this idea did not dawn on him. And as there was nothing more he could do that night, he went home.

Ruth was waiting in the darkened window when he turned into the walk, but hastened into the bedroom to pretend to be asleep. And again that light-headed feeling of relief flooded her with an almost sexual warmth. She suffered a faint aversion to her own emotion and for a moment disliked herself intensely for experiencing it. But she had no control over herself.

Since the assault on him by the deputies, she had suffered this stiflingly intense trepidation every moment he was out of her sight. She could not concentrate on her work; she was nervous and irritable, uncertain and absent-minded. All that day she had been contemplating resigning, thinking that if she quit now and left it up to Lee to sink or swim, it would resolve their unhappiness one way or another. Then she could be done with this terrible uncertainty. And if he failed and she had to return to work, it would not be difficult for her to find a job, for she would be alone. But at the last moment it was the fear that he would not be able to make it without her that kept her on the job—that any day he might quit his job and they would be dependent on hers again.

And now as he began cursing out the Communists as soon as he turned on the lights, she thought with a sudden aching apprehension that he had already done so, and felt betrayed by her love for him.

"What gets me down," he went on, "is they're not bound by even ordinary decency. There's no way to appeal to them."

"Now what did they do, Lee?" she asked, coming into the living-room to join him.

As he related how they had framed Jackie Forks to cover Luther's guilt, a slow resentment grew within her. At first it was simply because he had taken the part of another working woman when he had never taken hers. If Jackie had been a man, she would have admired Lee for it.

"It serves her right for spying on the company," she said acidly.

"But she was spying for us—for the union too," he said.

"She was spying just the same. And you've said yourself that you hate a sneak."

"But this was different—"

"What's the difference between a Communist spy and a company spy? They're both spies—low, degraded people."

"But the dirty part of it was for the Communists to use her, then frame her like this to cover for Luther."

"Maybe she did what they said she did. They would be in a position to know."

"But I know that she didn't!"

"How do you know?" she asked sharply, as the voice of intuition began whispering to her heart. "Were you there?"

"Oh, Ruth, don't always argue just for the sake of being opposite. Everybody knows it was just a trumped-up charge to cover Luther."

"But you just said they had proof." And now she argued only to quiet the silent whisper.

"You know how the Communists can manufacture proof; you've been around them enough to have learned that, I know."

"If everyone knew it wasn't true, I don't see how they could put her out of the union."

"You know how the Communists do things, Ruth. Hell! They got the floor and railroaded it before anybody had a chance to think."

"Weren't the organizers there—Joe and Smitty?"

"Smitty did try to stop it but Joe wouldn't do anything at all. If anything, he encouraged it."

"Well, if they don't want to do anything, why should you? It's more their union than yours."

"I just don't want to see anybody get framed like that. And I won't!"

Now her resentment grew because she doubted that he would do as much for her.

"I think you are being very foolish," she said. "Why should you stick your neck out because of what happens to a Communist spy? Anyone who would spy for the Communists would sell them out just as quickly."

"Jackie wouldn't!" he cried. "I know she wouldn't!"

It was no longer the voice of intuition, for in the sudden revelation of emotion she knew that he had gone to bed with this woman. At first she experienced that sick, lost, completely frightening sense of shock. For now all the strangeness she had noticed

in their sex life for weeks past exposed itself as an emotional in-
volvement. And she would rather he had murdered Luther, or had
been murdered by him, than for this to happen.

"Are you having an affair with the girl?" she asked, masking her
emotional chaos with a deadly casualness.

"Ruth, don't always be so crazy," he denied. "Do I have to be
having an affair with the girl because I object to her being
framed?"

"Then why should you be so upset about what happens to some
white tramp when worse things happen to Negro women every
day?"

"Aw, Ruth, I can't even talk to you anymore without having
you accuse me of the worse things you can think of."

"I'm not accusing you. I asked you."

"You accuse when you ask."

"You haven't answered."

"Are you having an affair with the manager of the plant?" he
countered.

"No."

"Well, no, then."

"Why couldn't you say that in the first place?"

"Because it's such a foolish question."

"If you could hear the tone of your voice you wouldn't think it
was so foolish."

"What has the tone of my voice got to do with it?"

"If you could hear yourself you would know."

"Aw, go to hell! Here I come in here trying to talk over a
simple problem on my job and you've turned it into an emotional
storm."

Now the instinctive protective coloration, as maddening in a
woman as her intuition, came to her aid, and she submerged her
first blind wave of terror by reviling him.

"You are the lowest person I know," she said carefully with intent to hurt. "You are willing to destroy your whole future for
some dirty white whore, and for your own wife who slaves for you,
you haven't a decent word."

"Slaves for me!" he shouted as the anger grew within him.
"What the hell you mean, slave for me! You're working for your
own damn self and always have!"

"If it was for myself, I would not even have my job. I would have a husband who supported me—"

"Well, get one then! Go get him now!"

"You probably wish I would go out and get some man to add to your support," she said, employing her sex to the full to hurt him where his inherent chivalry would not allow him to strike back.

"That is a rotten lie!"

"Why do you object to that? I couldn't be any more of a prostitute for you if I did go out and sell my body." And now it was his honor she sought to despoil: "You couldn't be any more of a pimp."

"Aw, Ruth, damn! Other women work too—"

"And you admire them for it!"

"I didn't say I admired them. I just said they worked too. You aren't the only woman who ever worked."

"Lee, do you have some uncontrollable desire for white women?" she asked conversationally. "If you do, just tell me and I will go out of your life and let you have all the cheap white women you want."

"Aw, Ruth—"

"If you want a white woman, go get one. Try to get one to support you like I have done—"

"I haven't asked you to support me. If you haven't wanted to work why didn't you quit?"

"I would have if you could have kept any of your jobs. If you thought about me as much as you do about every little white tramp who comes along, you'd have accepted the job that Mr. Foster offered you—"

"All I said was that other women work," he said, cutting her off. "And that started all this argument? Does that make their men pimps too?"

"If you were just one half as much a man as the lowest white bum—" and now it was his manhood she defiled—"you wouldn't put a white prostitute above your wife. That's why white men rule the world today."

His tight, thin face resigned itself to torment as he turned his eyes away. And now he groped for the words to tell her how it should be, or how it might have been, if she had ever considered her job in the light of a partnership instead of an individual enterprise. But he did not have any words that he had not already used in vain. So he said: "I'm going to bed."

She arose and began taking bedding from the linen closet. "I'm going to sleep on the davenport," she said.

He began undressing, cursing to himself.

At first she simply hated him, but finally the awful terror came again. For now that it had finally happened, she did not see how she could live without him. But God knows she could live with no man unfaithful to her for some white bitch.

Chapter 23

WHEN Jackie Forks was informed of her expulsion from the union by an anonymous telephone call shortly after the meeting had adjourned, her first reaction was utter shock. She had known that a victim would be offered, both to acquit Luther and quell the ugly talk of treachery, and from the first she had supported the necessity of such a move. Though her heart had been opposed to Bart's suggestion that she persuade Lee Gordon to denounce Lester McKinley as the traitor, as a good party member she had readily consented.

But that they would dare offer her as the victim had been unthinkable. For not only had she thought herself inviolable within the party, but sacrosanct within the world. Unlike the others who sought to escape racial and religious persecutions, she did not have to be a Communist. She was the kind of American whom even Hitler would have welcomed—fair, Aryan, and a pure-blooded gentile—and certainly she had nothing to fear in America. Even people as fanatical as the Communists could not believe they had anything special to offer her.

But it was not so much gratitude she had demanded from them as recognition, and her white gentile soul was utterly outraged that they would sacrifice her to save a nigger's reputation. She was outraged above her loudest claim to Marxist ideology, beyond her greatest sympathy for the oppressed, stronger than her most honest hatred of the oppressors.

In white anger she called Communist Party headquarters, and receiving no reply, called Bart at his home. Receiving her call shortly before Lee's arrival, Bart disclaimed all knowledge of her expulsion and refused to discuss it with her.

"You will regret this!" she said threateningly as she hung up.

Then she begin calling acquaintances high up in the Communist hierarchy. But they were either out, engaged, or knew nothing. Even the subtle warning contained in this did not lessen her blazing urge for vengeance. Nor did the later warning contained in her roommate's failure to call, which broke a rigid rule between them.

Alone with her unendurable outrage, she was mocked by the picture of Bart and Luther framing her just because she was white and they hated white people. She even entertained the idea of Lee's being involved with them. Was that why he had called, breaking off with her? The nigger! The goddamned nigger!

And as the seconds flowed like sand, her hatred for Negroes climbed like a blazing pyre. At first she hated three individual Negroes because of race, and then she hated the Negro race because of three individual Negroes. She hated their color, their souls, their minds, their character, their lips, teeth, eyes, and hair— hated them with an attention to physiological detail she could not have ascertained had she made love to all the adult Negroes, male and female, in the world. In this pathological hatred, the Negro became the bugaboo of Southern legend, the beast of Klanist propaganda, a distorted, monstrous, despicable object of her rage. And as her hatred rose, burning up all that was good within her, she became just so much rife white flesh, of common value on the prostitution market, good only in America for getting some Negro lynched.

And now when she recalled that she had gone to bed with one, and let him hold her white naked body in his black naked arms, her tautly strung, screaming nerves presented a threat to sanity. She felt as if she had consummated some self-pollution and imagined her body filthy, odorous, and contaminated by his touch. She arose and showered, scrubbed her teeth, brushed her hair, manicured and polished her nails, lotioned her body, and cold-creamed her face, as if to destroy by physical cleanliness not only the signs, but the fact of her debasement.

Now she was able to analyze with a degree of sanity what had happened to her. She had simply been sacrificed to the ultimate aim, which was pure and simple Marxism as she had learned it from the first. As a consequence she had no right to object since the logic of any other position would have been untenable. But even now her Marxist schooling could not lessen her sense of racial violation. She would not have minded being sacrificed to any other cause than the preservation of a Negro's reputation, she attempted to convince herself. But this she could not accept.

She went into the kitchen and made coffee; and drinking it, began to plan. Until then she had not realized how involved her life had become with the activity of the Communist Party. She had lived with Communists, talked their language, and thought their thoughts for almost three years. She had grown to be dependent on the party for all the decisions of her private life. And she had enjoyed it; she could not imagine life away from it. But now she found it difficult to think alone.

She did not want to be expelled from the party also, which she knew was inexorable unless she acted swiftly. Thinking it possible to force a retraction of the charges by mobilizing the support of the white gentile membership in a purely racial stand, she remained home the next day, telephoning white persons whom she thought important in party circles—motion-picture executives, producers, directors, city officeholders, business men, local politicians. And afterward she visited a number of them. But none would discuss the incident with her. Most denied membership in the party. Others denied knowledge of all party tactics. But many of them were willing to have an affair with her.

Before that day was over she had learned that though there were definite racial caste lines within the Communist Party, above them was Communism, the essence of which was fear. It was not so much a lack of sympathy which she met in the blank, rejecting stares at the first mention of the party, as fear of reprisal should they take her part. They had too much to lose to become objects of Communist attack, the first salvo of which they feared might be the sly accusation that they also were Communists.

Discovering on her return home that her roommate had moved, Jackie knew that all hope of retraction was gone. Now the only course open to her, she thought, would be to make a full confession involving Foster and perhaps Lee and throw herself on the mercy of the committee. But she would have to enlist some executive of the party to introduce the idea and convince the committee of its political expediency or it would do no good.

For this she chose a Jew, not so much with a cold-blooded deliberation, as with an inherent conviction that a Jew would always take the part of a gentile against Negroes. So she called Maud Himmelstein at party headquarters, catching her as she was about to leave.

"Maud, this is Jackie Forks."

"Yes, Jackie," Maud replied with a sympathetic cordiality in her usually rasping voice.

"Maud, I'd like an interview with you. It's terribly important."

"Is it about your—" the stub of her missing arm jerked spasmodically as she sought for the unobjectionable word—"trouble?"

"Yes, it is," Jackie admitted, not defensively, but inclusively, since in her thoughts all Jews, like Negroes, were guilty from the start.

But Maud experienced a sense of gratification over Jackie's coming to her, for she had bitterly opposed Jackie's sacrifice for Luther and wanted her to know at least one white woman was on her side. So she asked Jackie to call at her home that evening, giving the address in Boyle's Heights.

It was Maud's intention to befriend Jackie, perhaps offer to carry her case to the national committee over Bart's head. Secretly she hated Bart, as she did all Negroes, and it galled her to be in a position subordinate to his.

But Jackie's first words cut her to the quick, alienated her sympathy, and dispelled her good will. And this was the one thing Jackie intended to avoid, but the words poured from her involuntarily: "From the point of pure political expediency, Maud, you should not sacrifice a white woman to save a Negro. I'm not just thinking of myself; I'm thinking of the future of the party. You can't just have a party of Negroes and Jews." This was the way she thought.

Maud shriveled up inside, struck by a terrible hurt, for all the things she envied and desired and wanted to be were embodied in this young, personable, gentile girl whom she wanted to befriend, but who scorned her with these words. However she gave no sign of it as she asked with composure: "But do you think we could have a Communist Party without the Negroes and the Jews?"

"Oh, I didn't mean Jews—" Jackie hastened to amend, realizing too late her mistake.

But already she had bared her real emotions, and Maud accepted their reality with a blunt stoicism, forcing herself to say: "If you mean Negroes, you mean Jews also—and that includes myself," which was not an easy thing for her to do.

For out of all the many hatreds growing from her infirm body and oppressed spirit, the hatred of her own Jewishness was the most intense. She hated all Jews and all things Jewish with an uncontrollable passion, as an escape from which she had become a Communist. And yet she was as Jewish in appearance as the Jewish stereotype.

"But, Maud, you know yourself," Jackie argued earnestly, "with Bart at the head of the party it's getting so a white person is subject to any persecution."

"Now what is it you're trying to say, Jackie?" Maud asked in her rasping voice. "Are you accusing Bart on racial grounds of some attack on you?"

"You know it was Bart who had me framed—" Jackie began, but Maud cut her off.

"A white woman made the charges."

"At Bart's direction—and she was Jewish, anyway."

And even though Maud had braced herself against such racial slander, she winced again, and the stub of her missing arm jerked spasmodically. "I see you are determined to draw the difference," she said.

"You're making me do it," Jackie said. "You're trying to imply that white people are responsible for this when I know no white person would do such a thing to me."

"Is that why you committed this treachery?" for the first time accusing her of it. "Did you think you would not be disciplined because, as you say, you are 'white'?"

"You know I didn't do it, Maud, you know it!" Jackie sobbed.

"You know I'm being persecuted by all these vicious Negroes—"

"Lee Gordon came to your defense," Maud told her levelly. "He stood on the floor at the union meeting and claimed that you were innocent—and he's a Negro."

"I don't believe it!" Jackie gasped, shocked out of her urge to cry. For if this was right, then everything was wrong. "I don't believe it!" she repeated harshly, as outraged at being defended by a Negro as persecuted by one. "You're just trying to confuse me, to hurt me more—"

"By informing you that your lover came to your defense?"

"He is not my lover," Jackie said, blushing furiously. "I would not have a Negro as a lover."

"I was under the impression you had volunteered to recruit him—"

"By other means. I helped him with his problems and he always did just what I asked—"

"Because you are 'white'?"

"Yes, if you must know."

"Are you Protestant also?"

"No, I am Communist."

"Were your parents Protestant?"

"Yes, but what has that to do with it?"

"It is stylish now for a certain type of woman to say to Negro men with whom they are having an affair, that they are American, white, gentile, and Protestant, which makes them the greatest women in all the world. Is that what you said to Gordon to make him do what you always asked?"

"I hate you!" Jackie cried, bursting into tears as she rose suddenly to her feet. Turning, she fled rapidly from the house.

But Maud did not even move to close the door. Her hard, mannish features were set in hurting lines, with her eyes closed tightly against the tears. For a one-armed, dirty Jew, as she knew this girl thought of her, she had scored a singular victory. Yet, of the two of them, she was more deeply hurt.

The day following, the party paper reported the story of the union meeting with a front-page spread containing two column pictures of Jackie Forks, "The Traitor," and Jane Weaver, "The Exposer." Not only had Jackie Forks accepted the bribe to sell out the union and the Communist Party, the story explained, but in so doing had endeavored to cast suspicion upon a loyal, militant, entirely dependable party member whose name would not be mentioned out of respect to his feelings. As a consequence she had been expelled from the Communist Party ". . . for gross violation of party discipline and active opposition to the political line and leadership of our party, and for betraying the principles of Marxism-Leninism, accepting money for such betrayal, and deserting to the side of the class enemy, American monopoly capitalism."

Thousands of copies of the paper were printed and distributed by a score of party workers at the gates of the plant. The story dropped a bombshell among the workers, many of whom had no interest in the union heretofore. On the whole, the members of the union were embarrassed by the story, and many did not believe it. Lee Gordon was blindly furious, but Joe Ptak went about his business as usual, his hard, uncompromising demeanor giving no hint of his inner thoughts.

But the Communists were jubilant. For they considered their victory threefold. Not only had they cleared Luther of Lee's charges and blown into the open the "truth of the treachery," but they felt assured that they had accomplished a political coup d'état. For now they had established their position of leadership in the union's organizational campaign.

And this day Jackie returned to work, resolved to brazen it out despite the finger of accusation. For she was free, white, and twenty-one. But the other office workers made her job unbearable, even though Foster encouraged her to remain. For though he enjoyed to the full the whole incredible story as he reflected with broad amusement upon the union's embarrassment, the women with whom Jackie had to work manifested the instinctive American antipathy toward a traitor. They avoided her, refused to speak to her, and when she approached drew away from her as from someone filthy. So at the end of the day she quit.

In all the city she had not one friend. Dreading the return to her empty, haunted rooms, she stopped in a Hollywood motion-picture theater. Afterwards she ate dinner in a little restaurant on Hollywood Boulevard and walked herself to weariness. But once at home, showered, and in bed, she could not sleep. She tried to read, but though her eyes transmitted the words, her brain gave them no meaning.

For all of her consciousness was consumed with the thought of three black men—one who had persecuted her, one for whom she had been persecuted, and one who had defended her. And she hated all three of them indiscriminately, she told herself. But this was as far as she could get. Because this was a contradiction—if she hated the persecutor, she could not hate the defender. But she did, she told herself. She hated him because he was a nigger, too. And if this was wrong, then everything she had ever known was wrong and there was no meaning in anything.

And there was no meaning.

She had to get out! It was imperative that she get out! Out of such confusing, condemning, tormenting thoughts. Out of the city, the state, the world. She could not bear it! she told herself. Because if there was a contradiction in three black men—if one was brutal and one evil and one good—then she was wrong and her race was wrong and she was nobody. But she was white—white! And now it was urgent that she go where black was always evil and only white was good. But where could she go that the three black men wouldn't follow?—Death?—No! No! she cried to herself. Was it all so wrong and false she had to die when faced with what she'd been taught was never true? Wasn't being white enough to withstand any truth—enough to support her in the face of any contradiction?

She thought of returning to her home. But what good would that do? she asked herself. As she faced the I-told-you-so's of her staid and conventional parents, the three black men would mock her from the shadows. And she could not tell her parents of them, for her parents would only see two in reality and the third one in her own disgrace. Then she would have them to herself, in the stagnant pool of days, and they would rise from the dreariness and consume her brain. No!—Not home!—Now more than at any time she needed the excitement and physical freedom of communistic life and nothing less would do.

She thought of dressing and going out and picking up a date. But she was afraid of all white men now because of what she had been to one Negro man—and what he had been to her. To the soldiers and the sailors she'd be but another lay—and she was more than this—dear God, she was more than this. And yet she would not think his name.

Slowly in the terrible loneliness her body grew rigid as her mind willed that someone call her on the phone, and her heart cried out for just one word from anyone. And when midnight passed and that word had not come, she turned over and lay face downward and cried into the lonely night.

But daylight brought the hard, unyielding necessity of getting up and living. Now friendless and out of work in a hard hostile city, she was faced with the inexorability of human activity. The past was closed and the present moved and there was only the haunted future. What to do?

The formal notice of her dismissal from the Communist Party arrived in the morning's mail. She did not open it. When the house became unbearable, she dressed and went out, wandering— a stranger in a strange city. In the faces of the people in the street she saw the hard indifference of their eyes, the remoteness of their souls. She felt forsaken by humanity and terribly afraid.

At first she shuddered at sight of every passing Negro, little realizing their kinship of emotion. But as the hours dragged through her terrible hurt, within her grew a sense of affinity to these Negroes whom she shunned—for they were always terribly hurt. With some strange strength that this afforded, she went home to wait. For what, at first she did not know. And then she did.

For in the end her thoughts came back to Lee Gordon who had defended her, and she thought of him as having defended her, and the confusion left and the contradiction became the truth—there were these three black men side by side, and one was brutal, and one was evil, and one was good. For this was the truth, and knowing it for the truth, she wanted Lee Gordon that moment to hold her in his arms and pity her. And Jackie Forks, the greatest woman in all the world, was beaten. Yet she knew that it was better so.

The hours of the afternoon were spent in wonder at her emotions concerning him. And finally she could think the words: "In a way he's such a wonderful guy—and a man, yes, a man!"

It was then that she began to cry—crying out the horror and the strangeness of the world— "Oh, God, why hast Thou forsaken me?" The final refuge of anyone of any race. And it was as if she had been released from hell and with God's blessing was human once again.

And it was thus that Lee Gordon found her.

Chapter 24

THAT night alone, since Ruth had not returned to bed with him, Lee Gordon dreamed an involved and painful fantasy. But on awakening all he could recall was but the single line: "Thy immortal woman will hold thy hand."

He was assailed by such a sense of poignancy he all but cried aloud. All that morning he was haunted by the line. The tearing, hurting, exciting implication, pulled at his mind, and its simple melody sounded in his soul, stirring up those deep, hidden dreams of how it should be, of how he'd always hoped it would be, and how it never was.

"Well—ycs," Lee Gordon said aloud, and took the road to Jackie's.

By the still, damp tear stains on her cheeks, the softly moist lashes, giving to her features the charm of feminine despair, Lee Gordon could tell that she had been crying and had suddenly dried her eyes when he rang the bell.

He did not wait. It made no difference that they stood in the open doorway for anyone in the hall to see, because this was the world and they were the people and now was the discovery of their sexes. She came into his open arms, and for a moment longer he held her lips from his while he looked into her eyes and at the finely sculptured lines of her face and at the slight quiver of her mouth as if to etch it forever on his mind, and then with urgency they kissed. He could feel her lips trembling and breaking up softly beneath his. And he could feel her body trembling in his arms—And taste her tongue—And smell her hair. And the long, full moment lingered in the desperation of their embrace and would never end. In their awful urgency there was no end.

It was as if they had never had each other—had never had anyone—had waited for this moment to consummate their gender. The door was shut and neither knew who shut it. They groped across the room in a trance, never taking their eyes from one another's. Their fingers were stiff, unable to cope with the maddening intricacy of buttons, and they broke them off and tore their clothing in haste—now blinding and consuming, as if to make the earth anew and people it this instant.

It had been early afternoon when he had arrived, and now it was dark and she switched on the light and got up and closed the Venetian blinds. He got up and went to her and kissed her eyes and hair and mouth. They went into the bath and showered together, staring at each other as the first man and woman.

"You're beautiful," he said, not tritely or amorously, but with all the homage in the world.

After a moment she looked up into his face and murmured: "I am?" slightly questioning, the corners of her mouth quirking in beginning laughter.

Now barefooted and nude and dripping, leaving footprints across the floor, they went into the kitchen and scrambled eggs and cooked hamburger patties rare with brown sugar sprinkled on them. She split a loaf of French sour-dough bread, rubbed it with garlic, spread butter on it, and put it in the oven so the butter would melt. He washed and sliced onions and found mustard and green peppers. They put their chairs together so their legs could touch, and ate garlic bread, scrambled eggs, and rare hamburger patties sprinkled with brown sugar and spread with mustard and onion and peppers, and drank sour claret wine. And it tasted more delicious than anything they'd ever eaten in all their lives. From each other's mouths they took the food like children, and to each it tasted the same. In their five senses, in their sex and emotion, they had achieved a oneness in which their colors blended.

It was in their minds that the difference lay. In their inherent thinking to which they had been born and raised, that color made the difference. It was something they could not help, could not overcome. But yet they thought they had. And to each it gave a story of that afternoon—a different story.

To Lee Gordon, that afternoon became one more step toward the consummation of his destiny. Out of all the white women he might have or would want, this was the one who had meaning, the one who brought change. Finding it was Jackie who now needed comforting re-created the image of all white women in his mind and changed completely the structure of his own emotions. He pitied her, and to be able to pity this white girl gave him equality in this white world. With the equality of his pity for her he could now love her; and he did. He loved her desperately, violently, and completely.

And to Jackie Forks, that afternoon was the discovery of the world and the people thereof and the purpose of the people of the world. For to her came the knowledge that manhood was a many-colored thing and hers to serve the color of her heart's selection. And it was his, and he was hers, and she was of no race and of no color but only of the people of the world. For this was the way God made it, and now she knew it was the way He wanted it to be. And still there was deep within her the consciousness of race, covered over for the time by the consciousness of truth.

And thus they started up the ladder to the way it might have been.

"Why were you angry at me?" she asked.

"You mean when I left? I wasn't angry with you."

"You sounded hurt. Is that why you did it—to hurt me back?"

"I don't know," he said, his eyes on hers, and after a moment added as if thinking aloud: "To get something, I guess."

She waited so long he thought she would not reply, then she asked: "Did you?"

"Can't you tell? It makes now possible."

"I'm glad," she said, and after a moment added: "It seems like a thousand years ago, in another life, and I was very foolish then."

"You were never very foolish."

"I was always foolish, because I wanted you afraid of me."

"I was afraid," he said. "That's partly why I did it."

"Darling, why did you let me make you so afraid of me?"

"Of myself, too. Of how I might feel about you in the end."

"How do you feel?"

"Now?"

"Yes, now. And now tomorrow. And now always."

"I love you now."

"Oh, darling, darling, darling—"

And then they kissed again and got up and left the food because they could not eat anymore. They did not turn out the kitchen light or turn on the bedroom light in their urgency. And then it was after midnight and they showered again.

"You don't feel badly about me?" she asked.

"Why should I?"

"About what happened to me?"

"Of course I feel badly about what they did to you. I'd like to kill the dirty bastards!"

She had such a tired, warm, lovely, luxurious, satisfied feeling clinging lazily to him in the lukewarm bath that her emotions were diffused and the Communist Party seemed very far away.

"You shouldn't, darling. I'm not angry at them myself anymore. If it hadn't been me it would have been someone else."

"Why couldn't it have been Luther?"

"You should know why not, Lee. For the same reason the party hasn't framed you. They hate you—or do you know it?"

"I know it."

"But as long as you're a Negro, they're not going to touch you."

"For a long time then," he said and laughed, and it was not a bitter laugh. Then after a moment he added: "Rotten bastards!"

"Darling, you're hurting me," she said. "You're pulling my hair and water's getting in my eyes. And this is hardly the place for a political discussion anyway. Or the time."

"You're sweet," he said, and kissed her in the water.

"I'm sleepy, darling."

But when they had returned to bed she could not go to sleep. "You know, now that I am out of it, I wonder how I ever was a Communist."

"You were just playing at it. I could tell that when I first saw you."

"No, I wasn't. I was serious. I believed in it. And yet I've always known what they were like."

"Who doesn't?"

"I mean more than you could get to know if you were not a member. They wanted me to make you frame McKinley."

"I know. You should have gotten out then."

"I didn't think that they would do this thing to me."

"Why not you, baby? What was your claim to immunity from a Communist like Bart?"

"I—You know how everyone is, darling. You never expect anything to happen to yourself." After a moment she added as if it troubled her: "I talked to Maud Himmelstein trying to get back."

"The one-armed woman? What did she have to say?"

"It was a funny thing. At the time I thought she was only trying to hurt me. But after I had left her I had a funny feeling that maybe she wanted to help."

"I doubt it—" And then: "Jackie—"

"Yes, Lee?"

"Did you put the thing about the Rasmus Johnson case in my pocket?" Now he could ask.

And suddenly she was crying again. "Oh, Lee! Oh, darling! I don't know why I did it!"

The taste of tears; the feel of sobbing in his arms—

"But now it's different, isn't it?"

"You know it's different! You know it, darling! You know it!"

"And you are mine?"

"Oh, Lee! I am forever yours."

"Without regret?"

"Yes, yes, without regret, I am yours—"

Lost—

Gasping, choking, now breathing again. Now cooling. Tears drying. Talking again—

"I'm going to see Foster tomorrow."

"What good would that do?"

"I could get a statement and send it to the dailies."

"They wouldn't use it."

"They would if I put enough dirt in it about the party."

"But you'd have to name me. You'd be in it, too. It'd become so involved. I can't go through all that again, darling."

"You want to hurt them, don't you?"

"Oh, yes— No— I don't know what I want to do. All I want right now is for you to love me, darling."

"Baby—"

"Not like that. Not now. Not again. I mean in your heart."

"I do love you in my heart."

"I want you to love me like that, too. Oh yes, I want you to, darling. But I'm not used to so much at one time."

"Nor am I."

"But you've had a lot of practice."

"Not for you. There never was any practice for you."

"You overwhelm me, darling." But after a moment: "And there's your wife you have to think about, too, Lee. The papers would put our names together."

Now in the softly running silence: "Jackie—"

"Yes, Lee?"

"I'm going to leave Ruth."

"No, darling."

"But I want to."

"No, darling. That isn't the answer either."

"But I must."

"No, Lee. That would hurt her terribly."

"She wouldn't care," he said bitterly. "She wouldn't give a damn."

And now they let the silence run again.

"Jackie, don't you see? This is it! This is all of it! Nothing else will ever matter!"

"Oh, Lee, I don't want to hurt anybody. I've been hurt so badly myself I can't bear to see anyone else hurt."

"Did they hurt you so much, baby?"

"Hold me, Lee. Hold me tight, darling."

Then she was crying again—

"The bastards! The dirty, rotten, lousy bastards!"

Now the sound of sobbing and the shaking of her body in his arms—

"You know that night you played the symphony when I was going home—I had the strangest feeling that the earth was being lost and only heaven would be left, and I wanted so much to be in love with you I ached with it."

"If I could be that," she whispered as if in awe. "If I could be heaven and always have you in my heart."

After that nothing was real. It was fantasy, ecstasy, dread, and apprehension. And it was glory. They did not need a thing—neither people nor food nor sleep nor the world. There was too much of each other within the hours that they would never have. And the hours passed through this enchanted unreality, wired together and meteoric.

One of them he spent with Smitty in his office, tendering his resignation—thinking at the time: "I've always been a fool."—Because he had to give her something.

Smitty would not accept his resignation. "Take a few days off, Lee. You're upset."

"Yes, I am upset, Smitty," he said. "But after what the union did to Jackie Forks I am through with it."

"Lee, as I've said to you before, the union of workers is a bigger proposition than any one person, whoever that person may be."

"That may be true, Smitty, but you can not crucify people and expect to have a union."

"We don't have the union, Lee; the union is the workers."

"Or expect to have the workers—to have their confidence in order to build a union."

"We must have the workers' confidence, Lee. You know that. But if some one gets hurt, inadvertently, accidentally, or deliberately, the union will go on, Lee, and have the workers' confidence. No matter how much we might hate the fact of some on getting hurt—"

"Crucified! Framed-up—"

"Crucified, then. No matter how much we may hate it, we have to keep working for the union, keep our confidence in it, and keep building up the confidence of others. Unionization is a fact of salvation for the working class. The only fact. There'll be more and more people working toward that end. If not you or me, someone else. Only, I hope it will also be you, Lee. I like you, man."

"I don't have anything personal against you, Smitty. But I'm through with this union."

"Well, think it over, Lee. I'll wait."

"You don't have to wait, Smitty. I've already thought it over."

And later Jackie cried: "If our being together is going to hurt you, darling, then we shouldn't be together."

"Do you really mean that, Jackie?"

"Oh, darling, you know I don't mean that. But I don't want to

hurt anybody. Not you, darling! Not you! I want it to be the best
of everything for you."

"It is the best of everything."

"But you quit your job."

"Jackie, you don't understand. I had to."

"Why, Lee? Because of me?"

"Because of you."

"I ought to go away and leave you."

"Don't say that."

"But what about your wife?" For at some moment within each
hour Ruth was there between them.

And then she was crying again— She cried in his arms—at the
beginning and at the end and even afterwards as they lay in each
other's arms, spent—spent but not finished, not done, not through.
They cried out for a leveling, a fusing, a meeting, a togetherness of
spirit, and a communion of soul—a fulfillment of themselves in
each other.

They sought for it in music, confessing their emotions as the
records played.

And they sought for it in words. At sundown she read him love
poems with the bruised, splashed sunset in the window framing
her hair in a flaming aureole, while he lay on the davenport watching the motion of her lips and the expression of her eyes. They
laughed at a Shakespearean sally: "If sack and sugar be a fault,
God help the wicked! if to be old and merry be a sin, then many
an old host that I know is damned: if to be fat be to be hated, then
Pharaoh's lean kine are to be loved. . . ."

And that night they talked of skin color as if it were a casual
thing.

"I love to watch your muscles ripple. They're like fluid bronze."

"Where did you get this?" he asked, fingering the tiny scar at
her hairline.

"Playing when I was a little girl."

"You must have played awfully rough."

"I always play rough."

"And get hurt too."

And it was back again—the awful hurt. And she was in his arms
—the anodyne of sex—seeking, searching, hoping for fulfillment.

And sometimes it was almost sacred—but never quite. And sometimes it was weird as from phase to phase they ventured.

When the mood struck them, they dressed and went out, seeking it in the company of others. They went to shows, bars, the South Side, the beach, or just walking hand in hand along Hollywood Boulevard—at any time. Time meant nothing—only as an enemy. For they were two people bent on having everything there was to have of each other in their allotted time.

At first to Lee Gordon it was as if he had been in a shell or had been inanimate and was just coming to life. Food tasted better and skin felt softer and breasts were warmer and sleep was lovely. And that was when they almost reached it.

But they could not fulfill each other, for they had two strikes on them from the first. Out of their lives as they had lived them, came the shadow of their racial differences. And between them some time within each hour there was Ruth—and each time Jackie felt more like a whore.

Lee felt this in her, and he said as reassurance: "I'd like to have a son."

For a long moment she did not move or breathe, and then she asked: "What color do you think he would be?"

"Probably a beautiful sepia like McKinley's kids."

"That's it, Lee."

"That's what?"

"He'd be a Negro son."

"Well—yes." This was the first major disappointment.

But that was the way it was—if not Ruth, it was race, and most times it was both.

It hung over their heads, staining every moment with a blind, futile desperation, beneath which everything was distorted and magnified all out of proportion, so now things that should have been stirring became hurting, and minor incidents that might have sunk beneath a kiss grew into deep frustrations.

One day in a little cafe on Western Avenue they heard a recording of King Cole's *I'm Lost*, and that was the way she felt. Always afterward, wherever she was, sipping rum and cola at a bar, or eating barbecue on Central Avenue, it made her cry. And whenever anyone looked at her for crying, Lee Gordon wanted to fight.

He wanted to kick in the juke boxes and break the records. He wanted to strike out at anything, any place, that hurt her.

And yet at times, from this frustration of unfulfillment, he wanted to hurt her himself. He did not understand it. He was ashamed of it and tried to hide it. But she could see it in his eyes.

"Go ahead and hit me."

"I don't want to hit you."

"You can't hurt me any more than I am already hurt."

"Jackie, stop it! Stop it, please!"

"Why don't you? You want to."

"Why should I want to?"

They had tried so many things that sex was running stale. . . . But each time afterwards they went a little farther, for since they could not make it to the top, it seemed as if they would try it to the bottom.

The fifth night the telephone rang. She turned to answer it. "Hello—

"Now?—

"But I can't now—

"I'll call you back—"

And then she turned over to Lee. "It was some smart aleck producer who's been trying to make me," she said casually.

"What did he want now?"

"He wanted me to spend the night with him. He's always calling me up asking me to come to his apartment."

He did not answer, for the thought of her in another's arms was horrifying.

"He offered me a hundred dollars."

"The cheap bastard," he said, trying to keep it light.

Then, at the end of the long pregnant silence: "Lee—"

"What, Jackie?"

"Do you want me to go?"

"Go where?"

"To make the hundred dollars."

"Jackie!"

"I'd be a whore for you, Lee."

"Please stop it, Jackie."

"I mean it. I want to. I'd be your white whore and make you a hundred thousand dollars and the proudest black man who ever lived." Why not the fact with the feeling, since she could not be his wife and race would not let her be the mother of his children?

"Don't talk like that!"

"Why not?"

"Because it isn't like that."

"How is it?"

"You know how it is."

"Tell me."

"No, I'll let you tell me. How is it, Jackie?"

And then the drawing back—

"I didn't mean it, darling."

"I know you didn't mean it. But please don't say it."

"I won't say it any more."

But all that night he wondered if she had, and if he had been a fool for not accepting it.

So in the end he had to tell her: "I had a funny dream the night before I came to you."

"What was it?"

"I don't remember all of it. Just the single line: 'Thy immortal woman will hold thy hand.' "

The look for which from the first he had searched came into her ethereal features, and slowly, their eyes on one another's, they groped for each other's hands.

That day they almost attained the communion, fulfilling each other and themselves— But not quite.

For between them were their colors—race.

And his wife— Ruth called that night.

Chapter 25

RUTH sat in the window of the darkened front room, a framed silhouette against the soft, cool night, and stared down the walk toward the street. Beneath her feet was a tiny spot in the nap of the carpet where her agitated shuffling had flattened it the night before as she had sat there waiting for him. And now it was past twelve of another night and he had not yet returned. But her thoughts were so deeply absorbed in a dull, self-condemning agony that she would not have seen him if he had then come up the walk.

For it had been her lack of faith that had driven him away, she berated herself. Her childish theatricalism of sleeping on the davenport, as though one more night of sleeping in the bed with him would matter. And why should he be guilty because she had thought so? Was her faith in his fidelity so cheap it would not withstand a tone of voice? Was his every noble purpose to be debased by the unfounded suspicions of her jealous mind? Was it so impossible that he had defended the woman as he would have defended any victim of injustice?

She wanted to believe him, and her heart held out for this belief implicitly. But there was no support for it, no precedent, nothing in her experiences as a Negro woman to convince her that a Negro man's defense of a white woman could be for justice's sake. To believe it, to have faith in her husband's motive, would have been to contradict all that she had ever read or seen or heard of Negro men and white women in America.

But to doubt it brought agony unendurable. For that made him like all other Negro men lusting after white women, and more than the threat to her future, the knife of torture in her heart, was the fear that all eight years of her marriage had been nothing but waste. And this she could not bear.

But in the dead hours of early morning, her self-condemning ardor ebbed and self-pity came with a numbing sense of weariness. Her mother had warned her against marrying Lee, she recalled. Her mother had said at the very first that he was undependable— that he would be unfaithful and lead her the life of a dog. She wished now that she could go to her mother and cry out her heart in her arms. But she had never done that and could not now. Her mother lived in a different world—a world of values absolute in segregation. Should she make the long dreary journey to St. Louis only to announce that her husband had left her for a white woman, her mother would not be able to understand why she simply did not leave him and put him from her mind.

So she sat out the night alone, slipping down each passing minute into deeper despondency. Mercifully, daylight brought a change. Although she was dead on her feet and had a grinding headache, now it was anger that she nursed. By evening she had resolved to live her own life, to go her own way.

But nightfall brought worry again, conjecture, desperation. When she had not received word from him by eleven o'clock, she could no longer endure her own grim imaginings. Calling the union hall, she caught Smitty still at work.

"This is Mrs. Gordon, Mr. Smith. May I speak to Lee—if it's not too inconvenient."

"Lee? Lee's not here, Mrs. Gordon. In fact—" He caught himself on the verge of divulging that Lee had quit that morning.

For an imperceptible moment she waited for him to finish, then spoke rapidly to conceal that she had done so: "Oh! He said when he left this morning that he would be working late, and I presumed that he would be at the hall—"

She did not want Smitty to know that she was worried, yet she could not hang up without some definite information.

But Smitty had already divined that Lee had returned to Jackie's, and now he sought an explanation to relieve Ruth's anxiety. "We sent Lee to San Francisco on urgent business, Mrs. Gordon. He was terribly rushed and didn't have an opportunity to call you, but you should be hearing from him at any time now."

"Oh, thank you. My business wasn't urgent anyway."

"No doubt he has already sent you a message. You should receive it at any time."

He knew as he spoke that he sounded unconvincing. Nor was she convinced. But she was somewhat reassured by the fact that Smitty would go to the trouble to lie for him. That proved that he meant something to the union.

And now her hand touched her hair in a weary reflex gesture as the slow torture of his absence brought a recapitulation of their relationship, forcing an admission of what he meant to her.

She had always been in love with him from the moment she first saw him in the drugstore on Central Avenue many years ago. There had been a great, swelling happiness when he asked her to marry him. She had complete confidence in herself those first nights of love, the sense of assurance. She felt pride in him, in being with him, and the feeling that nothing could touch them—

Unaware of her action, she went back and stood in the window. Her muscles felt stiff and lethargic and her knees kept buckling, the strength gone out of them. She wanted just to stand there and never move until Lee returned.

Where before she had seen only the empty night, now she saw the rows of yellow flowers lifting their heads to the faint translucence of the city night. With a dry, blunt bitterness she recalled the enthusiasm with which they had planted them, the feel of the everlasting earth in her warm moist hands, the unbounded joy of the house at her back, knowing it was theirs after the long, lean years, now always, forever and a day. She remembered how it had been when they had first discovered that they owned the bed and the sheets were clean and they did not have to worry about what their landladies thought or heard, so passionate and wonderful. After a shower there was the nice, clean piney smell in the bed even in the heat of the day.

It was hot inside during the days, with the hot wind billowing the white curtains and sweat trickling slowly down the insides of her smooth tan legs. But the nights were always cool and there had been something ecstatic about going to bed in the cool of the night after a scorching day.

But that had been but a brief interlude in the grinding hurt of years, after his escape from the walled-in destitution of WPA and worse, and before her rise to individuality, when he had seemed contented in the post office and she had lived her life in their home.

Before, in the blue years when happiness had always seemed so far away and unattainable, there had been those times of awful fear and actual hunger—when he had felt the crush of circumstances closing in upon him, wanting to fight back, to strike out, but there had been nothing to fight.

The time when she had been sick, sitting in the one rickety chair in their second-story rented room, waiting for him to come up from the mailbox, which he haunted for a reply to one of his many applications for a job.

"Any mail?" she had asked, screwing around to look at him when he came into the room.

"No, there wasn't," he had replied, looking away until he could straighten his face.

But she had already noticed his expression, and her hand had moved in a spasmodic gesture as if to comfort him.

"Maybe the postman hasn't passed yet."

"Yes, yes, he's been by. I saw him. There just wasn't any mail, that's all." His voice had been so harsh that she had felt an odd sort of embarrassment for him. And then with a look of sudden contrition he had come over and stroked her cheeks. "Now don't you worry, baby doll, don't you worry."

"I'm not worrying. I just don't want you to worry."

He had turned to look out the window, down the street. "We got anything for dinner?"

"We—we've got some rice."

His lips had flattened. "You're not hungry now, are you?"

"No, I won't want anything until you do."

"I'll get something after a while." He was sitting on the table and looking down the street. "I just don't feel like going out right now."

Each, unaware of the other, had turned to look at the bare spot on the small side table where a radio, then in the pawnshop, had once sat. Glancing away, their gazes had crossed. And as she had watched the hurt go through his eyes, she had never felt so sorry for anyone.

"I'll get something after a while," he had said, but his voice had thickened from the awful hurt.

"Oh, I'm not hungry," she had said.

He had looked at her quickly again. "You've got to get back on your diet." Then he had looked away. "You're not well yet; this rice and stuff— I'm going to see some friends."

"I wouldn't, Lee. We'll get something. Everyone is having it tough right now."

"But not as tough as us."

She had waited the long afternoon for his return, and had seen the answer in his eyes even before he opened the hand in which he had carried the coin for two hours and nine miles— "A quarter."

She had never heard such helpless fury in his voice.

Together they had looked at it.

"You were never afraid, were you, baby doll?" he had suddenly asked.

She had twisted around so she could look at him, alarmed by the urgency in his voice. "Why, no, Lee. Why, no, I've never been afraid. There's nothing to be afraid of, Lee."

"You were never sorry for anything?" he had persisted. "You were never sorry for marrying me?" His voice had been husky with emotion.

She had been so terribly afraid but she had smiled. "No, Lee, why should I? I love you, Lee."

"I love you, too," he had said.

"We'll make it, Lee. We love each other. We'll make it," she had said, still smiling. And when she had no longer been able to smile, when the smile had begun to freeze in the awful fear that had come over her, she had turned abruptly away to keep him from seeing that she was no longer smiling.

And now the memory of it coming down the channel of the years brought the bitter question: at just what point had she begun to fail? In the self-searching of that endless night she could not believe it had been so simple a thing as just her job. It must have been something more—

If she had had a baby— She had wanted a baby, but he had never wanted children. Now she knew it had been because he had not wanted to bring more black children into this prejudiced world. But he had never said it. He had just kept putting it off, asking her to wait. In all that time she had tried so hard not to have a baby that when she had decided to have one anyway, she could not.

This she could not tell him, just as there had been so many other things within her thoughts she had never been able to tell him—at first because she had not wanted to worry him, and later because she had been afraid he would not care.

There had been so many, many things in the slow tortured movement of the years, while watching his slow disintegration under the impact of prejudice and feeling the tearing, hurting, awful inadequacy at not being able to help. There had been the sublime joy when she had first learned that she could absorb his hurts—the great feminine feeling of self-immolation when he struck her, the sharp hurt running out of his arm into her body.

Then came the slow knowledge that this was not enough—that what she could give him as a sponge for his brutality to rebuild his ego would never be enough. In this living, peopled world nothing took the place of acceptance; nothing could assuage rejection. A man could not be less than a man to the world and more to her. Whatever of a man the world rejected, she rejected too. For her values were common values and her thoughts common thoughts. And when she looked at her man and saw he was less than white, unwhite in a white world, that was what he was and there was nothing she could do about it. No matter if she should suffer hell for him and die a thousand tortured deaths, she could not change it unless she changed the way she looked at it.

And what had this done to her? Now she could see it in that dead dark before day, weary beyond words. She could see how she had lost to white values in a white world the man she had married —and how he had lost his wife. There had been nothing she could have done about it. She would have lost him whether she had gone to work or whether she had remained home. For down the line in her vision, colored by her country and her times, he had become less than his own image. Where once she had needed him to fulfill herself, she had sought to fulfill herself alone. And where her necessity had made him strong, her lack of it had made her stronger.

Society had put her in this place of advantage and she had accepted it, had accepted its values. She had accepted the condescending smiles of her white employers whenever she referred to him, simultaneously indulging her and denying him any claim to achievement. Even the foreknowledge that in a predominantly masculine society the pattern for oppression would be masculine too did not inspire the rejection of the values, for these were what you lived by, black or white, or else they killed you.

But, dear God, please send him back tonight, she prayed. And it will be different. I promise, God—

She rose and hunted for the Bible. Finally she found it, dusty and unused, wiped it off, and opened it. The line stared out at her: "They came unto the Sepulchre at the rising of the sun."

She went to sleep sitting in a chair with the Bible in her lap. When she opened her eyes it was early afternoon and the sunlight streamed in over her. And she looked at the Bible on the floor at her feet and did not believe. For now it was day and there were the merciless facts to face without faith, for faith was only for the dark.

Now she admitted to herself what she had long since known: that he was at Jackie's. And her imagination rose to torment her. She could see him kissing Jackie, laughing down into her face. His white teeth would be flashing in his lean, dark face, and his deep, wonderful eyes would be as impressed with himself as if he had accomplished something great to be holding a white woman in his arms.

A deep humiliation sapped the strength from her spirit. Why did it have to be a white woman of all women; and Lee of all black men? And why should this happen to her, who had never hated people for their color, who had never once thought that white women were different from her other than in their color, or better, or more attractive? It was all the more tormenting because she had never seen Jackie and did not know how she looked.

She went into the bedroom and looked at her face in the mirror and felt ashamed that she was brown. And this was the first time in all her life she had ever felt a sense of inferiority because her skin was brown. She powdered her skin a sickly white and painted with garish rouge and then screamed at her reflection: "Take off the paint, you fool!"

Crying hysterically, she flung herself across the bed and beat at the covers with tightly clenched fists. "You fool! You fool!" she kept screaming into the tear-dampened pillows, biting the covers, filling her mouth with the tasteless cloth as if clinging to sanity with her teeth. Finally she sunk into subdued desperation and lay crying quietly, holding on to her mind only by the strength of her will.

If she could only stop thinking about it! If she could just get her mind on something else! Please, God, just for a little while, she prayed. But the picture of him lying nude beside a nude white woman kept moving through her mind. If it would only stop there, dear God, with his lying with the woman and having her. But it would not stop. It went into all the details, moved him through all the motions, placing his lips upon her breasts and his hands behind her back. And yet it would not stop. It went through all the scenes that they had gone through together—their own sacred love scenes, profaned with this white slut. And even then it would not stop. It made a travesty of their own love and a mockery of the act. For she could see him holding this white woman in just that certain way—through her closed eyelids and the bed beneath and through the solid earth. And she could hear him calling her "baby doll," with just that loving tone of voice through the silence of the house and of her soul— giving to one white woman in these few days all the graces of their passion it had taken them years to acquire. And she hated her! God, oh Lord Jesus Christ, how she hated her, and all white women, and all white men, and the goddamned white world and the white babies in their mothers' wombs! She hated them!—

Though exhaustion had turned her body into a senseless hulk and dry rot filled her brain from the torturous imagining, she could not sleep. For one thin thread of hope, a ghostly thing not contained within herself but anchored to her will, not yet broken, kept her awake to wait for him.

With the coming of night came complete despair. She no longer cared whether he came or not; she only wanted to sleep— just to sleep a little bit. Just for ten minutes, God, for ten short minutes. But she did not sleep. Once she went off into a fantasy where he came back to brush his faithless lips across her dead mouth and caress her body with the formless fingers of her memory, and suddenly she became alert to think of him in Jackie's bed. And she wished that she could die.

That morning she knew that the thing within herself that had given life its meaning—the thing that unknowingly supported her personal ambition, that gave her the will to accomplish, the desire for self-importance—was the belief that above everything Lee loved her. It was not egoism or a defensive mechanism, but the essence of her life. And though in all other respects she could see him in relativity—his faults and his weaknesses, capabilities and inadequacies, thoughts and reactions, changing as her viewpoint changed—in his love for her she saw him as absolute. She would not recognize him otherwise, she knew—the expression of his face, the set of his body, the tone of his voice. She had one picture of him loving her that had never changed—although all other pictures against the light of living had suffered from comparisons.

It was this belief in the end that had given her personal security —the simple profound belief, over and above its fact or fiction— that had given her self-assurance in a world of hostile whites. Beyond the belief that he still loved her there was nothing. Now more than the certainty of his infidelity was this doubt in her belief.

She had not thought of returning to work because now there was no point in it. To her it had only had meaning in its relation to Lee, even in its equations of resentment. But even now she could not go in search of him. She could not beg him back. For now there was this doubt that might become a certainty, if she tested it like the certainty of his unfaithfulness. And when he did return, she would rather cope with the one than with the other.

On the sixth night she called him, driven to it. For the time had passed for him to return to her. Now it would be from necessity. But going to him, she could keep alive the one faint hope that regardless of his infidelity he still loved her.

Pride? What was pride in an extremity like this? She had no pride. Those six days in Gethsemane had taken all of pride. They had bruised her soul and mangled her mind to a weird infirmity as she clung to life and sanity with this one faint hope.

Lee and Jackie were in bed when the telephone rang. With that uncanny presentiment of guilt, both knew instantly that it was Ruth—and both hoped it was not.

Finally, as the phone continued to ring, Lee said: "You better answer it."

Watching Jackie's face whiten as she held the receiver to her ear, and her features tauten into sudden ugliness, Lee knew it was Ruth's voice, more than her actual words, that had so profoundly shocked Jackie, and wondered how the voice of Ruth could sound.

"He's not here," Jackie said softly. "No, he isn't—I tell you he isn't." And she hung up fearfully.

"What did she say?"

"She said if you didn't come home she would send the police here."

For a moment Lee could not speak and Jackie asked in a tight, frightened voice: "Would she?"

"I don't know."

"You ought to know!"

"Why the hell ought I to know?"

So driven were they by their fright, they were at each other's throats before they caught themselves.

"I'd better call her," Lee decided.

"Don't call her from here!"

"Why the hell not?"

"She'll trace the call and know you're here."

"She knows I'm here anyway."

"You'd better leave."

"There's no danger of her coming here."

"I don't want to get into any trouble, Lee."

"How in the hell can you get into any trouble?" he shouted, snatching the telephone. But calling his home, he received no answer.

Then the phone began to ring as soon as he hung up. Jackie answered, again denying his presence, but she turned on him with naked panic in her face. "You've got to go! She's coming with the police!"

And now her panic seized him. He jumped to his feet, scrambling into his clothes. She rustled about handing him the wrong garments at the wrong time, her nude body grotesque in its frantic posturing.

"Oh, goddamnit, you're taking all night!" she cried.

"I'm hurrying as fast as I can!" he shouted back.

"Here! Here's your tie!"

"Will you sit down and shut up!"

"I want you out of here!" she screamed.

Finally he started toward the door, unshaven and disheveled and incompletely dressed. She did not actually push him with her hands, but with her mind, and closed the door on his heels, locking it securely. Unorganized and demoralized, he started down the exit stairway.

Just as he turned at the landing, looking down, he saw Ruth at the bottom. He saw her thin, haggard body in the wrinkled, threadbare suit, and thought with a sudden sense of shock: "Good God, she looks old!"

And then for an instant they stood looking at each other. In her eyes, even at that distance in the dim light, he could see the hurt, overflowing like a flood of emotion running out of her. A sharp, constricting pain came up in him, solidifying in his chest. He looked quickly away from her, focusing on the wall, and went down the stairs to meet her.

"What are you doing here?" he said harshly. "What did you want to come here for?"

She could see in his face and hear in his voice his extreme attempt to be angry. Now, on top of all the rest, he was trying to build up a self-righteous indignation and a brutal rage that would impel him into striking her. And it did not matter. For at the first sight of him turning at the landing, the last thin thread of hope inside of her had broken. And as she stood there, watching him look at her and look away and come down the stairs to speak to her in that unnatural, grating voice, it was as if he were already dead, and that part of her to which this made a difference also died.

When it became apparent that she was not going to answer, he took her roughly by the arm and tried to steer her through the doorway. "Come on, I'll take you home."

But she held her ground with the strength of desperation. "I want to talk to Jackie."

"Come on! Come on!" he said, tugging at her. "There isn't any need of making any trouble."

"I'm not going to make any trouble. I just want to talk to her."

"She hasn't done anything to you and I'm not going to let you hurt her."

"I don't want to hurt her. I just want to see how she looks and talk to her."

"I don't want you to talk to her. What could you say to her?"

"I just want to ask her if she loves you."

"Come on! Come on!" he said, yanking at her savagely. "I'm not going to let you go up there and start any trouble. She's had trouble enough as it is."

"Please let me talk to her, Lee," she pleaded. "Please—I'm not going to make any trouble."

"Oh, come on!" he cried impatiently.

"Please, Lee, please. If you ever had any feeling for me in your life, please let me go and talk to her."

Since he had first looked at her, he had not looked at her again. Now he stole a glance at her and quickly looked away. But in that brief glance he noticed how red were her eyes from crying, and how swollen were her eyelids and the flesh all around them. Her face seemed loose; the skin was slack and fell in folds beside her jaws. She seemed so thin and broken. It was as if some inner support that had held it in shape all those years had suddenly broken apart. And he knew that it was not only because he did not want her to see the sickness and guilt and remorse in his own eyes that he did not look at her, but because he did not want to see the grief and sudden age showing in her face—as if not seeing it would keep it from being there. But he knew that it was there.

And suddenly he thought of all the times that she had said: "All I ever wanted was just to love you, Lee." Pity came up in him in overwhelming waves, and he was blindly furious with himself because he felt it.

He dragged her away and hailed a taxi and took her home. And now began the bitter necessity of facing themselves as strangers within their own home. She sank into a chair and looked at him as if she had never seen him before. And she never had, this Lee. Long ago she had ceased to brush at the slow growth of insanity that trickled through her mind, and now even the raw and eternal emotional hurt within her soul had no meaning. She was the calmer of the two.

"Lee, why didn't you tell me you were having an affair with the woman? Why did you have to let me find out like this?"

"I wasn't having an affair with her," he said.

"But you went to her without even telling me you were going to be away. You must have known that I would worry."

"I didn't know I was going to stay when I went there."

"But you could have called and told me you were there: I would have been hurt, but not like this. You have been through so much lately I could have understood that you needed some emotional release."

"I didn't need any emotional release," he said sullenly.

"Then that makes it worse. Why did you go to her?"

"I don't know, Ruth, goddamnit! I was sorry for her, I guess."

She was looking at him with a cold, dispassionate scrutiny, measuring the guilt in his face; but he would not look at her. He could not look at her.

"Do you love the woman, Lee?" she asked in that calm, deadly voice.

For a moment he said nothing, waiting for the answer to form within himself, and then he began to softly cry.

"I do love her," he said, and even then he did not know whether he lied or not. But deep inside of him he knew he told her this to hurt her, although he could not understand why he should want to do so at this particular time. Perhaps because she had so often hurt his pride and ridiculed his honor that he took his vengeance now, knowing that to confess he loved another woman was the only way. He could not understand himself at just this moment.

She did not move or flinch; nor did the calm deadliness of her voice change one whit. "You do not love the woman, Lee. You envy white men. That's why you want their women—because of what they've made of their women, which you could never do. You'd like to be the kind of a white man who could say: 'Here's fifty thousand dollars, go to Reno and get a divorce and enjoy yourself.' But you are a Negro. You are cheap and vicious and craven. And if you think you are going to marry this woman, you are mistaken. Because she wouldn't have you. I am the only fool who ever wanted you. And I don't want you any more."

She knew as she said it that it was not true and would never be true. She would always be in love with him, no matter what he did. But she sat there, rigid as death, watching him pack his bag and leave, and did not change a line.

"Well—yes," Lee Gordon thought as he returned to Jackie.

But Jackie was now thoroughly frightened and demoralized. She had heard vague stories of the savagery of Negro women where their men were concerned. She could picture Ruth attacking with a knife and cutting her to death. Never having seen Ruth, she now imagined her as a huge, dark Negress of tremendous strength and possessed of a vicious temperament, against whom she had securely locked and barred all the doors and windows of her flat.

But equal to her fear of violence was her fear of public condemnation. It had been all right to flaunt Lee Gordon before white eyes as a Negro male with whom she dared to have a sex affair. That was her own business as a prostitute's business is her own. Her body was hers to bestow on whom she pleased.

But to be caught in a Negro emotional mess—and as the other woman!—was altogether different. She could not fight with a Negro woman for the affection of a Negro man—or even bear the thought of it.

And now in this chaotic fear Lee Gordon became not a man, but once more a Negro. For over and above whatever passionate attachment she might have had for him was the simple fact of race. She would take him and have him and hold him and love him. And if she wanted him badly enough, she would fight for him with any white woman in the world. But she would not fight for him with a Negro woman—she would not sink so low, she thought.

And now at sight of Lee returning with his bag, trepidation seized her. "You can't stay here!" she said in alarm.

"Why not? I'll keep out of sight," he told her.

"It isn't that, it's your wife. This will be the first place she'll come looking for you."

Placing his bag on the floor, he closed the door behind him and halted just inside the room. She stood a few paces in front of him, as if to bar his coming further, and neither in their uncertainty made a move to touch the other.

"We're through," Lee told her. "She won't do anything."

"We can't fight her, Lee. Don't you understand that?"

"We won't have to fight her—"

"Don't you see what would happen? She's a Negro and you're a Negro and I'd be an outsider, breaking up her home. I couldn't do that to her, Lee. I couldn't take advantage of her like that. Can't you understand?"

"I told her that I love you."

"No, Lee, no! You didn't!"

"I already have, Jackie."

"Then go back and tell her that you didn't mean it! Tell her you were just infatuated for a time. She'll understand. And she'll forgive you, darling."

"She'll give me a divorce, Jackie."

"No, Lee, I can't do that to her."

"Don't you love me, Jackie?" he asked, so softly and so prayerfully.

"Yes, I love you, darling," she replied. "You know I love you, darling. That's why I want you to be happy. You go back to your wife and—"

"If you love me, Jackie, that's all that matters," he said, taking a step toward her.

"No, Lee," and she took a step away.

"Jackie, if you will marry me, I'll—" He broke off to watch her stoop to lift his bag.

Patiently, as with a little child, she extended it to him and said in a patient voice, dismissing him: "Go to a hotel, darling, and think this over. Then call me tomorrow. But call your wife tonight and tell her where you are. She'll understand."

"What's the matter, Jackie? Are you afraid of me?"

She could not tell him that now in her mind, in the whiteness of her soul, she was repelled by the very blackness of the skin that sexually had first attracted her. So she continued to simulate this sympathy for Ruth.

"I can't do that to a Negro woman, Lee."

"Why not?" he wanted to know.

"I couldn't do it. My conscience wouldn't let me do it. I couldn't take that much advantage over her."

"What advantage?"

"I'm white, Lee—white! Can't you understand? I'm a white woman. And I could not hurt a Negro woman so."

For a long, emasculating moment, during which he suffered every degradation of his race, Lee Gordon stood looking at the whiteness of her face.

"Well—yes," he finally said, and accepted his bag from her hand and went out of the door.

Chapter 26

H E WALKED fast through the dark streets of early morning, going nowhere. And a sickness came into his face, all up and under and around his nose and mouth and eyes. His muscles and his skin felt sick, and his eyes felt sick as did his stomach, and his soul felt sick.

Her being white was nothing newly found; she had been white at the beginning, and at the beginning, he recalled, she had used it as at the end. But he had gotten past thinking of her being white, and he had hoped that she had too. And now as the hurt came, it drenched him because he had gotten past believing that she would use it thus to reduce every' mood they had captured into nothing.

It was as if his heart had been taken out and beaten with a hammer. Because he had wanted to marry her, to adore, protect, and support her; to walk with her through life, defy traditions, and track fulfillment down. And to have her at his side he had been willing to pay whatever cost—his life, his honor, or his tears. No, not that she was white, but that she was the woman he truly loved. Now to have this extreme ardor of his self-immolation rejected on racial grounds was all the more agonizing because he had been defenseless from the first.

So he hastened through the deserted streets, not seeking a place to go, but trying to escape where he had been. But he carried it along in the dull, beaten memory of the words: "I'm white, Lee. White! Can't you understand?"

And this was her rejection, not the product of environment. For this was Los Angeles where many interracial marriages had brought success and happiness; where it was up to the people involved. As two people they might have failed, but they could have tried, he thought. She did not have to do what she had done to him, and this was the fact that hurt, for it removed all reasons but that she had wanted to—and made of him from the beginning just a beast to satisfy her sexual urges, or perhaps a therapy to ease her personal hurt. The realization was like salt sprinkled in an open wound. By this she had denied him all the qualities of manhood—soul, mind, spirit, emotions, and honor—everything but just one organ. And she had done so at her pleasure.

This in the end became the greatest outrage—not so much what she had done, as that she would do it. It was this racial advantage all white women have over Negro men, to employ or not according to their whims. Outraged by the indignity that they should have this advantage; that in this predominantly masculine society the hammer of persecution over the male of the oppressed should be given to the female of the oppressors. It was this that completed his spiritual emasculation. First, Ruth, his own wife, could not see him as a man; and now Jackie, who could, would not.

For a moment he contemplated calling her and saying vile and abusive things over the telephone. But he knew this would not make a dent in her white soul and only bruise his own; and she would know why he had done it—this more than the other decided him against it.

His mind went back, moment by moment, over all the time he had spent with her to see where he had failed. Should he have shown less excitement over her body, or expressed more emotion over her music? The first time she had let him have her, he had cried, he recalled. Was it weakness, then, that had repelled her? Or was it that he, Lee Gordon, did not have a soul? Was that it? Was that what all these people looked for within him and could not find?

Suddenly in the groping torment of his thoughts his mind came face to face with Ruth. He saw her as he had at the bottom of the stairway leading down from Jackie's, and he was rooted to the spot, somewhere beside a hedge on a lonely street in Beverly Hills. Perhaps she did not think he had a soul, either. But she had loved him—the only woman who had ever loved him. And as his mind scanned the period of his life, he corrected—the second woman; his mother had been the first.

And now came the sudden gouging realization that not only had he tossed away her love, but he had been willing, anxious, and eager to destroy more. Beyond the irremediable damage of this, he had offered the complete destruction of their lives, like the bloody head of Saint John on the platter of Salome. Now in the shadow of a hedge in the beginning dawn, to realize that he had done this to Ruth was inconceivable. And what he had done it for was now incomprehensible.

Was there some capacity for self-destruction in the traditional status of Negro men which only white women could release? Was it this capacity that made every act of interracial sex a gamble for one's honor? Was it the challenge or the threat; or just the human impulse, planted in Eden, to seek the forbidden?

But at this cost? Was the simple fact of lying in a nude white woman's arms worth this much to him? Was it the mere white legs and pinkish brown nipples of her breasts? Certainly she was no more noble in her soul than the wife he'd abandoned—nor more beautiful physically.

Or was it pity that had taken him back to her; and only pity afterward instead of love? But that he could have felt such a degree of pity for a white woman as to destroy the love of his Negro wife would take no form but lunacy in his present state of mind.

The questions passing through his thoughts added to his despair. It was more; he knew it was more. If he had not loved her, he had wanted to, so very much. And now he felt an emptiness, a betrayal, a loss not so much of what had been, as of what might have been.

It started him on the move again, not toward a destination, but to a conclusion whereby he could live through the day. He lowered the stark chagrin in his eyes unconsciously to the ground and hurried on, each step a separate torture. Later, when the taste of salt came into his mouth, he knew that he was crying and put down his bag to wipe his eyes. But seeing the bag again brought the realization that he had left Ruth and his home and quit his job—and for what? Had it been just for this woman, who in the end was no more or less than she had been in the beginning?—white!

Now this question brought the conclusion he had sought but did not want: that he, Lee Gordon, was simply this kind of a nigger. He had never been anything but this kind of a nigger, and never would be; and all the rest had been just so much self-delusion.

He caught the Santa Monica red car back to town and rode the yellow "U" car over to a hotel at the lower end of Skid Row. Stepping out into the bright sunrise, livid against the early morning desolation of the now-closed joints and flophouses, he felt a sudden affinity with all the other unkempt, unshaven, dirty, bedraggled, desperately sober bums in sight. Here at last was where he belonged, he thought. He had been heading toward it for a long time. And now he had made it. For this was the end of the line for all those who did not embrace the color of their skins and live by it, he told himself with cynical self-deprecation.

He saw a cheap hotel and entered it and rented a room without a bath. Once for a fleeting moment he thought of Ruth and how it might have been with her; and of Jackie and how it had been with her. And in the doorway going out, some tattered remnant of the man he'd always wanted to be halted him for a moment's self-appraisal. When he began walking again he knew where he was going and what he was about to do.

Eight o'clock found him, now showered and shaved, waiting in the anteroom to Foster's office, with dull, glazed eyes in his thin, sagging face, and thoughts so low he could not look into them. Now he was on the slave block, the next logical step toward the completion of his degradation. He had put himself here of his own free choice, out of his own conclusion that to live in fair comfort, relieved of the necessity to protest, his sexual urges satisfied by those who made a business of it, was worth more than all the freedom and virtue he had attained or hoped to attain. Now in the end he recognized the simple fact of his inadequacy to cope with both life and race. No doubt there were many Negroes who could do both with honor and integrity—and did so. He did not know. He only knew that he was not among them.

Ruth had been right about Jackie, after all, Lee Gordon thought with sudden hurt.

If he could just get it out of his mind! He had begun it. And now, please, God, just let him go ahead and finish it without so much awful memory. His mind soared and flared as he struggled to clear it of the memory of Ruth's eyes when she had begged: "Just let me go and talk to her—"

Foster passed through the anteroom, drawing his attention. He half rose, but Foster's glance just briefly touched him and went on, and he sank down again.

After a time the receptionist informed him that Mr. Foster was busy and requested that he wait. Now once again the choice was given him. He could have risen and left—and tried again— How did that verse go, out of his past?

> I've stood alone, deserted,
> And sweat my heart's red blood.
> I've seen the waves of failure
> Engulf me in a flood.
> I've felt the throbs of error,
> I've seen my fortunes spin;
> But by the living God I swear
> I'll try again and win !

"But not for me," Lee Gordon thought. Now, by the simple alchemy of events, this job, which once would have meant a definite advancement, was an admission of failure. He admitted this in seeking it. Within himself he was through. Ruth had always known that he was nothing without her, he thought bitterly. And he was nothing.

At eleven o'clock Foster admitted him, smiling cordially across his desk.

"Good morning, Gordon. Have a seat."

"Good morning, Mr. Foster," Lee said nervously, groping for the seat.

"How is the organizing coming along? Do you have all of our workers signed up now?"

"I don't know. I'm not with them any more." And now the falter was in his voice again.

"You don't say? As I recall, you turned down a very nice offer I made to remain with the union."

"Yes, I did. But now—"

"You're through with them," Foster said. "I'm sorry to hear that. Did you differ with them on tactics or objectives?" Although his manner still retained its polished charm, now there was the slight indication of contempt in it.

"Well—tactics, I suppose," Lee replied. "They're a bunch of dirty, rotten double-crossers, and I got out!"

"Is that so? There was a young woman in my office who got into some sort of difficulty with the union and was expelled." His sharp blue eyes searched Lee's reaction. "Did you know about it?"

"That was one of the reasons I quit," Lee felt compelled to admit. "She was innocent. The Communists framed her."

"So I heard. Do the Communists control the union?"

"No, not yet—"

"But they are working toward that end?"

"Yes, I suppose they are."

"It would work a definite hardship on all of the employees if the Communists got control of the union," Foster said, as a threat more than a remark.

"I don't think they have much chance of getting control." Lee found himself defending them involuntarily.

"Perhaps not. They are an untrustworthy lot—but wily. There was a colored boy, a big black fellow who worked with you, I believe. McGregor." Foster chuckled over the name. "I always thought he was a Communist. Was he a union organizer?"

Now Lee knew that he was being baited, but there was no way out. "No, he didn't have any connection with the union. To tell you the truth, he's a Communist Party organizer. We just let him work with us because at that time we felt that his help was valuable."

"Oh, I see," and Foster's sharp blue glance penetrated. "It's the union policy to accept the aid of the Communists. That's rather dangerous, though, don't you think?"

"They didn't make a rule of it. They just used McGregor because they felt I needed some help with the Negro workers."

"They didn't object to subjecting the Negro employees to communistic propaganda."

"McGregor didn't have much opportunity to disseminate any propaganda. And anyway, he's through now."

"He is?" Foster showed a surprise which Lee felt certain was false. "Why?"

"Well— I don't know," Lee said, avoiding Foster's eyes. "He— well—just quit, I suppose."

"Smitty isn't a Communist, is he?" Foster shot the question.

It caught Lee unawares. "Oh, I don't think so; I couldn't be sure though."

"I've always considered Smitty a square shooter." Now he was suave. "I have the greatest respect for him."

"Well—yes. Smitty's all right."

"As I told you before, Gordon, I am not opposed to the union as long as it is a representative union of the employees and not a tool of the Communists."

"Well, I'm not opposed to the union, either," Lee said. "I just couldn't put up with the double-crossing tactics of the Communists in the union, along with some of the officials."

"What officials?"

"Well, Joe Ptak—"

"Is Joe a Communist?"

"I'm not sure. But he upheld them when they framed Miss Forks."

"Then he's a Communist or he would not have done it."

"Well, I don't know. I suppose so though. I hadn't thought of him as a Communist, but as you say, if he hadn't been, he wouldn't have upheld them."

"Gordon," Foster stated, "you will always know a man by the company he keeps."

"Well—" and that was as far as he could get, because what this made of him he would not think.

"Now what can I do for you?"

"Oh!" Now again caught unawares, he lost his sense of tact. "About the job! You remember—the job you mentioned. I wanted to talk to you about it. I—"

"At that time, Gordon, the job was open," Foster said, cutting him off. "But it is no longer available. Perhaps I can place you in the assembly department."

Well, that was the way it went, Lee Gordon thought dejectedly. When you were down to the level of the boot, the boot was for you.

Standing, he replied: "Well, thanks, but I have my mind set on some sort of office work. You see, I'm a college graduate."

"Yes, I know. It's difficult for you colored boys with education," Foster said sympathetically. "There are so few white-collar jobs which you can fill."

"Well, I'll look around for a while anyway." He turned to leave.

"Do you have any definite plans?" Foster stopped him.

"Well, no. If I don't find anything today, I think I'll leave the city."

"Give me your address, Gordon," Foster asked. "If I think of anything before the day is out, I'll get in touch with you."

As he gave him the address of his hotel, Lee thought that was the end of it, and went out into the day. Walking down the street to catch the bus back to town, he saw Joe Ptak from a distance. But though Joe saw him, Joe did not speak, nor did he.

The bars were now open on Skid Row and he turned into one. But after he had ordered the drink and it had been served, he was afraid to drink it. He was afraid now to affect in any way the structure of his emotions, afraid of what he might do afterward, or what might afterward be done to him. He paid the bartender, turned about, and went out, standing in the hot morning sun, absorbed in vacancy.

The first terrible hurt had now passed and the shock of his chagrin had worn to a thin, constant humiliation in the back of his mind, depressing but not compelling. And the despondency was yet to come. It was as if he were drugged, or entering into some mental state resembling amnesia where he had not so much actually forgotten who he was, as that it did not matter.

He went into a restaurant and ate—what, he never knew—and then over to Main Street to a cheap theater. Nothing of the picture, whatever it was, penetrated his walled-in mind. He sat there in growing discomfiture until the one thought stung him—but she was white at the beginning. Then he arose and went into the street again.

A streetcar came to a stop. He boarded it, and when it came to the end of the line at 51st Street and Hooper, he alighted and began walking through the afternoon sun. At Slauson, seven blocks distant, he turned west and continued until the sun was in his eyes. But at the end he was where he had begun. Nothing had changed but weariness. And yet, turning, he kept on walking, north now, because it had to change, because one goddamned man couldn't keep on like this. Something had to break—his body or his mind.

His tall, gaunt frame sagging from the pull of gravity, sweat-soaked from head to foot, he plodded on, bone-tired. His legs were artificial things, hacked off and unrelated to the dead weight of his torso; and his heavy, wet coat, which he had not taken off since morning, was a vile and horrible growth out of the marrow of his bones. He walked from Slauson and Jefferson boulevards in Culver City back to his hotel on Fifth Street, more than twenty miles.

Now he would have to sleep, he thought, climbing to his room and dropping fully dressed across the bed. But he did not sleep. The ghosts of all his failures and of all his fears and trepidations and inadequacies began parading through his mind, until he lay trembling in the shell of what he once had been.

Then suddenly be began seeing Ruth—Her coffee-colored nakedness and crown of curly hair; neck curved out to wide, full shoulders like a handstroke; breasts like twin hills in that golden haze before some sunsets. And a face like a pale brown Madonna's with a ripely bursting mouth. Stepping slowly from the dirty wallpaper with those dark condemning eyes. "All I ever wanted was just to love you, Lee." And the thought tore through his mind: "My God, baby doll, what have I done to you?"

And for what? What had he expected—the woman to marry him? Love, honor, and obey him—and raise his nigger children on crumbs and love? Had he expected her to fight with his Negro wife and take him bodily? Or had he been looking for something he thought only a white woman could give him? And giving it to him would make her immortal—"Thy immortal woman will hold thy hand. . . ."

As the questions buffeted through his thoughts, his emotions became distorted and ran together like white-hot glass so that he could not differentiate among them. He could not tell whom he hated or whom he loved. And in this state his despondency intensified until it became solid to the touch.

He began to cry—slowly at first, just a soft leak of tears from the river of his eyes, and then more rapidly, until his whole body shook with wracking sobs.

If she had ever known—or even if he, himself had known—that underneath all of his resentment, all of the things he had thought of her, he had been proud of her achievement and proud of her. He had been proud of her femininity, of her fidelity, and how much it had always given him, even though he had always known that he was never worth it. And now there was this thing she should know that she would never know. She would never know about his crying out his heart because of what he had done to her. He was suffering his bitterest moment of regret for having destroyed in her what had meant so much to him, neither of them having ever known it until the time had passed.

In the end he would dry his tears and rise and continue living, a dry and brittle shell of what he might have been, because he could not do this simple thing to bring their togetherness again— go to her and tell her that he had cried. He was restrained now by the Anglo-Saxon trait of emotional repression he had inherited. He was a Negro whom it did not fit, but he was bound by it as he was by all white traits he had inherited.

Chapter 27

SOMEONE knocked.

Lee Gordon rolled over and sat up. "Who is it?"

"Luther."

"Well—yes," Lee Gordon thought. This would be in logical sequence. "Just a minute," he called, going over to the corner basin to wash his face in cold water. Then he unlocked and opened the door.

"What do you want?"

"I don't want to see you no more than you do me, buddy boy," Luther muttered, his huge apelike body in tan slacks and a white T-shirt filling up the doorway, "but Foster sent me."

"So you're still working for Foster?"

"He still got money and I still ain't. Are you coming?"

"For what?"

"For to see a man and get some money."

"What do I have to do?"

"The man will tell you what to do."

For just a moment longer Lee hesitated, then he said: "Why not?"

Luther turned without a word and led the way. Lee climbed into the car beside him, and without further conversation they drove out to Inglewood and turned into a driveway beside a small stucco bungalow. A man in his shirt sleeves opened the back door to admit them.

"Come in, boys, come in."

As they entered a small, immaculate kitchen, Lee instantly recognized the man as Paul, one of the deputies who had beaten him, and felt suddenly trapped in a deep well of shame that he should come back begging this man for what he once had had the courage to refuse. In this upsurge of emotion he could not speak.

But Luther began Uncle-Toming from the start. "How's tricks, Mister Paul," he said with a servile grin.

"Tricks ain't walking," Paul replied, but gave his attention to Lee.

"Aw, you got everything, Mister Paul," Luther continued in a voice so ingratiating it was sickening to hear. "Why'oncha give a poor boy a break?"

But Paul ignored him and addressed his questions to Lee. "All healed up eh, boy? No scars, no bad feelings, eh?"

"No scars," Lee replied finally, succumbing to the pressure of Paul's stare.

"No bad feelings, eh?" Paul said persistently.

"No bad feelings," Lee said stolidly.

"Got a little sense now, eh?"

"Got a little sense," Lee mumbled.

"That's a good boy." Paul laughed and clapped him on the back.

Sick from the shame of submitting to this, Lee sat suddenly in the nearest chair.

Now that this crisis was past, Luther went straight to the business. "Mister Foster said you got a little job for us, Mister Paul."

"I got a little dough for you boys," Paul winked.

"Aw, dough!" Luther rubbed his hands. "Now that's my language. What'cha want us to do?"

"I'm just going to give you boys a little dough. You're good boys and I'm going to give you a little dough."

"How much you gonna give us, Mister Paul?" Luther's smile remained white in his greasy black face but his eyes became small and cunning. "You know times is tight and things is high. Dough ain't what it used to was."

"Sit down, goddammit!" Paul cried. "You make me nervous with all that nigger cringing. By God, I believe you'd kill your own mama for a little money."

Luther sat unsmiling and suddenly solemn. "Well, now, Mister Paul, you can't blame a man for liking money."

"Now that's better," Paul said. "I'm getting tired of your niggering all the time. You tryna make a fool out of me?"

"That's just my way, Mister Paul," Luther replied in a flat voice now. "You can't coon a man for his way. That's just my way to try to make everything fine and dandy. That's the way I like things to go."

"By God, things will go like I want 'em to go!" Paul said, sensing Luther's resentment and challenging it. "You got anything to say about that?"

"Me? Not me!" Luther said, ducking his head like an artful dodger. "Don't get me wrong, Mister Paul. I'm happy 'bout the whole thing."

"You'd better be!" Paul said, relaxing into his lordly manner now that Luther had begun to fawn again. Sitting at the head of the table, he took out his wallet. "Now I'm going to give you boys a little money and I want you boys to keep in touch with me. I'll have a little job for you boys in a day or so."

Opening the wallet, he extracted a flat stack of hundred-dollar bills and looked from one to the other with a sly, taunting look.

Luther gave a long, expressive whistle. "You gonna give us all that money, Mister Paul?"

"What would you do for this much money, Luther?"

"Ain't no telling what I wouldn't do!"

Paul laughed, then looked at Lee. "How about you, boy?"

"Well—it looks like quite a bit of money," Lee forced himself to say, rapidly reaching the limit of his subservience.

"Quite a bit of money, he says! Boy, this money would buy you all the gals on Central Avenue!"

To that Lee made no reply, feeling the slow growth of heat in his brain.

"How much of that we gonna get?" Luther asked into the pause.

Paul slapped the bills against the table. "I'm going to give you boys one hundred dollars each."

"That all, Mister Paul?" Luther said, whining in his disappointment. "All that money and you just gonna give us a hundred dollars!"

"That's what I said."

"You know, Mister Paul, that ain't right. A hundred dollars ain't no money at all. I bet you got a hundred of them bills in that stack."

Paul laughed. "Just fifty, Luther."

"Fifty! And you gonna give us one apiece! That ain't right, Mister Paul. You oughta at least give us five apiece."

"I said one!"

"One! You expect me to do all this dirty work for one lousy hundred bucks!" There was the subtle hint of danger in Luther's changed voice.

But Paul scorned it as he jumped to his feet, a hot flush reddening his features. "Don't you argue with me!" he said warningly. Leafing two bills from the stack, he tossed them to the table. "Do you want it or don't you?"

Luther looked from Paul to the bills and slowly reached out and picked one up. "I suppose we gets some more when the job is done?"

"That's right. That's when you get some more."

Luther turned the single bill between his fingers as his greasy black features settled into flatness. But he said no more and did not look up.

Nor did Lee speak as he sat looking at the lone bill left on the table top, hoping with all his heart that Paul would not demand that he accept it or he would have to hit him.

But Paul had gotten over his moment of irritation and grinned at them again. "You boys look hot and thirsty. How about a cold bottle of beer?"

"Beer, did you say?" Luther began Uncle-Toming again, but now there was a difference.

"How about you, Gordon?"

"Well—thanks."

As Paul turned toward the icebox, Luther asked: "How's the missus, Mister Paul? Hope we ain't disturbing her."

"She's out," Paul replied shortly, bending over the open icebox to reach for the bottles of beer.

The instant Paul's back was turned, the curtain of submissiveness dropped from Luther's face and malevolence stood out with the shock of sudden nakedness. His neck roped like a growth of blackened roots and his thick white-shirted torso knotted with muscles. Abruptly he was caught up, metamorphosed, embodied with a violence that shed evil like rays of light.

Clutched in a presentiment of horror, Lee opened his mouth to cry a warning but it stuck in his throat like a rock. For before his startled vision, paralyzing his vocal cords, Luther rose like a great black monster, shook open a switch-blade knife, and stabbed Paul in the left side of the back, reaching for his heart. He saw Paul's body snap taut. A vacuum-tight concentration sealed his mind. He saw Luther stab Paul twice rapidly, low down on the right side. He heard Paul grunt. He watched him put his hand flat against the icebox and strike back with the other as he tried to straighten up.

Each stark detail poured into his consciousness to be forever etched in memory. But his mind would not take it, would not rationalize, would not perform.

"Mother—!" he heard Luther curse with an animal sound as he stabbed Paul in the side of the neck. He saw the muscles of Paul's neck tighten with the stab, saw the blood spurt in a geyser, saw his body strain to straighten and turn. He heard Paul's last gasped words, half cursing, half begging: "You don't have to kill me, you black son of a bitch!"

The next time Luther stabbed, the blade snapped off against Paul's spine, and Paul's body, like some gory gargoyle, began slowly crumpling to the floor. As Lee watched him fall dying, he saw his tremendous effort to live, and from behind his wall of nausea, came an icy trickle of horror down into his soul.

Then he saw only the blood—over and above all else the blood —surging down on reason in a gory flood. Blood welled through the white shirt, spurting from the white neck, over the floor and the icebox and on the side of the stove, splotching Luther's white T-shirt and slacks, dripping from his arm, clotting on his black greasy skin. And the smell of blood—sickish, sweetish, cloying scent—rooted him, nailed him rigid to the spot.

But when the body ceased to twitch and death came to what a few short moments before had been a man, it let him go. And now his mouth made chewing motions as he bit back the screams coming from his stomach.

Luther turned to look at him, huge and black and bloody, his flat face enigmatical but his muddy eyes menacing. Panic exploded in Lee's mind. He kicked back the chair, overturning it, and started toward the door.

"If you touch that door I'll kill you!"

The flat voice reached out and halted him, chained him in abject terror. He jerked back his hand, turned, trembling, fighting for control.

"Come over here and sit down!"

Charmed by the menace in the muddy eyes, he gave up his will, came forward and sat down as if to his own death.

"Now don't lose your goddamn head!"

In Luther's eyes Lee saw his own life hanging in the balance. He wanted to beg for mercy but could not speak. Fear had paralyzed his vocal cords and turned his breath rock-hard. But his thoughts ran on, down the dark line of irrevocability, his own imminent murder no less an actuality than the dead man on the floor. He could see Luther advancing, stabbing him in the chest, the throat, the heart. He could see his own blood spurting out his life, and knew that in his absolute terror he could not move a muscle to protect himself. He did not want to die like this, mutilated, without defense, black in a gory pool in this alien atmosphere. But still he could not speak.

And finally the murderous intent went from Luther's muddy eyes and in its place came urgency. Hurried but not hasty, Luther began to move, his actions as calculated as an automaton. Washing his knife in the sink, he returned it to his pocket and let the faucet run, wetting a towel. Soaping the towel, he tossed it to Lee.

"Wash the furniture, everything," he commanded. "Don't leave no fingerprints nowhere."

As Lee moved dumbly to obey, Luther squatted and took the wallet from Paul's pocket. Attracted by Lee's panicky haste, he glanced up and quickly cautioned, "Slow down! Slow down! Now's the time to take it easy. Get all them prints washed off. This son of a bitch is dead."

Unemotional and undisturbed as a man without a soul, without senses, without a nervous system, moving through a world where there was no retribution, no right, no wrong, no God, he looked about for a mop, and finding none, went through the doorway into the next room.

Out from underneath the domination of Luther's muddy eyes, Lee's flaccid subjection became panic again. He could not keep his eyes from Paul's bloody body. From outside, each sound in the night plucked at him and sent cold tremors of terror down his spine. Steps on the sidewalk, the distant barking of a dog, the sound of a motor, and the short, sharp laugh from somewhere close raked him raw, exploding in his mind the driving impulse to run again. And then he was running blindly and cravenly—but only in his mind. His body had not yet begun to move when Luther returned, naked to the waist, his black torso washed clean of blood and his muscles roping in the light. Lee's arm jerked with a reflex action and he struck himself in the mouth.

"How you coming?" Luther asked, swinging a dripping bath towel from his hand.

Finally, desperately, Lee found his voice. "All right."

"You get the chairs, the table, the door?"

"I haven't got the door yet."

"You get the walls?"

Lee shook his head.

"Get the walls too. And take it easy. Ain't no hurry. 'Cause what you do now gonna mean everything later on."

Lee nodded and went to work again. Fear had wired his mind so tight that now he was unaware of all his minor actions, and later was never able to recall what he did then. When he had finished washing down the walls, Luther said: "Take off your shoes."

Lee sat on the floor and took off his shoes.

Along with his own, Luther placed them beside the door. "Now you stand here too," he ordered Lee.

As Lee moved to obey, Luther wiped the floor with the wet towel then stood for a moment scanning the room. "Now get them shoes," he told Lee, "and when I turn out the light you go set in the car and don't move."

When the light went out, Lee did as directed while Luther washed the outside of the door, wiped the stoop, then backing to the car on his hands and knees, wiped off the entire sidewalk. He backed the car into the street, cut off the motor, got out, and went back and scoured the tire tracks from the pavement of the driveway.

"Jesus Christ!" Lee was whispering over and over to himself when Luther climbed back beneath the wheel.

"Shut up!" Luther said in a gritty voice. Unhurriedly he took his pistol from the glove compartment and stuck it in his waist band, then searched about until he found a soiled T-shirt, which he put on.

Driving back into the city at a steady twenty-five, he turned east on Washington Boulevard and drew to a stop in the dark deserted stretch beyond Sante Fe. Standing in the dark beside the car, he changed his slacks to a pair of greasy overalls he found in the luggage compartment, then got in and drove to the burning dump a half mile ahead and tossed his blood-stained clothes into the smoldering fire. From there he drove out to Belvedere and parked in a dark alley in the densely populated Mexican community.

"Now you can put on your shoes," he said to Lee, putting on his own, and when they had finished, he said: "Get out."

With the blood-stained bath towel he had brought from Paul's house, he wiped the instrument panel, steering wheel, and door handles, thoroughly and unhurriedly, and dropped the towel on the street.

"So he thought I'd sell my mama out," he said, showing his first sign of emotion.

Lee had not spoken since Luther had ordered him to shut up; he did not speak now because his mind was a blank and words had no meaning to him.

"Come on, let's get back to Hollywood," Luther said and turned to leave.

Long since, Lee had ceased to have a will, and when Luther moved, he moved as though he were a puppet controlled by Luther's will. Falling in beside Luther, he walked along in a daze, turning when Luther turned, stepping aside when Luther stepped aside. The fear was there within him, filling him, and outside him, encasing him. But with the stopping of thought, panic had gone. And as yet, as he moved automatically through the city night, thought had not begun again, and the panic lay dead.

In silence they walked down First Street to Rowan and stopped to await the streetcar. And in silence, sitting and standing side by side, they rode the long journey across town and climbed the stairs to Mollie's.

Mollie let them in, laughing suddenly at sight of Lee. "My God, when have you eaten last?" she greeted him.

"Shut up," Luther said and closed the door. Then he ordered her: "Call the police and report your car stolen sometime this afternoon."

"What happened to it?" she asked, suddenly sober.

"Nothing," Luther replied, then told Lee: "Sit down, sit down, you safe now, man."

As he went into the kitchen and took down from the cupboard a bottle of brandy, drinking long and noisily from the bottle's neck. Mollie followed him with her questioning gaze. Finally he came back into the room with the bottle in his hand and stood looking at her.

"I killed the son of a bitch," he said.

At the sound of his words and the sight of Mollie's red face growing bloodless white, Lee's mind was freed and his panic returned, overwhelming him. The muscles of his face began to tremble, and then his hands and finally his entire body shook as with the ague.

"Here, take a drink of this," Luther said, crossing with the bottle in his hand.

Lee reached for it, trembling, clutched the bottle, and tilted it, spilling brandy down his chin. As the fiery liquor struck his throat, he coughed and strangled. It was the sight of him that finally impressed Mollie with the enormity of Luther's announcement and released her from the senseless shock. Now she began cursing as a woman gone insane.

"You dirty, vicious, depraved maniac! Foul, filthy beast! And a fool! You've always been a fool! You and your stinking comrades! Unwashed, thieving, lying, cheating, murdering scum! A Communist! Yes, you're a Communist! All you vicious bastards! I'm tired of you! And all your nigger Communist mess! Pulling me down with you! With the rest of you self-befouling swinish degenerates! Black, filthy nigger! Get out! Get out of my house! Both of you! You murdering nigger beasts! You—"

It was not until her voice began rising on a hysterical note that Luther spoke. "Shut up!"

"Don't you dare tell me to shut up!" she screamed. "I'll—"

"Do I have to cut your throat too, woman?"

The cold, flat deadliness of his voice hushed her and gripped her in a sinister fascination that became sexual in quality as the hot blood flushed through her abrupt rigidity. She was ready again to lose herself in sensuality, because what the coarse animal brutality of this nigger did to her was more than any drug. It intensified the perceptions of her five senses to a sexual grotesqueness, where the merest touch of his hand upon her body produced a sensation either acutely exciting or nauseating—an aphrodisiac stimulant either way. And at such times the warm velvety surfaces of his arms could feel as delicious as silk against her fingers, and the rough texture of his kinky hair could leave the sensation of a bruise. The whiteness of his teeth, the yellowness of his eyes, the redness of his tongue, and the blackness of his skin became writhing hues in her frenetical ecstasy, and the animal sounds of his chewing exploded against her eardrums like the beating of tom-toms—building up this constant laugh of sexual bliss until at times she thought her guts would retch completely out. Now it was with an effort that she suppressed the laugh within her and prepared to face the emergency, as from the first she had known she must, as she had always known that there would be emergencies she would have to face, living with this physically dangerous nigger.

Carrying the telephone by its long extension cord, she went into the bedroom and closed the door.

After emptying the money on the table, Luther got a pair of scissors and methodically sliced the wallet into tiny slivers that he took into the bathroom and flushed down the toilet.

"Them's the little things that hang you," he remarked as he returned into the room.

For a moment he stood looking at the money, deep in contemplation, then slowly began dividing it into separate stacks. "It was me who killed the son of a bitch," he said, "so I'll take three fourths and give you one fourth. That's fair enough, ain't it?"

Now with the brandy and the sound of voices thought had returned to Lee, along with his consuming fear. He had seen a man murdered, and it had changed almost everything of his conception of life and death. In this fear it had made life itself just another bridge between two voids, but it had made the voids themselves so awful. But the horror of death made life no less dreadful, only more meaningless. And money was as nothing—to take or to refuse. Yet he did not want the money, because deep within him was still something that did not want inclusion in a murder.

So finally he said: "I don't want any."

With one quick, final gesture Luther bunched the stacks again. "You is a fool," he said. "Not only is you a fool but you is a square and a *lain* and a *do'*. The *peck* is dead, man, he's dead. And if we get caught they gonna kill you and me just as dead as he, and probably kill you first 'cause you ain't gonna have no money to fight it with."

"Maybe so," Lee Gordon said. "But I just don't want any of the money."

For a moment Luther studied him. "You're not thinking 'bout squealing, are you, man?" And again in his voice was that hint of deadliness.

"I'm not going to squeal," Lee told him fearfully. "You don't have to worry about that."

"I ain't worrying, man," Luther said in that cold, flat voice. "I'm just tryna make up my mind whether I'd be better off killing you now. 'Cause it don't make me no difference whether you're dead or 'live, so long as you don't try to kill me, too. That's what I'm tryna figger. If your conscience tells you to go down and 'fess, I may as well kill you as the state and try to keep on living myself."

Again in those muddy, menacing eyes, Lee saw his life tip over, but this time it did not frighten him. "You can kill me if you want to; I don't give a goddamn," he said. "I'm not going to squeal, no, I'm not going to do that. But you don't scare me any more because I don't give a goddamn whether you kill me or not. I've got nothing to live for anyway."

Luther continued to look at Lee with a sort of blind, frustrated fury, holding down the impulse to kick him in the mouth. "It's just you I'm thinking about, you goddamned fool!" The words burst from his lips.

He liked this kid. He had never liked anyone as he liked this kid, not even his own mama. And the simple son of a bitch didn't even know that he was trying to help him. So damn him! To hell with him! Let him take his own damn bumps! Luther thought. And mine too! Let him front his way on up to San Quentin and suck up all that fine gas they kept up there for fools. And see what his university education and his white folks' ethics did for him—

But when his sudden wave of anger had subsided, he still liked the kid. He could not help it, because inside of himself Luther was the kind of black man who, accepting the fact that he himself was only a nigger, admired another black man whom he thought intelligent and smart, who could compete with white folks at their own game and outslick them at their own count. The way he figured it, such a Negro should be smarter than any white man who ever breathed, having gotten the white folks' education and know-how from the white folks, their own damn selves, on top of all the nigger wisdom that had been kicked up his black ass. Even while trying to control Lee as Bart had directed, he had always been willing just to follow in his steps, be behind him, support him, or cut a son of a bitch's throat for him. Even when the deputies had cornered them, if the kid had just kept quiet, he'd have dug an out. For the way he felt about this kid was that peculiar, almost virgin love that the Negro hustler and criminal sometimes feels for the young, ambitious, educated Negro with sense enough to know the score—a sort of inverted hero worship that led them on to back these youths in what they did, as if it would make themselves bigger, more important men.

But Luther never thought of his feelings for Lee in just this way. All he knew was that he'd always liked the kid. And even now he did not fully understand exactly why—only that Lee was a nigger, and he was a nigger, too.

If Lee had been one shade lighter Luther would have framed him from the start. It had been his intention to do so when, sitting at the table in Paul's kitchen, he had first conceived the murder in his mind. But Lee's dark skin had saved him. He just could not frame a black boy for a white murder.

And even now, with Lee rejecting his proffered loyalty, spurning the money for which he, Luther, had murdered a man, Lee's color was still too black for Luther to take the next logical step, which would be to kill him too.

"You want half?"

"I told you I don't want any," Lee said, again refusing the offer.

"The trouble with you is you don't know yet you're a nigger." This was not so much in condemnation as with regret.

"I might be a nigger but I'm not a murderer."

"Maybe not the way you sees it. But they ain't gonna see it your way down in Civic Center."

"I don't care how they see it."

"Look, man, lemme tell you! My white folks are gonna cover me. You know why? 'Cause they know I'm a nigger and think in front that I'd do anything. And 'cause that's what they think they also think that if they le'e' me take this bump, or any other bump, that I'd take everybody with me I could take, and tell all I know and a lot I don't even know. Now what your white folks gonna do for you?"

"I haven't got any white folks and I haven't done anything."

"Look, man, just what is your objection?" Luther asked. Even a strange nigger on the street would take money from a dead peckerwood's pocket, he believed.

"Well—I just wouldn't kill a man for money," Lee said, trying to explain. "And if I took this money it'd be just the same as if I had."

"This man was a white man," Luther said as if that settled it. "He'd kill you for fun."

"But I wouldn't kill him unless I just had to."

"Then you is a fool. I never knew before just how much a fool you is."

What Lee could not understand was that to Luther the killing of a white man was not a murder, but a deed. And after the man was dead the deed was done—gone from his conscience like the swatting of a fly. Afterward the only thing to be considered was the avoiding of detection.

But to Lee, it was the same as any murder. So now he said: "Well—I'm a fool. But I'm not a murderer."

And now in self-defense Luther felt compelled to make an explanation that he had never thought he would even try. "Look, man, do you call it murder when you kill a man in this war?"

"I don't want to argue, Luther. I just don't want any money, that's all," Lee Gordon said. "I just want to sit here for a while and then I'm going to go."

"Look, man, goddamn, for all your education, they's a lot of things that you don't seem to know. In this goddamn world they's all kind of wars always going on and people is getting kilt in all of them. They's the races fighting 'gainst each other. And they's the classes cutting each other's throats. And they's every mother's son fighting for hisself, just to keep on living. And they's the nigger at the bottom of it all, being fit by everybody and kilt by everybody. And they's me down there at the bottom of the bottom. I gotta fight everybody—the white folks and the black folks, the capitalists and the Communists, too. And now I even gotta fight you. 'Cause everybody's looking out for theyself. Trying to get what they want. And cutting everybody else's throat. So I cuts me some throat, too.

"Look, you think I's a Communist. Sure, I 'longs to the party. But I is a nigger first. The party's realistic 'bout this business. They's realistic 'bout me. And I is realistic 'bout them. They done learned me, but they ain't won me. 'Cause I is looking out for Luther first. And if I is got any more looking out left, I is looking out for some other nigger like me second.

"Just like you always knew, I been taking Foster's money right straight along. And taking money from the party. And from my ol' lady too. And selling 'em all out. 'Cause why? 'Cause they is white. 'Cause to Foster I ain't nothing but a nigger. Ain't never gonna be nothing but a nigger. He gonna use me as a nigger to get what he wants. And the party gonna do the same. Only difference is I gets more from being a nigger for the party than being a nigger for Foster. But they both use me as a nigger in the same damn way. Work me today and sell me out tomorrow. Say I is a good boy and then double-cross me. What I wants don't count to neither one of 'em. And my ol' lady is the same. So I gets what I wants the best way I can.

"A few years back folks like Foster was selling out the nigger. Couldn't even get a nigger's job from the bastards. Today they's patting me on the back. 'Cause why? 'Cause they can use a few niggers now. Now they's the party. Yesterday wasn't nothing too good for a nigger in the party. Goddamn, all you'd a-thought the party was for was just to bow down and worship at the niggers' feets. Today they want something else. They done sold the nigger out. But if'n I can help it, don't nobody sell Luther out. 'Cause I sells 'em out first. I been taking dough from Foster and being a nigger for him. Now I done killed his stooge and tooken all the money. And what's he gonna do to me. Nothing! If you don't watch out he'll get your ass. But he ain't gonna bother with me. He gonna know I done it but he ain't gonna say one word. 'Cause if he do I is gonna tell everybody I been taking his money to double-cross the union. And he don't want that known. Then I is gonna turn 'round and tell everybody what I been doing and that the party knew about it and let me do it. So they gonna try to cover up for me too. 'Cause they don't want that known, neither.

"And I can do this 'cause I is a nigger. And I know I is a nigger. And what I do don't make no difference noway. It's what I know the people does to me that worries 'em.

"Do you think I love the Party? Or even believe in it? What the hell does I know about Marx? Or give a damn 'bout him? But I knows how to be a nigger and make it pay. If I can't make it pay one way I makes it pay the other. 'Cause if the white folks wants some niggers, let 'em pay for us.

"You and your idealism. A nigger with some idealism. Who is your ideal, George Washington? You gonna be like Washington, is you? You ain't gonna tell no lie? And what's it gonna get you? Look, I got the money. Not just a few lousy dollars what Foster thinks is all a nigger wants. But all of it. And I done gotten even, too. Even for that business back there on the road. All they done to you was sap you a little bit. But they ground me down. I couldn't take the sapping 'cause I ain't never taken one and now ain't no time to start. But I couldn't take the grinding neither. So now I got the money. And I got even. And I got my good old Communist Party. And I got my white woman. Plenty money and a white woman, too.

"Now what the hell you got? Nothing! Not even your idealism. If it don't be for me you'd 'a sold that too. And you ain't got nothing else to sell. You done quit your job. And your white chick done quit you. And you even lost your wife. Which only a weak-minded nigger would do for any white woman. 'Cause you ain't got to. You ain't expected to. They don't even want you to. All they wanna do is borrow you. Use you like Foster and the party does. Not marry you, man. All they wanna do is get their kicks. So get yours, man, like they does theirs. But here you go and let a little white stuff go to your head and make a damn fool out your-self.

"Join the party, man, and get all the white stuff you can handle. It ain't nothing but another hole, man, goddamn! Ain't nothing special 'bout it. And they's more of it than any other kind. They wanna give it to you, man. They solving the problem then. Your problem and they problem and everybody's problem.

"So do you thinks I gives a damn about the party. Look, man, as long as I is black and ugly white folks gonna hate my guts. They gonna look at me and see a nigger. All of 'em. Foster and the white folks in the party and the white women in the bed. But I is gonna always make it pay off, man, just as you could if you had any sense. 'Cause as long as I is black and ugly, the party gonna need me. I is gonna be they proof. Whatever they might do to all the other niggers I is the proof that they don't mean it. I is the proof that they always got the nigger to their heart. So that's why they gonna see to it I keeps my white womens. If it ain't this one it'll be another one. And they gonna make out like to me as if they thinks I is equal. And they gonna think I ain't. And I ain't gonna give a damn what they thinks. 'Cause I is gonna be they nigger, and they proof. And make 'em pay for it.

"Yes, I killed the bastard. And now I got more money than you ever had. Simple-minded sonsabitches like you will sell your stink-ing guts because you ain't never admitted to yourself that you're a nigger and never will be nothing else. But as long as I can help it, I ain't gonna let you do it and run the price on niggers down. 'Cause even if you is a nigger and don't know it yet, you don't have to be as cheap a nigger as Foster thinks you is."

"Well—yes," Lee Gordon said, and arose and left the house.

Maybe that was it, he thought—the one thing lacking about which all the misplaced emotions of his life would fit. Maybe it all came down to his being a nigger and never knowing it. But even if he was a nigger, what did they expect, for him to like it so? Was that what Ruth expected: for him to be her half-a-man and make her happy?; and Jackie: for him to be her black pimp and she his white whore? Maybe she had really wanted that, and he had been too much a fool to know it. But Foster? It was not reasonable that Foster should expect him to rat for a hundred dollars when he had refused the five-thousand-dollar-a-year job that had been offered him. Was that what a nigger was to Foster? At least he knew what Luther expected of him—to be a man without a soul. The white people had always said a nigger didn't have a soul, and Luther proved them right. Yes, maybe Luther was the only right one after all. For he, Lee Gordon, felt more like the murderer for having seen it done than did Luther who had done it. Being a murderer to Luther was just being a nigger after all, since being a nigger was being anything.

But still he didn't want the money. Only now he was able to realize that he would need it.

And now again without awareness of his direction, he had come to Jackie's door. But this time he knew what hidden impulse had brought him here: Luther's talk of his white folks. So this was his, Lee Gordon's, white folks—in the singular—one white woman who had gone to bed with him one day and put him out the next.

Well, why not? he asked himself, since now he had another presentation to catch her passing fancy—Lee Gordon, the murderer, the living example of what she had made of him. So he went in and walked up and rang her bell.

"Who is it?"

"Lee."

"Oh!—Lee!—Lee, what do you want now?"

"I want to talk to you."

"Haven't we said everything, Lee?"

"Open the door. I'm in trouble."

"Oh!"

She let him in as he had known she must—as any white woman would have to do for a Negro man in trouble with whom she had slept. But when she saw the fear in him, she wished to heaven she had not.

"What is it now, Lee?" she asked, hastening to close the door behind him. "Have you been fighting your wife?"

He went into the kitchen and looked about. Finding no liquor, he returned and sat on the davenport, beginning to tremble again.

"I'm going to stay here tonight," he said.

"You can't, Lee! You know you can't!"

"I have to!"

"Haven't you got any place to stay?" Her hands made nervous

gestures as she stood looking down at him, distaste etched in the fine-drawn lines of her face. "Have you left home, Lee?"

"It isn't that. I need an alibi."

A shudder passed over her body as she cried: "Oh, God, Lee. Have you hurt your wife? Have you killed her?"

"I—I—" He took a breath and said: "I saw a man killed tonight." And now he was crying, cravenly, abjectly, despairingly.

She fell to her knees beside him and shook him violently, furiously, scarcely restraining the impulse to beat him in the face. "Lee! Lee!" she screamed at him, her white face drawn in ugliness. "Lee! Lee! Goddamn you! Oh, goddamn you! What did you do now?"

And now the words came, pouring from him, overflowing, surging from his lips. He told her everything that had happened to him from the time he had left her house: of his dejection, humiliation, chagrin, of his scene with Ruth, of his despondency, of seeing Foster, and Foster's words, of Luther's visit, and Luther's words, the ride to Paul's, and Paul's words, and the words that Paul had said when he fell dying. He told her everything but what Luther had said to him at the very last. He did not know as he was telling her why he should tell her this—only that he had to share it, for it was more than he could carry. Someone had to help him with it, if no more than to listen. And now in the end, as at the beginning, he had come to acknowledge her supremacy, but of this he was unaware. Nor did she in her fear recognize it as an acknowledgment. Now their fear together was a solid thing, unbearable to them both.

"Goddamn you, Lee!" she cried, jumping to her feet. "I can't let you stay here!"

"I'm going to stay anyway," he said without moving or looking up at her. "And you're going to say I've been here all the time."

Out of sheer desperation she struck a sympathetic pose. "I want to, Lee. You know I want to. But I can't. Don't you understand?"

"This is one time you won't get out of it," he said dully.

"You hate me now, don't you?" she said softly, with tears in her voice.

"Well—yes, I think I do hate you," he replied honestly.

"Oh, Lee, please don't hate me!" she cried, for she was genuinely hurt.

"If it hadn't been for you, I wouldn't be in this trouble now," he said accusingly.

"But I didn't force you into it, Lee. I begged you to go back to Ruth. Oh, God, Lee, I didn't want you to quit your job. Don't you remember?"

"But you played with me," he went on relentlessly, for now it didn't matter. "And then you kicked me out."

"I didn't know you'd quit your job, Lee, and break off with your wife. Honestly, I didn't. I didn't want you to. Please believe me, Lee."

"But you could have known it, Jackie, knowing how I felt. It was just because you didn't give a damn that you didn't know it."

The grinding nonchalance of his accusations brought tears into her eyes. "Please don't say that, Lee, please," she begged. For she had not wanted to hurt him so! God knows she hadn't!

"I say it because it's true," he said in his dull, impassioned voice. "But I don't give a damn now, Jackie. You be whatever kind of bitch you want to be. But tonight you're going to alibi me."

"Lee, please believe me. Please, Lee," she said, sobbing and falling to her knees before him and raising her tear-stained face. "Look at me, Lee. Please look at me and say you believe me. I'm not bad. Not really bad. I've been mixed up and excited and have done a lot of things I wouldn't have. But I'm not really bad. I'm not the kind of person you think I am. If I hadn't been so all mixed up and hurt I never would have let you live with me. I never would have even gone to bed with you if I hadn't been a Communist. Please don't hurt me, Lee. I never meant to hurt you."

"But you did hurt me," he said, looking deep into her tear-filled eyes. "That's the difference, Jackie."

"Please don't, Lee!" she cried, clutching him by the trouser legs. "Please let's talk about it. If you really didn't have anything to do with Luther's m-m-murdering the man, go to the police and tell them the truth."

"You know what they would do to me, Jackie."

"They'd believe you, Lee. They'd have to."

"You know they wouldn't, Jackie. You know why they wouldn't. You know I'm a nigger, Jackie. That's why you put me out."

She flinched as if he had struck at her. "Please don't say that, Lee."

"It's the truth, Jackie. And you may as well face the truth: I'm a nigger. And nobody will believe anything I say. But if you say I've been here all the time, they might believe you—because you're white."

"Please don't do this to me, Lee. Please!"

"Face it, Jackie! Face it! Goddammit, I had to face it!"

Slowly, in resignation, she arose. "You're making me do this against my will, Lee," she finally said, "and I will always hate you for it."

Before she turned her eyes away, Lee Gordon stopped her, because now he had to know. "Jackie, I'd like to ask you something. What could I have done that would have made it different?"

Now the tears welled up again. "It couldn't have been any different, Lee. You know it couldn't have been."

"There was nothing I could have done—"

"Nothing, Lee."

"Then what did you expect from me?"

"Lee, please go. Please, Lee."

"I will go if you tell me this. Was there any way for me to have made you love me?"

"Lee, please. You're making me hate you now."

"You hate me anyway, Jackie, so hate me still," he said, and stretched out on the davenport.

Later, from sheer exhaustion, he dozed. She called the police. When they came for him she let them in before he was aware of what was happening. Thin-lipped and tight-faced, with the harsh determination ravaging the beauty of her features, she told them the story he had told her of Paul's murder. She told it precisely, coldly, and unhesitatingly, without once looking at him.

And as he sat on the davenport, listening, looking at the harshness of her face, he wondered how he had ever thought he loved her. He did not see her acute suffering beneath her ruthless shell, and he never knew how much it hurt her to do what she had done. He saw only this thing she was doing to him and he hated her for it. But now at last he realized that she would no more have given him an alibi than she would have appeared at a divorce trial against his Negro wife; that no matter what she might do in private, publicly she would always support the legend of her superiority—because in the end she would always find race her strongest emotion.

Without a word he arose and went out with two of the officers, while the third remained to bring her down to sign a statement. At police headquarters he was grilled for hours. But not once did he open his mouth to speak. It did not matter what they did to him, for all there was of him that could be hurt was already dead. Finally he was beaten with leaded hose into unconsciousness.

Chapter 28

FOR the first hour following Lee's departure, Ruth soothed her screaming nerves in a lukewarm bath. Then she went into the bedroom and lay uncovered in the cool darkness, telling herself over and over and over that she would not worry, would not think about it. He had returned to Jackie's but he would never be happy there. He would never be happy anywhere for what he had done to her. And someday soon when the novelty wore off, Jackie would tire of him and put him out. And that was the end of Lee Gordon as far as she was concerned, she told herself. For she would never take him back, no matter how he came. No matter if he came crawling down the street on his naked belly, with his bleeding heart held out before him in atonement, she would not take him back. Never!

He had not done this thing to her out of any feeling that she deserved it, but instead had offered it as a sacrifice before the shrine of this white slut. All of her highest hopes and ambitions and aims, and his own—whatever they were or ever hoped to be— and eight years of actual marriage, of those sacred peaks of happiness, caught and remembered, and those moments of togetherness, of themselves worth being born, had been sacrificed to lust. In the end, it was not so much the fact of fornication with this white woman, but what he had been willing and felt constrained to pay—not only of himself, but of herself, of racial evaluation itself, as homage to her white skin, making of a casual sexual fancy more than the highest honor, verily, a religious rite. And for this he would wear sackcloth and ashes the remainder of his days. For he would come back to her, she told herself. When the white scent had turned putrid in his nostrils and the scales had fallen from his eyes and he would see and smell the rottenness and falseness of the idol he had worshipped, he would come crawling back to beg for her forgiveness. But she would never take him back. Never!

But as the unsleeping hours beat at the iron of her control, it softened and wore away. For what did it matter that he had swapped all she had to offer for just six nights in a white woman's bed? What did it matter if he put every white woman who walked the streets above herself? What did it matter that in the end he had turned out to be a horrible, vicious thing whom she could not pity, but only despise? She loved him!—and could not live without him. In all her life she had never known another man. Once she had been so proud of having brought this to their bridal bed, but now she was ashamed that he had ever had it. But that did not change the fact: she had loved him in the beginning, and now at the end she still loved him. This, she could not help.

Dressing, she walked through the noonday sun to the corner drugstore and purchased a bottle of bichloride of mercury tablets and a bottle of sleeping tablets. She did not want to commit suicide. She just did not want to live any more and did not know of any way to do it otherwise. Back in the house, she made a solution of the bichloride of mercury tablets, but at the last moment was restrained from drinking it by the thought of how her suicide would affect Lee. She did not want to hurt him now. She had hurt him as much, and more, than it was in her heart to do. And he would hurt himself much more than she ever could.

But she had to go away, if only for a little while. The brief walk in the hot sun had begun a headache, already grinding down on her nerves. And her misery and despair had rooted in her brain. She had to get away, just had to. So she made a solution of all the sleeping tablets in the bottle and drank that, hoping that she would sleep for a long, long time.

She did not sleep. Instead she entered into a twilight stage of mental anguish. Her torture became part of her metabolism, paralyzing her body and corroding her mind. She lay writhing on the floor for several hours, gasping for breath. But it passed, and she arose, alarmingly weak, hanging on the border line of sanity, right back where she had started, hoping she could die. Neither thirsty nor hungry, but now moved by a nervous despair, she prowled about the house, from room to room, from door to window, lacerating her misery with the uncontrollable memory of her vision and cutting her heart to pieces with her undead hope. It was then she knew she had to die, now not because she wanted to, but because now she could no longer live.

But she could not go leaving Lee the slightest doubt but that she had always loved him. In her bedroom she sat down and wrote:

DEAR LEE:
My love for you is the same as it was when I first held you in my arms but time has changed and we with it and I find I cannot bear to live without you any more. I love you even now so much I cannot stand it and I am glad you loved me too one time.

I think God will understand why I can't live any more. Please put me away very quietly. Do not come to see me put away unless you regret every detail of your affair. Do not grieve for me, Lee. I died last night. Today I would not change one day of my life until a week ago. Loving you has been life for me. The silly little job was unreality, only you were ever real. Oh, my dear, it is death before I die to leave you whom I love more than life. It is not pride or vanity but the feeling that you do not love me any more.

God bless you and keep you and if I can help you after death only my love will do so.
Your wife, RUTH.

Inserting the letter in an envelope addressed to Lee Gordon, she placed it on the dresser and went out into the street again, intending to throw herself beneath a truck. Blinded by her headache, she moved with a vague, doped jerkiness, tensing and untensing with the waxing and waning of her determination.

Once an elderly white woman stopped her and asked if she was sick. The calmness of her own voice startled her. "No, thank you, I feel quite well."

After that she caught a bus, and when she could no longer bear the motion of the ride, got off. Out near the end of Slauson, unaware of where she was, uncaring, she found herself suddenly thinking of Lee again. It was as if he were beside her again, and she was stifled momentarily with an overwhelming desire to see him, to feel his arms about her, and hear his voice again. And as she went west in trancelike movement, eyes glued to the burning walk, the words came to her ears: "We'll make it, baby doll. We always have and we always will."

Not "we" now, Lee, she thought; it's not "we" any more.

Seeing another bus come to a stop, she boarded it and rode to the ocean and stood on the concrete embankment for a long time, looking at the waves. The sharp-tongued shimmer of molten waves, red in the late sun, was like a sea of blood beckoning to oblivion. But she only bowed her head and turned and came back to the city. At twilight she stood on the Sixth Street bridge over the Los Angeles River valley, looking down at the railroad tracks. Darkness came and she still stood, and then she found herself walking aimlessly through the streets again. Men spoke to her, cars pulled up and slowed, but she did not notice.

It was late when she opened the door and walked back into her house. For a long time she stood staring at the bichloride of mercury solution, berating herself because she could not drink it. Then she would be dead and this awful torture inside of her would be stilled forever.

"Oh Lee! Oh Lee! Oh Lee!" she cried aloud. Her voice was dry and cracked, but she could not cry.

After a time she lay across the bed and finally from exhaustion dozed off in a nightmarish sleep. The doorbell awakened her and brought her abruptly to a sitting position—nerves jangling, muscles quivering, mouth opening to scream. Then from some buried but still-living wish came the notion it was Lee, and she staggered groggily to the door to let him in. Outside it was gray dawn.

Two bulky white men entered and one said: "We're from the homicide bureau. Are you Mrs. Lee Gordon?"

"Has something happened?" she asked breathlessly, her hand flying up in a defensive gesture.

"Your husband has been shot."

Dull-witted and top-heavy, already at the end of physical endurance, she found the sudden shock of anxiety more than she could bear. As she fell, fainting, one of the detectives caught her and eased her into a chair. The other went to the kitchen to get a glass of water. Noticing the bichloride of mercury solution, he sniffed it, then filled a glass and returned, forcing it between her lips.

When she came to, her eyes were pools of pure terror. "Is he—is he dead?" she gasped.

"No, ma'am," the officer quickly said. "He's not hurt seriously. We didn't mean to alarm you."

"May I go to him, please."

"Oh, of course. That's why we came, to take you to him." Smiling down at her, he added: "We're sorry we alarmed you, Mrs. Gordon," and assisted her to stand.

When she went into the bedroom to prepare herself to leave, the one who had brought the water thumbed the other toward the kitchen. Turning casually to her as she reappeared, he asked:

"Did he appear worried about anything when he left home last night?"

"Oh!"—She gave a slight start—"are you speaking to me?"

"Yes, I was asking if your husband appeared worried when he left home last night."

"Oh, he wasn't home at all last night," she replied involuntarily, the sound of sobbing in her voice.

Returning from the kitchen with the glass of poison concealed in a handkerchief at his side, the second detective winked. Neither questioned her further until they had escorted her to the police car. Then before starting the motor, the first detective asked: "Wasn't your husband the young fellow who claimed he was assaulted by deputy sheriffs a short time ago?"

"Oh, that was what started everything," she sobbed. "He was beaten awfully."

"Never was anything done about it, was there?"

"He couldn't prove anything, but he knew who did it."

"Yes, that's it," the other detective said musingly. "A thing like that can start a man to brooding, especially when he feels he's the victim of an injustice."

"Oh, it was awful," she related. "It changed his whole attitude."

"You mean affected his mind?"

"Not so much his mind. It seemed to take the run out of him. No one could do anything and then the man with him lied about it. He didn't seem to care about anything after that—" The sobbing suddenly overwhelmed her and she cried: "Oh, Lee!—Won't you please take me to him now?" she begged.

They drove out Exposition in the early sunrise, and the detective in back with her continued softly: "It's too bad he got mixed up with those Communists. That won't do him any good."

"Oh, what has he done? What was he shot about?"

"We don't know yet. He turned up at the hospital with a bullet in his shoulder, and we haven't got him to say who shot him yet."

"She shot him! I told him she would try to hurt him!"

"You mean the white girl?"

"She didn't want him! She never wanted him! All she wanted was just to use him. Oh, Lee, you're such a fool," she said, sobbing.

"Is that what you and him were arguing about?"

"We didn't argue. He wasn't at home." She began crying as if her heart was breaking all over again. "He'd gone back to her."

"Did his buddy Luther tell you where he was?"

"Oh, Luther wasn't his friend. He hated Luther."

"Almost as much as he hated the deputies who beat him up, eh?"

"Oh, he didn't want to kill Luther. He just despised him."

"But he sure would have killed those deputy sheriffs who sapped up on him?"

"Oh, he didn't really want to hurt them. He was just so torn up all inside."

"So he got Luther to help him?"

She turned her tear-filled eyes on him in a puzzled look. "Luther?"

"Then when he came home and asked you to help him get away, you didn't know about his deal with Luther?"

"Deal with Luther—"

"He didn't tell you?"

"Oh, I haven't seen him since I went after him."

"At the white girl's?"

"He came out and took me home."

"That was when he pulled his knife on you?"

"Oh, no! We didn't fight. We were both too upset to fight."

"He told you then?"

"He said he loved her. But I knew he didn't mean it. He was so upset he didn't know what he was saying."

"He tell you what he was planning to do?"

"No, but I knew he was going back to her. I knew he was going to get hurt— Oh, Lee!"

"I see, that was night before last."

"Night before last—" she said. It seemed a million years in the past.

"Then it was last night he came and asked you to help him get away?"

"He didn't come home at all last night."

"But you didn't help him, did you? You told him to go back to the white woman and get her to help him, didn't you?"

"I didn't see him at all last night."

"You knew she was going to turn him in, didn't you? You knew that when you sent him back to her, didn't you? It was just as if you'd turned him in yourself, wasn't it?"

"Turned him in? Oh!" From the engulfing terror, her voice was smaller than a whisper. "What did he do?"

"He told you what he did," the voice went on relentlessly.

"You're confusing me!" she cried. "Oh, please, please tell me what has happened!"

"And you sent him to his death as surely as if you'd turned him in yourself."

"Please!—please!—" she begged, as the world began to turn, drowning her in tears.

"Then after you did it, you couldn't bear to think of what you'd done. So you tried to kill yourself."

"Please!—"

"You've been afraid ever since they beat him that he'd kill one of them."

And now the world was gone in sudden nausea.

When she came to, she was lying on a cot in the prison infirmary. The detectives and a policewoman stood about her.

"Mrs. Gordon, we are going to give you a chance to help your husband," one of the detectives began again. "As you know, extenuating circumstances tending to prove temporary insanity do a lot of good in a murder defense."

But now, even through her terror and exhaustion and the blind white headache burning out her mind, she realized that she had already talked too much. She made no reply.

"We want you to give a detailed account of your husband's activity from the time he was attacked by unknown persons on the highway until last night."

"But he didn't come home at all last night," she said, beginning again to sob.

"We know all about last night, Mrs. Gordon. What we are interested in now is what he did before last night."

She closed her eyes and refused to answer.

"Do you want to help your husband?"

If they would only go away and give her time to think—

"So you still want to send him to his death?"

"Oh, no!"

"Then tell us what he did after these people beat him. After all, Mrs. Gordon, it's not unnatural for a man to want vengeance."

"Please give me a little time to think," she begged.

"The boy goes up for arraignment in a few minutes, lady. There isn't any time. Either you want to help him or you don't want to help him. There's nothing to think about."

"I won't make any statement until I've had time to think," she whispered.

"Then we will hold you as an accomplice," the detective said threateningly.

If it was only what you could do to me, she thought, it would not matter—

When it became apparent that she did not intend to speak, one of the detectives nodded to the policewoman, and with the other one left the room. Ruth was booked as a material witness and taken to a cell.

Chapter 29

SMITTY had not given up on Lee, nor had he taken Lee's name from the payroll. For this he ran the risk of censure from the executive committee, but the risk was incidental—it was Lee who worried him.

Deep down Smitty felt a sense of responsibility for Lee Gordon. He liked Lee also, and to a great extent understood him. There was little he did not know of Lee Gordon's likes and dislikes, resentments and enthusiasms, antagonisms and admirations, his sudden animosities and just as sudden altruisms, and their sources and compulsions. As he had tried to tell Lee once, he did not find the Negro as strange as he did disturbing.

His sympathy for Lee had no bounds. Just to watch Lee's groping confusion tortured him, and many times Lee's behavior caused him actual pain. When circumstances forced him to deny understanding of Lee's attitude, when he fully understood but could not sanction it, he suffered a depressing sense of guilt.

As it happened at the time he had refused to take Lee's side against Luther, when he had believed Lee's story implicitly from the first. Watching the slow build-up of Lee's distrust of him following that incident was one of the tragedies of his life. But, goddamnit, Lee knew the Communists as well as he—how they were trying to get control of the union and fighting him under-handedly every step of the way. Lee must have been completely aware of the expediency of his stand. And yet he knew that Lee had con-demned him for it.

Later, he had watched this distrust blossom into full contempt, simply because he had refused to commit political suicide by fight-ing down the line for Jackie Forks. Of course, he had known, as had everyone, that she was innocent. But Lee had singled him out as her defender, and in his mind demanded that he die for her. And when he had refused to do so nonsensical and impolitic a thing, Lee had gone to her defense himself, knowing full well there was nothing he could do.

He could understand Lee's infatuation for the girl. He knew many white men with the same sexual curiosity concerning Negro women. But to these men it was simply a matter of going to bed with a Negro woman; while to Lee it seemed a matter of great importance—so much so that he had quit his job and deserted his wife for her. Nor did Smitty believe it was just because Lee loved the girl. No, it was the way that Lee must have her—not as just going to bed with a white woman, but as a mate, as the woman of his preference, with pride and honor and without shame, or not at all. And therefore he had felt compelled to defend her, even to the destruction of himself. Yet Smitty knew that it would be himself, Smitty, whom Lee Gordon would condemn in the end.

He was more puzzled than annoyed. What did Lee expect of people—that they take a stand and die at every minor crisis? But no sensible man could expect for one to make the stand alone and die without even beginning to accomplish that for which he died. Not even a Communist—an American Communist at that— would pick out a single millionaire, for instance, and condemn him for not giving up his millions while none other even contemplated doing so. Nor would it be of any benefit.

Yet, at every minor crisis, when a person failed to take a stand and make the supreme sacrifice, Lee quickly rejected them. It did not make good goddamn sense! No man would do it. Not even Lee himself—or would he?

These were the things about Lee that puzzled him: his seem-ingly headstrong bent for self-destruction against all reason and his blind revolt against injustice, yet as blind rejection of people working to rectify it. He could not understand how an intelligent Negro could reject and scorn and hold in contempt those who fought the Negro cause just because they did not die for it; or if they did die for it, how could he reject their memory because in some slight manner they had failed to live by it?

For example, there was the time when Lee had tried so hard to explain why the Negro worker must be given extraordinary privileges in order for him to attain ordinary equality. It was not so much that he had missed the point—he had seen quite clearly how this could be. But that a Negro, underprivileged to start, should ask in all sincerity to become overprivileged, seemed ridiculous, since they both knew that the attainment of simple equality and no more was itself an impossible goal.

And this was what he could not understand: a man fighting so blindly and desperately and dangerously toward a goal, and yet rejecting, denouncing, condemning each hand lifted to help him on his way—damning each slow step because he could not make it in one. That was it: if he couldn't have it all and at once, then to hell with any part of it. But to a man who was himself free, white, and over twenty-one, intelligent, and in an executive position, who seldom got anything he wanted and almost always had to put up with halfway measures, such an attitude was thoroughly bewildering.

What Smitty failed to realize was if he had been a Negro, without any other change, he would himself have lived in a raging fury. He simply did not have the imagination to put himself, a white man, in a Negro's place.

But though sometimes annoyed, exasperated, and often actually pained, yet deep down he did not condemn Lee Gordon for his attitude, because over all, he vaguely realized that this was Lee Gordon's way of making his stand for something better. And even though he knew beyond all doubt that in a Negro this was suicide, he had to admire Lee for it.

So when he read the report of the murder in the morning paper, it was not surprise, but trepidation, that shook him to the core. The report stated briefly that Deputy Sheriff Paul Dixon had been murdered early the night before in his home in Inglewood. Lee Gordon, a Negro union organizer, who a short time back had accused Dixon and three other deputy sheriffs of attacking him on the highway, was being held in suspicion of the murder. Luther McGregor, his accomplice, also his companion at the time of the alleged attack, had been shot to death resisting arrest in the home of his employer in Hollywood. The police attributed the motive to both revenge and robbery, as it was known that Dixon had had in his possession a large sum of money that could not be found. In the next column was a picture of Mrs. Dixon, who had discovered her husband's body upon her return from a motion-picture theater.

And though he knew that Lee was capable of behavior that would tear the face from reason, he did not believe Lee would murder anyone. His mind would not accept it. So his first conclusion was that Luther and the Communists had framed him in some sort of way, as they had done the Forks girl—or perhaps she had been in with them too. But no matter what had happened, Lee Gordon was still an organizer for the union council. He reached for the telephone.

Half an hour later the union attorney Steve Hannegan came into his office. "What do you think?"

"I don't think he did it."

"He could have," Hannegan said. "He had motive enough."

"I don't think the boy would murder, Steve."

"Let's get his story first."

But they could not contact Lee. His name was not on the blotter and the police denied holding a prisoner by that name. Nor would the chief of detectives, chief of police, or police commissioner profess knowledge of the prisoner.

"They have talked to the sheriff," Hannegan said.

"To hell with them!" Smitty said. "Let's get a writ."

"To apply for a writ of habeas corpus, I must present alibis to cover each minute of Gordon's time for hours before and after the approximate time of the murder," Hannegan said thoughtfully.

"Then we will present them," Smitty said.

Hannegan drummed his fingers on the flat desk top. "Sworn affidavits?" It was partly questioning, partly informative.

"I will get them," Smitty said. "I will go to—"

"I don't want to know about it."

"Then you don't know about it!" Smitty snapped.

For a moment Hannegan looked at him, and then said softly: "You like this boy."

"I believe in him, and I just don't believe that he's murdered anybody."

"Good luck!" Hannegan said.

Smitty did not find it as easy as he had anticipated. First, he drove to the plant to talk to Joe Ptak.

"To hell with Gordon!" Joe said.

"They'll execute him, Joe."

"That'll be good! The dirty quitter!"

Next Smitty approached Benny Stone because Benny was a Jew. But though Benny professed a desire to help, he pointed out the danger of complicity. So Smitty returned to the council hall and began appealing to the various union officials. He pleaded and cajoled, calling upon their union loyalty and becoming eloquent concerning their obligation to their Negro brothers. But neither the eloquence of his pleas nor the righteousness of his cause moved these hard-boiled unionists.

Finally, he himself was forced to alibi Lee to the union men. By swearing that he had been with Lee from nine o'clock the night before until one o'clock that morning, he finally persuaded eight of them to sign statements that Lee Gordon had been in conference with them at the union hall during that time. But for each signature he received five refusals. It was too risky, they all declared, and no one wanted any part of it. Those who signed the statements did so grudgingly, and with the express reservations that their statements be used only to secure the writ and not again if the case came up for trial.

If it were known that he had lied, Smitty would have been forced out of the union, he knew full well. He also knew that the risk he took not only involved the future of eight other men, but of the union. And it was not only the honor of these men, but their freedom, their security, and the security of their families. Yet he felt compelled to take this risk, not only just for Lee Gordon, but for the things in which he believed. And he did it quietly, seriously, and without pompousness.

He would not have done this for anyone but a Negro or some other underdog, but he did not know this about himself. All he knew was that he believed in a guy and was doing what he could to help him.

Again he contacted Hannegan, presenting him with the affidavits, and by three o'clock they had cornered a judge who gave grudging consent to the proceedings. But after scanning the affidavits the judge was not satisfied.

"You are forgetting, counselor," the judge said irritably, "that just a few weeks ago this Negro accused the victim, along with other officers, of criminally attacking him."

"We made no legal accusation," Hannegan replied.

"You were his counsel? He needs a permanent counselor, eh?"

"I am the attorney for the union."

"I see, and you believe this boy innocent of this crime?"

"I present the affidavits to support—"

"I am asking your opinion."

"My opinion is the Constitutional presumption of innocence—"

"Yes, yes, the stock speech! But you realize this is a charge of murder. If complicity is later disclosed you will be disbarred."

"Yes, Your Honor."

"And the men who have signed these affidavits will be prosecuted to the fullest extent of the law."

"Yes, Your Honor."

"I don't like this," the judge said. "These union men are unreliable; they will swear to anything. How do I know this isn't just another union collusion to effect this murderer's release?"

"If it has been proven that the prisoner is a murderer, if there is a single bit of evidence linking him with the murder, then I do not ask for his release," Hannegan said.

"I assure you, sir, you would not get it!"

"I petition his release only on the grounds that nine honorable, respectable men have sworn that he could not have committed the murder at the time of its occurrence."

"And I refuse it on the grounds that the prisoner had motive and has confessed—"

"To whom?" Hannegan asked, cutting in.

"To the woman who reported him."

"But not to the police?"

"We have her sworn statement—"

"To accept the word of one person as sufficient proof of another's guilt, in preference to the sworn statements of nine honest men, makes justice a whim and is abhorrent to our form of government," Hannegan said, again interrupting him.

"It is satisfactory to me," the judge said complacently.

"In that case, Your Honor, I will enter a formal protest of police brutality in behalf of the prisoner."

"Brutality! Brutality! Who's talking about brutality!" the judge shouted. "That's all you lawyers know! Has the prisoner claimed brutality?"

"No, Your Honor," Hannegan admitted. "We have not been allowed to talk with the prisoner."

"Then how do you state that he has been brutalized?"

"I state it, Your Honor, because it is ours to know—Your Honor's and mine—that any Negro arrested and held for the murder of a white officer, in any city, county, town, or township of America, will be brutalized by white law enforcement officers."

The judge gave him a long baleful look. "You make this charge on theory and conjecture."

"I stake my practice on it."

"For a Negro prisoner? You are indeed a union lawyer."

"I am, indeed!"

"Then I must have better proof of the prisoner's whereabouts than the word of union workers."

"Before you reach a decision, Your Honor, let me point out that it is more than the Negro prisoner's freedom I am seeking. At this time in our national history, during this war in which our form of government is imperiled by the forces of injustice, I seek the living manifestation of the justice for which we fight. Here in this city already are growing racial tensions. Many white persons, residents of this city, among whom is myself, have heard the word being passed about: get the niggers, get the pachucos, get the zoot-suiters. It is only by the administration of justice and fair play that this may be stopped. For this, more than the specific release of any prisoner, is my plea."

"Very pretty, Mister Attorney. But do you think the release of this Negro prisoner, accused of the murder of a white law-enforcement officer, will inspire the morale of our police officers, and encourage them to combat your growing racial tensions?"

"If it will not," Hannegan said softly, "then we may as well give up trying to continue with our present form of government and create one affording freedom and justice for the white race only."

Angrily, the judge signed the writ of habeas corpus and notification was served on the warden of the city jails. As Smitty and Hannegan left the judge's chambers, both suffered an aftermath of nervousness.

"Let us hope the boy is innocent," Hannegan said.

Suddenly Smitty was confronted by the awful immensity of his action, but greater than his apprehension was his amazement. That his hard-boiled realism had permitted him to take even a minor risk for as irresponsible a person as Lee Gordon now seemed incredible. Yet he had not only jeopardized his own future, but the future of eight other really good guys, and the future of the union. It was certainly not just because he believed one colored boy the victim of injustice—or was it?

"Let us hope," he said sincerely.

While waiting in the vestibule of the city jail for Lee to be released, a nervous, distraught woman stepped from the prisoners' elevator and searched the room with tortured eyes. Although he had never seen Ruth, with some intuitive faculty Smitty recognized her instantly.

"Mrs. Gordon?" he asked.

She turned, hope flaming in her deep, troubled stare. "Yes?"

"I'm Smitty, Mrs. Gordon, one of your husband's co-workers—"

"Oh, Mr. Smith!"

"How is Lee?"

"Oh, I was going to ask you. I haven't seen him; I've been in jail myself."

"For what, Mrs. Gordon?" Hannegan asked politely.

"They said they were holding me as a material witness."

Smitty muttered unintelligibly, but Hannegan's bland Irish face rolled back a wave of fury. Suddenly and without warning, Ruth began to cry again.

"Now don't worry, Mrs. Gordon, don't worry," Smitty said, trying to console her, appearing big and awkward as his hands made gestures of frustration and his face blushed with concern. "Lee will be free any moment now. We've secured his release."

Passers-by looked curiously at the three of them and Hannegan moved to block her from the stares.

Then Lee came out of the elevator, and when he saw Ruth standing there crying between Smitty and Hannegan, the emotional void that had swallowed him since his beating by policemen filled with a million tears. It was as if he had come back from death and knew that he was going to live again. Battered and bruised, he stood there, trembling slightly, trying to accustom his mind to this life that followed death.

She had not yet seen him but had felt his presence, and now when she looked up, their gazes locked and held. In that brief instant they crossed the River Jordan into togetherness again, and forgave each other for all the things that they had ever done. And they were safe again; they were in each other's arms, and her heart was singing thanks.

"Lee."

He let out his long-held breath. "I'm sorry, Ruth."

"That's all right, Lee," she sobbed, clinging to him as if she would never let him go.

Finally, ever so gently, Smitty drew their attention and, with Hannegan, ushered them toward the street. As they came down the stairs several police reporters converged on them, snapping questions, and a photographer shot a picture.

But Lee did not hear them. Although he was not looking at Ruth, his mind was absorbed with her and he could feel her eyes on him, overflowing with compassion and concern, and he knew it was more than he deserved.

"No statement," Hannegan said to the reporters, and a moment later Smitty hailed a taxi and they were away from it.

Sitting close to Lee and holding tightly to his hand, Ruth asked: "Did they hurt you much?"

Both Smitty and Hannegan looked away. And Lee too looked away, out of the window at the people on the street, and felt suddenly heavy with tears.

"It was like a funny dream," he said, and all three turned to look at him.

No one said anything else after that, and as they rolled along, Lee felt a sense of drifting in a sea of strange emotions, just light enough to float. He had no aim, no will, no purpose—he just went along. When the taxi stopped to let Ruth out, she said:

"I want to talk to Lee a minute."

Smitty nodded and Lee got out and walked with her to the door of their house, which looked unfamiliar now. But she did not say anything at all, just stood there waiting, the setting sun turning her tears to drops of blood.

He could not bear looking at her, and as he looked away he said: "I didn't do it, Ruth."

"Oh, thank God, thank God!" she cried.

He turned quickly to look at her again and suddenly he was overflowing; tears were streaming down his face and he was crying like a baby. Pulling his head down to her breast she let him cry.

"It's all right, Lee," she said. "It's all right now."

Then she kissed him, their wet lips together in the taste of tears, and he turned and walked back to the taxi—just riding along in this sea of strangeness. He did not know what was happening to him, or what was in store for him, only that for the moment now he was safe again. At the union hall they got out, went up to Smitty's office, and locked the door.

"Now what's it all about?" Smitty asked bluntly.

Automatically Lee said: "I don't know anything about it."

"Listen, Lee, we're on your side," Smitty said patiently. "We must know. Eight of our best men have signed sworn affidavits to alibi you, and we must know what happened."

Lee took a breath, and without looking at either of them, said: "Luther did it."

"Then you were framed!" He turned triumphantly to Hannegan. "I knew Lee wasn't involved in this."

But Hannegan was not so easily satisfied. "How were you framed, Gordon?"

While his gaze sought furtively for a place to hide, Lee searched his mind for a lie. "The Forks woman accused me to cover for Luther. It was a Communist—"

"Stop lying," Hannegan said, cutting him off. "No one was covering for McGregor. McGregor's dead."

"Dead!" His gaze touched Hannegan's cold, fixed stare. "God!" As the breath ran out of him. So Luther's white folks had not covered for him after all. "Was he shot?"

"Resisting arrest! Now let us have it. We can't help you until we know what happened. And you were not framed."

"Well—no, I wasn't exactly framed." Lee could not look upon the slow growth of bewilderment in Smitty's face. "I—" hesitating as the guilt moved in— "I—I was with him."

Smitty stared, his broad flabby face caught in startled disbelief.

But Hannegan coldly asked: "Had you gone with him to Dixon's house?"

"Well—" there was no escaping— "Yes."

"For money?"

"Well—yes. He came by the hotel and said Foster had some money for me—"

Smitty walked across the room and struck the wall a resounding blow with his open palm. When he looked about, his eyes were sick with disappointment in his mottled red face.

"Lee, goddamnit, why?"

"I don't know, Smitty, I don't know." Lee could not meet his eyes. "I was pretty low, I guess."

"You and the woman argued?"

"Well—it wasn't just that. It was everything. I had gone so far I thought maybe I just may as well go all the way, I guess."

The awful disappointment in Smitty's eyes now echoed in his voice. "I didn't think you would do that, Lee."

"I didn't either, Smitty," Lee honestly replied.

"Let's learn what happened first," Hannegan said.

"Well—" Now as if he had gone dead of all emotion, Lee reported in detail everything that had happened from the time Luther had approached him in the hotel until his arrest at Jackie's. All the workings of Smitty's slow-thinking mind, the amazement and repugnance and incredulity and slow growth of aversion, showed in his changing expressions; but Hannegan's face retained its cold composure.

"What happened before that?" he asked. "McGregor didn't just walk in and state his proposition coldly. What had you done to lead up to it?"

"Well—that morning I asked Foster for a job. But I only wanted a job," Lee added in defense. "I didn't go to him to sell out the union. That was his idea."

He looked up for Smitty to believe him and for a moment their gazes held. And when Smitty saw the pain of guilt in Lee's dark face, he could not help but feel sorry for him again.

"Why didn't you come to me, fellow? Why didn't you tell me what was troubling you?"

"Well—I had been to you, Smitty."

Smitty's face took on a hurt expression. "I don't understand you, fellow."

"I don't always understand myself," Lee Gordon said.

Again Hannegan brought the conversation back to actuality. "Are you certain you didn't leave fingerprints, Gordon?"

"I don't think so. It seems as if we wiped everything thoroughly." For an instance he was touched by the irony of Luther's insistence on this. "What I didn't do, Luther did."

"And you're certain there's nothing to connect you with the crime?"

"I can't be certain. I was pretty upset. I can't remember very well what happened after Luther stabbed him."

"I suppose I'd better talk to the Forks girl," Smitty said.

Hannegan shook his head. "I don't believe that will be necessary. I should think that by this time she will be far away."

"Perhaps, but I can check."

"You can, but her testimony is of no importance of itself. The only thing we worry about now is the discovery of evidence to place Gordon on the scene." Now when he turned his gaze on Lee, a troubled curiosity leaked through the clinical aloofness of his manner, and he wondered at the good Smitty saw in him. "Let's hope the postman doesn't ring again, Gordon. You'll hurt many good people worth far more than you."

"Well—yes sir. I don't suppose there's any use in saying I'm sorry."

For a moment longer Hannegan studied him. And then he said: "No."

Into the growing silence Smitty asked: "Then what can we do?"

"We can pray," Hannegan answered softly. Closing his brief case, he nodded and left the room.

"Thank you, sir," Lee called, but Hannegan did not turn.

A troubled expression touched Smitty's flaccid face as he searched his thoughts for understanding—because no one man could be as contradictory as Lee Gordon seemed. Sometimes on the surface he seemed just another rat, yet always deep from inside of him came the sense of something else, disturbing every judgment he might pass. Was this what being a Negro did to a normal man? he wondered. And what was there to do about it that he had not already done?

But even now, on top of all this, he was unwilling to give up on Lee. And he knew that however he might help, he would have to do it now. So now he resorted to harshness since all else had failed.

"Lee, I'm going to tell you to your face. You are one of the rottenest bastards I ever knew." Of all the times he had become so furious with white men who cursed Negroes, now he was doing it, and finding it unpleasant. But it was the last resort. "If it weren't for the fact I might get a lot of good guys into trouble I'd let you go up there and die, because you have proven to me that you are worthless."

Lee had never felt so much like a dirty dog—not like a nigger, not black and abused, just a common cur of any color. "I know," he said.

"But I'm going to give you one more chance," Smitty said. "And it's better than you deserve."

"Well—" There was nothing else to say.

"The organizing is not going along as well as we expected, and you are partly to blame for this," Smitty said. "Since both you and McKinley left, the Negro workers have lost interest. I'll be frank with you, fellow. We've put a lot of time and effort into this job —and spent a lot of money. Every union—every national and every local—in this country is watching us. We can't afford to fail If we don't get the Negro vote in the election next week, we are going to fail.

"Now this is the proposition, and I mean this. If you can get the Negro vote and we win the election, we will back you to the limit when the trouble comes. And make no mistake, fellow, Foster will be after you until he dies. But if we win the election, we will have a little money we can use for you. But if we lose the Negro vote, we fail. And if we fail, we're dropping you, fellow."

When Lee did not immediately reply, Smitty asked: "Do you want the proposition, or do you want us to drop you now?"

"Oh, I want it," Lee replied. "I'll try—I'll do my best, I promise you. But suppose I get the Negro vote and we still don't win the election?"

"Lee, I'll tell you," Smitty said. "That will be just too bad for you. When you went with Luther, you went to sell us out. And the only way I'll ever forget that will be for us to win."

"Well—thank you, anyway," Lee Gordon said.

"You've got six days. Report here tomorrow morning at nine o'clock and we'll see if we can give you a start."

Lee waited a moment longer, then started to offer his hand, but thought better of it. He went out and walked down the stairs. For a long depressing moment he stood in the hallway struggling to co-ordinate his thoughts. Then suddenly he became afraid again. He knew he couldn't do it. He should have told Smitty that it couldn't be done—not in six days, not all those suspicious Negroes.

He should tell him now, he thought. But Smitty would take away the union's protection. And the police would have him in jail again before the night was done. His eyes went furtive and he began to bite his lips. By tomorrow he could be on his way, he thought. Lee Gordon could be finished and somebody by another name suddenly in the world. He'd be a fool to stay and let them execute him, because Smitty meant what he had said. And no matter how one looked at it, Lee Gordon could not get the Negro vote out in six days. No one could. And Smitty knew it, he thought accusingly as he hastened through the doorway.

Outside Hannegan stood in the darkness, patiently waiting. "Gordon."

Lee jumped. "Oh! Mr. Hannegan!"

"Gordon, I waited especially to tell you that you have a friend in Smitty."

"A friend? Well—yes," he said, feeling forced to agree. "I guess you're right."

"I know that I am right, Gordon. I wouldn't let him down if I were you," Hannegan said, and stood waiting for Lee to go his way.

Smitty his friend? Lee could not see it. It was more as if he were Smitty's pawn, and Smitty some sadistic chessman. Six days to build him up to knock him down again! Confusion clouded his thoughts—suspicion, resentment! And that fourth apocalyptic horseman of the Negro mind, fear, trampled down the remnants of his gratitude. A friend? Smitty had never been his friend! But yet the small, still voice of reason whispered that somebody must have been his friend.

Chapter 30

THE murder was gone into another night. Smitty was gone, and the union; and the hard, merciless days that did not give a damn if a Negro lived or died were gone for this moment. Now in the world were only Ruth and himself, held motionless in the soft cone of light from the floor lamp as figures of expectancy. But what they expected, neither knew.

He sat on the edge of the davenport, bent forward, tense, eager. Etched in his thin drawn face were the ravages of guilt, but the contrition in his eyes petitioned her.

She sat across from him, limp in the big armchair, with eyes like candles of compassion in her tired, haggard face. Her hands, extending from the loose sleeves of an old cotton robe, were brown wax in the yellow light, and he thought with sudden anxiety, God, she looks frail—almost like a ghost in that big chair.

"You got on enough clothes?" he asked gruffly.

"Oh yes."

"You warm enough?" Out of all the things that he had done to hurt her, he was now concerned about her comfort.

"Yes, I'm plenty warm."

"It's cool tonight." Because even now, having come here for the purpose, he could not muster up the courage to face it.

"I hadn't noticed."

But it was there, so huge, so real that it was unavoidable.

"I've been with Smitty and Hannegan. At the union hall."

"Did they— Will they— What did they decide?"

"There won't be any trouble."

"You won't have to stand trial?"

"I don't think so. Hannegan thinks we got it beat unless they get some concrete evidence."

"They are wonderful people, Lee. You should be grateful to them all the days of your life."

"Well—yes. But Smitty said if I didn't get the Negro workers to vote for the union in the election, they'd take away their support."

"Oh, they're letting you keep your job."

"Well—" He had never told her that he had quit. "If you want to call it that. But the election is just six days away. And I can't get the Negro vote. Smitty knows it."

"Don't say you can't, Lee. I'll help you."

He looked quickly up at her, the question in his eyes before he asked it. "What about your job?"

"I've quit my job."

"Oh!" And then: "Ruth."

"Yes, Lee?"

"I was never in love with Jackie."

All motion went out of her body and for a moment her breathing stopped. But she did not reply.

"I was just sorry for her. I know it sounds foolish, but I think it's the truth."

"Then why did you tell me you were, Lee?"

"I think it was because I wanted to hurt you," he said with painful honesty. "I resented your job and your independence. I thought it took something away from me, and at times I used to hate you for it."

"But couldn't you have told me that? I would have quit then, Lee. The job was never of any importance." Nor did she realize how much this contradicted all her actions of the past.

"I thought it was. I believe it really was, Ruth. I don't think you realize now just how important it really was to you."

"But you were crying, Lee. That was the first time I ever saw you cry."

"I wasn't crying about that, honestly. I don't know why I was crying. About you, I think now. About you and I. Honestly, Ruth, I didn't love Jackie. I thought she needed me and you didn't, and I got all mixed up. I suppose I thought I was acting noble, and then the rest of it just happened I thought you were going to hurt her, and I was just trying to keep her from being hurt again."

"I wasn't going to hurt her, Lee. I just wanted to look at her to see whether she loved you. I would have known then—a woman can tell such things."

"I thought you might cause a scene and the police would come," he replied with the stupid candor possible only in a man confessing infidelity.

Although now his every word tore at her heart, she had to hear each bitter detail, because she was a woman. "Did she tell you I would cause a scene?"

"No, she wanted me to go back and make up with you."

"Really? She told you that?" As she looked steadily away, for now to look at him would be to see him naked in this white woman's arms.

"Honestly, Ruth, it never was anything—well—real. I don't know what happened to me."

"Did she have anything to do with your trouble?"

"No, I had left her when that happened. I'd gone to the hotel."

"Did she put you out?"

"Well—we had argued."

"She was frightened, was she?"

"I—well—I guess she thought you were going to cause trouble."

"Then she didn't know what you were going to do?"

"Oh, no. I didn't know myself. I don't even think Luther knew he was going to kill the man when we went there. It all happened on the spur of the moment. But I went to her afterward to get an alibi. That's when she turned me in."

"Oh! What really happened, Lee?"

For a long time after he had finished his story, they sat silently immersed in their private thoughts. Then finally he said: "I'm sorry it turned out this way, Ruth."

"I'm sorry too, Lee," she replied.

Whatever it had been they had expected, in the silence following both realized that it was not to come. The wounds were still too open and the memory too raw. Though now inactive, the hurt was in their blood like a filterable virus, dormant but uncured. He now hated Jackie's immortal soul, but thoughts of her white body still stirred its pungent passion. And though Ruth's love for him was deeply compassionate, inspiring the desire to comfort him, she could not touch his body—it was a very personal feeling.

The reunion had been made in mind alone, and the togetherness was an abstract thing. It was too soon, too weary for physical rejoining. She would have felt Jackie's presence in his every unfamiliar gesture, and imagined what he had taken to her in experiencing whatever new he now brought back. And if there would have been a forgetfulness of old harmonies, she would have hated him forever.

And vaguely, this was hammered through his masculine stupidity. So now he had to make the offer, since now it was hers to accept or reject.

"If you want a divorce—"

"No, Lee. Let's don't think about that now."

"Well—if you do. I still love you, Ruth—very much. But I know now that I'm no good for you. I'm not even any good for myself."

"Don't think about it now, Lee. The thing you must think of now is doing a good job for the union and getting out from the shadow of suspicion."

"I know. I'm going to try. I'm going to do the best I can. But in the meantime I'm going back to the hotel."

She didn't try to stop him. "If you need any money—"

"No, thanks. I don't need any money."

"Is there anything you want?"

"I'll need a suit and some shirts and things."

"Can I help you?"

"No, I can get them."

When he returned with the packed bag, she stood up. They had not touched each other, and did not touch each other now.

"Please don't worry about me, Ruth. I'll be all right. I'll be working hard."

"Call me, Lee, please."

"When?"

"Anytime—I'll be home."

"Well—good-by."

"Good night, Lee."

Emptiness assailed him as he went down the walk in the dark. He had never known how much he needed her until that moment. He was alone now, and afraid to be alone. Back in his drab, chilled, dimly lit hotel room, the night closed in on him, and loneliness was an unmerciful thing— And there was the blood! He kept seeing the blood all over everything— He sat on the side of the bed and buried his face in his hands—so afraid, he wanted to just sit there and never move again.

Finally he forced himself to get up and undress. The simple task of taking off his clothes required a special effort. But when he lay down he could not sleep. His body ached and his mind felt bruised, battered, insensate, but unstilled. Events of the past weeks paraded through his thoughts, forcing an evaluation that in his weariness he could not resist.

Being a Negro was a cause—yes. No doubt if he tried hard enough he could trace all his troubles to this source—his resentment of Ruth, the decay of their marriage, his entanglement with Jackie, his failing the union, and his failing himself. By logical process he could prove that he had been persecuted and oppressed by white people to the point of criminal compulsion.

But he was too tired of dodging and hiding and self-excusing, and too tired of that deteriorating form of acceptance which this inspired, to make the effort now.

For through it all, ran the one rigid realization, inescapable and inexpungeable: some white people must have been his friends right down the line from slavery. All of them could not have been his hateful enemies.

And now at last this brought him face to face with himself in the loneliness of the night. And he knew beyond all doubt that he could not excuse his predicament on grounds of race. This time he alone was to blame—Lee Gordon, a human being, one of the cheap, weak people of the world.

Being a Negro was a cause—yes. Thus far Luther had been right. But it was never a justification—never!—which was what Luther had found out in the end. Because being a Negro was, first of all, a fact. A Negro is a Negro, as a pine tree is a pine tree and a bulldog is a bulldog—a Negro is a Negro as he is an American—because he was born a Negro. He had no cause for apology or shame.

And if because of this fact his rights were abridged, his privileges denied, and his duties rescinded, he was the object of oppression and the victim of injustice. A crime had been committed against him by sundry white people. But this did not prove that all white hands were raised against him, because he still retained the right to protest and appeal, to defend his person and his citizenship courageously, and to unceasingly demand that justice be accorded him.

A fact, first of all! But if this fact could justify vicious, immoral, criminal behavior, if it could offer absolution, provide a valid excuse, or even pose a condition for sympathetic judgment, then the Negro was subnormal and could never fit into a normal society.

And now this brought the stark choice to his naked thoughts— he, Lee Gordon, a Negro, was either normal or subnormal. And if he was normal he would have to rise above the connotation America has given to his race. He would have to stand or fall as one other human being in the world.

And there would be white people, Lee Gordon knew, who could not conceive of this as a bitter choice—but that was only because they had never had recourse to this blanketing excuse of race. When Lee Gordon made his choice, he could not go to sleep. He doubted if he would ever be able to sleep again; because as a human being he was not very much.

By nine o'clock the following morning when he reported at Smitty's office, weariness had settled in his flesh and blood, slowing down the functions of his body. His eyes were glazed and bloodshot and he could barely think.

Chastened by a sense of guilt for speaking to Lee so harshly the day before, Smitty's greeting now was warm with encouragement.

"Buck up, fellow," he said. "You look as if you didn't have a friend in the world."

"I was told that I had one," Lee said respectfully, standing at attention before Smitty's desk.

"In that case you are fortunate," Smitty said. He had prepared a statement for the press which he now gave Lee to read. "See if you want to add anything."

Taking the seat across from him, Lee scanned the document. It began with the declaration that Comstock Aircraft Corporation had instituted a smear campaign directed at the union's effort to organize its workers. Then it made the definite claim that Lee Gordon, the only Negro organizer with the union, had been made the victim of planned persecution in an effort to discredit his race and promote antiunion sentiment among the Negro workers.

"After several fruitless attempts had been made to buy out Lee Gordon," it concluded, "he was brutally assaulted by deputy sheriffs who revealed they were acting on orders from Louis Foster, vice-president of the company. Failing to bring Gordon into line by this method, he was falsely arrested and accused of murder."

"I have nothing to add," Lee said, passing the typed sheets back. "But I don't quite see what good this will do."

Smitty grinned at him. "We're going to make a martyr out of you. Workers will always come to the support of an underdog."

"Well—let us hope," Lee said.

"Now get on out and report to Joe," Smitty said. "I told him you were coming."

But Joe Ptak would have nothing to do with Lee. "You worked here before," he said, his granite face unbending. "You know what to do. You're not working for me, you're working for Smitty. As far as I'm concerned, you're just a dirty rat."

Lee went out of the shack and down toward the gates where occasionally a group of workers lounged. But now only the guards were in evidence. Picking up a discarded copy of the company paper, the *Comstock Condor*, Lee read the caption beneath a Negro's picture: "NEW FACE IN THE PERSONNEL DEPARTMENT."

Following ran a eulogy to all the Negro workers:

In view of the excellent record made by our Negro workers, most of whom at the time of their employment had had no previous industrial experience, a Negro, Charles E. Raines, has been added to the personnel department to facilitate their future hiring.

Mr. Raines was formerly Director of a USO Center in the city.

Another Negro was considered for the position, this reporter learned, but upon discovery of his participation in the union's organizational campaign, his appointment was considered incompatible with the strict policy of self-determination which the company has maintained toward all union activity.

In accordance with the democratic principles carried out in all matters of employment and allocation of workers, two Negro journeymen have been promoted to leadmen. Now Negroes are employed in all departments and in all capacities throughout the plant.

We take off our hats to our darker brothers' initiative, industry, and enthusiastic cooperation.

Keep up the good work, pals.

For a time Lee stood there, carefully folding and unfolding the paper, his mind envisioning the Negro workers' reaction to these developments. It was not a brilliant stratagem, but he could see where it would be impressibly effective within the narrow limits of the time remaining before the election. For it would serve a two-fold purpose—first, the alienation of the white workers who would humanly resent special commendation being given Negroes for what they all had done; second, the alignment of the Negroes with the company in opposition to the union, by giving them some-thing to lose.

Lee Gordon recognized it immediately as the old political game that had been played on Negroes since time immemorial—give them something to lose, not much, just a little thing, and they would be blinded to all they forfeited by its acceptance. Presidents had played it along with ward heelers, and so-called humanitarians along with ruthless industrialists.

Give them a General in the army, Lee Gordon reflected, and you'd have them eating out of your hand while you Jim Crowed the other hundreds of thousands in uniform. Give them a power-less FEPC and they'd worship you as a great white lord, never once considering your negligence in enforcing the conditions of governmental contracts that would have made an FEPC unneces-sary. Give them a few black faces in the administrative bureaus of a Jim Crow capital and let the South run rampant. The Negro, in his overwhelming gratitude for what he received, would forfeit all that was his due. Lee Gordon knew—he had seen them do it, he was seeing them do it now.

To know this little sidelight on the character of Negroes and their leadership required no special acumen. Everyone knew that Negroes, in their enthusiasm to get ahead, would clutch at the first thing offered and pay with gratitude until death. But Lee had nothing but antipathy for all people who employed this cheap psychological trick—this taking advantage of the obvious weakness of a race—for it was an inhuman thing to do.

And maybe those who did it laughed about it in their secret souls, Lee Gordon thought as he stood there looking at the writing on the wall. Because it followed, as night follows day, that those who were the kind to employ this trick would be the kind to laugh about it too.

And now Lee Gordon could hear Foster laughing. He became afraid again, because Foster was laughing in his face. In a short time—perhaps even now as he thought about it—Foster would present an array of Negro witnesses to frame him for the murder of Paul Dixon. It was the logical sequent for a man who thought like this. In his slowly rising fear, Lee Gordon could see nothing to save him—not the union even though it tried. Foster would match witness with witness and no jury could be found that would accept the alibis of white unionists over the testimony of other Negroes.

Now Lee Gordon again felt impelled to run while he still had the chance. Returning to his hotel room, he packed his bags, but with his hand on the door knob, a wave of reason halted him. Once again he was held by the knowledge that he could run, but he could not escape; for what he wished to escape was not in the City of Los Angeles, or in the offices of Louis Foster, but within himself—not an actual thing, but a lack of something. He was a man in flesh and blood and bone, in brain and heart and senses, but in the indefinable essence of manhood there was something missing. Something in the hope that has kept man struggling throughout all history for a better world; in the faith of man on which were built all civilizations; in the charity by which man sought an understanding; in the love from which man has drawn man's humanity to man; in the self-reliance, honesty, integrity, and honor that have always kept man above the beast; in the convictions that are the measure of a man; and—most of all—in the courage by which men die for these convictions.

The vague realization of these deficiencies hammered on the shaping of his thoughts, but he did not analyze them thus. He simply knew that within himself there was a hole that needed filling, and that by staying to face his duty to the end he might in some way help to fill it.

So he forced himself to call on several of the swing-shift workers who had once joined the union. But from each he received the same cold reception. All had read of his arrest for murder and were distrustful of him, suspicious, and antagonistic.

"What you trying to do, get us all in trouble, man?" was the way one of them expressed it.

Nor would they listen to talk about the union. Mr. Foster was the Negroes' friend, they said. He was giving them a better break at Comstock than Negro workers were getting at any other plant in the city.

"We'd be damn fools to agitate the man. And that's all the union's going to do."

And this was true. "These were the words that Moses heard," Lee Gordon knew. But he would not lose hope, for losing that, Lee Gordon was lost.

If the press ran the story of his martyrdom, that would at least give him a conversational toe hold, he thought. Although all the papers had reported his arrest, only one reported his release; and that was in a paragraph on page nine stating that Lee Gordon, union organizer, held for suspicion in connection with the murder of deputy sheriff, Paul Dixon, had been released on a writ of habeas corpus.

And though the Negro weekly newspapers, which had carried banner stories on his arrest, planned to carry the full text of Smitty's statement, the next issues would not be published until after the labor board's election.

More than he realized, Lee had depended on the press to vindicate him, and now his disappointment was heavy in his mind. The inexorable curtain of circumstances seemed closing down upon him.

Until late that night he was awake, trying to devise some special appeal that might capture the Negro workers' fancy. But Foster had beat him to the punch. And he could think of no counter-stratagem.

Now his loneliness was his grave and he was dust within it. It was as if everything was dead and gone and was nothing, and had never been anything and would never be anything but a room of gray futility in an unpeopled world. It was as if the people going from the room had gone from memory too and had taken all reason with them, leaving only the steady hammer of remorse in the endless desolation. After that, sleep came like some horrible

Medusa, and he was drowning in a sea of blood—blood!—the goddamn blood is spurting from his neck!—

But the next morning he was up and trying again. It was discouraging, heartbreaking, thankless, as if pleading to painted faces on a wall—trying to sell a people Utopia when they already had Paradise. He was endeavoring to align Negro workers with poor white unionists when the rich white folks were "more than looking out for them." And Lee Gordon did not blame them for their refusal to listen. If he had been a worker at Comstock, he would not have listened himself. But he kept trying. There was this hole that had to be filled, and this was the only way to fill it.

By evening, with the pre-election union meeting three days off, he had secured the promise of two Negro workers to attend—two out of three thousand. Now he must not only face the desolation in his lonely room, but the certainty of failure.

Every fiber in his body cried out for him to quit. But he could not quit, because in this world men never can quit. Sitting there in the silence of his thoughts, he recalled the lines from the farewell speech of Lieutenant Colonel Noel F. Parrish to the Negro officers of the 99th Pursuit Squadron, which Jackie had read to him their first night together, a million years ago:

> No one can ask more than that you acquit yourselves like men. Each of you, and all of us, must prove first of all that we are capable of the dignity and nobility of manhood; that we can, when the occasion calls for it, fight and die for a cause that is greater than any one life, or any one man, or any one group of men.

If Jackie had given him nothing else, she had given him the memory of this. For this was what he had to do: to acquit himself like a man. But how? What could he do that he had not already done?

The next day it was the same. It was not so much that he was failing as that he could not get a start. One such worker as Lester McKinley might have made the difference—or even some such outside helper as Luther McGregor had been.

Slowly it dawned on him that even the Communists were opposing him. This he could understand. With the shooting of Luther McGregor had gone their chances of gaining control of the local. So now they would fight desperately to make the campaign fail. For to them unionism was not a matter of relativity, but a materialistic certainty—the important thing was that they control it. And though this was an added weight, it did not break him down.

That afternoon the weekly issue of the union paper came out with the story of his martyrdom. But the quick hope that this brought was soon dead. Though he had known of the control white employers can exert on Negro workers, never before had he been confronted with it. Now this fact, more than the abstract theory, confounded him. At last he could understand the full importance of the Negro worker to the union movement. For if the industrialist won them first, they were a hammer in his hand.

Late that night, until it was long past the hour for visiting on any pretext, he continued to call on workers. Few let him in, none welcomed him, and several slammed the door in his face. Now that Foster had put the union in bad repute, his prestige as an organizer was also gone. The predatory women no longer had an eye for him. It was dead end and he knew it.

Back in his room with its four blank walls of loneliness, he thought of Ruth. With his body crying for the comfort of her arms, he thought of her—with his sagging spirit crying for her love's support. There were the aching need for sexual consummation and the bitter obligation to make amends. Out from the endless desolation came her eyes to torture him, and in the dim light her body walked in a thousand different moods. It required a singular effort to keep from telephoning her—to refrain from seeking the consolation of her voice. But he had only failure to offer, and on top of all the things he had done to her, he could not offer this. He'd sweat it out alone. He had made it and it was his, and if he had made it hard, then he would have to soften it.

Early Saturday morning it began to rain. By the time of awakening, the city was caught in a cold, gray storm. With the pre-election meeting of the union to be held that night, it seemed portentous. For a long time after awakening, Lee lay there watching the rivulets run down the dirty panes, then he arose and went out into the rain. At eight o'clock that night he entered the union hall and took his seat in the assembly room.

Since the very beginning of the campaign, both Joe Ptak and Smitty had been trying desperately to get national officers to take part, but most of them had been tied down by heavy duties and their own union problems. Finally one official had been persuaded to come from Detroit. He appeared this night and found a truly disappointing audience. Lee was the only Negro present. There were only a few whites, fewer than at the very first meeting which Lee had attended.

The official addressed the group. But it was like talking to a corpse. Smitty was glum and morose. Joe Ptak's face was a stolid, impassive mask. Fear and defeat hung like a pall over the stage, and it was communicable. Those who had attended were the worse for having done so.

Throughout the meeting Lee sat silent and alone. No one spoke to him or nodded in his direction. After the meeting the union officials went out in a body, withdrawn and untalkative. Lee got up and went out alone. He had hoped for a word from Smitty, and it was with a depressing sense of letdown that he stood in the dismal rain, waiting for his streetcar.

Back in his hotel room, he sat on the side of the bed in his wet clothes and stared at the floor. After a time his thoughts returned to Jackie.

But he did not hate her now. He felt sorry for her. For she too was caught in this dirty hell of race, he suddenly realized. And it made her into what she was when she allowed it to, as it made him into what he was when he allowed it to—as it did all the people of the world caught in its values. He felt suddenly sorry for all of its victims—the white oppressors as for the black oppressed, the lynchers as well as for the lynched, the Nazis as well as for the Jews. They were all victims alike of this rotten racial hell—victims of others and victims of themselves. He just wished naïvely and wistfully that it wasn't so.

Finally he stretched out on the bed in his wet clothing, and as the cold virus seeped through his blood, it brought a fitful sleep. Heavy knocking on the door awakened him. Someone was calling him to the hall telephone. Smitty was on the wire and wanted him to come to the union hall. He took two aspirins and went back into the rain.

The others had left and Smitty was alone. He told Lee of their plan to stage a victory rally the morning of the election. It would not be a work stoppage. They would simply distribute banners and buttons among the day-shift workers, and employ a sound truck to urge them to parade for twenty minutes before the change of shift. The graveyard shift would vote on the way out, but if they could win the day shift, they would rally again with the swing shift.

Lee's assignment was to assemble a group of Negroes from the community, a hundred or more if possible, to parade with them at the beginning. Students, housewives, workers from other plants —it made no difference as long as they carried the union banner.

"Lee, I'm depending on you."

"Smitty, I'll do my best. But I doubt very much if it can be done."

"I told you before, Lee, and I'm telling you again: I won't accept failure."

"Well—okay."

Downstairs in the hallway he began telephoning Negro ministers. Three of the nine he called gave him appointments for early the next morning. One hung up at his announcement that he was calling for the union. The wives of the others informed him that their husbands were occupied with their sermons and could not be disturbed.

But the minister whom Lee particularly wanted to contact could not be located at that hour. Pastor of a large, unaffiliated church, Reverend Wilkins had inaugurated a progressive program of civic and community endeavor for his congregation, and Lee felt assured of his aid.

Then he telephoned the publishers of two weekly Negro newspapers. One would have nothing to do with the union, but the other, an elderly woman whose paper was reputedly financed and controlled by the Communist party, requested that he call at her apartment immediately.

Knowing that the Communists despised him as a person and were sabotaging his endeavor as a matter of politics, it was singularly galling to meet their satellites at every turn in the road. But he could not enlist any aid in the Negro community without coming back to them in the end, for all persons and groups in the community sympathetic to labor had been reached by the Communists first. As he sat on the streetcar through the rainy night, he prepared himself to swallow this bitter pill.

But Mrs. Jenkins had not requested his presence to humiliate him. Without comment she listened to his request that she run a special edition on Monday urging the Negro community to support the union campaign. He had the feeling that she had already known of the union's plan for a rally when she requested that he call.

Now she said: "I like to see our people take an active interest in the labor movement. That's our salvation. We're laborers—that's all we are and all we'll ever be—and we got to support labor for our own benefit."

"I knew that you would appreciate the necessity of our supporting the union, Mrs. Jenkins."

"I encourage our people at every opportunity to support labor. You know, I could get a lot of money if I was the kind to sell my people out. Big politicians from downtown are always out here offering me fifteen hundred or two thousand dollars to support their campaigns, and all I would have to do to be rich is just accept their money. But the welfare of my people is worth more than money to me. I want to know what they're going to do for the Negro, and what they're going to do for labor. And if I am not convinced of their political development, I fight them. But it costs money to run a newspaper."

"That I can understand," Lee said.

"Do you have someone to prepare the material?"

"We can send you the copy already typed up."

"Can you furnish the mats? Pictures of the union officials and group pictures?"

"I don't know about the group pictures. We can send you mats for all the officials."

"I think I have enough group pictures on file. If not, I can send a boy down to the *Times*'s morgue—they always have good union pictures they never use."

"That'll be excellent," Lee said. "Do you think you could get the edition on the street by noon Monday?"

"We'll have to work all day tomorrow but I think we can. We'll need about fifteen hundred dollars, and anything we spend over that I'll contribute out of my pocket."

Of course, Lee thought. He'd been a fool not to have realized that this would cost. And he knew the union had no money. But he had gone this far and had to play it through.

"I'd better call my boss," he said.

She led him to the telephone. He called Smitty at his home.

"Lee, you know we don't have that kind of money now. We've already overspent our budget."

"Can you spend anything, say for some leaflets to be passed out on the streets?"

"We can print our own leaflets, Lee. And we can't do that, anyway. We'd get into trouble distributing leaflets down in the Negro community. The military would have us on the carpet for subversive action. No, we can't do it. But if you can persuade Mrs. Jenkins to run an edition on her own account, it would be of tremendous help."

"I'll try."

But when he explained that the union could not afford to pay, Mrs. Jenkins said: "I would like to do it, Mr. Gordon, but I barely make expenses as it is."

"Well—thanks, anyway," Lee Gordon said.

Early the next morning he called on the three ministers with whom he had appointments. After listening to his request that they urge their congregations to support the union campaign, two said that they did not think it in the province of the church to support labor organizations. The third asked bluntly: "Are you a Communist, young man?"

From there Lee went to see Reverend Wilkins. Despite the fact that he had often heard that Reverend Wilkins was a member of the Communist Party and that Marxist scholars wrote his sermons, Lee had depended on his help. Leading a group of his members in a union parade seemed just the type of thing that Reverend Wilkins liked to do.

But after waiting for an hour, Lee received the note: "I am cognizant of the union's plans and am doing all in my power to help achieve a successful culmination. May God be with you and comfort you. Nathaniel Wilkins."

Now again having failed in all else, Lee went back to the workers. But it was Sunday. They were resting, drinking, or having fun. They refused to listen and resented his calling; they were tired of the sight of him. They taunted him and poked fun at the union and made asides about "white folks' niggers." But he did not stop. It was late when he returned to the hotel. He was low and discouraged. Finally he went to sleep.

As if by collusion, that Monday morning all of the daily newspapers blasted at the union. They reported that Communists were planning a rally at the gates of Comstock Aircraft Corporation in defiance of a military ruling against crowds. Editorials urged the workers to take no part in what might easily develop into a bloody riot. The police commissioner and sheriff were quoted as saying they would dispatch special details to guard company property. The general of the command, it was reported, had sent a warning to the union.

After reading the papers, Lee telephoned Smitty. "Are you going ahead with it?"

"We're going ahead."

So next Lee sought the aid of local executives of two national Negro welfare agencies. But the stories in the papers had frightened them off. They would have nothing to do with anything promoted by the Communists.

And now at the last, as at the first, Lee went back to the workers. After all, it was for their benefit, he thought.

At six it began to rain. He kept on through the rain. His head cold had become so tight he could scarcely talk. He knew that what he was doing was of no use, and that it served only to aggravate his condition and torture his mind. But he could not stop. Finally, exhaustion drove him back to the hotel. He sat on the side of his bed, dripping wet, and stared into nothing.

What he wanted most of all was to get stinking drunk. But he had no money to buy one drink. After a while he would get up and go down to the corner drugstore and get a package of aspirin, he decided. But for the moment he wanted just to sit.

Chapter 31

AFTER a while Lee Gordon's wet clothes warmed and the head cold settled over him like a blanket of indifference. It was pleasant not to care.

> If I should die before I wake
> I pray the Lord not bother . . .

Just before he sank into a stupor, a knock sounded and he staggered to the door and opened it.

"You are sick, man! Get off your clothes while I go call a doctor," Abe Rosenberg said.

"I am not sick," Lee replied. "I only have a cold."

"Definitive logic and instinctive disputation! You are ill, man, sick, in any terminology. And I am going to call a doctor. Because if you die you will be as dead theologically as materialistically."

For the first time in many days Lee laughed. "Rosie! Old Rosie! You are a doctor yourself, old man."

He gripped Rosie's hand as if he would never let it go. Rosie was touched. Even the hard shell of his insouciance was penetrated by emotion.

"Lee, boy! I came the minute I heard. I was in Sacramento attending business and read it in the *Daily World*. That Luther! That bastard!"

"Was a bastard. But what about him?"

"Tell me nothing, man! Do you have to tell me what I know! When I read it in the paper I said, 'That Luther, by hook or crook, has got my friend in serious trouble.' May his bones grow grain for Southern bigots! But don't talk about it!" He hushed Lee's quick denial. "Now you go to bed while I go—"

"I'll settle for some whisky and some aspirins," Lee said,—"no doctor though."

"Whisky and aspirin it is! Now you take a hot bath and get in that bed while I am gone."

Standing there watching Rosie's fat, frog-shaped body go carefully down the stairs, Lee felt the joy come back into living. The man must set his watch by God, he thought wonderingly.

He changed into his bathrobe and went down the hall to the bath. Rosie was sitting in the single straight-backed chair, having a drink and smoking a cigar, when Lee returned.

"No 'Nigger Hair'?" Lee laughed.

"No 'Nigger Hair.' I broke a tooth on the pipestem and had to give up smoking pipes. I look more like a Jew this way."

"You must have had some rugged thoughts to make you break a tooth," Lee said, climbing into bed.

"Accidentally I read a Hearst editorial one day. Now do you want the aspirin and some water and then the whisky?"

"Four aspirins and a fourth of a glass of water and a half a glass of whisky."

"Won't that make you drunk?"

"If it doesn't, I'll take another half a glass."

"That, too, is accountable," Rosie said as he prepared the tonic. "But you should be at home."

"I have no home. I had a home but I destroyed it."

"It is not given man to destroy that which he once has had. He may go away from it or it may go away from him. But destroy—it is not within his power."

"I went away from it. By the way, how did you find me?"

"Your wife. You have a wonderful wife, Lee. She is a good woman."

"That is one of the things you learn."

"Yes, love you know because you experience it. Perhaps because you can not escape experiencing it. But values you must learn."

"The hard way."

"No, with that I don't agree. The difficulty of such process is variable, relative to its empirical immediacy."

"Whatever that may mean."

"It may mean many things to you. What I mean is the learning of values is dependent upon their impact on you. You might never have learned the importance of being a Negro had not you suffered from it."

"So you think being a Negro is important?"

"To me? I do not mean to me. I mean to you, because you are a Negro, just as I am a Jew, and being what you are is as important to you as being what I am is important to me. If it were not so then we would be something else. The importance is not of your making, only of your learning. The importance derives from the whole, from the indisputable fact of existence. Food is important because it is food. It does not follow that it establishes its own importance; it is important because of its position in necessity, which is a component of existence. People are important not because of what they do but because of what they are. The fact of being people is important. Therefore it holds that being Negroes who are people is indivisibly important. People may be divided and races may be divided and nations may be divided, but the fact of their existence and the importance of the fact, are indivisible.

"But be that as it may. I didn't come here to lecture you on Rosenberg's evaluations of the principles of Marxism; I came to visit with you, to be of whatever help an unsuccessful Jewish philosopher may be to you at this time."

"You are a great help, Rosie," Lee said, taking another swallow of the whisky. The slow, warm, wonderful feeling of drunkenness was seeping through his blood, and he began seeing Rosie not as a Jew, but as a savior. "Just being here. I was getting pretty discouraged."

"The trouble? Is it over?"

"Well—no. It's just hanging. Smitty and the union attorney Hannegan got me out on a writ."

"I read in the newspaper."

"But you know the police are not going to let the death of Dixon go like that. There's nothing being said right now but you know they're working on it."

Rosie nodded. "And what do you do? Are you still with the union?"

"Not still, but back. I quit once."

"Not because of Luther?"

"No, after that." Finishing his drink, he asked: "Pour me another, will you?"

Rosie saw the sudden shadow that passed across Lee's face and knew intuitively it was Jackie that was the key he had sought to all the rest. Of course, of course, he reviewed to himself. Interracial premises must always be applied to the solution, or at least to the understanding, of purely personal Negro problems, since within the pattern of oppression all causation stemmed from the oppressors and it was merely the reflection that caused the personal problems of the oppressed.

"I recall now," Rosie said. "At the time I was so involved with my own minor tragedy that I did not give it the attention I should have. And since, it slipped my mind. You defended Forks."

"Well—yes. That started it."

"With all our Freudian repressions and penalized sex, it never needs more than a start to result in stark tragedy." Which many people did not realize, he thought. No self-respecting Negro man could have a white woman at below the value she placed upon herself. But to have all that she thought herself to be, and not only that part she considered expendable to sex, he would naturally build her up to more than what she was—which was where the tragedy began.

"Well—yes. But you were speaking of your own tragedy."

"It is of no importance."

"What is of importance to you, Rosie—the Communist Party?"

"Yes, the Communist Party is important to me."

"By the way, what was the outcome of your intercession for me? That was the last time I saw you too. And I left in a huff. But I wasn't angry at you."

"I know you weren't, Lee."

"I knew you were trying to help me. And I want to thank you for it."

"I was trying to help justice more than you."

"What did they do about it? Did you go before the state committee?"

"Yes, I went and stated my charges."

"It led to nothing, eh?"

"Yes, it led to my expulsion from the Communist Party."

"Oh! I didn't know. I'm truly sorry, Rosie. I know how much the Communist Party means to you."

"Yes, it was a tragedy, I thought then. I never knew how much of a Communist I was until I was expelled from the party."

"I am really sorry, Rosie. Please believe me." For now added to the list of all the others whom he had hurt was this little Jew who did nothing but try to help him.

"For what?" Rosie asked. "Sorry I am no longer a member of the Communist Party? But I am a member. That's what I discovered. I am a member for as long as I live and can never be expelled. They can prohibit me from attending meetings and taking part officially in Communist Party activities. But they can not restrain me from being a Communist and affiliated by ideology to all the Communist Parties in the world."

"Well, yes, that's because you believe in communism. But I am sorry you were expelled from the organization."

"Lee, I deeply appreciate your sympathy. But it is misplaced. I tell you, my expulsion is of no importance. Nor in fact is my belief in communism. Whether I have a belief in communism is of no great consequence, not even to myself, since communism is not a religious faith. It is the fact of communism as a way of life superior to all other ways of life previously in existence that is important—and my ability to see my own identification with this important fact. I do not believe in the absoluteness of communism, no! ; nor in communism as the millennium, but as a movement in the profound progression of materialism."

"Then, Rosie, what do you believe in if you do not believe in communism?"

"What I am trying to say is that I do not accept the absoluteness of communism—just as I do not accept the conclusiveness of any existence, or of any ideology, or of any theory. For nothing is static, final, absolute—all is progressive movement, in which ideologies, theories, philosophies are but steps, or rather facets, shades, parts of continuous change."

"You are preaching dialectics now."

"Dialectics, yes, but not preaching. More to the point, all that

I am saying is embraced by the absoluteness of dialectical materialism, which is itself relative, and proven by the immemorial movement of matter."

"That may all be so, but it is a more comforting assumption that it is man who progresses and that the movement of matter is a result of this progress."

"Yes, I am forgetting that you were educated in America."

"Weren't you?"

"I was educated in reality, which is a difference."

"Then you say there's no realism in America? That, I must dispute. You are looking at the illustration."

"No, I do not say there is no realism in America. I say there is a great discrepancy between American education and realism. I say that American education views realism as poverty and oppression, as a static condition of the masses. I say that this is spurious, for realism is the appreciation of truth, and truth is knowledge of the phases of change. I say that American education teaches a great contempt for what it dubs 'realism,' and the masses who reflect true realism acquire a great distrust for American education. But what I despise American education most for is its great contempt for knowledge. We live in a capitalistic state where what is called 'knowledge' must conform with bourgeois ideology; therefore education is maintained at a fixed standard of ignorance. But among the educators themselves it seems that intellectual curiosity would lead them to an examination of knowledge, or at least to entice the capitalist to look upon his own coffin."

" 'I agree with your hypothesis,' to borrow a phrase from my onetime sociology professor. Of course I wish that education would broaden to embrace some measure of the truth—the racial truth, at any rate. But you're too rigid in your judgment. Why should the successful white American accept the Marxian dialectic? —he's satisfied."

"No, you misunderstand. Not that capital should accept it, but that you, Lee Gordon, should understand it."

"Why should I understand it more than anyone else?"

"Because it will make you strong beyond your wildest dreams. Listen, this is no fragile dream, no sacred cow—this is what Lenin calls 'the living tree of living, fertile, genuine, powerful, omnipotent, objective, absolute human knowledge.' For dialectics 'alone furnishes the key to the "self-movement" of everything in existence; it alone furnishes the key to the "leaps," to the "break in continuity," to the "transformation into the opposite," to the destruction of the old and the emergence of the new.'

"Listen, matter progresses and man reflects that progress in the living brain. That is not only indisputable but beautiful. No—no, listen!

"Any capable geologist can cite with absolute authority a time when this planet was uninhabitable. He can name the geological ages when the first small areas of the earth's surface became habitable, when ninety-nine per cent of the earth's resources now available were unavailable.

"Man, in his vast conceit, thinks that he has harnessed matter. But it has been matter that has progressed and reflected in man the measure of its progress. Do you think man invents the elements? He discovers them as they are made. Gravity was not conceived by Newton, it is a law of matter recorded by him. Did man invent the process of combustion, which is the basis of this industrial age? Or could he have even conceived of the modern engine without the material reality of coal, petroleum, gas, reflecting their potentiality within his mind? He learns scientific truths, he does not make them.

" 'With me,' Marx wrote, 'the idea is nothing else than the material world reflected by the human mind and translated into forms of thought.'

"Listen, even with my limited ability to reason, I see the reflection of materialistic progress in every historical period of man's existence. I see it in the development of civilization from necessity. I see the reflection of mineral ore in great paintings, and hear the sound of trees in every symphony. I see the change on the face of the earth and hear its song in the culture of man. I see the necessity for all theory and ideology and experience in the absoluteness of the earth. I see our present industrial civilization reflecting the astounding release of materialistic resources.

"Listen, this is what I want to say to you: that matter is not a a static substance, but the infinity of change. And communism but the present reflection of a movement of this change. Make no mistake about this, Lee. Time, and the profound progression of materialistic change, will make all men communists—and then, make them more. Within this movement, a tiny part of it, more symbolic than representative, more indicative than causative, is the socialist state of Russia and the small communistic movements throughout the world.

"It is not so much that communism is ideal as inevitable in this historical pivot of change. So what if it seems too rigid for the human factors of existence? It will be—and then something more. The profound proof is that progress has taken place and the people have not been able to escape it.

"Luther was a murderer, yes, but he was a Communist, too. Maud is an anarchist, but she is a Communist, too. Harry, a boy I know, is an anti-semitic, Negro-hating Southern gentile, but he is a Communist, too. It is of no special significance that now among the Communist Party are great hordes of rats and heels, but that they be people of revolutionary zeal. For at this pivot of change they are the people who reflect the change, and are now more important historically than all your Morgans and Rockefellers and Vanderbilts.

"That's why you are important, Lee. You are a Negro of revolutionary potential."

Rosie paused to get his breath and Lee lay admiring him.

"Rosie, I like to listen to you. You have the ability to make me feel important in the world. But frankly, my potential points more toward execution than revolution. I didn't tell you everything, but I am still on the spot." His position had been turning over in his mind as he listened to Rosie and now he brought it out for reassurance. "You've been reading of the rally?"

"How could I miss it with the smears all over everywhere?"

"Well, if we don't win the election, the union is going to withdraw its support from me."

"Why? I don't understand? Are you being held responsible for the whole campaign?"

"It's not that." Lee took a breath. "You see, I sold the union out."

"No! I don't believe it."

"It's true, though. At least I tried to sell them out."

"And they discovered it?"

"I told them. I had to. When I was—well, explaining about the murder."

"I see. And you are afraid that Smitty means this?"

"I don't blame him. I think Smitty is truly my friend. But I am certain that he means it."

"I do not want to know any more than you want to tell me. But can you be convicted for this murder?"

"Rosie, I don't know. That's what worries me. Without union support I don't have any defense. It depends on how far Foster pushes it."

Rosie was so long in replying that Lee was forced to ask: "What do you think?"

"Are you asking for the truth, Lee—for what I really think? Or do you want comfort?"

"I want the truth of what you think. I'll take another drink, too."

"I am an old hand at this business of rallies and elections," Rosie said, pouring him another drink. "If the rally is successful and the union wins the election, Foster is not apt to do anything. There will be no point—that is, unless they have concrete evidence against you. But if the rally is a failure and the union loses the election, he might make trouble, because your conviction would insure the company against the union for some little time."

"Maybe I'd better not go out there tomorrow."

"No, you can't dodge Foster by staying away. You have to see it through."

"Foster is a vindictive man. If he saw me in that parade he'd never forget it."

"Yes, Foster—he exerts great influence on the workers, doesn't he?"

"Tremendous."

"But he will pass. Men such as Foster are passing now. Just as the rugged individualist of the last generation has passed, the capitalist maneuverer of human destiny under the guise of political liberalism will also pass. As far as men may determine their own destiny, it will soon go back to the people."

"That won't help me tomorrow morning."

"No, Lee, nothing will help you tomorrow morning. If you were with Luther when Dixon was murdered, you will feel Foster's power."

"What if nothing can be proved connecting me with the murder?"

"Then you will not be prosecuted. But as a Negro you will be persecuted. As a Negro you will face your darkest days in the near future. When the war is over, reaction will set in. There will be no peace, for those who can establish even a temporary peace do not expect or want peace. There will be only the beginning of another war. And minorities will be crushed. For it will be capital's last stand and it will be a bloody bitter stand. But the handwriting is already on the wall. This is change, Lee, and out of the rivers of blood will come a different world."

"Rosie, I have a great respect for your historical interpretations. But as one individual Negro afraid of being framed for a murder rap, they do not encourage me."

"No, Lee, you must face it, friend. You may die for the murder of Paul Dixon. But once you resolve your indecision toward life and embrace your own reality, you will not be afraid to die."

"I think I have done that, Rosie."

"Then you will not be afraid. All people die—that is a little thing."

"I am still afraid, Rosie."

"You will not be when the time comes. Death will be but another change in the infinity of change. You will return from the reflection of matter to the matter you reflect. But the movement of which you have become a part in your resolution will go on. Lee, it is not that you are with the labor movement, but that you are a part of it; not that you support a cause, but that you are the cause. That is what makes you important, Lee."

"Thank you, Rosie. But now I am a little drunk."

"Yes. Then I must say good night. You have my address and my telephone number?"

"Somewhere."

"I will leave a card."

When Rosie stood, Lee could see the lines of fatigue in his face, and he knew suddenly that Rosie had been working to save something in him in much the same manner as a minister works to save a condemned man's immortal soul. He felt suddenly grateful to this grotesque little man.

"Thank you for calling, Rosie. Thank you."

"You will be all right, Lee," Rosie said as he opened the door. "You are a brave man."

Chapter 32

T HE room was filled with sunrise when Lee Gordon awoke. The moment he opened his eyes he saw a different life. His cold was cured without hangover and his mind felt clean without doubt. Gone was the depressing sense of failure, the bitter thoughts of yesterday—and in its place, an inner excitement, a keenness of the spirit and a zest for things to come. He tingled with that gladness in a perfect day. This was the way he'd always wanted to feel, and never had before—because this was the way that life could be wonderful.

Throwing back the covers, he let the sunshine warm his blood. And then he went down the hall to the bath. The sharp, cold needles of the shower filled him with an eagerness to face the day, and now he reviewed the prospects of the rally with confidence. Anything seemed possible on a day like this. Suddenly he had the feeling that they were going to win. Never before in all his life had he felt that he would win at anything. It was like a breaking-through, a getting-there—like arriving at a wholeness.

Without warning, song broke from his lips, that great inspirational battle hymn of the Christians . . . "Oh when the saints . . . go marching onnnnn . . . Lord I want to beeeee in that numbahhhhh. . . ." From what religious recesses of his past this came, he did not know, but it filled him with a poignant sense of laughter.

Now as he shaved he noticed the age in his face and discovered his first gray hair. And he was glad to realize that he had safely passed his youth. ". . . in that numbahhhh," kept running through his mind.

For such a day as this he chose a jaunty slack suit and left his head bare to the sun. Hunger paid an early visit as in many years gone by. But now asking for credit at the greasy beanery where he ate was an easy thing to do. The ham and eggs tasted better than ham and eggs had ever tasted and the sour-faced Greek served him a second cup of coffee on the house—and with a smile.

"So you wun-na the sweepstakes, eh?"

"The sweepstakes, they wun-na me."

As he stood outside waiting for the streetcar, images moved before his vision in startling clarity. Sounds came into his ears with clean fidelity. He saw the dirty façades of the buildings and the filthy tatters of the bums, and heard the foul obscenities of decayed minds. He saw the ravages of dissipation in the faces of the winos and the reeking ruins of syphilis in the bodies of the whores. Yet everything he saw was with compassion and all he heard was with a prayer. And the odor of garbage from the uncleaned gutters gave place to a fragrance of friendliness in this living world. Just life itself was pretty wonderful—a thing the dead would know. It was a strange and shocking thought, but it did not affect him so because he felt so untouchable, so buoyant, so light, so living up on high.

The streetcar came and with the mob he pushed aboard. His race made him one with the sullen-faced Negro workers from the South Side who filled the car from door to door, but his spirit rejected them. How could people be so sullen on a day like this? So of them all he only saw a lovely dark girl with a proud red mouth and eyes like purple muscadines. He smiled across at her and her replying smile lit up the faces of all others.

And now he thought of Ruth without hopelessness or remorse. He was surprised to find that he could think of her like this—as the queen of the kingdom of his heart and the mother of their children yet unborn. A flood of poignant yearnings rolled back the tearful yesterdays, and he saw tomorrow as the resurrection of a dream. With this song in his heart to serenade, and this newly born life to place at her feet, with the enchantment of a California spring on his side, how could he help but win her back? And when he had, they would set out yellow roses down the borders of their lawn for constancy. And in the cool, dark evenings they would lie together in each other's arms and talk of the future. Because now he knew that when all of this was done and past, it was going to be wonderful again—so much better this time because of what they'd both been through. Maybe it would be like it should be, like it could be if they tried. Maybe she'd see in him what she'd been looking for, maybe this was what kept singing on a laughing note. And suddenly he was laughing again.

Now he saw the city that he had never seen, though it had been ten thousand times within his eyes—the pleasant little shops on Fifth Street toward the Square, sunlight on the buildings—delicate pastel tracings against the blue—and two wedding gowns in a shop window like petals of eternal hope; and the faces of the people of the race—the human race—each with its story of the crusade.

And he thought of Rosie's words and wondered, was this but the reflection of the immemorial movement of matter within the living brain? Was this ceaseless human struggle but facets of continuous change? His heart cried out against it— God made hope to spring eternal from the human heart— Those were the words that were beautiful. And who could say what words were right and what were wrong— Or that they both were not the same, as long as mankind made the struggle?

Changing to the bus at Pershing Square, he was enclosed by the stream of early-morning workers. But he did not feel lost or black or unimportant, but a part of it, contained by it, as a ripple in the river of humanity. And this was how it should be, Lee Gordon thought—and how at last it had finally come to be.

But as they bumped and rolled through the city in the sun, the days came back to charge him with the cost—that afternoon, a lifetime ago, when news of his employment by the union had put him briefly in the stars, and this morning when now at last he felt alive in the living world. But in between there were the fear and bitterness and hurt, not only to himself but to Ruth, to everyone and every thing that he had touched. The face of the earth had changed for him during those fifty days. Values had taken new meanings and people new forms. But had he spent too much of other people? Had he spent too much of Ruth? Had he paid too great a price in human suffering for the change that he had bought? Only the future knew, and it was to the future that he looked.

Now again, as at the very first, he watched the rolling expanse of gray-green meadowland assume angles and take shape and reveal itself as the sprawling assembly of camouflaged buildings that were Comstock. But now he felt the wonder of his native land, its might and power and its parenthood: ". . . our nation an improving nation, and the best nation of them all. . . ."

He hitched up his trousers and hurried toward the union shack. Approaching from the rear, it seemed empty and deserted. He changed direction and headed toward the plant. As he came out into the side street across from the parking lot, he looked up and saw a line of deputy sheriffs, blocking off the street, the brightness of the day, blocking off hope and happiness and his future in the sun. Spaced evenly apart, they were numberless it seemed, a row of white helmets running down the slope of diminishing infinity— not the workers on parade, but power, the wages of wealth. So this was the company's answer, Lee Gordon thought, the voice of Foster! It broke unions, but did it make men? And he was suddenly raving mad.

Squaring his shoulders and tensing his muscles, he walked toward the line to pass. But a heavy hand reached out and stopped him.

"Your badge, boy. Let's see your badge."

"I have no badge."

"Then what are you doing here?"

"I am a citizen and this is a public street."

"No more. This is a military zone and you can't pass without a badge."

He stared at the adamant face, seeing its each minor detail in his helpless fury. "I say it's the street."

"You can be hurt, boy. Get on."

He turned abruptly. But as he stalked down the street his rage ran out. What could he, one lone Negro man, do against this army? Better see Smitty first and work with the union. But as he neared the union shack, he saw Benny Stone detach himself from two policemen and saunter toward him. He started to speak, then noticed Benny brushing off a sleeve. He jerked another glance to the two policemen, past them to the deserted shack, then back to the two policemen. Sight hung there, and thought and conjecture and memory, and even the day itself hung there, on the blunt, red faces of policemen, so suddenly discovered. Policemen!

And then he was moving again. But his mind was a Pandora's Box that he dared not open yet. Casually he cut across the street, circling toward the parking lot. He could feel the gazes of the policemen digging into his back, measuring his height, weighing the manner of his walk. Fighting down the impulse to break into a run, he climbed the guard railing and went down between the cars.

Union men were all about—organizers from other unions, volunteers from other locals—moving in and out between the cars, approaching the workers, and passing out union buttons, arm bands, placards, and banners.

One stopped Lee. "Wear your union emblem, fellow."

Lee looked blankly at the man. Then he accepted the button, pinned it on his shirt, and wrapped a band about his arm. "Thanks, fellow." But his mind was not yet functioning.

As he came out of the parking lot on the other side, he saw the union sound truck facing down the street toward the company gates. Surrounded by a score of men, it was the hub of activity. The deputy sheriffs blocking off the street on which the plant faced were thicker here, and four policemen stood near by. Even from where he stood, Lee could feel the tension of the crowded scene. Every minor motion seemed deliberate. He jumped the rail and hurried toward the truck with the feeling of walking into danger.

As he approached, Joe Ptak opened the back doors of the truck. Beyond, he saw Marvin Todd's blond head high over the others as he moved quickly to call the policemen's attention to something down the street. He saw Joe's thumb motion him into the truck. He looked inside and saw Smitty frantically beckoning. Everything was posted on his brain, but all for future reference. Now he only moved without a loss of motion and swung inside the truck.

It was to Joe Ptak he first turned, drawn by the change in Joe's attitude. Joe was dressed in the shiny blue serge suit, complete to vest, with soiled gray shirt and tie, as Lee had first seen him, and his hard blunt features were the same. For a moment they stared at each other. Then Joe ran his two fingers through his bristling shock of iron gray hair, and for one brief flicker his stony stare relented.

"Okay, boy."

"Okay, Joe."

Rigidity settled back into Joe's granite face as he quickly closed the door.

"Lee—"

He looked at Smitty in the cab's semigloom and saw it painted on his face. A stunned look spread slowly down his features. "I know."

The operator of the sound control looked at him and looked away.

"They have a warrant out for you," Smitty said.

"I know," Lee said again, his mind groping for the best thing to do. "Then I better give up, Smitty. No need of getting you into trouble now." The slow, forced deliberation of his voice reached out to Smitty's face and shaped it.

"No, wait, Lee. Just stay here in the truck for the time being."

"Won't they look in here?"

"Not right away. They have already. The main thing now is the rally. Later we'll think about you."

"But I'll mean more trouble, Smitty, if they catch you hiding me."

"No, wait, Lee," Smitty said again. "We've already sent for Hannegan. We've got those affidavits to think about."

"Oh!"

"Just keep out of sight."

Lee knelt down behind the microphone stand and gathered in his thoughts. A numbed, dazed expression came into the ashes of his eyes. He did not feel abused or persecuted, just defeated in the end, just caught in the fall of that sudden disaster hanging always overhead—not that it was unexpected, just that it had to happen now, when happiness had seemed so close and life had looked so wonderful. Now Ruth would never know. This was the thought that brought hurt.

For once again he was a burden, an obstacle, and a liability, at the very time he needed most to be an asset. When the fate of the union hung in the balance, perhaps of all of the world— "As Comstock goes the West Coast goes. As the West Coast goes the nation goes. As the nation goes the world goes." Lost !—for the want of one black man !

It was not only this, but more : He was jeopardizing the very freedom of these good men who were taking up their time and thought protecting him—fellows who normally hated his guts. Benny Stone had given him the warning. Marvin Todd had blocked off the cops. Joe Ptak had given him a vote of confidence. It was not because he deserved it—just because he was a Negro.

In the end it came back to the beginning, back to the legend of Georgia, that a Negro was the white man's burden. He was nothing but trouble for anyone—no good in the world. He never had been any good to anyone—not to the union, not to his wife, and not to himself.

He raised his head and peered through the small side window as he tried to collect his thoughts. He must determine what to do. He could not let these good guys take another rap for him. But there was no escape. The four policemen had divided; two stood behind the truck, two in front. He could not even give up now without getting the union men into trouble. They had committed themselves by hiding him. And what could it bring them but ruin, ignominy, perhaps imprisonment? His head jerked spasmodically from the hammer of his thoughts.

He looked across the parking lot at the workers crowding along the edges of the guarded, barren street. He saw the union workers trying to form a line. But there was no space within the lot and the deputies kept them from the street. The workers stood and looked, as if they had come more to view the rally than be a part of it.

"How do you think it'll go ?" he said to Smitty.

Smitty was hurt. A feeling of failure had overcome him. It showed all through his big, flabby face and in his bright, protruding eyes. "Lee, I don't know. It looks like Foster's got us beat."

"It looks that way, Smitty."

"I didn't think he would do it," Smitty said, as if talking to himself.

"Do what ?"

"Call out the cops. I wrote him a letter and told him that we did not intend to cause a work stoppage."

"Oh ! Did you think that would mean anything to Foster ?"

"I thought he'd at least be fair about it." After a moment he said : "You got to believe in something, Lee. And I've always been a sucker for people."

Lee flinched as the knowledge of Smitty's belief in him spun out its special hurt. "Is Joe going to break the line ?"

"He's going to try."

Lee turned to look through the window again, tortured by the hurt in Smitty's voice. This was his, too. This failure of the rally was more his than anyone's. And this breaking down of this big bluff man's belief in human nature was his. But what could he do ?

"Why don't you have Joe line them up down this street first ?"

"That's an idea." Smitty spoke into the microphone, "Joe, why don't you try lining up the workers on this street first ?"

The blaring metallic voice drew everyone's attention. Lee saw Joe directing the workers toward the side street. Joe's stocky barrel-chested body, clad in the dark blue suit, seemed impregnable in the sunlight as he rode herd on half a dozen workers and forced them into a line. But most of them remained within the parking lot.

"Workers of America !" Smitty appealed to them. "Now is the time to assert your democratic rights— All of you—brothers in the union—accept the emblems and placards from the volunteers among you . . . line up behind your union leaders in orderly fashion . . . when your leader gives the signal march in orderly fashion up and down the public street before the plant—"

When the voice ceased, the silence closed in. A few more workers moved to join the line. But most just stood and stared. Over them hung a pall of abnormal tenseness. Lee could see the sullen animosity in their faces. It was as if now at the showdown they hated the union for bringing them to this. Most were Southern migrants. Within their lives until this moment the extent of their hatred had been toward Negroes. Now it was as if against their wills they were being forced to hate rich white men whom they had always feared, still feared. But they did not want to appear as cowards. So they hated the union for maneuvering them into this unacceptable position.

"Did you get word from the army forbidding the rally?" Lee asked to break the silence.

"No, that was just newspaper talk."

Now Lee saw a group of Negro workers standing in sullen silence behind the white. He was struck by the similarity of these workers of two races. Now that both faced a common enemy with equal reluctance, there seemed no difference but color. And why should there be? Lee Gordon thought. All had been born on the same baked share-croppers' farms, steeped in the same Southern traditions, the objects of the same tyranny that, together, they had not only permitted but upheld. They were bound together by their own oppression rendered by the same oppressors—their fears and their superstitions and their ignorance indivisible. Only their hatred of each other separated them, like idiots hating their own images.

"Is it doing any good?" Smitty asked.

"They're listening. Maybe they'll fall in when Joe breaks the line."

"Brothers, take up your banners and march for your union," Smitty tried again—"your union, brother workers of America. Do not be coerced or confused or threatened. You have free choice in the selection of your union. This free choice is guaranteed by the laws of the United States Government. The National Labor Relations Act gives you the right to join unions. The law says yes, brother workers—"

And now a few more came into the line.

"It's taking hold," Lee said.

He saw Joe Ptak grab two fellows bodily and shove them toward the line. The fellows drew back and said something, and Lee could see the hard uncompromising gesture of Joe's rejection. He should be out there with Joe, he thought. That was where he belonged. Then he saw a tiny group of a dozen or more come from between the cars and move toward the rear of the line.

"Some more are coming—" He broke off as he read the forward placard: "The Communist Party Supports Labor!"

His thoughts ran bitter. After all that they had done to undermine the campaign, they would come! While the rank and file trembled in the indecision they had helped inspire, they themselves would be on hand. They must be seen. It must be known. It was the line—not right, but revolution!

Words of Rosie's tugged at his memory and cut loose his thoughts in strange omniscience. "Time, and the profound progression of materialistic change, will make all men communists." And from some minor chord of memory echoed its root in Marx, "The victory of the proletariat is inevitable." It struck him as a funny time to recall it.

"Keep on, Smitty, you're doing good!" he said aloud.

"In union there is strength," Smitty began again. "Without a union, you are helpless. It is too easy to cut wages of unorganized employees. It is too easy to ignore or violate seniority rules. It is too easy to misuse the speed-up. This is true, whether your particular employer is a basically fair employer, or basically unfair to labor. Without a union, even the fair employer, under pressure from without, will make mistakes costly to his employees and costly in the long run to himself and the industry. Vote for your union. It is the only practical step you can take today toward bettering your present condition and safeguarding your future—"

But if the rally failed, they would not vote the union in, Lee Gordon knew. These workers would not vote for failure.

His flitting, hunted gaze picked Rosie from the crowd and watched him stand at the edge of the parking lot and look about. He knew that Rosie was looking for him. From where he knelt within the truck, he could see the disappointment come into Rosie's face when he failed to find him there. And now he wondered what effect his arrest would have on Rosie. It would probably cause him to perjure himself into prison. And this was what he had for everyone it seemed—the Gorgon touch.

"In the midst of this war for justice and liberty—" the voice of Smitty carried on. "For fraternity and equality—we bring you the manifestation of the democracy for which we fight—"

But through Lee Gordon's mind kept running one refrain. What was this thing that made meaning? This thing that brought change? What could he do for all these people who had befriended him?—for Ruth? for the union? for Rosie's simple faith in him? What could he do to avoid the hurt he held in store for them?

Overhead the metallic voice blared persistently : "What do you want?—a job? security? the right to live decently? to live without fear? to educate your children? to fulfill your democratic heritage? Your union offers you this future!"

And what future had Lee Gordon ever offered anyone? Lee Gordon thought.

Smitty glanced at his watch. "It's past time for Joe to start."

"He's starting now," Lee said as he saw Joe Ptak step to the head of the line.

"Let's hope, Lee, let's hope, boy." Now Smitty leaned toward the microphone with new life in his voice, "Line up, brothers! Line up! March for your union!—"

Lee saw the deputy sheriffs close in before the line of workers.

"Have no fear. You have the right to march. The law says yes!—"

For a moment the tableau held, two suspended lines caught in that moment of time. It seemed suddenly like a battlefield before the battle has begun, with two opposing forces arrayed against each other. Lee sensed the drama of the moment. It made him bite down into his lip and tightly clench his fists. Then suddenly in that telescoped instant in history the zero hour sounded on which the future of the world might hang.

But what kept ringing in Lee Gordon's mind like some forgotten liberty bell was not the words of Rosie nor the words of Marx, but the words of Jesus Christ : "Blessed are the meek, for they shall inherit the earth."

Then Joe Ptak began to move. In one hand he carried a long-handled union banner. The other hand hung free. His iron-gray head bobbed slightly above the indomitable hunch of his shoulders. Behind him the others began to move. A slight wave of motion swept across the parking lot, stirring the first faint signs of action. The deputies shifted on their feet. One drew his gun, then quickly holstered it. Each stark detail showed with photographic clarity in the California sun.

Lee saw a deputy step into the path of Joe Ptak. He recognized the face of Walter. He saw Walter put out his white-gloved hand and push Joe in the chest. He saw Joe brush Walter aside with one uncompromising motion. He saw the moment hold again as if all time was tangible. A cold chill tingled down his spine. He felt his mouth getting big inside from the explosion of air, felt his muscles getting tight clear up from his feet.

He saw Walter swing at Joe with a blackjack. He saw Joe duck, still holding to the banner, and with his one free hand knock Walter down. He saw the workers behind Joe move up. He saw the other deputies close in from all directions. He saw the tide begin to break from the parking lot.

"He's done it! He's done it!"

He saw the deputies club a worker across the head, knock another down, and kick still another in the face. For as long as he could hold his breath, the scene was lost in motion. Then he saw the workers back up from the deputies' assault, saw them break away, and saw the tide from the parking lot slow down and halt. He saw the deputies quickly draw their guns. He felt his hands getting wet with sweat.

Now he saw Joe Ptak alone and deserted in the street, fighting all of the deputies at once. He saw a deputy stand directly behind Joe and swing a long night stick down across Joe's skull. His eyes followed Joe's staggering recoil from the impact of the blow, and saw him catch his balance, shake his head, and bore back in.

He heard the workers scream curses and yell threats, and saw the tide surge down from the parking lot.

He saw the line of deputies quickly form again, saw the blue-steel gleam of many guns in the bright sunlight, and saw the tide of workers halt before what looked like certain death.

But alone in the street Joe Ptak fought on. Lee Gordon saw the sticks descend again and again across his skull until it did not seem that a man of flesh and bone could stand. But Joe kept fighting and taking his toll.

Lee Gordon felt so great an admiration for this one man's gallant stand that it tore him up inside. "Fight 'em, Joe, goddamnit, fight 'em!" It filled him with an exaltation to be on this man's side, and now he was with him in heart and body and soul. And when Joe went down to his knees from the weight of the blows, Lee Gordon went down too; and when Joe still fought back on his knees, Lee Gordon fought beside him and felt each separate blow.

The spectacle of this unconquerable man sealed the workers in awed silence. Nor could Lee Gordon find time to breathe.

He saw Joe get to his feet again and turn, and now he could see the streams of blood down Joe's face as he fought on without thought of ever quitting. He saw the final blow and saw Joe fall as some mighty oak. And even as brutal a man as Walter could not find the villainy to kick Joe in the face, which was the expected thing.

Now Lee's eyes went down the ragged line of workers to see who might come to Joe Ptak's aid. No one moved. But they did not look defeated, only poised, held on that breath of indecision. It needed but a spurring-on, a calling-out, an incident to set it off.

Suddenly in that tense line of watching workers his gaze came upon the face of Ruth, and it claimed his whole attention. She was pressing forward desperately toward the front where the fighting had taken place. He saw Rosie head her off, saw them standing there, and saw their eyes search the crowd for him once more. He looked quickly away from the thoughts that showed in their actions.

Now he saw the deputies rolling the unconscious body of Joe Ptak over on his back.

"Take that man to the hospital!"

The metallic voice from overhead ran shock down through his skull. He felt his eyes jumping as next he saw the deputies cross Joe Ptak's legs and stick the handle of the union banner in his crotch so that it stood erect. There was blood on the banner now —and blood on Joe's hard, uncompromising face, looking up from the pavement of the street, down but undefeated.

He looked back at Ruth and saw the agitation in her face, the worry and concern. And he could not help thinking of what it would do to her—the degradation and dishonor, a woman scorned in the eyes of the world because her husband had been convicted of a murder—the grief inside of her, the protest and the fear, and the knowledge of his innocence she would have to carry— not for just a day, but for all of the days of her life.

"What you are doing to our organizer is brutal and inhuman!" the voice overhead cried out.

"The next son of a bitch that crosses this line gets killed on the spot!" a deputy shouted back.

The workers booed, cursed, yelled, taunted. But no one moved.

"Somebody ought to do something for Joe," the operator said.

"I'll go get him," Smitty said. He climbed down from his seat and let himself through the back doors, quickly closing them behind him.

Lee watched him squeeze his way through the crowd. He saw the deputies halt him. He saw them argue and gesticulate. He looked toward the line of workers. They did not look quite beaten yet, but still held on that breath of indecision. He looked at Rosie. And now at last he looked at Ruth again. For a long moment he studied the flower of her face—and thought of how it might have been.

Now once again he turned his gaze on the long line of deputy sheriffs, cutting off the success of the rally, the future of the union, the movement of the working people of the world. He felt overcome with a helpless impotence. All he could bring these people was more hurt. All he had ever offered anyone was hurt—Ruth and the union alike, Rosie and all the other good guys who had befriended him, and all of these poor workers who would also suffer because of him— Thoughts flashing like sheet lightning through the turmoil of his brain—Joe Ptak, lying there unconscious in the sun, who had done the best he could for the thing in which he most believed—the disappointment in Rosie's eyes—the hurt in the face of big, bluff Smitty, the only white gentile he had ever known to be his friend (was his faith in human nature to be lost?)—and Ruth!—"All I ever wanted was just to love you, Lee."

A thin flame came alight in his mind, burning ever brighter. Words spun through his thoughts : "When the occasion calls for it—" Not tomorrow, or an hour hence. But now! For the time was running out!

It was as if all of his life was coming to a head; the good and the evil, the high and the low, all of the things that had ever happened to him and all of the things he had ever done and the things he had not done, coming together into meaning. It was as if this was the moment he had lived for—not the choice of a conclusion, nor the facing of a fact, but this was the knowledge of the truth.

He straightened out his legs, flexed the muscles to ease the cramp.

"Tight quarters," the operator said.

"It is that!" Lee Gordon said.

He moved to the back and opened both doors. As he jumped to the ground he saw the startled faces of the two policemen. He saw them move toward him but he was running.

"Halt! Halt or I'll shoot!"

The words pushed him on to greater effort. He fought through the mass of workers, pushing them aside. When he reached the line of deputies he heard Rosie suddenly cry : "No, Lee ! No !"

And Ruth screaming : "Lee !"

But he did not look around. He pushed with all of his might into the chest of the deputy in his path, saw him fall away. Ducking beneath the blackjack of another, he was through the line. Out of the corner of his vision he saw the gun of Walter come leveling down on him. And from the parking lot he heard a worker cry : "Don't shoot that boy !"

He reached Joe Ptak, snatched up the union banner, and holding it high above his head, began marching down the street.